Sheila is a retired teacher of Modern Languages and English as a foreign language. Until lockdown, she had only written a few articles for magazines and Christian poetry. Inspired by attempting a memoir on her spiritual journey, she decided to use her experiences in education. Sheila travels in England, Europe, Canada and Australia to create family stories dealing with anthropology, racism, spirituality, mental health, indigenous art and belief systems, relationships, sexuality and counselling. In her retirement, she has studied Romanian, spiritual direction, indigenous spirituality, post-colonial theology and writing.

Sheila Longman

The White Bookshelf

AUSTIN MACAULEY PUBLISHERS™
LONDON • CAMBRIDGE • NEW YORK • SHARJAH

This is a work of fiction. Names, characters, businesses, places, events, locales, and incidents are either the products of the author's imagination or used in a fictitious manner. Any resemblance to actual persons, living or dead, or actual events is purely coincidental.

A CIP catalogue record for this title is available from the British Library.

ISBN 9781398490390 (Paperback)
ISBN 9781398490406 (ePub e-book)

www.austinmacauley.com

First Published 2023
Austin Macauley Publishers Ltd®
1 Canada Square
Canary Wharf
London
E14 5AA

Table of Contents

Part 1
A Significant Symbol

The story of a family of an Oxford professor living in a beautiful house but each family member has a trauma to overcome. Both parents lost loved ones because of the Second World War. Both the son and the daughter were abused by people they trusted. Daniel underwent harmful therapy and Alice's life was scarred for years by a man who let her down badly.

Their love and support for each other helps them get through and leads them to unexpected paths through life. They have to look back and deal with the past before they can move forward and experience faraway places and other cultures.

The compassion of this family provides a legacy for others drawn into the circle and for the next generation.

1 The Berlin Wall

"Come and see! Quick! People are pouring through Check Point Charlie. The Wall is open," Thomas yelled.

Esther was in the kitchen preparing soup. Daniel was with Charles in the lounge, both of them at the grand piano in the big bay window at the far end of the room. Alice was curled up in a leather armchair in the corner of her father's study next to the white bookshelf.

Her father had chosen the house just outside Oxford when the children were toddlers. It was a rambling Victorian house with large rooms downstairs, and two floors above. The guest bedrooms were under the eaves. Most of the walls were white but when the children became teenagers they chose their own decoration for their bedrooms. The large lounge with the grand piano became a music room for Daniel. The television lounge was in a smaller room at the back of the house. Father's study was Alice's favourite place. He was often working there himself or receiving guests but when it was empty and she was at home she always read and wrote or browsed the bookshelf. From early childhood she had loved that room. As a toddler she often read sitting under the large desk. Now she was in her usual pose listening to her father calling out.

He ran to each room and flung open the doors and called for his family to come to the television room.

"Check Point Charlie is OPEN!"

Everyone dropped what they were doing and hurried to see the spectacle of history unfolding. Esther stood behind the settee where Alice and Daniel sat right on the edge of the seat.

Thomas stood with Charles next to the armchair, gripping the top. Esther had tears running down her cheeks. No eye was dry. On the screen soldiers had hesitatingly opened the bar and let the thousands of marchers through to the West. They were crying, leaping and hugging each other. The guards stood helpless and bemused.

The news had spread within minutes. Schabowski had ruffled his papers during the Press conference. He had explained that Krenz was making new arrangements and that passes would be issued for people to go through to the west. The journalists pressed him, cameras and microphones in his face.

"When?"

He shuffled the papers, looked down and answered, "Ab jetzt." From now on.

It was a mistake, of course, but it was too late. The crossing points let the crowds through to the waiting groups of reporters on the other side of the Wall.

Esther had followed the news of the last few days very avidly. The marches had started in Leipzig, the town where she had been born. Every Monday people gathered outside the Nicholaikirche and then left with their pastor to march peacefully around the Leipzig ring road. Since the visit of Gorbachev and the resignation of Honeker there had been many changes in the DDR. The new leader was promising travel rights. Marches took place in every big city and grew and grew each week. Thousands of citizens made efforts to leave the country often crowding into the Embassy of a neighbouring country, Czechoslovakia was first. Crowds were climbing over the barriers and they camped there until special trains took them out. Parents left children, families left pets and chaos reigned.

The cameras switched from Berlin to Leipzig. The walkways over the ring road were lined with armed guards. There was shouting from the crowds below, "Wir sind das Volk!" Esther wept aloud, "That's my town. Look at the armed guards. What courage!"

"I was born the year that they built that wall. Now look. They said that Krenz had given permission to shoot. What stopped them?" Daniel, Alice's older brother, earnestly watched as the cameras panned the people, the banners, the soldiers and their guns.

In the early eighties, Alice had stood at Check Point Charlie with Herman. They had observed the wide brimmed caps of the Communist soldiers. There were no crowds that day, just a small queue of people showing passes to go through from the West to the DDR.

Herman was her first serious boyfriend and they had come to Berlin for a weekend from Reutlingen. They were planning to stay with his parents in Aachen where they would be working out their possible future together.

Weeping like her mother, she thought of Herman and wondered how he was experiencing the shock of this late November evening. Seven years ago they had walked hand in hand along the Wall to look at the artistic graffiti.

"I've seen Mum's photos of people trying everything possible to get through as the wall was being built." Daniel explained. "One soldier even jumped over the barbed wire; others jumped out of windows to land on the west side. Friends were holding blankets to catch them. At least one lady was actually killed making the jump."

Esther had lived in Leipzig until late 1938. She had been put on a train by her parents into the care of a Kindertransport organisation. She was only five years old. She had finally grown up with an English family but never lost her attachment to Germany.

Charles put an arm round Esther, "Could you never go back, Esther, after the war?"

"After the war the Charltons joined the hundreds of people trying to find survivors from the camps. They checked the Berger family from Leipzig but found no survivors. In 1948 they adopted me so I became Esther Berger Charlton. I grew up with this loving couple and called them Mum and Dad."

"I am so sorry. I did not know."

"They always encouraged me to be in touch with my roots. They guided me to learn German and even to pick up some Hebrew."

"Do you attend a synagogue?"

"No. I visit sometimes but I became Anglican like the Charltons. I believed in Jesus and I really loved the church."

"I am so glad you took Alice and me to church while Dad was with voodoo tribes in Africa!"

"Nigerians also sing great hymns!"

Daniel, the musical older son often teased his father about the strange spirituality of the tribes he studied in Nigeria. Thomas had become an expert on the brasses, bronzes and artefacts of Nigeria and had written his PhD thesis on these tribal people and their belief systems.

In 1989, now grey haired and nearing the final years of his career, Thomas was more often at home than travelling. Esther, used to being alone, was able to endure the times when Thomas was abroad for long periods, even when they had two small children. They began their married life in a flat in central Oxford. Esther was working as a translator while her husband was writing up his thesis and made life-long connections with anthropologists in Nigeria, When Daniel was two and Alice was a baby he bought this big house on the outskirts of the town. He had a study installed with a large white bookshelf. Artefacts adorned the walls and shelves.

Thomas loved his wife deeply. He had not dated girls when he was spending long periods in Nigeria, then returning to Marsden College, Oxford. He was in his mid-thirties when they had married. This distinguished research student, tall and thin with straight brown hair had virtually fallen in love at first sight. Esther was studying German, French and Hebrew at another Oxford college. She had long, black, wavy hair which she let hang loose. She tended to wear long, flowing, flowery skirts. Esther was bright, intelligent and interested in many things but she was alone in the world. Her adoptive parents had both passed away. They were not young when as a childless couple; they had taken in a little German Jewish refugee in 1938.

He dabbed his eyes and turned to Esther, "You might be able to go to Leipzig if they allow visits, if the Wall stays open." Esther got up and hugged him.

"Thomas I would love that. I want to go to that church which started the prayer meetings and the marches."

"Alice, we must both go with her. It is our heritage." said Daniel.

Alice Leah Hartley, with her Jewish middle name was aware as she grew up that her mother had some scary parts to her childhood. She had negative feelings without understanding why. As an adult she had learned about the war and of course knew about the atrocities of the Nazis.

She hated to connect that with her loving mother and she developed an inner fear of her own emotions and of her mother's emotions. It was as if a dark cloud hung above her and she did not want it to burst over her.

Esther had only been to Germany once. She had been brought up as an English child, lost her German accent and done well at school. The Charltons had not been great travellers into foreign countries. They had taken Esther to the lovely areas of England, the south coast, the Yorkshire Dales and as far as Scotland. They had an invitation from a close friend to visit the Black Forest in Germany when Esther was a teenager. Surrounded by her mother tongue she remembered several words and understood much of what was said to her.

Since the amazing visit of Gorbachev to Berlin the whole political situation had begun to change. The Hartley family had followed the news and could not quite believe how marches and demonstrations filled every bulletin. Esther had a few memories of her birth town and Alice was quiet. She returned to the study and found herself weeping. She wept for the joy of this historic moment. She wept for the memory of Herman and also in anticipation of the emotional toll of sharing her mother's pain in the city of her birth. Alice was somewhat nervous at the prospect of making a family visit to this town. Deep down she dreaded going through more emotional turmoil. She was nevertheless interested in seeing her mother's city. She wanted to see the famous Berlin Wall again. The stories of escapes and deaths were well known in the West.

Sitting alone, Alice began to recall the last time she had made an emotional trip a few years earlier. She had gone to support Derry and his family in some difficult family research; a pain which was not her own.

She wiped her sore eyes and drew comfort from perusing the bookshelf. This had always been her place of escape; books on Africa, books on Australian aborigines, books on tribes with strange art work and scary masks, books on Germany and books on strange languages. Seven years ago, in this very corner, she had wept over Herman while her Dad held her in his arms.

It was nearly a year later that she had been introduced to Derry.

"Hello, Alice, I am Derwent Barnes. People call me Derry or at school I was often DB."

Oh, no! she thought, *Not another lost soul from Dad's tutorial!*

But she managed to greet him politely.

Now, watching history unfold she wondered if Derry would know what was happening because she knew he was somewhere in the Outback of Australia.

Thomas was professor of Anthropology at Oxford. He travelled less these days after he had completed his PhD on Nigerian brasses and culture. He was tall, thin and kindly with receding grey hair and a trim beard. Many students feared the rigour of his teaching and of his demands on them, but they had great respect for his knowledge and wisdom. They were also drawn to his gentle and compassionate character. Some sadness in him drew those who struggled with their own sadness.

If Alice complained about the frequent presence of a young man in the holidays, Esther would explain, "Dad lost his older brother, Robert, in the war. He was just old enough to join up and was sent to Egypt. He was only 19 when he was killed. He and Dad were very close. We named Daniel after him, Daniel Robert Hartley. Dad loves to reach out to the young men, mostly very brilliant but nursing some kind of pain."

"I know I am being selfish but I want him to myself sometimes."

"So do I!"

After this incredible news about the Wall, Alice was getting a headache. In her leather armchair she made the decision to talk to her Mum and really encourage her to go to Leipzig. She would promise to go with her. She hoped that her Dad would be free to come for at least some of the time. She and Daniel would do all the planning.

Alice worked in London as a translator, mainly of German. She had applied to study for her BA in London University as she felt rather stifled and intimidated by the atmosphere of Oxford. She needed independence and to be away from the earnest young men from the Anthropology Department. She shared a flat in London but often returned to Oxford to see her parents. Her brother, Daniel also lived in London with Charles and their visits often coincided. The brother and sister were very close and spoke to each other every week.

She still felt emotional, with that same sense of fear, when she remembered the trip with Derry and his family. He had come to her home for the first time in the summer of 1985, a year after she had left Herman.

He was tall and thin like Thomas with straight brown hair. He was very intense and focussed on his research. He seemed fairly withdrawn and did not chat easily. However, after a few weeks he sought out Alice and Daniel for D and Ms, or 'deep and meaningfuls' as he called them.

Alice related quite well with him. She had noted that sometimes when he was reading at a desk, his elbows on the desk top, he would lean over with his head in his hands and his brown hair flopping over. She wondered if he had shared his pain with Thomas.

He wanted to know why she was studying Urdu in SOAS. She explained that after completing her BA Hons in German, she had followed in her mother's footsteps and done some translation work in both French and German and to help her get over a broken relationship with a German boy, she had taken up something very different. Derry asked nothing about this broken relationship. He always kept a certain distance from her but was happy to play tennis in the garden or sit with her discussing studies, philosophy or religion or some other academic subject. He had not talked about his family except to say that he had a married sister in Epsom.

As ever she had been inspired by her father's books to consider studying a very different language. Her flat mate in London had found an advert for teachers to give survival level English lessons to Muslim ladies.

“That’s me!” She exclaimed. Even with her translation work she could fit in the classes. She looked around for a short course in Urdu so she could communicate with her students. She was accepted at SOAS.

Derry was very pleased to discuss her findings as she tried to familiarise herself with Pakistani culture. He would sometimes talk about the tribes he was studying in Australia.

A few weeks into the following year, his older sister Madeleine turned up at the house. Their long talk together led to the decision to follow up some research on their family history. She was curious but would not ask him any questions as she felt it was a sensitive area. She had never even asked him about his unusual name.

“Derwent is a river, isn’t it?” But she left it at that.

She was about to meet his sister and get drawn into their research.

2 Bad Blood Barnes Derry and Dadirri

Madeleine Walker was so very different. She was shorter, quite plump and with curly blond hair. She was the mother of two teenage children whom she had left with her husband, Roy and her parents, Bob and Clara, in Epsom. She had come to Oxford to work on her brother. She was not unannounced because she had phoned Derry and asked if she could stay for a couple of days. She had important things to talk about. Esther was pleased to put her up.

"Thank you so much for having me. Please call me Maddy, everyone else does. You have such a lovely house!"

"My Granny has died recently and there are things I need to talk to Derry about, but you can't hurry Derry, he will need time to make decisions before he leaves the country again"

Derry took Maddy to his room. He did not come down for tea but Esther offered tea to Maddy who was very glad to come to the lounge. Alice found her easy to talk to and very willing to chat openly.

"How is it your brother has such an unusual name? I was too shy to ask about it." asked Alice to break the ice.

"My parents were driving with me in Derbyshire a few weeks before he was due. We were on holiday and visiting an aunty. They were driving over a bridge when Mum started yelling and moaning. She thought her waters had broken. Dad stopped the car and ran to a phone box. He called an ambulance. I was scared stiff, crying and screaming. I can still remember when the ambulance came and took her to hospital. We followed the ambulance and as we crossed the bridge we saw the sign River Derwent. Derry was very early and while he was in intensive care they decided to call him Derwent. At school his friends called him DB but at home he became Derry."

Alice noticed Maddy's eyes were a little red. She had been crying with Derry. "Are you OK? Do you want to talk about it?"

She needed to pour it all out. Alice was a good listener and was very pleased to learn more about this quiet, serious, withdrawn house-guest.

Grandmother Kit had just died but knowing she was ill she had asked to talk to her daughter, Clara with her husband, Bob.

Clara had then shared the information with Maddy because Derry was in Australia. Bob was unable to speak about it all right then.

Kit was a tough war widow with a vindictive streak. She had not been delighted when her only child, Clara said she wanted to marry Bob from next door. They lived in a row of terraced houses outside Brighton. Bob and Clara had almost grown up together but he had been sent into a Children's Home when his mother died. He was only five. Kit had been very fond of her neighbour Lucy, Bob's pretty young mother. In spite of living in various Homes, he returned to see his grandfather from time to time. He had always been interested in books and grew up to work with them. He found a job in a library. He was promoted and had a steady career with training and prospects for the future, so Bob and Clara were married and moved to Epsom. In 1952 Madeleine was born.

"I grew up hearing the term, Bad Blood Barnes," she said, "I didn't understand it, but got used to it. I was about nine when I was staying with Granny Kit and she decided to tell me about my Dad's family. I had vaguely picked up that Dad had an uncle who was in a place called Broadmoor."

Grandparents and aunts chatted together in the parlour, the front room with the aspidistra on the table, kept only for guests. Maddy could hear bits and pieces but was too young to understand what they were talking about.

Kit told the nine-year-old that her Dad was the son of Lucy who was single when he was born. She was about twenty. She and her younger brother lived with their father who was a widower.

When little Robert was born, Christopher, the young brother, who was a labourer was sent away from home by his father.

Lucy and Robert lived with her father until when Robert was about 4, Lucy became very ill. She died when he was five. Grandpa could not cope with the grieving little boy. He asked for him to be fostered or to be put in a Home. Bob returned on frequent visits to his grandpa between foster homes and children's homes. When the old man died, Kit took in Bob for visits because she had been so fond of Lucy.

The Barnes scandal had taken place before the war but Kit had been caught up in the trauma of it all.

"Kit decided to tell my Dad about his Uncle Chris when they were expecting me. She swore him to secrecy and he has only just told us."

Chris was in Broadmoor but they did not know why. Kit told Bob that this uncle was in fact his natural father. At 17 he was a strong labouring lad and that he had had his way with Lucy, a slight and pretty young girl. When Bob was born the granddad threw Chris out.

Lucy wanted to keep her baby so she was able to carry on living with her Dad.

"On that stay with Granny Kit when I was nine, she told me that Chris in Broadmoor was my Dad's natural father. He had got his own sister pregnant. The news would have shattered my Dad. That explains why he was such a depressed and angry man. He was so often angry with Derwent, not too bad with me."

Why had Kit decided to tell this to Maddy when she was so young? She had also told her that Chris had done something terrible so he had to live in this prison hospital. She also swore Maddy to secrecy.

"Why did she tell me like that?"

"Perhaps she was finding it too hard to keep the secret any longer." suggested Alice.

Clara had talked a little to both Maddy and Derwent but had never spelt out the whole truth. Maddy never understood what this Bad Blood Barnes was all about but in 1984, when Kit knew she did not have long to live she called for them. Bob was always reluctant to see her but this time he knew it would be the last.

Kit gave them some more details about what Chris had done and Clara decided that her children, who were now adults, should now know about the past. She little realised that her daughter had kept part of the secret all these years. Chris Barnes died in Broadmoor and his story was repeated in the local Press. Kit saw the paper but kept it from Clara and Bob. It provoked her to tell them more. Bob kept the paper away from Maddy and Derry.

Maddy was in Epsom and Derry was either in Oxford or in Australia. When Kit died Bob broke down. Clara persuaded him that their son and daughter needed to know in case they found out through the Press or through someone else.

"They were so upset, Alice. They were really worried about how we would take the news. I am so fed up with secrets and scandals. Please help me; please persuade Derry to come with me to research the crime that Chris committed. This was our grandfather. I have made a start with contacting Broadmoor but Derry has suffered all his life from Dad's temper. He can now understand why he was so angry and often depressed. Bob was so worried that the bad blood would come down through his son. We need to let Dad know he is not Bad Blood Barnes and that we love him. Derry needs to understand that too, he has not got bad blood!"

Alice felt privileged to be asked. She thought of Derry with his head in his hands, his hair flopping over his book.

Maddy went home and contacted the chaplain at Broadmoor. He was kind and helpful. "Many people do what you are doing. It is better to know the whole truth. I will send you some papers and press cuttings." It was a terrible story.

Over the next few weeks she returned with the papers and a court report from Lewes Crown Court. Before returning to London, Alice had her D and M with Derry. She hoped he would agree to deal with it before he left for Australia in the autumn to complete his PhD.

"I do hope it does not bother you, but Maddy told me what your family is dealing with right now. Derry, please do help her. I will help you and I will drive you both to the places you need to go to. You know that we have had to face my mother's past tragedy. I understand that it is hard for you."

"You are so kind and thoughtful, Alice. I think we would both like you to come with us when we go to their local library. Can you spare the time? I need to support my father."

"I had such loving support when I broke up with Herman. That was a hard time for me. We all have our demons!"

"It would be great if you could drive us. We are bound to be going through shock and pain. I am so grateful to you. I have told your father a little of the troubles but I did not know as much as Maddy and Mum. You take after your Dad."

"Do I? What a compliment!"

"I am so looking forward to my next trip. I have just discovered an Aboriginal lady who has become a teacher and an artist. She gives talks and has a lot to say about my subject, *dadirri*."

"Dadi what?"

"I will explain it in detail when I get back next year. It is rather complicated but to find someone who speaks English and deals with this culture is wonderful. Unfortunately she lives in the Northern Territory and I am working in Queensland so I will have to travel a bit to meet her."

Maddy's next step was to go to their library to see the microfilms of the old newspapers. Alice drove Derry to Epsom and she camped overnight on Maddy's floor. The next day they went down to the library in the coastal town.

"We won't call on Mum and Dad this time. All too much."

The brother and sister were quiet on the last hour of the journey. They all walked upstairs to the microfilm machines and asked for the November 1938 version of the Sussex Daily News. They were led to drawers with rolls of labelled films. Derry threaded the film and wound it on. Alice looked around at the four other people using the huge machines. There were scraping noises, squeaks from the machines and flashes from the moving images on the big black screens. He wound more slowly as the correct dates came nearer. There was a strange stuffy smell as the drawers were opened.

He stopped on a headline, GUILTY BUT INSANE. Sure enough this was the article they wanted. They could magnify the centre screen and read the small print more comfortably. Chris Barnes had been sentenced to life imprisonment for the murder of a child. Little Maisie, aged 5 had been declared missing one evening. Her body had been found the next evening under a bench in an allotment.

Who was Maisie? Did Clara know? Alice saw the shock and pain in Maddy and Derry. Alice looked up at some higher shelves and noticed some black files marked *The Times.* She pointed them out and asked if they could have the copies of the same dates.

Derry scrolled down, winding the film back off and starting again with the longer reports in *The Times*.

CHILD KILLED BY INSANE MAN was the headline this time. Alice looked over their shoulder as they read the tragic story. They asked for the articles to be printed out as the quality of the texts was not very good. They saw mention of an expert witness who had examined Chris and had given his opinion at the trial. The local neighbours seemed to like Chris, a kind man who did odd jobs and helped out. He loved animals and children. He was a labourer and gardener. He was married to Gertrude but they had no children of their own.

More details came later from Clara when they had finished their scrolling. They paid for copies once more of all the reports of the expert witness. Derry and Maddy made an appointment to go to the Angel, Islington to the Family Records office. Having given the relevant birthday dates, they were handed giant tomes to look through.

They discovered that Chris had married Gertrude in 1927. In 1932 they legally adopted Maisie. Chris had fathered Maisie with a young teenager who lived nearby. Gerty had eventually agreed to adopt her and bring her up. Maisie was two by then.

Chris had never seen his son, Bob and was unaware of what happened to him after Lucy died. His father would not allow him back in the house. Clara did not know how he had met Gertrude and married her, but thought he had probably rented a room in her house. Clara did not get to meet Gerty or Maisie.

They read through their photocopies back at home. Alice returned to London, Derry to Oxford and Maddy to Epsom. Derry and Maddy met a few more times to make decisions.

The court report was headed 'Remarkable evidence from Brain Wave Machine'

William Grey Walter had been developing EEG machines at a neurological centre in Bristol. The judge was unfamiliar with such inventions and thought it was not worth bothering with. The results, however, were read out in court. An abnormally slow electrical rhythm from the left frontal lobe of the brain was detected. This was associated with epilepsy and some degenerative change in the brain. Gertrude had given evidence that some years earlier, Chris has fallen and become unconscious for a short period. He was told he could not go into military service.

Alice researched this expert and discovered later that he had gone on to have a distinguished career and had written a book called *The Living Brain* in 1953.

Chris had taken Maisie to the allotment and come back without her. The police recorded that he had no recollection of having taken her there and that he had no idea where she was. The next morning he had said, "I think she is under a bench."

Neighbours had seen him go down the road with Maisie so the police searched the allotments and found her little body. She had been strangled with the cord of a Venetian blind. There was no evidence of 'interference', noted the report.

Alice thought of Herman when mental health issues were mentioned but the research to her was like any other research. She remained at a distance away from it, but she could see the effect it was having on Maddy and Derry. They were silent, shaking and shedding tears at times. Maddy's own teenagers were healthy, lively and showed no signs of epilepsy or mental illness. Bob had long carried the secret which had eaten at his confidence and filled him with a fear he could not face.

Back in Oxford by the bookshelf, Alice talked with Derry.

"I feel we should go to Maisie's tomb and Chris's tomb and say some prayers."

"That's a wonderful idea, Derry. Will you take your father?"

"Yes, we'll do it together. Maddy is so much better at communicating than me."

Alice made no offers. She encouraged him to write out the prayers and to get some flowers for the tombs. She hoped they would cope as a family. Derry and Maddy talked it over with Bob. Maddy rang Alice to thank her for her help.

"He's even inserted a spiritual bit."

"Yes, he told me. How are you dealing with your Dad?"

"We have filled him in and reassured him that we love him and really admire his work in the library. He and Mum will come with us to Broadmoor and the cemetery."

Maddy would collect them and drive them and meet Derry there. Alice saw the shattered young man.

"Would you like me to drive you there?" she offered despite herself. "That's very kind. Let me think about it." Her heart went out to him.

He, like her father buried his emotions by delving into his anthropology, music, artefacts, rituals and tribal life.

Her special place was the study but her brother Daniel's was the lounge. He had started playing the piano when he was two and seemed to have a natural gift. He was destined to study music and spend his life in music. He had learned the violin but his favourite was the organ and the piano. He collected hundreds of CDs and spent his free time in concerts. Alice spent hours in the kitchen with Esther learning how to cook. She enjoyed this as relaxation. They often chatted in German as they worked. Thomas was often in the study with students or African visitors.

Thomas knew that Alice was very careful with his books and always replaced them on the right shelf so he encouraged her to use them. There were times when he was happy to talk. She could pour out anything to him. He loved his brilliant children and the fact that they were following such different paths. Alice and Daniel had a loving relationship. She had had a few boyfriends before she had a serious relationship with Herman but Daniel had no girlfriends. She introduced him to some of her friends who played tennis with him but although there was laughter and fun and some of the girls were very pretty, he never showed any interest in them. He related well to the other students that Thomas invited home, but Derry became the only frequent visitor in the holidays over several years.

While Alice waited for Derry's response she thought of Christopher, Bob and Herman. She had left Herman in 1984. Her relationship with him had caused such pain and damage that she had lost all confidence and trust in men. She had lost interest in new relationships and put all her focus on her Urdu studies and her translation work.

"Are you busy?" Derry put his head round the study door.

"Come in, Derry. How is it going?" He was packing for his Australia trip.

"Slowly. It is so hot in the day and then at night it can go down to freezing in the outback."

"Wow. Between 30+ and 0 in 24 hours!"

"Alice, I would be very grateful if you would drive me to Broadmoor and the cemetery."

"OK. We must sort out a day convenient to everyone."

"I've written some prayers. Would you read them?" Alice sat down again and took the papers from his hands.

He had hand-written them in his tiny scrawl.

In the act of forgiveness and repentance we are on holy ground.

We are in a realm beyond our comprehension, the realms of principalities and powers mentioned in Ephesians. There are strongholds being broken.

Before God in the name of all my family I come to forgive Christopher Barnes for the evil he did. We are ignorant of the influences and forces that caused his actions.

We are aware of the pain and destruction he caused to all his family and his descendants. We bring before God the abuse of his sister, Lucy, her pregnancy and early death.

We bring before God, Robert, his son and ask that God's grace, mercy and peace will be with him and his family.

I forgive Christopher and ask that his soul may rest in peace.

I ask God to break over our family the shame, guilt, melancholy, depression and anger that have been the fruits of Christopher's life. I commend his soul to God.

"Oh, Derry, that's beautiful and so sad. It says it all."

"Thank you, Alice. I hope I can read it without weeping."

"Why? Weep, go ahead and weep! That is real!"

"Here's another one for Maisie's tomb."

In the name of the Barnes family, the descendants, siblings and relatives of Christopher Barnes, I bring repentance before God for the evil which he wrought upon Maisie.

I ask forgiveness for his evil action in taking her life. I know that Maisie is safe with God.

I ask God to bring healing on all persons damaged by Christopher, and to break the power of evil over our lives.

In the Name of Jesus Christ, Amen.

Alice let her tears flow.

"Perhaps Maddy will read one. I am not sure what she will want to do."

"Send them to her. She will have time to read and think then. Those are the prayers of a man who feels deeply but has avoided facing the truth. I think you will find you can get on better with your father in the years to come."

It was a beautiful, sunny late summer day. The two cars met at Broadmoor where the chaplain showed them to the grave. Derry read the prayer, his voice breaking a little at times. They placed very large white lilies on the tomb.

On the journey to the little town, Alice let him be silent. She put on one of Daniel's organ CDs.

Maddy had found out how to identify Maisie's grave and as the cars arrived in convoy, she walked straight to the 1938 section. They stood around the headstone with its angel, a little girl angel with spreading wings. Maddy read the prayer and they ended with the Lord's Prayer. They all hugged each other and Alice stood back a little to give them some privacy. They each put down a circular arrangement of bright coloured flowers on the bare tomb.

"I'm going to tell my husband and children all about it. There's been enough secrecy. I will take some photos. No use keeping it from the next generation."

Maddy hugged Derry and held on to him for a long time. She took his arm as they walked back to the car park.

"I am sure that will help all the family." Alice felt it would be natural to hug him but she held back. He had never hugged her nor greeted her with a kiss in the past three years.

Perhaps he is gay like Daniel. she thought. After that week she would not see him again for months. In Oxford he would spend time getting advice from

Thomas on his thesis on aboriginal spirituality and culture. He would go to Epsom to see Maddy and her family and then to Brighton to see his parents before catching his plane to Cairns.

"He will soon be Doctor Barnes!" Alice looked forward to hearing about his thesis and the Aboriginal word he had mentioned.

Back at home, Thomas was in his study so she went to her room. She did not know what she felt. She was just aware of an unrecognisable set of emotions. A cloud of confusion filled her mind. She had shared a big part of Derry's life and experienced real empathy for a sadness that was not her own. She thought of the young mother of Maisie.

"Did she ever know what happened to her little girl? My mother was adopted and had to face a terrible loss. The Charltons had been very loving grandparents before they died."

After Derry's departure she sought out her father for a cosy chat.

"I need a break from the sadness of Derry's family, Dad. Tell me again how you met Mum" She loved the story.

"I was over 30 when I first saw her. I had been in Africa for so long and was looking forward to spending time in Blackwells. I had not had any opportunity to date girls but when I saw her, I just had to speak to her. She was asking about Hebrew-English and Hebrew-German dictionaries. She was tall and slim, wearing a long flowery skirt which swished round her when she moved. Her long, curly black hair was hanging loose.

"Hebrew? What for?" He said he was not very good at chat-up lines. However, she had responded, "I'm studying German and also Hebrew. I am of Jewish origin."

"We ended up having a coffee in the cafe outside, the same one now used for Morse episodes. We dated for nearly two years and then…"

"Then you proposed to her in the Pitt Rivers Museum, upstairs on the balcony, next to the shrunken heads!" Alice laughed.

It was 1987 when Derry returned from Australia with his thesis complete. His doctorate ceremony had taken place in Cairns University. He showed the family the photos of the bright coloured gown and large hat, so different to the black of English universities. He had been sent to Cairns for his PhD as the research needed to be done in the outback. He met up with Alice in London and they sat in the Royal Festival Hall overlooking the Thames. She often chose riverside places for meeting with friends.

"Welcome back Dr Derwent Barnes!" Alice had greeted him.

"I want to return to your home because I want the opportunity to thank your father properly for the help he has given me. And you too, Alice, I want to thank you. I could not have got through without your support."

"Well, I doubt I shall get to read your thesis soon. One day I'd like to. You will be very welcome at home again. Tell me about that 'dadi' word."

"*Dadirri* means something like our Christian meditation. It translates as quiet listening and stillness but it has a much deeper meaning. Stanner, the anthropologist wrote a lot about it in the 1960s and I used his works heavily. There is also the aspect of being aware of nature's silence and nature's sounds. The Aborigines are very attached to 'Country', 'Land' and 'Songlines' and I have included chapters on these topics. It has done me a lot of good and I will look out a Christian meditation group when I settle in England.'

"Do you know what you will do?"

"I can lecture. Oxford has already booked me for some lectures this year and next. I don't think I am right for teaching, giving tutorials. I am better at public speaking and answering questions and possibly at writing. I must find a more permanent base in Oxford or London until I go back to do some follow up research."

"Religion? Spirituality?"

"No, ecology and the environment. You know the Australian army is sending its recruits into the bush to learn from the tribes about how to find water in drought and what is poisonous and what is good to eat in the mangroves or in the bush." He was becoming more animated than she had ever seen him. He loved this work.

"We are slowly realising what a wealth of knowledge will disappear if we put all Aborigines into reserves in houses like ours."

"Did you meet that Aboriginal teacher you mentioned?"

"Yes, briefly. She has agreed to see me again. She is called Mary Ruth. She has a lot to say about the environment. You would like her and her art work. You really must visit Australia one day. It's not all wild bushland. There are some beautiful places."

"Perhaps I shall make a trip to visit you during your next long research program." He soon made his trip to Oxford when Alice returned home too for the weekend.

His hair had been cut very short because of the heat but by the time he came to Oxford it had grown a little. She remembered how it used to flop over his face when he was reading at a table. He sat in the lounge eating the biscuits that Esther had just made. Thomas came in and scooped up a handful as he made his way to a chair near the piano.

Derry opened his bag and unrolled a huge canvas. There was a very colourful depiction of men, kangaroos, lizards and a river in true aboriginal style, dots and little hash lines, but with modern colours.

"Thomas," Derry stood up, "Esther and Alice, I want to give you this canvas for your home. It is not tourist tat. I bought it from a tribal elder. I want to thank you for welcoming me into your home and your family during the past three years. You have all given me more than you can ever know. Thomas, I was privileged to study under you, under such a gifted, kind and generous professor. Esther you have treated me like a son. Alice you have shown me such understanding and sensitivity when I invaded your privacy and called on your support for me and my family."

Esther stood up, walked over to him and hugged him. She held him for a while and then took his hands.

"Dr Derwent Barnes you have been very welcome. You have been an exemplary house-guest and you will always be a friend wherever you go and whenever you need a base in Oxford."

They spread the canvas over the grand piano and Alice went over to Derry and put her arms round his neck. She felt his arms hugging her round her back. She had hugged no man like that since she left Herman. She drew back and gave him a kiss on both cheeks.

"More French than German! Thank you so much Derry and congratulations." He went back to his bag and pulled out an envelope.

"This is a more formal thank-you for you, Thomas. And Alice, I hope you will like these." He passed her a small box with Reef pearl earrings from the Great Barrier Reef.

Alice was so surprised and thought they were beautiful. "Thank-you, Derry, these are so special!"

"Give me your lecture dates in Oxford." Thomas asked, "I would love to come and hear you speak. I'd like to know more about Aboriginal spirituality and do some comparisons with the tribes in Nigeria."

"Comparisons? Have you done others?"

"Not academically, just ideas. Tribes worldwide, there is an increasing interest."

Sitting in the study, Alice remembered those events and conversations from two years ago.

Now, the Wall had fallen. What a significant decade they had gone through; the 1980s had been significant for Daniel and for Derry and for Alice. They had all suffered from some very challenging problems and needed to go forward on a new path. Now they would concentrate on preparing the trip to Leipzig with Esther.

3 Student Life: A Significant Decade

At the beginning of the 1980s, Alice had been preparing her A levels when Daniel was accepted at Durham to pursue his music studies. She went with Esther to help settle him into his digs and fell in love with the city, the cathedral, the castle, and the river views. Thomas was in Nigeria and Esther was due to join him there for a holiday.

"It's strange. He went to Africa to see Egypt and the desert where Robert died but he ended up in the jungle. I blame the Pitt Rivers. He was always fascinated by that place and the African artefacts."

"Are you worried about going there?"

"A little but he is with a tribe he knows well and the University authorities take better care of their people than they did a few years ago."

On their return from Durham, Esther prepared her luggage and Alice worked hard at her A levels in French, German and Religious Studies. Daniel invited her for a stay in Durham at the end of his first year.

"Alice, I need a serious talk with you before I have one with Mum and Dad."

That was unlike her brother. She looked out at the skyline and the castle as the train drew in. Daniel was blond with blue eyes. He dressed quite formally and did not go around in sports clothes; jacket and trousers were more his style. He too had wanted to study away from Oxford. He was fairly conservative but he felt he needed some fresh air. He had enjoyed his interview at Durham and was glad to study Music there. Alice saw him on the platform looking drawn. She thought of herself as the tougher of the two and had been aware of his sensitivity in the rough and tumble of sibling life.

"Daniel, you look so thin! Haven't you been eating?"

"Come and see the standing stones at the cathedral and we can catch Evensong. Great choir!" he said. Alice was enthralled by the giant pillars of the cathedral with their different designs carved round them. She loved looking at Celtic Christian origins and bought some ear-rings with the snake like, twirling, twisting, winding patterns from the standing stones. The serious talk came in the Italian restaurant which had a bay window overlooking the river Wear.

During the glorious, moving melodies of Evensong, he had leaned over to her.

"I have not been coming here regularly. I have been going to a charismatic church which meets in a kind of empty factory."

"What's a charismatic church?"

Daniel started by explaining that on Fresher's Week he had met these very friendly young people who welcomed him to their church. It was an informal fellowship with hundreds of young people. He had been overwhelmed at the warmth of the welcome and the enthusiasm of the worship. Some sat, some stood, some danced around to the music group who led a long, unbroken time of worship. The hymns were short and repetitive but most people raised their hands, closed their eyes, or looked upward with a great smile. They believed in the gifts of the Holy Spirit. Some people went up to the microphones on the platform and gave messages.

"God wants to heal you. Someone with a serious back problem is here and God wants to heal you. Come forward and we will pray for you."

A few people responded and little clusters gathered round them, put hands on their shoulders, head and back and prayed aloud. A few of them fell over.

"I had never been in any church with such a sense of worship, love to God, trust in God and a very real expectation that He was working in our lives and would perform miracles." He took a sip of wine.

"I went for several weeks. One week a preacher jumped up and down and preached about our over-sexed society."

He warned that it was God's purpose that all sexual activity should be within marriage. The congregation had clapped and he led them all in prayer. He asked them to repent and make a vow to God that they would remain celibate until God led them to the right partner.

"That got me thinking. I knew Mum and Dad would want grandchildren but I did not want to get married as I knew I was only attracted to men."

"So you are gay!" Alice whispered. "Well yes, same-sex attraction, they say."

"So this church does not like people to be gay?"

"Let me explain."

Daniel sipped his wine. He had felt he should go forward for prayer the following week as the next topic for the sermon was same-sex attraction. The preacher had ranted somewhat about the depiction of gay life in the media.

God created Adam and Eve. Two men or two women having a physical, sexual relationship is an abomination in the eyes of God. He read some verses from Romans and said that God would not have forbidden this behaviour if He did not intend to change people's evil desires. When he stood at the front an older Elder prayed over him. "God wants to heal you but it will not happen all at once. You need to change your mind set."

He was invited to make a regular date for prayer which would be a conversion for him. Daniel wrestled with his emotions. He would love to fall in love with a girl and become a father.

"Do you want children, Alice?"

"Probably but it is too soon. I am too young to think about it as I have years of study ahead of me. That sounds exciting for you."

Daniel had felt excitement and hope as he attended the prayer times. They met at the Elder's home with his prayer partner, another student from the University.

"I had to start with confession." He had recounted his boyhood fumbles in the school toilets. He explained he had never had intercourse but had fantasised about boys he found attractive.

Next came the cleansing prayer. His filthy mind had to be cleaned out.

"What you desire is an abomination to a Holy God. He did not create you like that and He wants to heal you." They wrote some Bible verses out on cards so whenever he felt attracted to a man he should pray and read them aloud over and over again.

"Do you not know that the wicked will not inherit the kingdom of God? Do not be deceived. Neither the sexually immoral nor idolaters, nor adulterers, nor male prostitutes nor homosexual offenders will inherit the kingdom of God.

"Flee from sexual immorality.

"He who sins sexually sins against his own body."

"Week after week I was told that God would give me over to sexual impurity, *for the degrading of their bodies with one another."*

"Daniel, that's terrible. It does not sound like a God of love."

"They wanted to perform an exorcism on me. They said I had demons inside and they needed to come out so I could be clean."

"Really? Did you agree? How did they do that?"

Daniel had tears in his eyes. The Elders lit candles and he was asked to kneel down. Then he had to prostrate himself before God. They took it in turns to call on God's presence. They yelled, "Come out! Free him! Let him go!"

"They touched me. They touched me, Alice, you know, they touched me to cast out the demon of lust."

Tears now rolled down his cheeks.

When they stopped yelling, Daniel was sobbing and shaking. They sang quiet hymns and anointed his head with oil, softly wiping it over his forehead.

The Elder proclaimed that the demon had gone and now he had to work at cleaning his thoughts.

"You will be tempted and tested."

"I was a gibbering idiot and could not wait to get away from them."

Daniel had left them and walked along the river bank. At the bridge he had considered jumping off but he thought that he was too good a swimmer. He followed the footpath into some trees and wept until he could weep no more.

"Alice, nothing changed in me over the next few months. I had been told to start dating girls and I saw that some in the fellowship were very pretty. I found it difficult to face total failure and felt I could not go to the fellowship anymore."

Alice took his hands across the table.

"Daniel that can't be right. God would not lead you to kill yourself when you went for His help. We must talk to Mum and Dad and see if there is a vicar or counsellor who could give you some advice. Write to them and tell them you think you are gay. Dad will be back from Africa in August."

"Dear Dad, he could cope with anything. You can tell him anything."

"Alice I feel very disturbed because these Christians meant well. They really believed in what they were doing. When we met there was always a time of worship. They would sing songs about the love and the power of God. The worship times with the singing in tongues were so beautiful. You could totally accept that God was capable of doing any miracles. At the start I believed that this was God working in my life. I knew I was gay when I was very young. Boys at school messed around with each other but I saw most of them move on to girls. I never could. After the first weeks I was expecting to feel different. I tried very hard but nothing changed inside. I began to ask God to show me if I was on the right path."

"And you only had these people to talk to about it all?"

"I felt I owed them. I should not let them down. They were kind and invited me to their homes for meals. When we had the meetings they always started with hymns and declarations of the power of God. They lit candles, made an atmosphere and they shouted when their own expectations came to nothing. I never lied to them. I told them that I felt no different."

Daniel addressed his letter to both parents. He loved and trusted them. Alice thought that some of Dad's waifs and strays had been gay. She thought back and realised that she had never known any gay people in her circle of friends. She was certain that her parents would be understanding, perhaps disappointed, but realistic. She was right. Both of them hugged Daniel and assured him that they loved him and would support him. They encouraged him to change his studies and leave Durham.

Daniel applied for a place in the Royal School of Music in London. He wanted to concentrate on the organ. He left Durham and lived at home while he waited. He took up a few organ playing engagements in local churches. He took up a place at the RSM and began an intensive course of organ playing. He was like a different man.

He met Charles, never Charlie or Chas, always Charles. He became a frequent visitor at the Hartley's, as did Daniel to Charles' family, the Carmodys in Surrey. Thomas and Esther enjoyed a couple of quiet years as both their children were happy in their studies and both were aiming for high honours.

In 1982 Alice took up her German BA in London. She was advised to find a holiday job in Germany in the summer to perfect her fluency and her accent. She travelled to Reutlingen near the Black Forest to work for some months in a home for disabled children, the Georg Stiftung. The children had mainly mental disabilities and learning difficulties but a few had some physical problems and wore neck braces or leg braces and walked with crutches. They were divided into family groups in separate houses. Each house was purpose built with bedrooms and toilets and shower rooms. There was a large communal area which served as dining room, sitting room and play room. Alice loved the daily routine and the weekend walks into the hills where they would all pick wild strawberries. Nothing was as delicious as these crushed berries spread onto bagels. On free days she went into the town, visited Tübingen and went on trips to the Black Forest. The staff from the other houses could meet in the canteen in the evenings. She soon noticed the Schwäbish accent of many of her colleagues but then there was Herman Kreuz. His accent was different.

“I’m from Aachen and I am a Bible student in Switzerland.”

“What are you studying?”

“Theology, the Bible and how to be a missionary.”

“Where are you aiming for?”

“With a name like mine, what else should I do? I don’t know yet. Africa perhaps.”

Alice told him about her father’s studies in Nigeria. He was dark haired and good looking. He was casually dressed and put on a crumpled suit for Sunday services.

The tolling of the local church bell haunted Alice for years. She thought of her mother’s start in life in Germany and of the holocaust. The toll of the bell, the single note lasted for a long time and filled Alice with a sense of the tragedy that had been overcome in this land.

Herman sat strumming his guitar in the canteen. She told him that her brother was studying music. Nearly every break she noticed that he came to find her. He explained that he was the only son of elderly parents who had suffered during the war.

They arranged to have their free days together when possible and one weekend they travelled by train to Berlin to visit the Wall and the museums. They walked around the famous Zoo before returning. He started to put his arm round her and they often walked hand in hand.

He greeted her with kisses and she fell in love with this gentleman. She stared into his dark brown eyes and noticed that sometimes they held a different expression.

She tried to discuss some of the authors she had studied.

“I prefer the modern ones like Böll and Mann but you **have** to do Goethe. He is like our Shakespeare!” He did not know these authors. He had not completed his Arbitur but had left school to work in a Chemist’s before deciding on Bible School. He was already 24 so she was aware of a degree of mystery about him.

“You need practical experience to be a missionary.” It sounded like an explanation or an excuse.

She asked him about the war. His father had been in the army and was slightly injured in the fighting with the Allies near Aachen. His parents were well into their 40s when he was born. Most of the bomb damage had been cleared up by that time. Aachen stands on three borders and was badly hit as the English and American troops invaded after D Day. He promised to take her to the

Dreiländerecke, a post to walk round to be in Germany, Holland and Belgium. They declared their love for each other and began to kiss more seriously. They dreamt about the children they might have and wondered where they would end up working. She planned to research some missionary societies to see where her own gifts could be best put to use. The Bible school also had contacts he could follow up when he returned.

They planned for her to spend time in Aachen and perhaps make decisions over engagement and their future. Alice really wanted him to come to meet her family first.

There were certain aspects which troubled her but she was so in love that she found ways to dismiss them. He talked about being terribly academic but he had done no higher studies.

When she invited him to Oxford he explained that he could not afford the fares. When they talked about the Nazis and the war he revealed a deep anger. His father had returned in 1946 an injured, broken and depressed stranger. Herman had a few more weeks before he was due to return to Switzerland. She said she would pay for an air far for him for the next long holiday. He could come to meet her parents and they could fly back to Aachen together.

He held her tightly as she got on her train to go back to her studies.

"You could give up your studies and come back and marry me." She felt such love for him. "I am only 19." She said nothing more but inside she knew she would never give up her studies and was happy to wait until they were over. They wrote to each other twice a week at least and phoned each other. Often his letters began with phrases such as 'Why did you write so late? What have I done? What did I say to upset you? You have not replied yet.'

Alice bought him a ticket from Koln/Bonn airport to Heathrow. They embraced and could not easily let each other go. Daniel drove them to Oxford. Thomas was in Nigeria and missed this first visit. Esther chatted away with him in the kitchen and learned about his family and his aims in life. They played cards and backgammon together.

They flew back for the Aachen visit. Her memory of that time was not a happy one. She went full of hope and love and returned broken.

She loved the city of Aachen, the historic cathedral, the street sculptures and the beautiful countryside around it. The Kreuz parents lived on the top floor of a small flat in a block which they had moved into when their house was destroyed by British bombs. Dad was already 70 and had difficulty getting up and down the stairs. He had several hospital appointments to attend. His wife would care for him and do everything for him. She also gave Herman many hugs and often stroked his head. She was 67 but still active and capable. She offered to go for a walk with Alice to the cathedral where Charlemagne was buried. Outside they sat by a beautiful little bird fountain. She asked Alice what her plans were.

"I will probably do missionary work with Herman when he has finished at Heilberg."

"Oh, he left the Heilberg Bible School last year. They did not treat him properly. They should have taken his side against the Georg Stiftung but instead they sided with the home so he had to leave. He is back at the Chemist's now. He'll be alright there. He'll get on there."

Alice felt immense shock that he had not told her of such a huge life change. She felt very nervous about asking him. She was incredulous that he had met her family and not said anything about this terrible news.

Had Herman asked his mother to tell her? Why had he said nothing when her letters had told him about her contacts with missionary societies?

She saw the black look in his eyes when they returned and he told her to walk with him to the hill outside the city. They held hands and he gradually walked with his arms around her.

He told her a tale of conflict and lack of support at the Home. "They are too proud."

"Herman, why did you not tell me? You know I had some interviews with some of the Missionary Organisations. Why? How could you NOT tell me?" She was crying now.

"Loving someone is more important than education. If you love me you can give up your studies and come to Aachen and marry me. I am going to get work in the Hospital Pharmacy and you could get work anywhere with your German and French." She felt despair. Could she trust this man? She was still weeping when they returned home.

"Herman, I love you but I cannot stop my studies. I can marry you when they are over. I could probably even get a job in the University here."

Herman was sweating and panting. He went into his bedroom and lay on the bed.

His mother heard him and came into his room with a bowl of water and a cloth. She began wiping his head and neck, arms and hands.

"It's manager's malady." he said. His mother sat next to him, stroking his head and muttering "Hermansche, Hermansche," as if to a toddler. He fell asleep and she came out to Alice.

"He cannot cope with conflict. Let him sleep. You are too studious for him, too much brain and not enough love." Alice was dumbstruck.

"I have to take Papa to the doctor tomorrow morning. Please take Herman a coffee before you decide what you are doing."

"I will."

He was still in bed and his brow was still covered in beads of sweat when she took him the coffee. She put it on the bedside table and he grabbed her arms as she sat on the edge of the bed.

"You did this to me! You say you love me. Prove it! Show me!"

She leant over and kissed him on the lips. They held each other for a while but then he pulled her down to the bed and began pulling at her blouse. He rolled on top of her and pulled at his pyjamas. He pinned her down with one arm and tried to get her skirt off with the other.

She yelled "No!" a dozen times and struggled to free herself. He was furiously kissing her all over her shoulders and neck and forced his tongue into her mouth. She managed to pull one arm free and gave him a heavy slap across the face. The shock made him stop.

"Herman stop! That is not love. That is rape!"

He did stop but suddenly he grabbed the coffee and threw it over her. It was not scalding but uncomfortably hot. He slid off her and fled to the shower. Sobbing, she wiped herself at the kitchen sink and went to find another top. She pushed everything quickly into her suitcase and checked she had her passport and wallet.

She ran down the stairs and heard him open the door above her. She was grateful he had not attacked her any more but was determined to go and never return.

"Sorry. Sorry. Please come back!"

"Fertig!" She yelled. "It's over." He was still in his pyjamas so he could not run after her into the street. She quickly ran around a corner and went into a shop. She waited to see if he was out on the street. No sign.

Alice walked quickly to the station and got a train to Cologne.

She would stay a while in a hotel to recover some equilibrium and then change her ticket to fly home early.

Once she was calmer she rang her best friend at the Reutlingen home. Anne was a sympathetic listener. She explained that after she had left him, Herman became angry and was very rude to the other staff. The director told him that they could not tolerate his bad language and bad temper and that he should pack and leave immediately. He had insulted the director, the staff and the home.

Alice asked to speak to the director and told him how sorry she was for Herman's behaviour. She liked and respected the director very much.

"He tried to rape me so I have run away to a hotel." she explained.

The director said he was not surprised. He had gone after the young girls who worked there even after she had left he had been touching Hannelore and forcing his attentions on her.

"I think he needs help. He has something like manic depression. I had to report him to Heilberg and the head told me that they were planning to expel him on his return from Reutlingen, because he had also shown anger inappropriately and had shown too much interest in the young girls."

"Alice you worked well here. You are young and naive. It is not your fault but you have been saved from a very unhappy marriage. You had no way of knowing he had such serious emotional problems"

The next day Alice rang Daniel. She had listened to his tale of woe two years earlier. He was just right to talk to. He put up with her tears and sobs and did his best to reassure her.

She then rang Esther.

"My darling, I am so sorry. He was such a charmer. He was so gentle while he was with us. In the end you will recover dearest and you will meet a better man to love. It is a great mercy that you did not marry him."

She posted a letter to Herman when she left the hotel in Cologne. She pleaded with him to get some psychiatric help, to seek out a counsellor. She made it clear that although she was in love with him, she would never marry him, never have a future with him. She wished him well and that he would find someone else who would love him.

At her Oxford home she wept with her mother and with her father. She read for hours in the study when Thomas did not need it. She stood in front of the bookshelf and a sense came over her that the last two years would eventually fade and that she would be doing different things and the bookshelf would still be there. She had a sense of peace. She saw books on Germany and the holocaust, books on Hebrew with the fascinating script from right to left, the dots, the squiggles and the shapes in such neat lines. She found books with Aboriginal cave paintings and books on India with some Urdu script. She did not realise that as she flicked through them, seeds were being sown for her future.

She had read the stories of the terrible way the border line had been drawn between India and Pakistan, sometimes through the middle of a village. Muslims and Hindus who had lived in peace together in the same towns were then killing each other. There were massacres on both sides as the Muslims left their homes and walked to the new border to form their new homeland.

Doing her best to put Herman Kreuz behind her, she returned to London to complete her BA German, still aiming at a First Class Honours. She had an inner hunger for something different. This was when the door opened for her to teach Muslim ladies and learn some Urdu herself. It was also during the next year that Derwent Barnes had come into her life and that she had got involved with his family problems.

The Urdu classes were something of a relief for her. She could keep her mind off Herman and concentrate on these lovely Pakistani ladies who had such a different life. They came mainly from the Rawalpindi area and had never been to school. They could not read or write in their own language. When the story cards were spread out on the table, however, the ladies automatically picked up the one on the right to answer the questions. They thought in a right to left line.

They usually wore beautiful, coloured, silky clothes, the shalwa chemise. This was not warm for them in the winter. In November, some of them wore flip flops. She tried to guide them to put on tights or socks and cardigans on the top of their own dress. Her first student whom she taught one to one, invited her to Ramadan celebrations. This lady had married her first cousin at 15 and now had 5 children, three girls and two boys. The second boy was born with severe disabilities. He could not speak, sit up alone, or walk at all. He knew he was loved as his parents both spoke to him and he would smile and move his head.

Alice found the husbands rather loud and brusque but realised that they had never encountered an independent woman with a car who had the freedom to go where she liked.

"You speak better Urdu than me!" Said one of them. Their main language was a dialect from their area of Pakistan and they rarely communicated in Urdu.

When the Wall came down she was still teaching a couple of hours a week and continuing to do some translations for a firm. She tried to move beyond survival level language to role play in her classes. She wanted to prepare them to deal with callers at the door, with the doctor and the teachers at their children's school. There was excellent resource in the Community English Class office. The flash cards were of everyday situations they would all recognise.

They had no idea what role play was and had never experienced it before. They did not know how to use their imagination. She started with how to deal with an unknown caller to their house. She spread out the pictures of doors with numbers.

"This is your door." She gave one lady a card.

"You are calling at the door. You are with the Gas Board" She gave another lady a card.

They failed at the first question. "What is your name?" The caller answered with her own name. "Where do you live?" The lady ignored the card and gave her home address.

What they really loved were the party games. They brought generous curries and finger food like samosa but also enjoyed the English cakes. The favourite game was at the Christmas party. They sat in a ring around a small table and chair. A big bar of wrapped chocolate was on the table with a knife and fork. On the chair was a scarf, a jacket and some gloves. They passed a ball around the ring and whoever was holding it when the music stopped had to go to the table, put on the clothes and try to open the bar with the knife and fork. The laughter was so infectious.

The word for owl was similar to the word for potato. When she tried out her Urdu with the ladies and told them that the potato was in the tree, they had a good laugh.

She was happy and had made no efforts to seek boyfriends since 1984. She had lost her confidence and found that she could never trust a man, including Derry. He kept in touch on his second trip to the Northern Territories. He sent post cards of Cairns and the Great Barrier Reef when he touched base with Cairns University. He was in the outback for months at a time. He probably did not even know that the Berlin Wall had fallen.

Those last years of the decade passed very quickly. Alice moved into her own flat and put all her efforts into her work and her teaching. She went out with friends, went to concerts with them and with Daniel. Charles had changed his name to Hartley by deed-poll in those days before Civil Partnerships and same-sex marriage. Most people thought they were brothers.

Alice was beginning to think of furthering her studies, getting a Masters and a PhD in German. She decided to wait until after their trip to Leipzig.

Unification took place a year after the fall of the Wall. Esther hungrily watched all the documentaries and read all the magazines that came out. The situation became clearer. The currency was regulated one D Mark for one DDR Mark. New rulers took over and the rebuilding of the East became a priority.

Spiegel Magazine had an article by a pastor from a Lutheran Church in Leipzig. He was coming to speak at the Goethe Institute in London. Alice was often there for films and talks. Esther came to London to attend this talk with her.

He told how during 1988 churches were seen as a safe place to be, to voice opinions on the DDR regime and to organise marches. Now, the young people who had flocked there were leaving for the West. Even the churches had not been totally safe. Spies were sent in and reported back to the Stasi.

Esther spoke to the pastor at the end and introduced herself. She asked if they could come and visit him when they came to Leipzig. He was very warm towards her and offered her family the use of one of the church flats during their stay. One link led to another and she was given other names of pastors who also had an interest in the Jews of Leipzig.

Alice had her talk with Daniel. He wanted to go to the famous Gewandhaus for a concert. He did not want Charles to come with them as he felt it was a private family visit and they needed space for their own emotions. He too feared Esther's emotional reactions

"She had kept so much inside over the years. She has talked more about Dad's dead brother than about the death of her own family."

Alice put behind her all memories of her teenage relationship, of Daniel coming to terms with his sexuality and of the difficult emotional time with the Barnes and focussed totally on her mother's story. Esther needed to find out anything she could about her family in Leipzig.

Deep inside, Alice was full of dread.

She bought street maps of Leipzig and found information on the history of the city in the Goethe Institute library. She saw that it was not far to Weimar and Wittenberg. Daniel thought they could easily get to those towns.

The film, *Geteilte Himmel* from the book by Christa Wolf was showing there one evening. Esther came to London to accompany Alice. The story of lovers separated by the Wall prepared them emotionally for what they might experience in the old East Germany.

4 Leipzig

Professor Thomas Edward Hartley was given an award for his work on the tribes of Nigeria, the relationship he had with the tribes and for his charity foundation. His family stayed for the ceremony but flew to Leipzig immediately afterwards. He had a few lectures to give about the award and planned to join them after a few days. Like the tolling of the bell in Reutlingen, the name Leipzig provoked a deep emotional reaction in Alice.

This was a new decade and new experiences lay before them.

They spent the first few days getting to know the city. In the flat they found old street maps of the city centre and noticed that all the street names were different.

"I suppose Deutsche-Sowietische Freundschaft Strasse is no longer valid." Daniel smiled.

It was beginning to be a thriving international trade centre. *Leipzig kommt!* was the slogan on the many posters on the walls. The town centre was a mixture of old and new. The University tower was nicknamed *The Tooth* because of the shape of the roof of this glass and metal structure which dominated all other buildings. There were photographs of a church with a spire that the Russians had demolished in order to build it. The face of Karl Marx was still there in the metal sculpture on the front wall. Near the Gewandhaus were wide open spaces, tiled with low walls, streams and fountains. The three of them made a dash to the Buchhandlung opposite. On that first Sunday they went to the Thomaskirche which had been the church of J S Bach.

They would save the Nicholaikirche for when Thomas joined them. They filmed each other next to the huge Bach statue outside.

Pastor Michael invited them to have a meal in his flat on the floor below them. After supper he showed them his Stasi files. Large black folders were filled with reports and letters. Tears rolled down his cheeks as he showed them a report from people in his congregation whom he had considered as close friends.

"I cannot blame them. I know they would have been threatened by the Stasi that the man would lose his job and his children would not be able to go to

University. They knew that I had foreign contacts and thought I was receiving money from abroad. I was not, but if any visitors came, that went into the reports. We knew we could not trust everyone so we trusted no one. Sad situation for a church."

He advised them to go to the old Stasi HQ which was now a museum. The imposing building straddled a corner and was called the Rundeecke. A feeling of fear and dread had emanated from this building with its strong wooden doors and wide steps up.

As Alice went up the steps she began to take in the atmosphere and relax. This was recent history and not part of her mother's story. Upstairs screens were playing the video tapes which the Stasi had taken in 1989 of the marches around the ring road. They sat and watched the armed guards standing shoulder to shoulder on the footbridges.

The camera switched to the crowd and suddenly a circle would appear over a face and that face was enlarged for identification. On another film young soldiers were seen weeping in their barracks. They had been told to be prepared to shoot on the crowd on the next march when many extra thousands were expected. Some of them knew that their mothers and other family members would be marching.

Esther was amazed, "Egon Krenz had given the right to shoot but nobody fired a shot!"

"Something in the ether" was in the Telegraph report.

The atmosphere had been electric. In June the Chinese army had shot and rolled tanks over their own student demonstrators. 'Could that happen here? Yes, it just could.' However 'Wir sind das Volk' and 'Neuer Sozialismus, neue SED' were the banners being carried.

'Keine Gewalt!'—no violence, was scrawled on the banners outside the Nicholaikirche.

A few days earlier police arrived with dogs and bundled the leather jacketed youths into the vans, beating them with truncheons. Now they could read 'Deutschland EinigVaterland!' held aloft as the marchers made for the ring road.

Downstairs there were some amusing exhibits; there were rows of glass jars on shelves. They contained large blobs of cotton wool or rolls of felt.

"They were used to wipe a chair where a suspect had been sitting. He was made to sit on his hands so they would sweat. The cotton wool would wipe the chair and be stored in a jar. Tracker dogs would sniff it and follow the suspect or pick him out in a crowd." Daniel had read the notices.

He laughed and pointed to the very obviously false moustaches and hair dye.

In the cellar room was a stack of what looked like concrete in the middle of the floor. To one side were giant bath tubs. As the marchers had gathered outside and made attempts to break down the doors, the officers inside tried to destroy as much as possible from the files. They soaked the paper in the baths then emptied them on to the tiled floor for the next pile to be thrown in.

Visitors were invited to take a handful of the dried, mashed paper for a Mark or two and to buy a file cover with the hammer and sickle. Daniel and Alice took one each.

"The title of the exhibition is very apt!" Alice said, "Macht und Banalität, Power and Banality!"

The reports were unbelievably trivial;

'Sat alone in cafe. Went to bus stop. Got on bus.' The three of them had a laugh.

Esther drew their attention to a large photo of the soldiers standing in a tight line on the outer steps of the building. The lights of the cameras had caught their shiny, black boots. They held their guns tightly as the marchers approached. The crowds were holding hundreds of candles and some came up to the step and placed their candles at their feet next to the threatening boots. The photo appeared in Spiegel, in the Press and on the television news.

"It was like spiritual magic." Esther was deeply moved.

"The road sign was also in a photo, *Leipzig Heldenstadt*, was printed there. Town of heroes!

"Thank God we never had to live under such a regime. What courage! Such bravery!" Daniel added.

"Germany is such a beautiful country with beautiful cities and countryside but such ugly things have happened here. Look what they have achieved since the Nazi times and now since the Reunification. They are really working at being a united nation, modern and non-threatening."

Had she spoken too soon? They walked towards the attractive market place. They had lunch in Auerbach's Keller, the famous, historical restaurant linked to Goethe and his works such as 'Faust'. Ahead, they noticed large crowds waving flags and shouting. A group of mainly youths dressed in black leather, held red, white and black flags, no swastikas but a similar design which evoked the now forbidden symbol.

"Neo-Nazis!" Daniel pulled his mother and sister in another direction but suddenly dozens of soldiers or police with dogs walked quickly in front of the crowds. Yet another group was approaching with banners about Sozialismus! They did their best to separate the two groups and send them down different streets. A look of horror spread over Alice's face and they all backed away to where they had come from.

That evening Daniel went to the airport to collect Thomas. They had been surprised at the very inadequate airport building. It was small and metallic, not quite corrugated iron, but that is what they thought of when they stepped outside for a taxi.

"This is no better than an African airport." said Thomas. "And this is aiming at becoming an international trade town!"

"They will rebuild it. They will do it very well!"

Thomas was introduced to Pastor Michael.

"I have an invitation for you tomorrow. Pastor Langman will be delighted to meet you all. He has close connections to Israel. You will notice this as soon as you go into his study."

Esther wanted to go to the station where she had last seen her parents when they had put her on a train with many other children. They went there first before walking to the Langman flat. There were even postcards of the station which had a frontage and architecture more like a gigantic palace. In the main entrance a modern cake stall was selling cherry streusli. Above was a giant screen showing the Barcelona Olympics.

Esther said that all she could remember was a glass roof. The space inside was immense. Sure enough the glass roof was there, spanning the platforms with arches.

"It must be more modern. The station was damaged by bombs in the war." Alice opened her history booklet. The floor area had pale tiles like grey marble so the light dominated the station. There were over 20 platforms but the sign system had not been renewed. Old fashioned signs showed the destination of the trains and the number of the platform.

The four Hartleys slowly walked the length of the station. They found a train going to Weimar.

"The town of Goethe and Schiller," said Alice, "and the link town to Buchenwald."

"Mum can you remember anything?"

She could remember the big space and that she was holding her parents' hands. Dad had a suitcase and Mum held her doll. They all knew the doll, still in her bedroom in a little glass cabinet with the old photos. Her parents handed her over to the Refugee Children's Movement representatives. Her mother was not crying.

Esther remained in silence and looked upwards for several minutes. Thomas put his arm round her. She had a smile on her face. This was a holy moment. They stood in silence.

Alice began to fear the intensity of her mother's pain.

"What she must be going through! But she looks happy."

How long did that moment last? Eventually Esther spoke, "It is like the spiritual magic of the Rundeecke. I could see crowds of angels in white all over the roof. They had feathered wings slightly open. They were just standing there all over the roof area in the arches. I am sure terrible things happened in this station but that was an image of hope."

"There is hope now Mum." Alice hugged her mother.

They began their walk across town. Not far from the old Deutsche-Sowietische Freundshaft Street were elegant blocks of flats with balconies. Pastor Michael had warned them, "Never walk on the same side as the flats, take the park side. Bits of balcony and concrete are often falling off. They will be renovated soon."

They saw the broken pieces of concrete and the iron work of the balconies hanging down. Pigeons were flying in and out.

"People still live there. They have coal fires and have to carry the coal from the cellar up all the floors." Michael had explained.

'Umleitung', Deviation was a sign they saw all over the town as well as on the roads which approached it. There were huge piles of earth in heaps at the side of the gigantic holes in the road. In the centre of town was a McDonald's, the first new western cafe to go up after the 'Wende', the big change. They chose a more German looking cafe and studied their map.

"The New Jewish Cemetery is not far; shall we go there next?" Thomas suggested. He appreciated that the Charltons had done their research after the war. One Berger was named as victim in Buchenwald but no Bergers were on any other lists, certainly no survivors. Many of the Jews were moved from Leipzig to Theresienstadt on a death march. As the war was coming to an end the Nazis tried to hide as much evidence as they could, even blowing up some gas chambers. The forced marches caused many deaths and unnamed Jews were placed in outside tombs. Two generations of Bergers were probably buried there.

The four Hartleys stood together in front of the building just inside the gates of the cemetery. STÄRKER ALS TOD IST DIE LIEBE was carved above the doors.

"Stronger than death is love" read Daniel, "How beautiful!"

They looked at the tomb stones with the Star of David and noted how many had a date of death in 1940.

"Can you face a visit to Buchenwald?" asked Daniel.

"Let me think about it," answered Esther. "I am sure something will tell me that I should and I know that I will find nothing new there." She pulled out the photos that her parents had put in her little case. She had not brought the doll.

"God give you peace!" She wept a little.

"You need a couple of days and if you go we will all be with you." Thomas held her again.

"We could go to Weimar anyway," Alice said, keen to see the literary museum and perhaps the balcony where Hitler had stood to rouse his people in the early days.

Pastor Langman lived in a first floor flat in an elegant building not so damaged as the others they had seen. Esther led as they walked into the study. It was not a big room but as they squeezed in they saw the large menorah on the table, the Star of David on the wall and a large photo of Langman at Yad Vashem. An Israeli flag was in the back corner and they stood around a big armchair which was covered with a sheepskin.

"This is where I pray. I was given it as a gift when I went to Israel. As soon as the wall came down I went there."

Moved and impressed they asked him to explain more. Under the communists they had been taught that the holocaust was the fault of the imperialistic west and not of the good communists who stood up to the Nazis.

"I knew that was not totally true and that the people in the east were equally guilty. The West Germans had repented and made a huge effort to make relationship with Israel soon after the war. I was never allowed out to travel there. I made as many contacts as I could."

There had been a strong Communist Resistance in the war and many were imprisoned. Nevertheless this pastor felt he should lead a Repentance trip to England in 1995, fifty years after the end of the war. He had contacts with an English Bishop who would join him in Coventry.

"I was deeply affected by Yad Vashem. I was given the sheep skin there. On my return I set up a charity to help the poor Jews in Russia to come out and go to Israel. This block of flats has the refugee families staying until they move on. Russia was prepared to let them go because they were uneducated, peasant stock. They had not been allowed to use the Hebrew tongue or Yiddish and they spoke only Russian. The Lutheran church provided the furniture and clothing they needed. We had a fleet of mini buses in Dresden and here at the station.

"Some of them wore pots and pans round their necks. Many did not move on quickly because of the conflicts in Palestine. Some decided to stay in Germany."

"Which station?" asked Esther. When he affirmed that he meant the Hauptbahnhof of Leipzig she exclaimed, "The angels! That explains the angels. God is blessing your work!" She told him the vision she had seen.

"On Sunday evening we have our ecumenical praise and worship service in the Petrikirche. Please do come and join us. We never forget Israel."

"Spiritual magic." whispered Esther.

Their sad visits were broken up by a concert in the Gewandhaus. Daniel was in ecstasy. The beauty and power of the music brought healing and peace to them all.

Esther said that she would go to Buchenwald and then they could visit Weimar. There was still Luther's church in Wittenberg for their last day. Alice battled with her own fear. She remembered Derry and the Chaplain's words;

"Better to know the whole truth than just a bit. Your imagination runs wild with the bit you know."

Buchenwald was in every way as bad as they had dreaded. They expected to see the well-known *Arbeit Macht Frei* on the gate but instead the gate had *Jedem das Seine*, Each to his own. How bizarre. How meaningless. How cruel. They walked slowly and surveyed the vast area where the barracks had been. Instead, there were the stony rectangles with just the number of the huts displayed.

Few buildings remained; the crematorium, the officers' block and the Medical Experiment block and a bunker with cells.

"Charles would never cope with this." Daniel read the plaques with the names of some special people commemorated, a pastor, a communist leader.

In the museum the information cards were all in Gothic script. Many contained that same propaganda. This vast camp imprisoned Poles, Gypsies, Russians and Jews and hundreds of children. There were pictures of their liberation in 1945. Outside the camp stands the stunning memorial. Eleven brass statues, beautifully depicted, overlook the wide stretch of countryside below. They represent the determined struggle of the 'antifascists.' The animate looking figures are placed in front of the memorial tower.

The Hartleys stood again in silence. They all thought of Esther's parents and grandparents. Starvation on the death march was the best that they could wish for them. The cruelty of the medical experiments could not be contemplated. They went back to Leipzig. They did not feel like eating or visiting Weimar.

"Let's have some soup" suggested Thomas and tomorrow morning we shall go to the Nicholaikirche in the morning and the Petrikirche in the evening. Silent and overwhelmed they were all pleased about that.

The 'tooth' tower was a welcome sight as the train drew into the station. They found a shop and bought some soups to make up at the flat. Sunday would be another roller coaster of emotion.

They walked through the market where there were no crowds that morning. They could admire the yellow ochre painted, arched building which was along one side. They retraced the steps of the marchers to the Nicholaikirche. Joyful, crowds of people sitting on the white benches between the high fluted columns, they sat listening to the music. Uplifted by the choir and by singing Lutheran hymns they tried to put Buchenwald behind them.

In the bookshop of the church they found a CD Rom about the church and the demonstration and a photo book with all the slogans and the famous candles and boots picture.

After a good lunch in a modern restaurant and a siesta back at the flat, they left for the Petrikirche.

Pastor Langman met them at the door. It was old, in need of renovation and extremely large. They were led in to the rows of chairs and immediately before them stood a giant menorah. Next to the altar was a screen with the words of the hymns. A small music group on a platform to one side strummed guitars, played a keyboard and some flutes. Daniel had a flashback to Durham. Suddenly Hebrew appeared on the screen with a transliteration.

Everyone sang in Hebrew.

Shalom, shalom, evenu shalom alehem. Baruch haba ba shem Adonai.

Blessed is he who comes in the name of the Lord.

Thomas said, "This is worship. This is reconciliation and repentance."

"It's wonderful!" said Daniel.

There were a few more German and Hebrew hymns and Pastor Langman then took the microphone.

"Now we sing in English to welcome our visitors today." He explained who Esther was and how she had been born in Leipzig but rescued in 1938.

"Ascribe greatness to our God, the Rock."

Daniel remembered it from the Durham charismatic fellowship.

"His work is perfect and all His ways are just.

"A God of faithfulness and without injustice, good and upright is He."

Several people came to speak to them at the end. There had been no ranting sermon but an encouragement to take these words seriously.

"Hard to sing them after Buchenwald." said Daniel

"And after Herman, and after Maisie." Alice said to herself.

"I have another one for you to sing when we get back home, Bonhoeffer wrote *Von Guten Mächten treu und still umgeben.*"

"How do you know that?" asked Daniel.

Alice had studied his prison letters as part of her BA German course and had read that he was in Buchenwald shortly before he was moved to another prison where he was hanged in 1945 barely days before Hitler killed himself.

"What a tragedy. What a loss. He was a wonderful man and he left a sweet, young fiancée behind. Their letters were not at all lovey-dovey but rather erudite and instructive. He always tried to encourage her to trust God."

Thomas became his educational, pastoral self when they returned to the flat.

"We have had a demanding time, interesting of course, but we have walked with Esther into her early childhood. We have encountered the terrible end of your grandparents and great grandparents. We have seen the evil cruelty that man is capable of. We were planning to go to Wittenberg tomorrow, to Luther's church. We shall not do that but we shall have a quiet day, possibly each of us alone in the park. We need to stop and contemplate, look at nature and prepare ourselves for returning to our normal lives. One day we shall return and see Weimar and Wittenberg and revisit the friends we have made. We will no doubt see some improvements to the roads and buildings and of course we shall go to the Gewandhaus.

“We need to assimilate what we have experienced and what we have felt. We may need to weep some more. Esther will not be in a good state. We must give her space and show understanding.

“Let’s not forget that hymn by Bonhoeffer. I think it will help bring us healing.

“We must face our reactions and not run away from them or try to escape. In time we will not know any more answers but we will accept the mystery of our Christian faith. We will find healing in different ways; walks, music, work but most of all we need to talk, not necessarily to each other but to a counsellor or spiritual director, or even a good friend you can trust.

“When Derry is next in England let’s ask him about his experiences but not put too much on him concerning our Leipzig trip. He may ask. It is not his way, but only tell him about it if he does. I think having a perspective on European history might help him too.

“I feel very privileged to have shared this journey with Mum and both of you. Our lives will never be the same again. We shall see things differently. My African studies give me something relevant right now. I’ll wind up with this thought; there is the concept of Ubuntu in the tribes. Find out more later, but in summary, it translates as, *I am who I am because we are. A person is truly a person only in and through other persons.*

“We are academics but never be afraid to be humble enough to learn from primitive tribal people. There is a lot to learn.”

“Dad, thank you so much” Daniel said.

“What a wonderful thing to say” Alice could hear the Reutlingen bells toll in her mind. “Being quiet and listening to nature. That is Derry’s Dadirri.”

The story of Herman was now in a different perspective and was fading away. She decided to write to Derry and tell him that she was more and more interested in his thesis and was ready to read it all.

5 Derry Returns

Alice produced a copy of Bonhoeffer's hymn and an English translation. They found a music sheet for Charles and all met up before Christmas in their Oxford home. When she read '*Lass warm und still die Kerzen heute flammen.'* (Today let candles send their radiant greetings.) Alice thought of the candles by the Stasi boots. She wished she were an artist as she would have loved to have a painting of this powerful symbol.

Charles played the melody and they all sang along, first in English and then in German. Charles and Thomas did not know so much of the language, but they appreciated the words all the more when they heard of the life and death of the author.

They looked at the Aboriginal canvas on the lounge wall. Alice would have preferred it in the study but there was not enough space on the walls because they were already exhibiting spears and masks from Africa. In the lounge they had taken down the landscape which came from Thomas's parents. Before his departure, Derry had taken instructions from Thomas and Esther and got the canvas framed. It was so imposing he chose a plain, dark, narrow frame with no visible cord. It looked very striking and was clearly visible from the grand piano.

Alice had begun to write more regularly to Derry. This time he sent more than the usual 4 lines on a post card and gave her more details about his research. He had found that it was not possible to make a clear dividing line between dadirri and the concepts of the knowledge of nature. It was all one. Alice looked through the books on the shelf and found a few dated copies without the bright, modern Aboriginal art and not much information on their belief system.

Two coincidences then occurred in Alice's life.

Her parents had decided to go on a real holiday somewhere totally new. They wanted a restful holiday and Esther made the rule of no tribes and no research, just a tourist trip and exploration of a new environment. They sat at his desk looking through maps. If they took two months they would ask Daniel and Alice to look in at the house and stay some nights. South America or Asia? Esther went into the lounge and the Aboriginal canvas caught her eye. She went out again, forgetting why she had come in and said, "Why not Australia?"

"Of course. We have never been."

"Sydney Opera House and the Great Barrier Reef but no tribes and no research."

"We could call on Derry if he is in Cairns when we are there."

"No hours of discussion on tribes with him either!"

"That's decided then. I'll write to him and find out when he will be available and tell him we are doing the tourist thing this time."

In her new London flat, Alice sat by the window to answer Derry's last letter. He **had** asked about their experiences in Leipzig. She decided to start with the two churches and the Stasi HQ. She told him she was learning about English dadirri. She had contacted the World Communion of Christian Meditation and found there was a small group meeting not too far away.

Esther rang her to tell her about their plan to go on holiday to Australia.

"We will try to look up Derry but Thomas has promised; no tribes and no research." Alice was thrilled.

"He did kind of invite me vaguely, once, but I have never decided on such a long trip." She posted her letter to him, having added that her parents would soon contact him about their proposed holiday.

Next morning there was a packet from Derry. Inside he had put two CDs with Aboriginal style meditation music. It was not all didgeridoo but a modern composer had added nature sounds, birds mainly and modern instrumental sections. His letter surprised her.

"Alice, I would love you to come out to Queensland but before that I need to have a D and M with you. I am planning a brief trip to Oxford and London before Christmas so we can have our talk. In Queensland you would be in civilisation not in the outback. I think I will arrive in England in a couple of weeks. I do not have too many commitments so you choose the most convenient time to suit you. I hope you enjoy Didgeridoo Dreaming and Uluru."

"Oh, good, we can make plans with him when he is here." said Esther.

Alice arranged to meet him at the Royal Festival Hall. She liked being near a river for serious talks. They had a very natural hug and Alice felt more relaxed as she gave him a French style peck on both cheeks. Derry did not seem totally at ease. His hair was short again and he tugged at the front part as if his floppy fringe were still there.

"Let's have a drink." They bought a glass of wine each and took it outside as it was not too cold.

"OK. D and M. What's it all about this time?"

"It's about you, Alice. It's your turn. I think you should tell me about your unhappy teenage romance." She did not expect that. She had imagined some issue in his studies or with his family. Why did he want to know now?

"Derry it was so long ago. Why do you want to know about it now?"

"Because you were very hurt and I think that you are still single because of that relationship."

This was not the Derry she was used to, "And you are still single?"

"Yes, I am. I cannot use my work as an excuse. There is another reason I have not found the right girl to marry. I have met plenty of pretty, young anthropologists in the universities and in the outback…"

"But?"

"But I have always loved you, Alice." She swallowed some wine and felt waves of electricity go through her head. She felt shaky.

"Really, Derry? You have never given the slightest indication that you had feelings for me."

He saw she did not draw away from him but leaned forward, so he took her free hand and held on to it.

"Think of the situation when I met you. You were still a teenager and you were the daughter of my professor. I made very sure that I did not take advantage of my position in your home. I purposely shut down my feelings for you. I was already some years older than you."

She put down her wine glass and reached for his other hand.

"Derry, I thought you were possibly gay like my brother. After Herman, I felt I could never trust another man."

"What's more, you were in an upset state. You were grieving." They remained holding hands across the table.

"You were a professor's daughter. All your family were academics. I came from a very different background. My aptitude for study was a foreign country for my parents. Madeleine had married early and had children. They all had respectable jobs but I could never be considered on the same level as your family and your lovely home. I fell in love with you that first summer but told myself there was no hope for me. I loved your parents and Daniel like my own family. I could not stop coming because I so respected your father and needed his tuition.

Your mother was like an angel, so sweet and capable and kind. I had to learn to leave my feelings way behind when you helped me through our family trauma."

Alice felt her eyes sting. She felt an unlocking in her inner being.

"Most boys, men even, try the touching first. They try to attract me into kissing and cuddling. Not you, DB," she had never called him that before. She smiled at him, "We always had D and Ms but we never discussed our own personal feelings."

He lifted his right hand to her face and stroked her cheek.

"In the outback, Alice, sitting on the red earth, seeing the tribal men stamp their feet in the sand and wail, I could only think of you. When you wrote and said you would consider making a trip to Queensland, I could hardly contain the sense of hope."

"Well, Doctor Derwent, all these years you have been in my life. I did sometimes want to show you affection but your constant distance convinced me that I was just like a sister to you. This is so strange. This is so new for me."

Derry let go of her hands.

"We need to get to know each other in a different way. You possibly need some time. Let's talk again tomorrow."

"DB, I will tell you about Herman and the damage that the relationship did to me, but not now. Yes, we can meet tomorrow but right now I have a huge wave breaking over me and I just want you to hold me."

He stood up. A public place, oh dear. He went round to her chair and she stood up and put her arms around his neck. He held her tightly to him and she put her head on his shoulder. How long did they stand there?

"It's not that I have waited eight years for this moment because I had no hope at all, until last year. I had my dreaming. You have heard of Aboriginal dream time?"

She became aware of so many things in those moments. There had been a degree of deep, inner healing in Derry after those ceremonies to bring to a closure the scandal of his grandfather. He had felt liberated and had gained confidence. As he held her she was aware that she loved him. She drew back and smiled, "Aboriginal Dreamtime, nothing to do with our dreams. I have done some reading of your thesis." Alice turned to walk.

"Let's walk down the river, across Westminster Bridge and sit in St James' Park" she almost whispered. They held hands as they walked then sat on a bench watching the pelicans, the other birds, the fountains and the palace. He put an arm round her shoulders and she leant on him, taking his other hand.

"It's too soon for you to make a decision, Alice. You are in shock. I have loved you for a long time and right now…"

"Kiss me." Alice cut him off. He took her head in his hands and kissed her lips a few times and then they had a long, lingering kiss.

"I would not let myself love you. I was locked in. I think I have always loved you and wanted you to be in my life." They smiled and kissed again.

"It would be very easy for us to go back to my hotel or your flat and make love but I really want you to have time to be realistic with yourself. Have some space away from me. Of course I want to marry you and make love to you, but we have both come through some sorrows. We need to assimilate this new love between us!"

"Assimilate! That's Dad's word!"

"It is wise."

"You are so wise like him, so in control, so trustworthy."

"Let's go back now. I know where I stand but I want you to have time to get over the shock and then be sure that you love me and want me too." Hand in hand they walked to Victoria and kissed goodbye.

"Where shall we meet?"

"The British Museum."

"Really?"

"If we were in Oxford it would be the Pitt Rivers."

"Dearest Alice, about 1.30 tomorrow afternoon? I'll wait on the steps by the main entrance."

"I am a member so I can take you to the Members' Restaurant."

"I am not sure I will be able to eat."

"Dear Derry. See you there."

She could not remember walking to her flat. She was in a dream. He had really loved her and waited all those years. He had never tried to seduce her or even touch her or indicate in any way how he felt.

Lying on her bed she knew she would agree to marry him. She had never trusted anyone else. Her mind went back to Broadmoor and the seaside cemetery and to scrolling down the microfilms. She thought of the tennis games in their court in the garden and then the beautiful painting he had bought for them. He had given her the Reef pearl earrings. She thought of their talks on philosophy, religion and anthropology in the study, in the lounge and even over the dining room table.

Derry felt so relieved that he had managed to communicate his love to her and that instead of rejecting him, she had discovered that she loved him too.

"But she must be sure. I've shocked her, changed her mind set, stirred up her emotions, her desires."

There were not too many crowds on the Museum steps that winter day. She saw him standing there when she arrived a little early. They ran towards each other and hugged and kissed.

In the restaurant they found the most secluded table possible and ordered some wine, saying they would order food later.

"Salmon special today. Don't leave it too late."

Derry started speaking, "Alice, my lovely Alice you have done so well, even though you were so hurt in Germany you worked so hard to get your First in German and then you studied Urdu instead of going on to a Masters. You taught Muslims. What a girl!"

"It was my salvation!"

"Alice, how are you now?"

"I am so excited and in a whirl. I thought I would remain single and perhaps get a PhD."

"No one else courting you? Alice will you marry me?"

"Yes, Derry, I will marry you. I realised that I have loved you for a long time but I had killed all my feelings out of fear."

Derry pushed two little felt boxes over towards her. He opened the tiny box to show her the diamond ring. She pulled it out and gave it to him to put on her finger.

"I think it fits." She tried to turn it.

"We can always get it adjusted in a jeweller. I had no idea of your size."

"Derry, it is beautiful! I love it."

The main diamond in the middle shone and glistened between two little stars either side. "Do you wear the earrings?"

She pulled back her hair.

"I put them on specially."

"So romantic." He pushed over the second box and opened the lid. Inside was a Reef pearl necklace which matched the earrings.

They sat gazing into each other's eyes.

“I don’t know how to thank you, dearest Derry. I love the necklace too.”

“You know that my parents got engaged in the Pitt Rivers, on the balcony next to the shrunken heads.”

“That’s typical of Thomas! And Esther still said yes!”

“It’s amazing, but they wanted to see you because they are planning a holiday in Australia and were hoping to call in on you.”

She explained that they wanted a two-month break in a place they had never been to before. “Mum did not want it to be Africa. She survived the last trip to Nigeria but after Leipzig, she wanted a new experience, a new perspective. Did you realise that her whole family were killed in Leipzig? They want to be tourists and see Sydney Opera House and the Great Barrier Reef. No tribes and no research is her rule.”

“Fine. I know just the place for them to stay in Cairns and just the place for our honeymoon!”

“Let’s drive to Oxford. I’ll ring them but I won’t tell them about our engagement until we arrive!”

They did manage to eat the salmon and then walked round to Russell Square where in her study years she had often sat contemplating her life.

“He was tall, dark and handsome and a real charmer.” She began giving Derry the outline of her romance with Herman. “He was a Bible student aiming to become a missionary somewhere in the world. We fell in love and planned a future together. He wanted me to stop my studies and marry him. He found it hard to accept that I could not do that. It was not until I went to his home town, Aachen and met his parents that I discovered that he had lied to me, fooled me. He had very serious emotional, even mental problems. I never saw it when we were in the Black Forest area. I was 18 and had no wisdom or insight. When I did suspect there was a problem, I buried it as I was in love. We did some interesting visits to the local towns and countryside and went to Berlin to experience Check Point Charlie actually functioning. In Aachen, a beautiful town, his parents lived in a little flat. They were very old, around their 70s and his mother treated him like a toddler, stroking his head and hugging him very often.

“He had lied about everything. He disgraced himself at the Children’s Home and was sent back to the Bible school and then they expelled him. Both places had seen his bad temper and inappropriate behaviour towards young girls, and then his bad language when challenged. All those months he wrote to me, visited me in England and said nothing."

"You were so young. I am so sorry."

"That's not the worst." She explained that Herman had insisted that love was more important than education. If she really loved him she would marry him now and give up her studies. She would easily find work in Aachen. He had some kind of 'fit' when she resisted him and he attacked her and tried to rape her.

"Oh, Alice. No wonder you were so emotionally damaged. Rape?" She described what happened and that she had packed her case and run away while he was still in pyjamas.

Terrified she had hidden in a shop.

"I booked into a hotel in Koln, not far from the airport. I had a few days to compose myself and ring my Mum. Dad was in Nigeria."

"What an ordeal!"

"My parents were wonderful!"

"So were you! As you said, it damaged you."

"I could never trust again. I was so relieved when you showed no interest in me. I kept away from all relationships for years."

"Everyone is damaged in some way. We can put it behind us and make a new start."

It was too cold to sit outside for long. SOAS was not far so she walked round to show him where she had studied Urdu. It was too far to go to Burnton College where she had studied German.

"Oxford next."

"My car is in Cairns!"

There was so much to sort out; telling both families, when and where to get married and what to do in their future together. Would he balance research with wife and possible family like her father had done? Then there was the Hartley's trip to Australia.

Alice was so excited when she got out of the car and ran to her front door. Her mother noticed the ring immediately.

"Oh how lovely. Congratulations to you both!" she rapped on the study door. "Thomas, come here now please! I am so delighted!" Alice went into the study first as her father got up from his desk.

"Thomas, they're engaged!"

"What?"

"They are not just here to discuss our trip!"

Thomas hugged Alice and then shook Derry's hand but then hugged him too.

"Well, that's wonderful! About time! You could have warned me but I am so pleased."

It took a while for them to settle down with each other. Derry told them about a holiday centre that they would love near Cairns.

"We shall have our honeymoon there! They are very keen on the environment; it is an ecotourism centre but it is also very luxurious.

"Right now it is very, very hot. In English summer it is their winter with temperatures of 21-27, more like our summer here but much easier to cope with."

"Well, you don't want your parents with you on your honeymoon. We need to sort out our dates!" said Esther.

It was an exhausting time and it was a happy time. Derry was able to stay in England until after Christmas.

Daniel and Charles were due for Christmas Day too. Brother and sister sat in the lounge and decided that they both wanted their loved ones to experience Leipzig and Berlin.

"It is our heritage through Mum," said Daniel who could not stop smiling about their engagement.

Daniel was performing more and more in concerts which were broadcast on Radio 3 and Classic FM. He wanted Charles to go to the Gewandhaus during their trip and he decided to make contacts to see if they could perform there sometime.

Some well-known film stars, such as Dirk Bogarde, had 'come out' recently and declared that they had a life-long partnership with a man. That is what Daniel wanted, a life-long partnership with Charles.

Charles' family were conventional and conservative. They had realised he was homosexual as early as his teen years. They accepted that he would never marry, and although it hurt them and disappointed them, they accepted his boyfriends. When Daniel came into his life at the Music School, they thought so highly of him that they welcomed him into the family.

Alice took Derry into the study and sat him in the leather armchair. She dragged over a footstool and held his hands. She explained how much this corner had meant to her since she was two. She was still in a bit of a dream, but she felt it was important for her to try to reassure Derry of her love and total trust in him.

"After our honeymoon, I am quite prepared to look for work in Cairns. I know you will have to be away from me for long periods and I am prepared for that too. If I can ever be of use to you in the outback, I will be delighted to do that too. I think I will try to get on 'the pill' before we go so we have the time to sort out our future without worrying about me getting pregnant."

"Are you sure? I have been thinking about that too and as we are in an unusual and uncertain situation that could be the best solution. I would love a family but it would be very difficult while I am still researching in the outback."

"Do you have a base for sleeping at the University?"

"In anticipation of you accepting me, I bought a house in Cairns as a base for us."

"A house!"

"Wait till you see it. It's only an old Queenslander, old but roomy."

Esther decided they would return to Leipzig the year after their Australia trip and then they would also go to Israel and to Yad Vashem. Since the time in the Petrikirche she had sought out the Messianic Jewish organisation in England. She hoped she could attend some meetings from time to time. She wanted to be in touch with her Jewish identity. She wondered what Alice would do with her London flat. She might lose her place to stay there. Alice would also not be available to look after the house while they were in Australia.

Derry made enquiries at Marsden where he had begun his Oxford studies and met Thomas. Some alumni were able to get married in the beautiful little chapel. The best offer was June, straight after all the examinations. In May Alice would resign and get her luggage transported to Cairns.

"You probably won't need anything warm and heavy. Bring summer clothes and one or two warm things for the outback frosts."

Thomas and Esther felt so blessed to have both their children and their partners at home for Christmas. They would miss Alice and had some heartache that any grandchildren could be Australian citizens. They still had their health so they hoped to make regular trips to see them like hundreds of other families.

Bob, Clara and Madeleine were delighted that Derry was marrying Alice.

"I thought you were an item already. Will we have to save up for a trip to Oz?"

"Perhaps. But our long-term future is uncertain."

Christmas Day was idyllic, a roaring wood fire in the lounge, a turkey and all trimmings meal and the six of them seated around the table in the dining-room. Esther had bought a small menorah for the table. Thomas, in his usual practical and organised way said he would transfer a sum of money for them to use as they settled in Cairns instead of buying presents here. After the wedding, the couple would go straight to Thala for two weeks and then move into the Queenslander.

Thomas and Esther would begin their stay in Sydney, travel to Uluru and then come to Cairns for a train tour into the outback before going to Thala for their final two weeks. Derry dealt with all the bookings in Cairns.

They were packing and preparing to see Derry off. Thomas arrived home one afternoon with a shy looking young man.

"This is Edmund. He's going to spend a few days here." Daniel laughed, "Will he need my room?"

"He can start off in the guest room."

Alice smiled and recalled how she felt when Derry had first arrived; Esther was pleased that she would not have an empty house when her son and daughter left.

Alice drove Derry to Heathrow and she wept as they hugged their goodbye. "Six months used to be nothing. It feels like an eternity."

"And to me. I hate leaving you so soon. I'll return in May, as early as I can so we can get to Leipzig."

"Leipzig, it is an interesting town but it was a difficult visit. We met some amazing people, went to a Jewish Cemetery and to some lovely churches. The worst was Buchenwald Concentration Camp. Mum's whole family died. She still needs to recover as she was traumatised. She was five when her parents saved her life by giving her to the Kindertransport organisation. She can still remember her parents and grandparents and her home. That's why she needs to go on a holiday"

"It's not surprising that she was traumatised. She told me about the Messianic Jews, an excellent healing place for her." Derry picked up his bag to leave Alice.

"I will have a lot to do when you have gone. Mum will come to London to help me choose a dress."

"Do you want me in tails?" He was used to the formal dinners at Oxford, Degree, Masters, PhD and special occasions in Anthropology.

"Wear what is comfortable for you my love. It does not have to be tails. I am sure you would not use formal suits in Australia."

"I will also have your thesis to read and I will do English Dadirri with the Christian Meditation group"

"That's wonderful! We shall see what there is in Cairns. It has limitations. There is much more going on in Brisbane."

"Does Cairns have foreigners who need English?"

"Oh, yes. There are even some Africans in camps not far away, Sudanese refugees fleeing the war. There are different tribes and they sometimes carry on their conflict in the camp." The last call for his flight was made.

"God bless my love."

"God bless dearest Alice. Goodbye until May."

He walked through the barrier. She could hardly see as she returned to the car park. She took a while to work out the ticket machine then drove to her London flat.

At Meditation group she told them about her fiancé's research and read out some of the relevant passages.

"We could arrange for him to come and give a talk at the Meditation Centre in Islington." said the leader, Abigail. Alice's heart leapt for joy. During the next few months, they became firm friends. She found it easy to talk to Abigail and share parts of her life with her.

"WCCM definitely has centres in Australia and they have a big schools project to introduce Meditation into schools."

"I'd love to be involved with that. My long-term future is rather blank. Derry has several more months of research to complete with some Aborigines."

Alice found it difficult to find a dress. She rejected the marshmallow style dresses with off the shoulder, sleeveless styles. She wanted something simpler, less revealing. Esther suggested she had one made. The dress had a scooped neckline with sleeves down nearly to the elbow. The skirt fell with some tiny pleats from just under the bust. Across the bust were two rows of ochre-coloured beads with aboriginal design circles to break the lines. The pattern was taken from part of their canvas painting. The silk skirt fell gently to her ankles and moved elegantly when she walked. Her long, wavy hair would be partly clipped up to hold the small head piece with a short veil. She was very pleased with this dress and wondered what Derry would choose.

She decided to rent out her flat in case they needed it in the following two years. In mid-May they all met up again. Derry arrived with a huge suitcase with a special suit section. She held on to him as soon as he reached the barrier at Heathrow and could not move for several minutes.

"How is it possible to feel such happiness?"

Derry had his old room in the house. He met the new house-guest, Edmund who would stay while Thomas and Esther had their holiday after the wedding. Alice and Derry travelled by train to Heathrow and met Daniel and Charles. This time they did not ask Pastor Michael for accommodation in his Leipzig flat.

They booked into a hotel in the town centre and went first to the Nicholaikirche and noted how much more information there was in the bookshop. There were so many photographs of the marches, the armed soldiers and the speakers on platforms. They made day trips to Weimar, Wittenberg and Berlin.

In Wittenberg Daniel stood at the main church door reading the 95 Thesis which were printed on a metal plaque. He had a deeper sense of history and of what was owed to such courageous people of the past. In Weimar apart from the literary giants, they stood in the square and saw the balcony where Hitler had given his speeches to the admiring crowd below. In Berlin they went to the Check Point Charlie Museum, the holocaust memorial and the glass domed Reichstag.

Derry agreed with Daniel that they needed a perspective of European history.

"What did you write your thesis on?" Derry asked Alice.

"The Baader Meinhof terrorism in the 1970s." He looked surprised. "I had read a lot about the years between 1945 and 1965 and the after effects of the war on the young generation."

"I suppose they had to face that their fathers and grandfathers had been Nazis?"

"What insight. There were books by psychologists about *The Fatherless Society.* The Mitscherlick husband and wife team explained how their emotions fed into the sense of freedom from the fascist way, the rebellion and 'free love' commune ideas of the 60s. They felt guilt and shame and strong rebellion against their society."

"Can I read your thesis?"

Charles was a sensitive man. He was virtually in tears reading the names of the over 200 hundred people who had died trying to cross the wall near the wall on a plaque near the Brandenburg Gate. It had been built with barbed wire and breeze blocks at first. One soldier had even jumped over to escape before it was too late. The photo was in the English press. Then the mighty concrete slabs appeared. They had become the graffiti art gallery. Some slabs remained as a token to remind everyone. A photo book of the length of the wall had been made and some small stones from the broken wall were on sale at high prices.

At Check Point Charlie, Charles had another weep when he saw depictions of the many ways people had tried to escape. They had first tried tunnels under the wall. A book and film had been made about this very dangerous activity. Several had nevertheless succeeded. They were shot if they were caught. There was a whole organisation at work. Secretly people from the West helped them get out and waited at the exits of the tunnels with minibuses to take them to safety. There had been spies and traitors of course, as well as earth falls and near suffocations. Then there were the efforts to get over the wall; flights in little planes or gliders or flying machines of some kind.

Some desperate people had adapted their cars to have a secret compartment under the back seat so they could drive through the check points. The dangers were immense.

'Why ever did the communists not see that their system was so bad that people risked their lives to get away?' Charles spoke.

In Leipzig they were all aware of his sensitivity and made sure they took him to the Gewandhaus.

"We will not go to Buchenwald this time. Charles would hate it so much!" Daniel said.

Instead, we will try to get links with the concert hall and see if we can do some piano concerts there.

In Leipzig they called on the two pastors and two other churches. Derry was particularly impressed by the museum in the Stasi headquarters. The dangers got worse because the Stasi realised the ingenuity of desperate people. This was the Wall of protection for the socialist state. They saw a good example when Pastor Michael took them to the old border between East and West outside the town on the way to Frankfurt via Bad Hersfeld. The Wall building had doubled and between the two walls was 'no man's land'. It had land mines, was patrolled by soldiers with dogs and was looked over by armed guards in a watchtower which looked very like those in the concentration camps. Daniel pointed out the contrasts between the condition of the roads and the buildings either side of the old border. There was still a lot of rebuilding to do. A factory was spewing out filthy white foam into the river.

“Let’s offer a series of charity concerts,” said Charles, “and give the money to a charity for some rebuilding for a school or hospital.”

“Great idea!” said Daniel. “We could try and time it to coincide with my Mum and Dad’s visit next year. The BBC might help us.”

“I’ll help you too,” Michael said. “I do know people in the Gewandhaus and there are several big churches which would love to invite you to play.”

Daniel and Charles were pianists and organists. They played individually and as duets. Sometimes they played two grand pianos opposite each other and sometimes they played two organs, a pipe organ and an electronic, digital organ. Their reputation in London had been growing and they had begun receiving invitations to play in other cities, mainly Cathedral cities in England.

Their future plans were beginning to take shape.

6 Thala

What could be more idyllic than a wedding in Marsden chapel? Sadly, the blossom on the boughs which hung over the grassy grounds had long dropped. Alice used to love sitting on the bench under the pink flowers in the spring. Some of the choir who remembered Derry offered to sing. One sang a solo of the Bonhoeffer hymn in both English and German.

Derry wore a black suit with a white silk waistcoat and tie. His hair was still short so he had it cut to a more flattering style instead of just bush convenience. Abigail and other friends had been invited. Derry's old colleagues also joined in and made the journey to the restaurant reception a noisy one with pots and pans and balloons.

Esther cried of course, but so did Thomas. He watched the shy young man he had invited to his home become a professional and loving son-in-law.

Everything was stunning and so admired by the guests. Daniel and Charles wore matching pale grey suits with silk waistcoats and ties. Edmund had been invited to the ceremony and the reception. Derry made sure he was with others he knew once he could take his eyes off his beautiful bride.

"This was me once," he said to Edmund. Alice observed Derry's caring behaviour. Edmund was due to house-sit for them.

Just like Dad, she thought. *I have married a gem.*

"See you in Cairns!" She said to her parents as they departed. "Look after our clothes"

She changed into a pale blue, silk Pakistani style shalwa chemise. Derry wore a light blazer in navy blue with white trousers and an open neck shirt. This time the stopover was Brisbane but the flight time was still over 24 hours in all. Anyone who observed them in the plane and the airports guessed that they had just got married. A taxi took them from Cairns airport to Thala, just about an hour away.

They passed a sign to Port Douglas and turned right down a wilderness track to Thala. "Port Douglas is a lovely little port and town. You will love it."

The long track took them down through the rain forest and upwards to the central building, stopping at the bottom of a huge flight of wide wooden steps. The steps and walls were in a beautiful light, shiny wood.

"I'll wait for you to check in and then drive you and your luggage to your lodge,"

"They do have transport, but that's fine if you don't mind waiting."

The entrance was a wide-open reception area with art works on the wall and a huge Aboriginal style sea eagle above the desk. Thala means sea-eagle.

There were little shops and glass cabinets selling reef pearls, perfumed natural oils and other attractive items.

The smartly dressed staff were very friendly.

"We can show you the restaurant and bar area before we drive you to your lodge."

"We have a taxi waiting so we will come back for a drink when we have unpacked."

Keys in hand they returned to the taxi and saw how undulating the paths were.

The lodge was spacious; a wooden building on posts buried into the hillside. A little wooden bridge led to the front door.

"Wow!" said Alice as she walked in while Derry paid the taxi driver. A beautiful bathroom with both bath and shower and basin was on the right. There were several spot lights, some spotless, soft white towels and soaps and oils on the side by the huge mirror. Ahead was a little corridor leading to the lounge. On the right was a giant king size bed with tasteful, plain silky covers. Some beautiful photographic art work hung above the bed. On the left was a bar with a fridge and chairs with writing materials. Above the shelf was a large television screen. Next they went through to the lounge area with armchairs and a low table. The back wall was all glass with a door leading out to the balcony. The view was unbelievable; a panorama of small islands and patches of rainforest meeting the coast line and of course the blue, blue sea. Alice stood on the balcony, in total isolation with paradise below them.

"Derry it's so amazing. Thank you so much my dearest husband." They hugged and kissed. "Can we eat here?"

"We can but just wait until you have seen the restaurant!"

They unpacked and had a quick wash and then headed off for the restaurant in the reception building. There were little swimming pools in the rocks on the way down and other lodges among the trees as they walked up. Friendly people greeted them as they passed. There were various entrances into the restaurant and lounge instead of going up the front steps. The wooden roof was almost circular with evenly spaced beams to hold it up. Under the roof was open space with a panoramic view over the ever-blue sea. The tables were set out so residents could eat with this view. Some of the beams held bird feeders. Bright coloured humming birds flitted in and out, flapping their wings while drinking the nectar. Wooden shutters could be drawn if wind and rain interrupted this paradise.

They looked through the menus.

"Crocodile and kangaroo! Will you try some one day?"

"Not today, though. We are pretty tired. There's a private beach we can walk down to and then back up if we have the energy. Come and have a drink in a melon in the lounge and you can see what activities are on offer."

"Activities?"

"Like you have never known before."

True enough, there they were on the cards; birding, coconut Odyssey, Sky watching, beach combing, meeting the Aboriginal Elders, boat trips to Green Island and the Great Barrier Reef, then massage with oils and hair dressing. 'Advanced Ecotourism' was on the posters. 'All the soaps and oils and shampoos are from nature.'

The rock pools were available without booking. In the smooth barked eucalyptus trees Alice could see bright coloured birds.

"Lorikeets."

"We'll never want to leave!" said Alice.

Their melons arrived. Each huge melon had a straw protruding from a hole in the top. "What is it?"

"Coconut milk and some spirits."

"You will notice the contrast when you come to our Queenslander. We'll go there one day and then you can think how you would like to decorate it and what else we might put in. We won't be there forever. When we know what we are doing we can buy a proper house somewhere in the country".

They felt too tired for a luxurious meal that evening, so they chose a small salad in their room on the balcony.

From Brisbane the plane had flown up the coast right over the Reef. The views and the colours were spectacular.

"Reef trip first?" asked Derry.

Their love making was gentle at first and then demonstrated the hunger within them after years of frustrated desire. In the morning they showered together and then made love on the soft white towels across the bed.

They had breakfast with the humming birds and then walked down to the beach enjoying the soft sand but having to avoid rocks and spiky vegetation. They even saw some snakes in the rocky areas on the way down. They were about an inch wide and no longer than a metre.

They writhed away quickly, black with red markings.

"I don't think they are dangerous. There will be info about them in the lounge."

"How did you find this place?"

A colleague, one of the pretty young anthropologists told him she was spending her last weekend there and invited him for a farewell meal before she left. He immediately chose it for a honeymoon if Alice said 'Yes.'

After the first three days when they had done the Reef trip and the night walk, he asked her if he could take her into Cairns and visit the Queenslander. She knew he would be lacking in confidence, so she was determined to be as positive and as hopeful as she could even if she hated it.

They took a taxi and planned to take his car back if he could get it started. The streets of Cairns were like an American road map, parallel lines crossed by several main roads, a grid of straight lines leading to the coast or to the bush.

Their street had wide grass verges and rows of mainly wooden houses on both sides. They were nearly all old Queenslanders. They are built on stilts. The steps up were fairly steep. He unlocked the front door and walked in down a corridor. On the right were doors into four rooms; on the left was a bathroom which had been decorated with sea shells. It was tiled in blue and had a bath and shower fixture with a curtain over it. Ahead was a large open space, an all-in-one kitchen, lounge and dining room. There was a master bedroom on the right at the end. The bedroom and the glass back door overlooked the long garden, a playing field and tree covered hills in the distance.

"That's a lovely view."

"School playing fields. Could be noisy sometimes."

In the big bedroom there was already a double bed and some shelves with towels and bedding.

"First we'll get in some lounge furniture and better dining table and chairs. You can let your imagination run riot with decoration. I've got another smaller canvas from the same genuine Aboriginal tribe. I got it framed in Cairns. Choose your wall."

Some of the walls had been painted, some papered and others left as bare slats. She had a look into the other rooms; no doubt guest rooms. The first was the biggest.

"I know what I want to use this for. Tell you later. Derry it's lovely."

She opened the back door to find a small balcony and a flight of steps down to the grassy yard.

His car was in the garage, a separated section under the house with a locked door. People often use this space for washing machines or freezers.

"I asked colleagues to rev her up and take her for a drive while I was away. I hope they did."

He pulled open the double wire gates and Alice watched him get into his little beige car. She had noticed that in general the cars seemed bigger than those in England, but not this one.

He turned the key and it came to life. "Well done kids!"

He closed all the gates and the door again.

"Do you want to go back inside before we go back to Thala?"

"Yes. Do we have pen and paper?"

Alice went from room to room getting an idea of the sizes. In the open plan area she found crockery and cutlery and pots and pans for two. She noted how he had thought of everything, even tea towels. He knew she would turn it into a colourful, artistic home. While job hunting she would get to know the Cairns University, quite a way out of town, up the north coast road. She would also contact the educational establishments and the shops with decorating materials. Outside the main town were several large shopping centres with all kinds of shops. He drove her on a detour to the main esplanade before they returned. She noticed that most buildings were quite low except for the luxury hotels on the sea front. There were holiday flats to let and casinos, restaurants of all kinds and a play area for children.

"There are other beaches off the north road going up to Mossman and the Daintree. There's an Aboriginal centre. We **could** tell your parents about it but it might break the no tribes, no research rule for your mother."

"It's such a beautiful area!"

"There can be downsides. We have had cyclones. People had to evacuate and sleep in the shopping centres. Road signs were ripped off and flew down the street, lethal. Houses can be destroyed!"

"Have you experienced this?"

"Yes, two years ago I was on a break in the University. That was the safest place." Back at Thala they had a swim and decided on the crocodile meat for supper.

"Rather like chicken."

Their love making began in the shower.

Next day was the walk around Port Douglas. They were amazed at the size of the luxury boats in the marina.

"Film stars, celebrities."

They went to the 'historic' church, a lovely little white painted building on the grass bank by the sea. It was about 100 years old. The shops in the inner town area were old and charming, and those in the modern shopping area by the sea were bright and clean but lacking in charm. They did most of the activities except the massage. That was out of their comfort zone. They thought they might buy the oils and try it on each other.

"You could use a car of your own when I am away. I usually take mine as near as possible to Bush camp, but there we have big off-road vehicles to use."

"I could cycle."

"When did you last cycle?"

"In Oxford before going to London. Far too much traffic there. How far is it?"

"About 45 minutes by bike. Faster by car."

"I'll decide when I have seen it by car. I noticed some used car plots not far from the esplanade."

That evening it was 'Meet the Elders.' Alice could not stop her tears when she watched their presentation. She was so moved to share the experience which had taken Derry's attention and motivated him all these years. She loved the clap sticks and the didgeridoo, the body decorations, the dancing and even the not very musical sounding song. She listened out for patterns but could not identify any. She watched the puffed-out cheeks when they made animal sounds, bird sounds with the didgeridoo. Then they listened to the 'story telling' all in English for the tourists but an important part of their culture as they talked of the land, the formation of the creatures and of human beings.

"Not quite Genesis, but we all came from the earth!" They tried out the oils that evening.

"Alice, I never realised that loving you would be so powerful."

"I love you Derry, my man with three names."

"We are so blessed."

"D and M?" she said after breakfast. "Balcony or beach?"

"Balcony."

"Derry, I was deeply moved by the aboriginal presentation. I want to learn more about them. I would like to know some and talk to them about their lives."

"You must join their educational organisation, AIATSIS and go to some of their conferences in Canberra. They have music CDs and DVDs and books for instructing. It can be your project when I am away."

"If ever there is a chance for me to come into the Bush with you and learn about their art and their food. I'd love to join you."

"That can be arranged. You must meet Mary Ruth, the teacher I mentioned. She is helping me with my book on their concept of nature. I reckon I will need another 12 to 18 months before I will have completed it."

"My mother used the phrase 'spiritual magic' in Leipzig. I told you about her vision of angels and of the fact that the armed soldiers never fired on the crowds. This Aboriginal presentation had the same spiritual magic for me! I really want to share as much of your research as possible."

Derry was clearly moved.

"And they were my salvation." He said, imitating her words.

In this talk she impressed on him how she valued him and respected his work, his care and thoughtfulness. They made love gently and slowly. He had chosen the balcony because he felt sure they would want to express their love after talking about unknown and difficult decisions for their future.

"Reality now, my love. Back to Cairns."

The buggy took them down to the car park and they could only just fit the cases in the beige car. It only just managed to go at all with all the extra weight.

Outside the gate he stopped and asked her if she had a bottle of the oil with her. She was able to find one. He took her hand and at the front door. He put a little oil on his finger and wiped the door handle and the lintel.

"I bless this house in the name of God the Father, the Son and the Holy Spirit." Inside he went to every door and did the same.

"It feels like a Jewish ritual." said Alice. "It is certainly a Christian one."

"First I shall find a group of Christian Meditation. I feel it will play an important role in our lives."

"I agree. When you come into the bush with me we shall ask them to do dadirri with us." They unpacked, made some tea, made the bed and surveyed their new home.

"Tomorrow we'll go to Cairns University and then buy a bike or a car for you."

About 25 minutes out of town the University was a modern campus with grey tiled floors, a red roof and high windows. They arrived in his office where there was an open plan section. Some students were working there, some using headphones. He stood on a chair and clapped his hands. Most looked up and he heard "Welcome back!" a few times.

"Sorry to interrupt you but I would like to introduce you to my wife." Most got up and came to shake his hand. A large black lady hugged her and smiled. "I'm so excited to meet you Alice. Welcome to DB's work place. I'm Jane. I'm looking at the role of women in the Aboriginal tribes."

"I am Jake. Hello Alice. I am with DB in the bush doing roots and berries." He beamed.

"Welcome. Just wait till Christmas. You'll be hot! I am Connie, a botanist"

"Steve! At your service. I'm here writing up most of the time. When your husband is in the wild I will be here for you. I can put my hand to most things; help out if anything goes wrong at your house. I'll give him my home number and you can call."

"Thank you so much. What's your field?"

"Good question. I am looking at the dark side, problems with drugs, alcohol and abuse in the reserves or the Aboriginal areas of town. Some of the reserves are in a terrible condition. Have you heard of John Pilger? He is an investigative journalist and he did a whole TV programme on reserves. I am mainly interested in drugs, where they get them, how they pay for them and who the dealers are. I do speak with police but have to keep that quiet or they would not talk to me. It's a very sad side of Aboriginal life."

Alice was fascinated. She longed to be involved in both the good and the bad of Aboriginal life.

"So you're DB here?"

"I gave them the option."

"You'll always be my Derry."

"You have a beautiful wife, DB. Don't worry when you are away I will make sure she is OK. She can come and meet my wife and kids." Steve shouted.

They thanked Steve and set off for the car lots. She looked at 3 or 4 and chose a dark red one which had enough room for luggage and even small items of furniture. She drove it into the garage and the beige one was left on the verge outside.

She had until mid-August before her parents arrived in Cairns. She knew they would love Thala.

"I will take them to the Mossman Aboriginal Centre because I want to go there!"

"When they leave, you will leave too. That will be strange. I shall have to make some friends so I'll start with the neighbours."

On the left, the Queenslander was beautifully kept and decorated. A dog barked and wagged its tail when the door opened.

"Gday, Frank. Meet Alice, my wife."

"So glad to meet you. Congratulations." He turned and yelled, "Susie come and meet DB's wife."

Alice was given a warm welcome. They were an older couple with grown up children now living away from home. Zippy the dog was very friendly.

"I love dogs. Could I walk with you sometimes?"

"If you show me your wedding photos…" Susie smiled.

"I always wanted a dog when I was a child but it was not possible because of the foreign travels."

They chatted a little before they went to the house on the right. That was not quite so well decorated but there were flowers growing in the garden. An Italian couple lived there. The Benettis were delighted to meet Alice.

"I'm Maria. Welcome to your new home." She spoke fluent English with a slight accent. "Perhaps you will be able to advise me on curtains, paints, papers to decorate."

"I'd love to. I know where the best shops are. It has been empty for quite a while."

They left to eat out and then do some grocery shopping the next day. He drove to Palm Cove. It was a delightful beach just a short drive up the northern coast road.

Alice stood and looked at the view.

"It's almost like Thala!" There was a small cluster of islands on the left and rows of palm trees along the beach. There were surfers in and out of the waves.

"What a lovely place. We must bring Mum and Dad here." She chose a large restaurant out of the many in this little town.

"I am in love with you and with Cairns and with the Aborigines."

"I can only think of loving you right now."

They started talking about his research and she asked what he would be doing next with his team.

"Top end. Up north. Time with Mary then back to write it all up. Next time it will be Queensland with you. If you find a job, make sure you can get time off for such trips."

Alice could not get off to sleep. Derry seemed deep in sleep so she got up and stood at the window looking over the hills, now just black shapes with an occasional twinkling light.

She thought back over the many D and Ms over the years and wondered why she had not taken more interest in the Australians before. She realised that she had so concentrated on her father's studies. She had enough on her mind.

"I'll meditate." She decided. Still standing at the window she looked out onto the hills and slight streaks of light behind them. She had been taught the John Main system, using a mantra or prayer word. The one he suggested was 'Maranatha'. No way was she taking that one. It had four balanced syllables but she chose 6 instead from Bonhoeffer's hymn;

'*Dein Licht scheint in der Nacht. Your light shines in the night.*' She usually used the German.

She soon sat down on the bed and then felt sleepy enough to lie down and drift off.

Thomas and Esther had greatly enjoyed Sydney and Uluru. They were tempted by the Ghan train journey but chose to save such an expensive trip for a future occasion. They flew to Cairns and took a Savannahlander trip instead. Alice and Derry met them at the airport and drove them to the station amid excited chatter.

Derry took their big cases in his car and Alice took them with their smaller cases for this local train journey.

"Hard to see Uluru and not speak with the tribes," said Thomas. He had kept his word and played tourist and not anthropologist. The Ghan would have taken them to Alice Springs and then they would see the buses for Uluru.

"It's magnificent and mysterious. I have taken lots of photos and it is a different colour in nearly everyone." They boarded the silver train and left for a four-day tour. They passed hours travelling through scrubland and eucalyptus forests with ant hills resembling grave stones. There were cattle and wallabies to be seen. There were picnic stops with very basic refreshments and then overnight stops with a hot meal. One night they were in a caravan but ate with the owners who ran a small wild life sanctuary. Esther held a little joey which curled up under her tee-shirt.

"Prickly claws!" she cried. Around them were wombats, koalas and wallabies.

Another night they slept on bunk beds in the train. They were given extra blankets as it was so cold. Primitive toilets and washing facilities were in the station building. Their favourite stop was Cobbald Gorge; tall, coloured volcanic rock formations rose above the smooth water in the gorge. The boats stopped their engines so they could sail in silence across the wide and narrow stretches of water. Crocodiles were sunning themselves on the tiny beach area.

There was a look round the Undara Lava tubes formed by active volcanoes which had spewed lava over the land millions of years ago. Esther especially loved the stops at the charming little stations they passed through. Kuranda was the nearest to Cairns. The station appears on post cards as it is covered with plants and flowers. At some places the rocks towered above the station while in others the station was high up so they were looking across a vast red desert-like area where they were told stories of floods, broken bridges, roads washed away.

After their four days they looked at maps to see where they had been, expecting to see a railway line reaching into the bush. Instead they saw a tiny hook of line which went in and back. It had taken them four days to travel along that tiny hook of rail. They remembered how vast this country was. The track had originally been built by refugees who had come to earn money in the mines. Several were from Italy and they had remained after the mining had shut down, to work in vineyards.

The arrival of the train was an event for the small townships. As the train slowed down families walked towards it. It stopped for them to get on and the children came down the aisles with goodies. Some had put on fancy dress.

"What a lovely touch." Said Thomas looking at the spaceman wrapped in silver foil standing next to him.

Alice picked them up at Cairns Station in her red car and took them to Thala. Derry joined them there with their luggage.

"We'll let you settle in and then tomorrow we shall come to supper with you and see what other trips we can do together. First we shall show you our house in Cairns. I am not sure you will want to have a meal there when you have seen the restaurant in Thala."

They met up for part of most days. Port Douglas, Cairns and Palm Cove were all visited.

"There's a place I want to take you to about an hour north. It's an Aboriginal Tourist centre. Will that break your rule?"

"Derry had mentioned the Skyrail and another Aboriginal Centre next to it."

"Oh, Tjapukai! Yes, we can do that too. There is a fantastic but expensive gift shop. The Sky rail takes you up the mountain to Kuranda. The view is amazing. Then, you can come down again by rail, if you haven't had enough of little trains!"

"I'd like to see the lot. Thomas was very well behaved at Uluru." Esther was smiling.

Derry wanted to spend a morning with his team at Uni so Alice asked Maria Benetti if she would tell her where there was a furniture shop.

"I will come with you!"

They drove into one of the big commercial centres just outside town. Alice found some of the roundabout systems very confusing and was pleased to have her guidance. She was very pleased to find what she was looking for and placed an order, hoping that the dining table and chairs would arrive in time for the meal she wanted to give her parents.

At Tjapukai they watched the presentations which were very similar to the one at Thala and made great use of the shop for gifts for Daniel and Charles. It was quite different at the Mossman Gorge centre. There was a shop and outside were buses to take them into the bush. At the entrance, scarcely clad natives waved burning twigs and leaves over them for protection and cleansing.

"That reminds me of the sweat lodges for the Native Americans." said Thomas.

They had been warned to wear strong shoes and were glad they did when they walked over rocks and stones and prickly plants. They were surrounded by flying things and small beetles and other unidentified creatures scurried across the path. The wild, rocky river wound and descended into a cascade. While walking, the guides told them the stories, the history, the culture and the development of the centre. There came a time a few years earlier when more respect and appreciation of the natives and their skills became almost the norm after the terrible racism and harsh treatment of the tribal peoples who were not even considered as fully human.

Thomas made sure he took all the contact details of this project. Alice noticed.

"I really want to learn more about these tribes. Derry is going to take me into the Queensland bush with him on his next trip."

"You will be all alone when we leave!"

"Yes, but I have a lot to do, job hunting and my neighbours and Derry's team are very friendly to me. But I know I will miss you all."

Thomas was inspired. Over the Thala supper he suggested to Derry that when his ecology book was published, they could do some research together.

"We need to find a University centre in America who would work on a three-way comparison with us; spirituality, rituals, culture in African tribes, Australian Aborigines and the Native Americans."

"Sounds great! We need to have a think, see what funding we could get, set out a study plan and decide where our base would be."

Esther laughed, "I knew it!"

"Ok. No more now. We'll work on it later. We could perhaps have the base in Oxford as there are three different places to travel to."

"I have a team in Nigeria who could do most of the work there while we concentrate on Australia and America."

Alice and Esther smiled at each other.

"We'll never keep them apart and we'll never keep them at home."

The Queenslander was number 42.

"The meaning of all life and the universe! According to the Hitchhiker's Guide to the Galaxy!" Derry had laughed when he first saw it.

Alice bought some picnic plates and cooked them a mound of roast vegetable for the meal together. She had seen it on offer at a Garden Centre and thought she just about had enough pots and pans to produce this for four. They planned the final meal together at Palm Cove as they sat around the old table. The next day the furniture was delivered. Alice asked the men to take it upstairs. She would find out later how to get rid of the unwanted chairs and tables. She invited her parents to come into the large spare room. There opposite the window, standing against the longest wall was a white bookshelf.

"Now you need a leather chair!" said Thomas. Her trunks and boxes were yet to arrive. "And a desk, a small one!" She smiled with delight.

"We'll do it, Alice, we'll pursue this new research project!" He hugged his daughter.

7 Alice in the Town

A large taxi took Thomas and Esther to the airport and the little beige car took Derry to University where he would travel with Jake to meet Mary in the Northern Territory. They had all wept a little when they separated.

Alice bought town plans, a detailed one and a tourist one. Susie took her to a park with Zippy and Maria returned with her to the shopping centre and advised on paint and paper.

"I quite like the bare wood in places, very natural looking."

Her trunk arrived but she did not unpack it until the nascent Study had been decorated. She stood looking at the empty white shelves. They were not as sturdy as the one at home but they were strong enough. The ready-made shelf fitted almost perfectly. There was a space for a notice board and some pictures at the far end.

Steve turned up one afternoon.

"Hello Alice. Come to mine, meet my family. Got time now?"

"Yes, I have. Thanks so much."

Steve's wife, Jeannie was mixed race. Alice was delighted.

"There aren't many pure bloods left. I have English and Aboriginal blood in me. My Mum was one of the stolen children." Alice looked forward to understanding what all that meant. The two children were a pale coffee colour but their hair was very black and curly.

Alice was so pleased to meet all these new people. She ordered a television and DVD player and had her laptop installed. With map in hand, she walked around Cairns to get her bearings and find schools and offices. She registered her interest with her CV in two Translation companies. They wanted Japanese but said they sometimes needed German. She went to senior schools and the University to make them aware of her availability to work and asked around for any classes for teaching English for refugees or foreign residents as well as any needs to teach Aborigines from the outback who had not learned more than a few words of English.

In her trunk she came across an old DVD of a Wim Wenders film she had studied. It was called *Alice in den Städten*, a road movie about a little girl called Alice who was travelling with someone around German towns. Some of it had been filmed in Wuppertal. Although she had been fascinated by the rail bridges where the characters often sat or walked, she had never wanted to travel there.

I am Alice in the town! She thought as she looked through for more. Then she found Werner Herzog's Australian film. Where the Green Ants Dream. She could barely remember the story but a scene had impressed itself on her memory. The huge, yellow bulldozers were about to tear up the earth when a group of Aborigines sat down in front of them.

'Just mow over them!' said one boss and was fortunately dissuaded by the others.

She invited Jeannie to come and watch it with her. It was a story of the conflict between Aboriginal land rights and the advance of modern technology.

"It has happened often. White men just do not understand land, country and sacred places." Alice wondered if the green ants would succeed in holding back this progress.

The next few weeks passed quite quickly. Alice in the town discovered a modern Roman Catholic Cathedral and loved the bright interior. The stained-glass windows ran around three walls depicting the story of Creation. She loved it and decided she would attend a Mass there. It was not far from her number 42. She had not yet tried out the several small Anglican churches in the town. As she read the notices on the board, the words Christian Meditation stood out to her. She took down the details and longed to join. She bought a large candle that she planned to light every evening when Derry was away. It got dark so early. By about six, darkness fell as the sun set so there were no long summer evenings in the garden.

In one of the big markets, perusing the books, she found an old copy of '*A Town Like Alice'* by Nevil Shute. She recalled reading it when she was in her teens.

She piled up the pillows by the bookshelf.

"I must get a chair!" She could not remember all the story except that an English girl had married and Australian. There was a Japanese prison camp with some traumatic events and then a love story as the girl and the Australian had found each other again after the war. The part that interested her most was the way the girl tried to cope with life in the outback. She had hated the house at first. Then there were dramas in the bush with floods, herds of cattle, and the flying doctor. Alice was relieved that she would probably never encounter that kind of adventure. The couple had had some children and Alice found herself longing for a baby with Derry.

"It would be so good for him." She envisaged him holding a new born son. "Perhaps we'll find a river to name him after."

She ached for Derry but they had managed to speak when he went into Darwin.

In her new home, Alice decided to do some painting herself. She started with the walls of the study. An off white covered the wooden slats well. She imagined the artefacts which would eventually go on the three walls. She measured the space for a desk and thought she would place it sideways on to the window so she could see the hills outside and the bookshelf inside. This would be Derry's study when he was home and she would either share with him or use the dining room table.

The Christian Meditation Group proved to be very welcoming. It was held in a luxurious looking house with a sea view. The street was lined by beautiful, smooth, white barked trees, she was given the name 'melaleucas'. By the sea front were darker trees with thick, arching roots forming a dome like structure at the base of the wide trunk. The botanist, Connie was needed, "Figs!" she told her later.

The group met once a week with occasional get-togethers, for socials and more serious Days of Reflection. The people were from different denominations. The leaders were Richard and Fiona who attended a Catholic Parish in Edmonton, one of the regions of Cairns. The other regular members were Simon, a retired teacher and Sandrine an artistic housewife. Alice told them about Abigail and her group in London. She explained that her husband was a research anthropologist and had studied dadirri and Aboriginal spirituality. The group was familiar with the term and its meaning.

"We have some Aborigines who come sometimes and they help with the Days of Reflection and lead some 'awareness' sessions."

"Sandrine brings her art and craft and sells some on these days." Simon explained. "What were your subjects?" asked Alice.

"English literature and Woodwork. Strange combination but I always loved woodwork and I still do some in my workshop at home."

Alice used her German 6 syllables for the 30-minute silence. Each week a member brought a reading which would lead into the silence. Gentle music played as they gathered and sat down. At the end they had refreshments on a table with some WCCM leaflets. Alice picked some up to take home.

"When is your husband back?"

"Not totally sure. End November, early December, I think."

"Oh you poor young bride. We'll invite you for some meals."

"I'd love that. I'm decorating the Queenslander he bought. We do not know where we will be next year."

Simon asked about the research. She explained about the botanist and the team working on plants, nature and ecology among the tribes.

"When he comes back he'll have to work on his book. He is based at Cairns Uni but I met him when he was a student at Oxford."

Alice enjoyed the supper in the luxurious dining room. Richard asked how Derry had become interested in anthropology.

"I am ashamed to say that I have never asked him. I have taken if for granted. My father is also a research anthropologist but he works in Nigeria."

"Quite a family!"

"Mustn't forget my brother, Daniel Hartley, the pianist and organist. He performs in Leipzig and London and several other places. Sometimes he is recorded by the BBC and I am so proud of him."

"And you?"

"I followed in my mother's footsteps and studied German and went into translating, oh, and I taught English to foreigners, Muslims actually."

Alice soon felt at home with this group and hoped she could see Sandrine's art work and Simon's woodwork when she was not painting and decorating, Alice spent her time with Zippy in the spacious parks of Cairns, not always with Susie. Her gentle rhythm was broken by a call from a German Engineering Company who asked her to translate their reports for their international workers. Her work slowly began to grow. She longed for her calls and cards from Derry. Steve called at least once a week after University and then invited her to join him on his next trip to the Aboriginal township just outside Cairns.

"Will it prepare me for my trip with Derry?"

"I hope not!" He answered

Alice was disturbed, even horrified by what she experienced with Steve. He left his car near a small store and walked past two or three very spread-out shacks. The roofs were of corrugated iron, the windows were very small. A few men and women sat outside on the ground, leaning against the wall. Children and older boys ran around the dry grounds. The adults stood up. They could not take their eyes off Alice. The children came to hold her hand and lift their arms to be picked up. She asked one mother about her home. She had no kitchen so they cooked on an open wood fire outside. There was one tap with cold running water, one narrow shower in the corner. The room was L shaped and around the corner was the sleeping area, just mattresses spread out with pillows and blankets on the floor. Seven of them slept there. Alice held herself back from asking about schools, doctors or transport. More was slowly revealed. A thin girl who looked about 9 or 10 took her hand and showed her a cotton reel with crochet work.

"I do." said the girl.

Alice praised her. "What's your name? I'm Alice."

"Queenie." She replied and when asked her age, she said she was 15.

The store sold cigarettes, bread and a few vegetables but mainly there were stacks of dried food packets and tins.

Steve gathered 3-4 youths around him when they stopped kicking a ball. The ball was punctured and malformed.

"Come and talk to Alice," he said. They sat together on the ground. "How's it going?"

"OK." They nodded.

"This month, any drugs, booze, smokes?"

"Not so much. I had some beers." Alice noticed empty cans on the ground. "I had some smokes. Guys came from the town."

"Pills?"

"Yep. I've nothing left till next week."

"Do you eat meat?" asked Alice. "Kangaroo, wallaby, Mum cooks it."

"There's a creek near the school, we sometimes fish." Steve kept them talking and offered then to meet up for a football game with some others.

"I'll get you a new ball." said Alice.

"Careful," whispered Steve. "They'll ask for all sorts if they think you are rich!"

Steve had another chat with the lads individually. He was neither police nor social services, so they chatted in a relaxed way. Steve then walked over to another group of shacks. Outside were some prickly trees with items of washing spread across them to dry.

Alice looked around at the other shacks, the thin sleeping dogs, the broken bits of cars.

Steve put his arm round Alice as he walked her back to the car.

"This is the unseen Australia, the hidden and secret Australia. Think of the luxury homes a few miles down on the coast. It's so unjust and it hasn't changed for decades!"

She brushed a tear away.

"I feel so ashamed. Can I offer some gifts? A football?"

"That would be OK. That's enough for now. My issue is ICE, Crystal Meths. They get it in spite of the poverty. It leads to crime and some forms are so dangerous that it renders the user out of control and violent. Dealers come and sell for very low prices and then return later, when the kids are hooked and sell at greater prices."

"Oh, Steve, how terrible!"

"When Derry takes you to the Bush camp, it won't be anything like this. The tribes live very differently and try to live by the old ways, be self-sufficient and ecological. They have avoided being so corrupted."

Alice was emotionally upset for a couple of days and felt unable to buy any more furniture. It seemed like an insult to the Aborigines she had seen. She invited Jeannie to bring her children round to draw some pictures. She bought paper and felt-tips and some cakes and drinks. While they sat happily drawing rockets and cars, she told Jeannie how she felt about her visit with Steve.

"You come to accept it. You can't change anything. It's not just here; it's over the whole country. The powers that be move exceedingly slowly. There are a few pockets of hope but generally it is still a picture of struggle and despair."

"There's room for a proper football pitch and changing rooms. I wish we could get something built. There must be some activists trying to make the government change things."

The rainy season was beginning so Alice had to learn when to give up driving as the rain, like rods of milk, started to fall. No visibility at all. It was getting hotter and hotter both day and night. Alice put on the fans and felt tempted to buy an air conditioner. She tried not to pour out her sorrow about the visit when Derry rang, but she mentioned she had been and he seemed to understand instinctively.

"Dearest Alice, we need some furniture to live, we cannot deny it to ourselves because of Aboriginal poverty. I am not sure how we can help but the research we are doing will bring it more to the attention of the government and bring a greater appreciation of their gifts and skill and the disgraceful way they have been treated in their own land."

"Dear Derry, I want to think about what we could do." Alice let her mind think around what a charity could provide what was needed. Her father had done something similar in Nigeria.

The more she thought, the more overwhelmed she felt. The problems were much deeper, more complicated, more political and of course more historical than she had imagined.

There were breaks in the rain but the wind was growing stronger. On the TV news Alice saw the warnings that a cyclone was heading for the north Queensland coast near Cairns. That same evening Steve arrived with Connie. They braved the wind to get out of the car and run up the steps. 'Hello, Connie. Welcome! Come in.' Alice held hard on to the door which was taking a blast from the wind. Steve pulled back his hood, "This is serious. Your first cyclone after a few months. I've bought some rolls of tape for you."

Alice hesitated to ask why. Steve and Connie started to unroll the wide tape and cover every window with crosses. He threw a roll to Alice. "Back door and panels! It can stop the glass flying if you get a direct gust."

"Both Steve and I live in solid houses with a cellar. You could come and spend the night with one of us. We might not be in the direct path but we will feel the winds anyway."

Connie broke off from her tape work for a minute. "Last one was just north of Townsville so Cairns got off lightly."

"When will we know about the direction?"

"In a couple of hours it should be clearer. It is monitored all the time."

"Can I decide then?"

"Too late. You could not come out in it. We might also lose power even if it is not the worst."

"You are so kind. Thank you so much. I would really like to try and live through it here."

"You might be asked to evacuate into the shopping centre."

"If that does not happen, I'd like to stay."

"Can I stay with you?" asked Connie.

"You really want to do that? I can give you supper!"

"I'll ring home and we can eat while there is still some electricity." Steve went home and Alice put on her Australian Meditation music. Soon it was impossible to hear it. The radio report said that the direction seemed to be south of Cairns in the Innisfail, Babinda area.

Alice could not believe the roar of the wind, the shaking of the doors and windows and the crashing of objects outside. The squalls of rain were like the river cascades. Alice did feel terrified as it was all much worse that she expected.

"Derry won't have this at least!"

"They get cyclones over the top end and the Gulf of Carpentaria but not at the same time! He'll be OK."

"There's only one double bed. Do share it."

"We must pull it away from the window as far as possible."

They lay down fully clothed and tried to close their eyes. Impossible. Talking was also impossible. The noise of the wind was too much with intermittent crashes. Hours passed before there was any indication of the rain softening or the wind slowing.

Just before dawn it seemed not to be so noisy. They both looked out of the window. At least that glass was still intact but it was too dark to see the extent of the damage outside. The power suddenly came on.

"It must have been turned off because the power lines have fallen over the street. The worst must be over. Alice, well done!"

"I was terrified. I chose this life and I wanted to live it instead of escape from the bad parts."

As the light of dawn arose the wind had dropped but not stopped. They put on hooded coats and opened the back door. One glass panel on the left had cracked. In the garden were things she had never seen before; bins, toys, broken pieces of wood, metal bars and street furniture and broken bits of everything.

"Careful as we go." Connie went down the steps. "Few broken roof slats, broken blind, curtain sucked out but no major damage."

They picked their way through the debris and walked around the side under the stilts.

"Oh, dear, garage door broken off." Alice tentatively followed as Connie went round to the front. "Power line or phone lines hanging low but the post is just bent." The reports stopped. Alice wrapped her arms round herself and stood there crying.

"They will bring skips to the street corners and we can clear up then."

They sat indoors. The tape had stopped the glass breaking into bits and flying into the room. “Wow! Wow! Wow!” said Alice.

“Got coffee and breakfast?” asked Connie keeping cool and calm.

“Sure. Coffee first. Thank you Connie. Thank you so much.”

“You’re welcome. Alice, Derry will be frantic if he is near a screen or a radio.”

When Connie had left to survey her own garden damage, Alice went to see both her neighbours. They had very similar damage and a very frightened Zippy. Alice cuddled him but he wanted to hide under the bed. Some outer doors were broken but at least the stilts and beams were solid. Mid-morning the phone rang and a frantic Derry asked how she was. She described her night to him and praised his two colleagues who had come with tape.

“They both said I could stay with them but I decided to stay and Connie stayed with me! Isn’t that kind?”

“Dear Alice I am so glad you are OK. I have seen wooden houses end up as a pile of rubble. There are some reels of tape in the garage, in a drawer.”

“Of course!” laughed Alice.

“Not long now before I can get home. Ten to twelve days.”

“I have had some translation work to do for a German Engineering Company.”

“Well done.”

“Maria has taken me to some shops to get paint. I have made a start. Bright red OK?”

“What?”

“Any other colour requests?”

“I trust you! See you soon my lovely one.”

It took all of 10 days to clear up. Alice rummaged through her cases to find some gloves. At least the roof did not seem to be leaking. Every neighbour was out doing the same when the skips arrived. Steve gave her the names of some workmen for the repairs.

“Roof first. But they will have a lot of work round the town!” Gradually normality was restored. When the debris was cleared from the roads, Alice took Maria out for lunch and to accompany her when she chose a desk and chair and an armchair.

"Leather is probably not a good idea. I do not know how long we will be here." She walked past some wicker chairs that would be in an English conservatory.

"There are nice thick cushions for them. They will be comfortable." Maria encouraged her. She put away all thoughts of a desk resembling that of an Oxford Professor and looked for something modern and simple, attractive and functional. She found one with a chair that she thought would fit in the right-hand corner and still leave space for two wicker chairs and space to walk in without a squeeze.

"Big enough for a computer and Derry's files." The chair space was on the right with a set of drawers on the left.

Alice recalled how she had enjoyed setting up her new flat in London, choosing colours and designs for herself. She experienced the same sense of freedom now as she had Derry in mind when she chose the furniture. She was amazed that he had bought this house for her with a double bed before he knew she would accept him. That surprised her; did he somehow know that she loved him? She was tempted to paint one room red to shock him.

Next came the new curtains and blinds. While in the centre, Alice bought a football.

"There's a game at the Aboriginal township."

"Are you going? You're brave!"

"They have nothing. The poverty is terrible. The kids get booze and drugs and live with no hope for a future."

The day came when she drove to the township where Steve arrived in a minibus with several young lads and a set of portable goal posts. From one of the shacks a young girl emerged carrying a blanket. Alice smiled and the girl lifted the blanket and passed it to Alice. When she unfolded the top she saw a recently born baby barely a foot long. Alice held the little boy who snuggled into her breasts and slept soundly. She stroked the stick-like arms and legs and his black head of hair. Tears rolled down her cheeks and a wave of new emotions washed over her and through her.

8 Alice in the Outback

Alice sat in her armchair by the white bookshelf which already held some of her books and DVDs, reading through the pages of *A Town Like Alice.* She read how the English girl sat at a table with her husband to prepare him for the plans she had for the isolated farmhouse and for the nearby town. She loved how the author had described the way she was sensitive about her husband's feelings. There was no indication of conflict, anger or even annoyance.

"Just like Derry. I hope we can always be like that!"

Daniel had already heard about Thala.

"You can also stay with us as long as you wish. There are luxury holiday apartments in Cairns but Thala is different. Charles will love it! If you book, remind them who you are. You might even get to perform, there's a grand piano in the lounge."

This holiday became the plan for next summer when Thomas and Esther were going to Israel.

Even though Derry was very preoccupied with preparing his notes and recordings for the journey home, he thought about his sister, Madeleine and decided to try and invite her, the whole family in fact to come for a holiday. He realised they would have to get some guest beds and perhaps a bed/settee for the lounge.

Alice felt very strange when she saw the little beige car arrive and drive up on to the grassy verge. She thought he looked thinner as he stood up, banged the door and leapt up the steps. It was a very happy and relaxed reunion.

"I am so sorry that so soon after our wedding I had to leave you for so long! That was unkind and almost inhuman."

"I made the best of it. That is the nature of your work, my love." He walked through to the open area.

"Find your study!" She opened the door to show him in. "Oh, Alice, that is wonderful!"

She held back on expressing her new feelings until after they had made love. She almost whispered to him, "Derry, I am so longing to have a baby with you."

He kissed and caressed her, "We can make that a priority and work everything else round it."

"You are serious?"

"What you feel is the most important thing in my life. If you want us to have a baby now, I will start planning a work schedule."

"Even if we are still here for the birth?"

"Other people manage to combine work and family life. We could not invest in a better house just in case our new base turns out to be in Oxford if our project is accepted."

"I got through a cyclone in this house. I can have a go at motherhood."

"I am so grateful for you, my love."

"Have you got any river names for me?"

They had a blissful few outings before the Outback trip was due. Derry went with her and Steve to the next football game at the township and to Sandrine's art therapy project. At the township Alice made for the shack where the girl and her baby had been. There was no sign of her. She asked around.

"Baby die," was the response. Alice stood paralysed and frozen. Derry walked around the shacks while the boys were earnestly engaged in their game with Alice's new ball. Derry stopped to look at a thin horse tied to a hook at the back of one shack.

"No water." He sighed. "Steve's doing such a wonderful job here. It is not part of his research but he puts time and effort into getting to know them so they have some confidence in him.

"He's really working on ICE and trying to get Jake and Connie's help to find some healing medicine, a kind of antidote, Bush Medicine."

"How come it is so bad?"

"The male suicide rate is unbelievably bad. There is a school but their attendance record is terrible. They have lost their own identity and any sense of hope for their future or that they have a value."

"Baby health?"

"Everyone's health. They have many illnesses which are no longer dominant in urban areas; renal problems, ear and eye infections, diabetes. Many of their parents are part of the lost generation. The government and some churches thought it would be better for children to be taken away from their family and brought up in a Mission orphanage. No one considered what trauma would be caused by the family break ups. When we go into the Bush we will meet some

Elders who are working with an anthropologist to restore some of their old ways. The Elders are trying to pass down their knowledge to the young generation."

"It's overwhelming!" said Alice.

"Certainly there are no quick and easy solutions. We have so much to learn from the Elders. It will soon be too late."

She felt relieved to join Sandrine in yet another shack on the outskirts of a large park on the edge of town. It was untidy and ramshackle. The central table had piles of tiles, papers and textiles. One wall was draped with a large piece of net material which had been painted with waves of blue and purple. Sparkly jewels had been stuck on and embroidery in contrasting greens and yellows formed the underwater plants.

"It's not an exhibition, explained Sandrine, "but we do have one or two to get funding. The people who come here are disabled, mentally ill, unwell and struggling with something." Some of the art works had been done by people who were talented, black ink line drawings of local scenes, water colour landscapes and acrylic portraits. On a side table stood a structure in cardboard and paper cups. A colourful collage struck Alice.

"It's by a young man who was a drug addict and has been in a clinic for rehabilitation. He is doing well and it helps him to sit cutting out pieces from the magazine stack and spread them on a huge sheet of paper on the floor and work out a design."

"This is a really good project, Sandrine. I am so glad Alice found your Meditation Group. I look forward to joining you. We are going to do dadirri in the bush soon with one of the tribes I have been working with."

Alice visited a doctor to get advice about stopping the pill and trying to get pregnant. She found the doctor helpful and encouraging. She was given advice on how to stop the pill completely and advised that they should wait for her regular periods to happen for a couple of months.

Their trip came after the rainy season. Alice found the heat very difficult to cope with. She was alright until she had to actually move and do something like cook or clean. They sat on the balcony when he talked her through the 5-6 days she would be with the tribe.

"You will be ritually welcomed and then we shall have a session of quiet listening and awareness. We shall sleep in one of the shelters they build themselves. The women will demonstrate basket making and the men, canoe building, possibly even didgeridoo making, they will talk about their methods of land control and their medicines which date back hundreds of years. You will see the plants that we have gathered for the research."

"It's so different from the urban areas. Sometimes they leave the township to spend time with their families, or to avoid the police."

"A baby I saw there, died."

"I am afraid that often happens. Not enough medical care, not enough milk. At times the Social Workers come and just take the babies."

"It's tragic and disgraceful."

"It's centuries of racism and a negative mind set." He took her hand and kissed her for a long time. "We are so blessed." He smiled at his beautiful young wife knowing they might be parents in the next year.

"Being pregnant or having a new baby is no time to go to the Northern Territory and meet Mary."

Before the trip, Alice spent a morning at the Uni with Connie because she wanted to understand how the team worked together. Connie showed her the fridge with all the plants she had studied and Jake did the same with the roots and berries. Steve's agenda was a little different but he looked at the healing properties of these plants which could bring relief and healing to drug addicts. There would be a chapter on this aspect in the new book. Alice noticed one box with a red strap and buckle round it.

"They are the ones you cannot eat. They are poisonous. Quite deadly." said Jake. "A professional photographer will come and take all the photos and label them ready for the book before we get the manuscript to the publisher. Then there's Jane's work on women. A little to the side of this issue but there will be a chapter on their knowledge of cooking methods and especially how to make some poison nuts edible!"

"Derry is the brains. He has piles of notes and recordings from Mary and he has to organise it all. It will cover ecology, spirituality, philosophy and nature itself," added Jake.

Alice had some translation to write out and some oral interpretation for a business meeting for the international partners of the German company. The director congratulated her on her accuracy and fluency. She told him about her German born mother. She was relieved that her first natural period arrived before the trip.

On their last evening they had supper with Richard and Fiona. They talked about some aspects of their lives and experiences of Meditation.

"The bush will be a contrast for you," smiled Richard sipping his wine.

"When we have our next Day of Reflection you will be invited to speak to us about your work."

Derry was pleased but explained that he needed several quiet months to write up the new book.

Alice took his arm when they left, "You are becoming famous, Dr Derwent, I have a booking for you in London!"

The little red car drew into the Bush camp. Alice locked it up when they had transferred their luggage to the off-road vehicle and then climbed in with Bobby the Aboriginal driver.

The paths were marked with deep ruts from large tyres. Sipping water almost constantly, they passed ant hills, cattle, kangaroos, wallabies as they took about three hours to reach the tribal area. They crossed a creek, bumping over the stones.

"It broke down in the middle in my book!" said Alice.

"Book?"

"*A Town Like Alice*." she answered.

"Don't know that one." She smiled at him and was not surprised. She thought that he would not know the Green Ant film either.

"Tell me how you first got interested in anthropology."

"Round the fire tonight. It's too bumpy now!" They stopped shortly after the creek and saw the shelters and the billy-cans over logs outside.

"Roast goanna and potatoes tonight." announced Derry. They left most luggage in the van and put their sleeping bags in a shelter. Derry could only just fit in.

The Elders came to greet them. Smoke was waved over them and the Elders spoke to their ancestors to introduce Alice to them.

The women then hugged them and so did the male elders.

They were invited to sit in a large circle. Some of the natives held clap sticks and didgeridoos. Their singing still brought tears to Alice's eyes. There was then a prolonged silence. Alice did not use her German anchor word but expected some instruction.

One lady stood up.

"Now we move to our own place. We will listen to nature, the movement of the trees, the insects, the breeze, and the animals around. No thinking. No words, just listening."

How long did they sit listening? She recalled her mother's spiritual magic but then found she could focus on listening. She stopped every thought and closed her eyes. She heard sounds all around her including the breathing of some of the others. She felt a presence around her and inside her. The presence went down and down and down inside her to her stomach. She lifted her hands up to the sky and held them there, feeling love and power flowing through them to her head. The intensity made her open her eyes. It was nearly totally dark but the sky was such a colour that she thought she was looking at a painting. Purple, red, orange and yellow streaked across the horizon. Birds were silhouetted on the twigs of some trees and huge black shapes flew across the camp.

The clap sticks began and everyone stood up and moved back to the circle. The closing song was in English and was clearly a Christian song called '*Deep Waters*.'

Everyone hugged everyone else like sharing the sign of peace.

On what looked like a banana leaf, they ate roast goanna meat and potatoes with mugs of water.

"Right, Derry dear, tell me how you got into this."

"Well I did A levels in Geography, Geology, Economics and Natural Science. I was not sure which path to take for a degree course. One of my teachers took time with me. My Dad was in a bad mood or seemed angry all the time. He wanted me to leave school and take up a trade or work for a firm. My teacher asked me some leading questions. I had to go away and write down what made me feel excited, what so gripped me that I could not let it go, what I longed to look into? Thinking like that was refreshing. I was inspired by the formation of different countries and the movements of tectonic plates and volcanoes. I could not wait to find out about strata of rock formations. I saw a video about ancient Rock Art in Africa and Australia. I was surprised to discover how old they were and that Australian natives dated back over 40,000 years, the oldest known people in the world. The teacher noticed that Economics had not figured in my list. He asked me if I knew about the people who had produced the art and I said I would love to know about them and their culture."

Derry was advised to look up Anthropology and see if there were any aspects which grabbed his attention.

"DB, if you choose to go for that, make for Oxbridge. You should get straight As." Derry had always felt grateful for this guidance and eventually his father was so pleased that he had a place at Oxford that he accepted his son's choice.

“I met the professors, including your father. He changed my life.”

“He is a remarkable man. I love him dearly and I have a special bond with him. I love Mum too of course, but I have always been aware of her inner pain without understanding what it was exactly. We all understood after the Leipzig trip.”

“Thomas adores her. I am sure his love has brought her some healing.”

“We could always talk to Dad about anything at all. I cannot imagine how it feels to know that all your nearest and dearest died so horribly.”

“Some of the Aborigines bear that kind of grief.”

The next day Alice was invited to watch some of the tribal skills which date back many centuries.

“Part of the Irukandji tribes; this is not their daily routine,” explained Derry, “but they are always happy to show visitors. This is actually how they live in the bush, though, and you will see they use metal and modern tools. We’ll see the weaving first.”

It was a laborious task. To get the strands to weave the ladies began by pushing and bending down some narrow trees until they snapped, or they simply chopped them down. They took a trunk about a metre long and hacked off the outer bark with an axe. After that most of the work was done sitting cross legged on the ground. Alice recalled her Junior School days when she sat with her class, cross legged on the shiny wooden floor. Here she got better at it as time went on but she was very conscious of what was crawling around in the woodchips under her legs.

Using the back of the axe they then beat the strands of bark which they had peeled off. They found softer strands in a deeper layer and pulled it apart into long, narrow strips. One girl rolled and rolled the strands on her thigh until they were thin enough to plait. Onto this length of plait they threaded the pale strips and began to weave strips of slightly different colours along and across the fronds. After a while they could define the emerging shape and see that a bag was being created.

Making canoes was equally laborious. The men used ropes and strong sticks to shin up tall, straight trees. Again it was a matter of peeling off the bark. On the ground men held sticks of 3-4 metres long to poke under the bark and push the knife on the end to cut off the sheet of bark. These sheets took three or four men to carry and were treated in both water and fire.

Several men worked on one canoe. They shaped the treated bark, put in holes and sewed the sides together and bound them to thicker branches. The front was very pointed, shaved, shaped with sharp tools.

"However did they do that without knives?"

"Bones, always bones and sometimes some sharp stones a bit like our flint."

An Elder brought over a hollow tube of wood, the trunk of a narrow tree. He used another solid stick to hit trees nearby.

"Hear, some good, some too solid. Termites eat inside, then it is good."

He held up the hollow tree and thrust his stick down inside and scraped out the extraneous material. He blew down the tube and made recognisable didgeridoo sounds.

"Now paint." He showed her some half-painted didgeridoos. They had been smoothed down and dotted lines were beginning to appear. This art work was taken very seriously and each lizard or snake had a meaning. Alice tried to blow down but no sound came out.

"I can't do it either" said Derry, "It is called circular breathing, you breathe in and out at the same time."

This was a presentation for me. I would have to live here for weeks to see real life. Alice thought.

Next morning they drove northwards to a salt water lake to meet Paul, the anthropologist and the Elders. Paul was showing them his mapping work when the Aborigines arrived.

Alice and Derry were invited to stand in the shallow waters to be introduced to the Spirits and the ancestors and to have prayers of protection.

One Elder took the boys deeper into the water and handed them a spear each. He was teaching them to spear fish.

"Now, metal tip, before we use bone in wood." Explained the grey-haired man. They loved the challenge but did not catch many. On land again they soon cut down branches and built a primitive high jump. They placed the straightest stick across two uprights with notches cut into the top. The young people had brought battery-controlled tape players and had modern pop music in the background. One girl pulled down a large fruit and cut it open. She pulled out fluff.

"Fluff good for pillow." She showed them how to rub it in their hands. The boys jumping were not too successful either. The fell and rolled in the sand and laughed.

“Turn off. Turn off.” Shouted the Elder pointing to the tape recorder. Then he cut a large branch, shaved it in places with his knife and passed it to one of the boys.

“Try, put in ground.” Then he spoke in his own language.

The boy smiled widely when he jumped right over the high jump with the help of the sturdy stick.

Paul took up the fruit with the fluffy insides.

“You cannot believe how capable the different tribes were thousands of years before the white men came. It is so rarely spoken of now. They were farmers and managers of the land. Recent archaeologists have found drainage ditches and stones used to crush plants.”

“Derry has researched dadirri, spirituality, culture and now he is working on Bush medicine, plants, concepts of nature.”

“How interesting! There must be more awareness these days. The government has recently discovered their skill using fire for land control. They used fire sticks to burn certain areas to help new growth. It is being studied right now. Are you also an anthropologist?”

“No. Just Derry’s wife. I teach and translate German. We only married this year.”

They both felt they should return to camp now, before darkness fell. There were the usual fond farewells and Alice felt very privileged.

They met Bobby for their drive.

“Bats!” he yelled pointing to the large black shapes fluttering above their heads. “Much bigger than I have ever seen.” Alice instinctively covered her head.

Before they left the camp Alice saw some of the collections of the roots they had been working on. With no fridges, most of the trial and error took place in the laboratory in Cairns.

9 Family Affairs

Derry spent long hours at the Uni manipulating all the material. He was often in conference with the publishers. He wanted to make sure that his colleagues received adequate acknowledgment and to oversee the photography, such an essential part of the chapters on food, poisons and medicines.

Daniel and Charles arrived for three weeks at Thala. They hired a car so they would not be dependent on Alice for lifts. She asked them if they would be interested in visiting the woodwork studio of a friend from the Meditation groups.

"He produces beautiful, artistic pieces. A souvenir or gift to take home?"

"We do like woodwork; that sounds good."

Alice had suggested a visit to Simon after the last meeting. Outside the house, Alice explained that it would be Daniel her brother and his partner, Charles. Simon smiled, "I am very happy to meet them. I have never mentioned it before but I also have a partner, a man called Eugene. Some Christians find it hard to accept gay partnerships."

"They've been together since the early 80s. And you?"

"We've been together for over twenty years but we have only shared a house since our retirement. I was in a Catholic School and it could have caused offence." Alice smiled. She had guessed Simon was gay and was so pleased to be able to include him and Eugene in their circle of friends.

"What did Eugene do?" She asked.

"He was a doctor in the hospital specialising in spinal deformities. He is a part-time consultant now in a private clinic."

Alice had to buy some more cutlery and crockery to entertain her growing list of friends and family members. Maria went with her as usual.

"I don't want expensive things because I may have to find a home for them if we leave." She made home cooked meals for her brother and friends. She told him about the cyclone and the Bush trip. Daniel saw her corner in the study.

"Do you still have D and Ms?"

"Well actually no, we do not need to, now we are together every day."

"When is he off again?"

"It's an unknown. We'll know more when the book is published. Did you know Dad is trying to organise a three-way comparison with Native Americans?"

"Yes, he mentioned he was not getting much response from the USA."

"What's next for you and Charles?"

"We are going to Sydney Opera House on the way home! Then we have several bookings in Leipzig and London."

Alice remembered her times there, especially that first visit when Derry was so far away and not part of the experience.

They visited the local sights and enjoyed each other's company. The visit to Simon was very pleasant. Eugene was a very distinguished looking man with silver hair and beard. They all loved the workshop and Daniel was drawn particularly to the bird relief sculptures in dark, polished wood, Daniel and Charles found it difficult to choose.

They ended up with a package of 5-6 birds for friends and for their own home.

Daniel asked Alice what her own plans were, more study or more time in the outback with Derry.

"I want a baby," she smiled. "That would be wonderful!"

"I won't name him after a river!"

"And a girl?"

"I want a Jewish name for Mum."

A few weeks later Madeleine and Roy and the teenagers, Kyle and Zara arrived to spend a long weekend in Thala and two more weeks staying with Derry and Alice. Hearing of their dates, Alice bought more single beds for the spare rooms. Maddy and Roy could use the bed/settee in the open plan room. Alice was already planning where the nursery would be. They all went to Green Island and went snorkelling on the reef. Their favourite place was Palm Cove with the many restaurants and bars and the wind-surfing on the beach. Many a beach Adonis took long looks at Maddy's pretty daughter. Alice was aware that Kyle seemed to spend time with his uncle Derry. He seemed to be very fond of him.

Maddy sat with Alice when Derry was away in his publishing world.

"Are you thinking of having a family?" she asked without embarrassment.

Alice gulped and smiled, "Well, yes we want a baby as soon as possible." Maddy leapt up and hugged and kissed her.

"He'll be such a good father!"

"I think so too. I hope I don't fall pregnant or have the birth in the hot season."

"You must plan your dates." said Maddy. "You cope so well with everything. I love you like my own sister."

'I love you too, dear Maddy.'

Kyle and Zara were determined to return to live in this beautiful country when they finished school. Madeleine imagined the day when she would lose both of them. Roy had enjoyed it all and taken it all in his stride, but he was a 'home' man and looked forward to being back there again.

After the two visits, Alice decided she would make Steve's work with the Aborigines in the township a regular commitment. She was not sure how she could be of use but she hoped the situation would develop and she would find a way until she became pregnant.

She was just settling into another routine with Derry focussed on his book when Thomas rang to say that they would both like to come out again for a few weeks. Could they stay?

"We might have a treat weekend at Thala but we would like to spend time with you if you can manage that. How's the white bookshelf?"

"Waiting for Derry's books."

Derry and Alice gave her parents the bedroom and slept on the bed/settee. They enjoyed going shopping for groceries and sharing the cooking at home.

"Derry has invited me to spend time in the Uni. I reckon we need a day to try to set up our project. You and Mum can do something together."

"Lovely! I know just the park to take her to, Paranella."

"Let's have a meal out together at the end of the day. We shall all be tired. Palm Cove?"

Alice looked forward to time alone with her mother. She wanted to understand how she was after Leipzig and Israel and she wanted to share her desire for a baby. The drive took just over an hour. They happily walked through ornate arches, bamboo forests and flowering shrubs. They had a coffee and found a bench overlooking the distant sea.

"How did you feel in the cyclone?"

"Terrified. I'd probably go elsewhere if it happens again. We can evacuate to a shopping centre or stay with friends in a solid house, one with bricks!" she smiled.

"I miss you. How are you my darling?"

"I am happy in all that we do but there is one thing…" she hesitated, "Mum, did you long for a baby when you got married?"

"After a while, yes, I saw babies everywhere, in prams on the street, in people's arms, I was surrounded by them and I began to have a great longing. Daniel came along quite quickly."

"Oh, Mum, that's what I'm like now. I was on the pill when we first came out as we both thought it would not be sensible to have a baby until we knew at least which country we would live in. But now, I don't care. I just want a baby."

Esther put her arms around her daughter.

"I think this desperation does not necessarily last in such an intense way. I think you may well regain some equilibrium if pregnancy is delayed. Darling, don't let it dominate you. It can be a destructive force if no baby comes or if there is a problem of some sort."

"Would you like to be a Granny?"

"I would be delighted."

"Do you think I might have a problem?"

"No, but we can never tell in life. When you were about two, I also longed for another child. Dad was away in Africa for a long time and when he returned I was desperate to get pregnant. It never happened. Quite soon I was counting my blessings and I really enjoyed you and Daniel, especially when Dad was away. I learned to look on it in a different way and became very content."

"Thanks Mum. I shall try to relax and not feel so devastated when my monthly appears." She felt relieved and saw how the Aboriginal baby's death had got to her and intensified her own longing. She determined to enjoy every moment of this uncertain time.

They both wondered how their men were getting on.

"Thomas will be very disappointed if he does not get funding."

"Before we talk about that, tell me how Leipzig affected you."

Esther talked about her emotional reaction. She did not like to speak about it as she feared it would prove too painful but she had found a bereavement counsellor.

"At first I could not look at the pain of their deaths; just imagining the torture, the agony for my Mum. She helped me face it and helped me see that as we could not know the truth we did not have to always imagine the worst. She gave me some other Jewish testimonies, some worse than mine. Reading about how they came to terms with the unthinkable really helped me cope. She said that the support of loved ones was very important in the healing process and that finding a way of serving, helping others could also be a real help."

"You served us and Dad and students like Derry."

"That's when I looked for a Messianic Jewish group, I could feel in touch with my roots, my family and see if I could find a way to serve through them."

"For the Aborigines, roots and ancestors are very important and meaningful."

"I live too far to go each week but I have discovered some elderly people who live alone so I go to them about once a month."

"Well done Mum! They will love you for that."

They returned to Cairns and to their men, promising to speak together more often. Thomas and Derry were feeling very enthusiastic about the three-way comparison project.

"We'll talk to Cairns Anthropology directors before we go home. Did I tell you about Canada?" Thomas grinned as he untwisted his napkin.

"Canada?"

Thomas explained that there were so many projects going on in America but that he had heard of a Native American with a PhD who was running a Christian Community. He intended to follow that up.

However, one of the American links led to a college in Winnipeg. They showed real interest in building a connection with Australia.

"First Nation people are the same people as the Native Americans. They were in tribes long before the border was made. They have the same history." Derry added.

"I'd love to go to Canada," said Esther, "And see the Niagara Falls and the Prairies."

"Well, the college has contacts with an Indian, or First Nation Reservation right in the middle of the Prairies!" exclaimed Thomas.

A surge of hope filled Alice. *I'd love to go to Canada too, but…* She thought to herself.

Before they drove home they stood on the dark beach under the waving palm trees. A few twinkling lights could be seen on the islands and further up the coast. When their eyes adjusted to the darkness they looked up at the myriads of stars in the sky.

10 Amaranth

'Tribal Medicine and Nature Management in Australia'

Derry had to attend a series of book launch meetings in Sydney, Adelaide and Melbourne and in the north to meet Mary. Alice went north with him and was delighted to talk with this interesting Aboriginal teacher and artist. He took at least one colleague to each lecture and launch. They would have to return to Oxford for the English launch, but before they left some good news arrived. The funding for the research was approved and the perimeters for the study were accepted and Dr Koda Keith Blackhill was invited to Oxford.

Alice did not want to stay alone while Derry toured the Universities but she was very sad to leave Cairns after she had settled in so well. The new project to include a Native Canadian would take them in new directions but she hoped it would not be too long before they could return to live in Cairns.

While Derry was on his tours, Alice sat in her familiar corner in Oxford reading the thick, heavy tome. The dust cover and inner covers were decorated with one of Mary's beautiful paintings. It was no easy read; a very detailed, academic book, it was aimed at students of anthropology, ecology and medicine. She flicked through the pages of photographs with the descriptions of their properties. At the back were the portraits and biographies of each of the participants. After the Foreword, written by her father and before the Introduction was a dedication to the tribal peoples and to 'my wife, Alice Leah Barnes, without whose support and encouragement, I could not have completed this study.'

On the cover in bold print was his name Dr Derwent Barnes. She noticed that in Darwin people came to him and addressed him as Dr Derwent. In the next few years he was often addressed in this manner in academic circles.

Derry suggested that he and Thomas should go to Canada to meet Dr Koda before he came to Oxford and that Alice and Esther should join them for a holiday. This suggestion was taken up willingly by everyone. Derry no longer needed to have a base in Cairns and it was with a heavy heart that Alice left her first home and all her friends in her life there. They let number 42 to PhD students.

"We have two homes, both let to others! My London flat is on a two-year let."

"And we shall have to find our own home in Oxford when we return from Canada."

"We have lived in too many places for too long!" Alice smiled and hugged Derry. "Yes, we need our own home."

Dr Koda was very happy to welcome his new colleagues to his office and study area in his Winnipeg College. Derry and Thomas stayed in college rooms for these days of consultation and planning.

Koda was a forthright man with an edge, a sharpness, when he spoke about Dakota Sioux and Lakota Sioux, and as he said 'my people'. He seemed to function out of an inner anger. He was as tall as Derry with long, shiny black hair worn in a plait down his back. He was broad chested and very solid looking and wore highly decorated leather boots.

"I was Keith at school. I was taken into a mission boarding school when I was small. The standard of education was good, unlike most of the others. Natives were too often considered as good for nothing."

Derry and Thomas sat like students in front of his large desk. He spread out the papers and held one up.

"The perimeters: 1. Family, clan and tribe. 2. Appreciation of the Natural World. 3. The Supernatural and Spirits. 4. Belief systems. 5. Art. Yes, very good. I can contribute a lot on number 1. I did my PhD on the Law and First Nation Groups. Do you want to begin with any particular area of interest?"

Thomas smiled, "Well done on your PhD, excellent subject; different interpretations of the Law, so very necessary. I would go for art as I have done a lot of work on Nigerian artefacts."

"Brasses. Nothing like that here, but wood, totem poles, decorated wigwams and of course rock art." responded Koda.

"You know the BBC have started taking an interest in that and there have been several documentaries on Australian rock art."

"Tourism level?"

"No, actually, much deeper than that. Real Aboriginal contributors treated with great respect."

Derry butted in, "I have spent the last few years on medicines, plants and ecology in Australia."

"The supernatural and belief systems are behind everything. You cannot separate them." Koda added in his forceful way.

"So like the Aborigines."

Thomas and Derry were pleased to have time together when they went to explore the city. "Cut and dried. Sharp and sure. Indigenous pain underneath." said Thomas.

They enjoyed the Forks, a big market area near the river, the museums and the cathedral. "Our ladies will love it!" said Derry.

"Tomorrow I will take you on a visit to the Prairies and to a Reservation. We shall stay a few nights with friends." Koda had said.

The second night Koda invited them for a meal at the Forks so they explained to him that their wives were coming to join them for a holiday after their initial negotiations.

Long, straight and almost featureless roads stretched ahead of them. Derry recalled the roads in the outback. They had not asked Koda about his family life as they did not feel at ease with him yet.

They drove West along the main Highway to Portage le Prairie and then headed north.

The house was to be found on the left, twelve kilometres along the gravel road off Highway 261. They were surprised to note that the speed limit was 60mph even along the Highways. Uncertainty and insecurity gripped them after driving for a few minutes along the unmarked road. The road disappeared on the horizon far ahead. All was silence and stillness. There were no buildings visible in any direction.

They had driven due west from Winnipeg along Highway 1. The straight lines and 90-degree angles on the grid like map of Manitoba, belie the reality of the vast expanse of prairie and wilderness which spreads between them. Telegraph poles linked by thick, drooping wires, line the wide, straight roads. They came to some railway crossings where a train was passing. They could not believe the length of the trains and waited at least 20 minutes before the bar opened.

"Some people bring stoves and brew up."

"I gave up counting carriages after about 100!" said Derry.

Koda noticed that they were looking at the wide ditches either side of the roads.

"For snow." He explained. They arrived at the crossroads of Amaranth and saw the few stores and houses, a church and a petrol station.

"Welcome to Amaranth!" said Koda.

The northern, narrower, white stony road made a chalky cloud behind the car. The large white, wooden bungalow stood in a wide property; woodland, fields of alfalfa, grazing land for a bullock and old wooden outhouses, one of which was the house where Koda's friend Curt was born.

"I was at school with Curt for some years after mission school. He has a smallholding, horses, cattle, plants. His children have grown up and they live away from home. They are glad of visits."

Thomas and Derry began to warm to Koda. The clouds of dust had announced their arrival and Curt and his wife waited for them in the car park. Curt greeted Koda with a hug. "Welcome! Welcome, meet Pearl my wife."

Their hosts were very warm and welcoming. Their home was cosy, comfortable and well decorated. Each room had wall hangings, tapestries and embroidered cushions.

"You know the way, Koda, and Thomas and Derry you can share this room at the end of the house. We have two beds and a bathroom."

Pearl brought beers and nibbles for them all. Koda behaved like a different person and seemed very much at home.

"How's Shining Star?" asked Pearl. Thomas and Derry swopped a smile. "Very well, thanks."

"What a lovely name. How many children do you have?" asked Thomas.

"Three, the oldest is 7 and wants to be called Wayne, the other two are girls, 5 and 2, Silver Star and Bright Star. I expect they will want white man's names when they start school."

"A pity. Such evocative names." said Derry.

"We'll visit the rez tomorrow. If it rains the roads are difficult." They chatted about their plans when their wives arrived in Winnipeg.

Thomas said that he and Esther were booked to visit Toronto and Niagara. Derry thought that he and Alice would remain local.

"Come and spend the weekend with us. We have a Homecoming and I am sure you'll enjoy it all." Derry explained that he would hire a car and gladly return to Amaranth.

The First Nation Reservation was on the other side of the town. There were rusty, old petrol pumps near the entrance.

"You need vouchers to fill up here. It is cheaper here."

Koda parked and they walked over to the houses which resembled holiday chalets with big satellite dishes on the corners. The chalets were in better condition than the Aborigine homes in shacks. Some of the chalets had wire fences around a garden. Others had no fences at all. They walked past broken cars and other debris.

"How familiar!" said Derry.

"You will see the same in Cairns." Derry told Koda. Then a small group of young appeared. "You will not believe this, here is Tom, Dick, Harry and Pete." said Koda smiling.

There was a long, thin chalet with a table and benches outside. It was the Bar. They sat together to chat as Koda explained that the boys had agreed to help Koda with understanding their relationship with the police. There was a small Police Station in Amaranth with two cells. "Curt takes his turn at being night watchman if a drunk is being held overnight." Thomas and Derry enjoyed listening to Koda's Question/Answer session with the boys. It sounded off the cuff but they saw that he had an agenda but knew how to phrase his questions and encourage the boys to speak about their life, their dealings with the police.

"Visitors?" He sounded like Steve in the Township.

"Some. Young ones live on the edge of town but like coming to the rez. One old man teaches us Lakota language and they come too."

"An old lady teaches the girls to make bread, Indian style cakes and shows the plants they can cook."

"There are so many similarities it will be hard to find contrasts." said Derry.

"You will find some." The chat went on for over an hour. Derry noticed that the boys were better dressed with tee-shirts, sports trousers and shoes. Thomas got them talking about school and their families. Some were 'half-bloods'.

"We was Injuns, now we are First Nations but we still answer to Indians but not to Redskins, Red men, or savages." said one of the boys.

"I should hope not!" said Thomas. "Be proud of your roots. You are Native Canadians."

Another long building was a clinic which was opened for a few hours two or three times a week. They found a small school and a chapel.

"Curt and Pearl want to take us to a big holiday park. We must look out again in case of rain."

"Any rock paintings?" asked Derry.

"We could visit Lake of the Woods but it is a long way."

"I'll hire a car when Alice arrives and we could drive there. We are staying local while Thomas and Esther go to Toronto and Niagara."

"Sure." said Koda. "You must bring her for a meal with my family."

"That would be great."

Curt and Pearl were so pleased that they would welcome Alice and Derry for the 'Homecoming'.

"You can also see my shop where I get my threads and materials."

Derry asked for ideas of what they could take for them as a gift for their stay. Koda suggested chocolates, flowers or fruits.

They drove home chatting about their next research steps. Koda dropped them back to the College. Thomas booked a flight to Toronto and Derry hired a car. Thomas put Alice on a plane to Winnipeg and he and Esther flew off to a hotel near Niagara Falls. Derry drove to the airport to meet Alice. He booked a town centre hotel for the night so they would be near the road to Portage.

As usual, they stood and hugged for a long time.

Alice was delighted with the unexpected invitations. They shopped in some of the underground passages for gifts for their hosts in the Prairies. They made love in their cosy hotel room. They thought they would abstain in their twin bedroom. They chatted a little about their hopes for a baby and decided that back in Oxford they would consult a doctor and check that neither of them had any problems.

That weekend in Amaranth afforded them an experience of a community, a life-style, a history, and a culture so different from their own. They were outsiders participating in a family celebration. They had decided on these dates in ignorance of their significance. Every few years, anyone who has ever lived in Amaranth is invited to return for a weekend of special activities. They were immersed into the world of pioneers and native people.

The residents were the descendants of Anabaptists, Mennonites and many other German or central European groups, who had sought religious freedom and a new life in the prairies of Canada nearly two centuries before.

They were shown books with records of past Homecoming. Most families could trace their roots back to the settlers in the eighteenth century. Everyone knew Curt. He, like most other locals, was a farmer, an office cleaner, a part-time fireman, a part-time policeman. Everyone seemed to help with everything in the little community. Many were related through decades of intermarriage.

The curling rink was the centre of the Homecoming activities. It was without ice in those temperatures of 30 degrees. In the rink were the Registration and Administration desk, the live bands, the BBQ supper, the church service, and the display of handicrafts. On the tracks of the surrounding sports ground, were races and games of all kinds; Drag races, Horse Shoe Tourneys, horse races and pig scrambles. The program began with a pancake breakfast.

Dishes from China, Thailand and the Ukraine were on sale alongside the pancakes and maple syrup. The word 'perogies' caught their eye. They had no idea what they were. It was much later when they hesitatingly prodded their forks into the heavy, white dumplings that they discovered they contained bacon, onion, fish or fruit. They were a Ukrainian specialty.

The Parade at 10.30 was the public opening of the events. They rushed to the general store to buy sun cream and mosquito repellent when they knew this meant standing by the roadside for more than an hour. A lone piper wearing a kilt, started the procession. Behind him walked the newest recruit to the Royal Mounted Police who had the honour of leading the line of floats. There were modern fire engines, tractors, and cars and flag waving "Mounties" astride black cock-horses.

At the end came the original pioneer wagons and the natives with their huge drum. The five drummers wore ordinary T-shirts and jeans, their long, black hair tied in pony tails. They sat in a circle on a float around a huge, flat drum, which they banged with deep, resonant, thundering strokes with the drumsticks which looked like bull rushes with thick, blue, fluffy heads. Native girls in jingle dresses sat on the floor between the drummers and a small, white tipi. The Pow-Wow was due to start at 1.00pm according to the program, but they soon learned that First Nation time is not the same as Canadian time.

By three o'clock, crowds who seemed to know when to come assembled as the display began. The men dancers wore bright coloured fringed tops. Down the front of their chests hung the white bone ribs strung together with leather thongs and beads. Two eagle feathers stood out high from red Mohican style head dresses. On their backs they wore a highly decorated, circular shield, to which were strung dozens of brown eagle feathers. In their hands they held bird claws on sticks with downy feathers. Their smiling, unpainted faces prevented them looking fierce. One dancer wore glasses throughout the display and he took sips of water from a plastic bottle, hung in a pink nylon bag on his child's push chair. Their feet clad in soft leather moccasins pounded up and down to the drum beat and the wailing of the tuneless Ojibway song. The women and girls wore long, loose, bright coloured dresses, with layers of soft bell like metal pieces sewn in tight rows, producing tinkling, jingling sounds as they danced. The high-pitched wailing and the sonorous thuds spoke through this bright, light hearted display, of the pain of their past—lost land, lost lifestyle, lost identity—and the pain of their present—a Reserve without the dignity of the tribal village, a reputation for crime and alcoholism, a lifestyle where some desperately try to hold onto the language and culture, using the traditional crafts to gain respect and earn a living in their new kind of wilderness.

The little community seemed to include their local First Nation People with affection in this Homecoming. Bead work, bark work, quilts and woodwork were on sale in the upper rooms of the rink. Native sellers were ready to explain the symbolism in the designs.

To inexperienced outsiders, this colour and warmth contrasted with the bleakness of the Sandy Bay Reserve.

At the Sunday service an enthusiastic keyboard player led them in a few old hymns but no one attempted a sermon. After this, and before the grand finale, they were invited for a swim in Lake Manitoba by a group of Mennonite friends who had travelled in a large camper van. While the men and boys wore shorts and shirts, and in no way looked different, two girls in their twenties wore calf length flowery dresses, buttoned to the neck, with puffy sleeves to the elbow. Their long hair was tied back unattractively. While the boys changed behind the bushes, these girls padded barefoot across the sandy shore and paddled fully clothed into the water; another ethnic group trying to hold on to their beliefs and traditions in the same way as the First Nation Peoples.

The little community of Amaranth made them welcome at their Homecoming. It has now become a meaningful dot on the map of Canada. For Derry and Alice, it conjures up the images of racing pigs, dancing natives, the strains of 'Amazing Grace' in the curling rink, the smell of pancakes, the cool waves of the mighty lake, the limitless prairies, the hundreds of dragon flies buzzing in the scrub at the road sides at dusk.

Alice loved the drum beats and remembered the German tolling bells.

“That was quite an experience.” Alice said to Pearl. “There is so much to learn. I had lots to learn about the Aborigines in Australia.”

The clouds seemed to be darkening but so far it did not rain. Curt drove them to the park where they loved the walk round the lake. Then they drove to another town to the sewing shop. It was 16 miles away. There was a small row of shops, a grocery and then Pearl’s favourite store. A man wearing a Turkish style hat greeted them. There were many shelves with rolls of materials as well as displays of silks, tapestry materials, frames and even paints. Alice noticed something very strange. On one set of shelves there were rolls of cotton materials with Australian Aboriginal designs.

“How come you have these?” Alice asked. “We have just returned from over a year in Australia”

“I am trying them out. They seem to be quite popular.”

Back home they saw the rain pouring down. They ate in doors and Curt had to go down to the basement to check flooding.

“It is unusual for it to rain so heavily at this time.”

Next morning when they looked out of the window they saw several inches of water in the car park and noted that the field opposite had become a lake. The rain had stopped but the ground was very wet.

“I will escort you to the main road. The stone roads are dangerous in heavy rain. You have to go slowly. They have probably had to cut the road both north and south of here. Our neighbour in the north is away so I must go there and check they are not flooded.” said Curt. “Cut the road?” asked Derry.

“There’s a machine or we do it with a shovel. We cut a ‘v’ shape so the water can run across the road. You can only drive slowly over it.”

After their affectionate farewells, Derry was very grateful for the escort to the main road to Amaranth. They soon came across a car in the ditch. A young girl was standing by the roadside phoning for help. She did not look at all frantic.

“I will check with her on the way back.” Curt waved.

They reached the crossroads and the more solid road back to the highway to Portage. Alice was feeling a bit queasy after that hair-raising drive. They returned to their hotel and then had a very interesting walk around the Forks. Alice admired the many shops with Native artefacts, fringed dresses, feather head dresses, moccasins and dream catchers. They walked by the river until it was time to go to the Blackhill house. Shining Star wore her long hair loose and came to the door holding Bright Star in her arms. Alice reached for her but she cried and whimpered and held on to her mother.

"She'll come a bit later."

Koda and Derry planned their next step, a visit to Oxford where he would spend time in the Anthropology Department.

"I reckon you might be able to stay with Thomas but you could also have a room in college. Have you been to England?"

"Yes, London when I was a student. I'd love to visit Oxford and Cambridge and their ethnic museums."

"That can be arranged. When you are here we will plan the trip to Australia. I am based in Queensland."

Alice ventured to the corner of the room where Bright Star was sitting on cushions playing with dolls and teddies. Gradually the toddler accepted her and sat on her lap.

The food was traditional white man's food, roast chicken and vegetables as the Blackhills had feared upsetting their stomachs with native fare. As they were planning a long drive to the Lake of the Woods, they did not want to take any risks.

It was a very pleasant evening with the two older children sitting at the table.

"I was a nurse, they called me Susan then, but when Koda achieved his PhD we decided to revert to our tribal names. Wayne is just Wayne for the time being!"

"We'll call on you when we get back."

Koda handed him a card. "Here is my friend and colleague in Sioux Narrows. He will take you by boat around the lake to see the art and he will be very helpful to you."

It was another long, straight drive to Kenora On the map the lake was hardly a blue dot besides the larger Lakes Winnipeg and Manitoba but it was actually 100 miles long with a winding rocky shore line covering thousands of kilometres. There were also thousands of islands in the lake. Some were tourist spots with large hotels but most were uninhabited and wild. Derry and Alice walked hand in hand by the lakeside watching the pelicans and cormorants along with the loons, or Great Northern Divers.

"I have never seen any birds quite like that." said Alice, who had been surprised to see the black and white striped neck and the almost geometric design of the black and white feathers.

They strolled into the old town and admired the native murals on some high shop walls. Alice wanted an early night while Derry made contact with Heinrich.

While Kenora was a sizeable town, Sioux Narrows was a tiny village around the lake. It was a beautiful, scenic drive passing the pine forest on one side and the lake on the other. After the buildings in the little village there was a picturesque, wooden bridge to cross to reach Heinrich's house.

"You must speak German!" said Alice.

"Yes, but a rather old-fashioned German. My ancestors were refugee Anabaptists in the sixteenth century. I don't use it much here."

Alice told him about her mother.

Heinrich lived on a rocky peninsula. His spreading bungalow looked out onto the lake at every angle.

Walking around the rocky shore he warned them that bears sometimes came into the woods and down to the lake. They talked about the winter when the lake was frozen to a depth of about two metres.

"I have a skidoo so I can cross the lake to the shops, most people here have one as well as a snow blower to clear the paths so they can get out."

"Such a different life!" Alice smiled, thinking of the outback in Australia

Heinrich explained that the rock art had been photographed and catalogued. The boat ride was wonderful as they sailed between the flocks of birds and round and round, island after island.

"They are hundreds of years old. They used a red pigment and painted their hands before pressing them on the rock." Derry remembered the Aboriginal technique of spraying the paint around their hands, sometimes spitting and sometimes using a tube.

On one of the bigger islands they found more prolific rocks with crevices and caves. There were paintings of hunting scenes and creatures.

"So like Australia." said Alice.

"Up north, near Inuit country you will find Xray style animals like in Australia." added Heinrich

"Thomas will love coming here. He will work with Dr Koda and then take him to Australia to see the 40,000-year-old paintings in the Northern Territory. I hope Koda will bring you in on the research."

"I'd like to invite you to a restaurant in Kenora for supper. It is rather special."

"That's very kind, but please let us invite you to thank you for today."

Alice wanted a siesta before they met at the restaurant. It had a tower like, glass restaurant at the top. They ate the local fish and loved sipping the white wine as they looked out onto the setting sun over the lake.

"You are looking pale, my love."

"Too many boat rides and fish!" laughed Alice.

In the morning Alice felt sick and had to rush to the bathroom. She sat on the bed recovering, wondering, hoping, thinking. Her last period, due just before the Canada trip, had not come. Could she possibly be pregnant?

They had one more night in Winnipeg and a farewell visit to the Blackhills. "See you in Oxford in November." said Derry.

They drove to the airport to return their car and caught the plane to Toronto to join Thomas and Esther on the flight back to Heathrow.

Esther and Thomas had greatly enjoyed their time at Niagara and in Toronto. Derry told him about Heinrich and the rock art.

"It was great to see the falls in real life, but Mum has not been feeling too good for the last few days."

"Strange, nor have I. What's the problem, Mum?"

"Tummy upsets." she replied

Home and then straight to a doctor, they decided.

11 Joy and Sorrow

Derry and Alice remained at the house while they were dealing with medical matters and said they would house-hunt after all that.

Alice told Derry that she had missed about two periods and started being sick some mornings so she was feeling hopeful that at last she was pregnant.

"Dearest Alice, that is wonderful but let's get it checked out. I will always love you even if we cannot have babies."

A scan confirmed the good news; Alice was expecting a baby in spring.

Thomas and Esther were thrilled. While Derry and Thomas were working at college, Alice started to look at housing in the local area. She guessed this project would take at least three years and she longed to have a base which was her own home. She could sell her flat in London to help financially. She also thought ahead to Derry's trips with Koda and Thomas to Australia and she hoped she could take their child with them. She really longed for their Queenslander life in Cairns.

Alice and Esther went into town to buy baby clothes, cot, bottles and toys. Alice knew that would cheer up her mother while she waited for tests. They thought Daniel's room could be right for the baby.

She sat in her favourite place, probably over thinking about houses and possible future plans. Derry could end up in any university in the country after the research. He might even become a professor. Her mother came and sat with her and they worked through baby names.

"Boy, Thomas in there somewhere but perhaps Derry will want Robert for his father. Girl, a Jewish name."

"Alice was the name of Thomas's grandmother and Leah was your Jewish name, as was Daniel with Robert for the late brother. A grandchild, that's so good."

Derry had to force himself to concentrate on his work. He was so excited that he was to be a father. 'Derry's son', 'Derry's daughter', was like a mantra in his head. He had the same strong desire as Alice, to show his child to his colleagues in Cairns.

After a few days Thomas and Derry and chosen most of their team; Connie and Jake could handle the botany if they wished.

"We need a theologian who is interested in indigenous spirituality.

"You have a vast knowledge of African spirituality but we need someone to help look at the other two; complicated, because it is such an integral part of every aspect of the culture." Derry explained. They both searched through their contacts around the world.

Esther had some tests, colonoscopy, scans and blood tests and was invited to bring her husband for the results. The surgeon's words came as a great shock to them and a wave of pain swept over them.

"I am expecting my first grandchild!" Esther spoke with despair.

"Congratulations, Mrs Hartley, you have something worth fighting for. We will do our best for you."

Cancer, the dreaded word. Esther had a cancerous tumour in her bowel and the doctor was proposing surgery to remove it. Alice and Derry wept with her.

"I will fight hard to recover and meet your baby. I'll fight with all I have got."

"It is such a shock as she had no symptoms until the final days in Canada. New life in Canada and cancer in Canada." Thomas muttered.

He took some days off as he could not focus on his future work. He was often sitting in his study in silence and in darkness.

Alice tried to persuade him to start Meditation. It would help with shock and grief. Esther went to see her Messianic Jewish group and told them her sad news. They promised her their support in any way she needed. Thomas determined to support her too and asked Derry and Alice to delay house-hunting.

"I have some ideas of what we could do with this house. But please stay with us until Mum has recovered and the baby has been born."

"Of course we will stay." they replied.

Alice spoke to her baby and sang to him or her. She sang the Bonhoeffer hymn as well as English hymns and songs including 'Ascribe Greatness' from the Leipzig service.

Alice made a brief trip to London to see Abigail and her Meditation Group. Abigail was so happy for her and so sorry for her mother's cancer diagnosis. She loved sharing with Abigail as it was always good for her. She felt they could talk about any subject at all. She described her life in Cairns and explained that she felt she blossomed in her own home. She enjoyed her independence.

“What did you do in Canada?” asked Abigail

My father and Derry went first to Winnipeg to meet Dr Koda, a real ‘Indian’. He is a First Nation Academic and has a native wife and three children. Mum and I joined them for a holiday.

“You mentioned floods and Prairies.”

“An unforgettable experience. Koda had friends in a house, miles from anywhere on the Prairies but near a Reservation.” Alice described the ‘Homecoming’ and the Rez.

“I think this baby may have been conceived in Canada.” Alice smiled. “Best of all I loved the Lake of the Woods. If ever you can get to Canada, go there. The distances resemble Australia, five hours driving between stops.”

Abigail shared her teaching stories. She saw her parents each week but did not always attend their church; too narrow, too strict. She loved the Meditation Group where different denominations were represented. She showed Alice some of her reading; Thomas Merton, Cynthia Bourgeault, Dorothy Day. Alice talked of her longing to settle in a place called ‘home’. She was not looking forward to more upheaval as Derry and her father worked on the new project. Alice was feeling happy when she returned to Oxford. Before going home she had a stroll around the Pitt Rivers Museum.

She felt she was getting in touch with her childhood.

Dr Koda was due in November and decided to take a room in college when he heard of Esther’s illness. He was told he would be very welcome to meals with the family while Esther was waiting for an operation date. In fact he ate most meals with the Hartleys and Barnes.

“When we have done our work we might have some medicine to contribute from our Medicine Man.” Koda said.

Derry and Koda planned their studies and made a priority of finding a spiritually wise person to assist them from any country at all. Koda had very pleasant times with the whole family as Esther was coping well and although weak from blood loss, anaemic even, she was able to welcome guests and make conversation.

Koda proposed that Heinrich and Thomas concentrate on all forms of tribal art in the three countries.

“Connie and Jake have a great deal of material already. I think they should regroup it into roots in the three countries, toxins, leaves, healing medicine and so on, separate them out so they can analyse and compare each element. I hope we find a theologian with ready formed insights on indigenous spirituality."

Derry was not sure that was the best approach to compare natural medicines. He thought the regrouping should be wider; rituals of natural medicine, healing plants as a whole, but he would leave it to Jake and Connie to decide.

Daniel and Charles came up for a day to see Esther before she had her operation. "We'll come again when you are home after convalescing," they promised.

Daniel was very upset about his mother's illness.

"I hope it is not linked with the stress of her going to Leipzig"

"Stress can cause illness, but she has made so many new contacts since that visit. She and Dad returned to Leipzig and met the pastors again. Here she has found a group of Messianic Jews and worships with them regularly and visits the elderly. I do hope it is not that stress but just one of those things."

Sensitive Charles had a weep when he greeted Alice. "You are going to be uncles!" Esther smiled at him.

"We are so thrilled; Uncle Daniel and Uncle Charles sounds so good.!" He smiled at Esther. "What haven't they got yet?"

"Baby bath." They took Esther to the shops to choose a bath for Alice.

Derry took Alice to the Cotswolds for a quiet weekend after Koda left, right at the end of the month. After Christmas they would concentrate on looking after Esther and encouraging Thomas.

They sat by the log fire in their guest house, Alice on an armchair and Derry on the floor next to her so that he could talk to their baby. He had often done this at home too.

"I have a blessing for Miriam or Hartleigh." He smiled.

"Hartley?"

He spelled out his new idea. "Miriam Esther for a girl and Hartleigh Thomas for a boy."

"Give me time to think about it. You DO love unusual names but I rather like the sound. What will he get called, I wonder, Hart, perhaps?"

"I think the whole name might stick!"

"Tell me about your blessing." Derry drew out a paper.

He said there would be another when one for the baby when he or she could be seen in the cot.

'Loving a baby is one of God's greatest blessings.

In the name of the Father and of the Son and of the Holy Spirit. God give our baby inner peace and contentment.

God grant baby good health.

God grant us wisdom to bring baby up with love. We thank God for this new life.

God enable baby to help and serve others.

God give baby a happy heart and a clear mind.

God protect baby from evil people and from the evil in the world. God open baby's eyes to our wonderful world.'

Alice had tears in her eyes.

"I am sure baby moved as you said the blessing."

Decades later, Alice would read these words again and go into silent contemplation.

12 New Beginnings

There were two hospital visits for Esther and Alice.
"Do you want to know what it is?" asked the nurse holding the scanner over Alice. "Baby is doing well."

"Can I see?" Alice pulled her head up to see the indistinct image on the screen. She could make out the head and the legs.

"Is it Miriam or Hartleigh?"

"Miriam."

"A little girl first. How lovely."

Esther and Alice hurried home to share the news that Miriam Esther was on her way. Esther's appointment was not such a delight, but the surgeon, having given the statutory warnings before any surgery, told her that the long-term results depended on how far the tumour had eaten into the wall of the bowel. If it turned out not to be a high-grade tumour she could possibly avoid chemotherapy and radio therapy.

"As it is early December we will try to have it all over with before Christmas."

Esther was on iron tablets to reverse her anaemia. She had not noticed any blood loss but it had been significant enough to make her weak if she walked far. Derry and Alice suggested that they have a silent Prayer Meditation together before the operation. Thomas joined them. Derry leaned over to him, 'English Dadirri.' he said.

They held hands as the Australian music played and then held 15 minutes of silence. Alice used her Bonhoeffer phrase but had no idea what the others had chosen. They all appreciated the intense silence, peace and calm.

Esther was being given key-hole surgery. When she awoke and tried to move she still had tubes attached; one for urine, another feeding some clear medication into her arm. Within a day she was able to sit up, get out of bed and stand. She had to learn how to move without pulling at the metal clips in her abdomen.

"I'm not hungry." Esther said when food arrived. "Just try a little."

"It looks very nice but it is a waste of food." Esther obediently swallowed 3-4 mouthfuls. The next few days passed so slowly as each little step of progress was marked by great relief. Thomas and Alice had arranged some home helps, a cook for a few days a week and a cleaner twice a week for ironing, washing and the usual housework.

It seemed a long time but after two weeks Esther was able to get in and out of bed without help and walk up and down stairs.

Daniel and Charles offered to take charge of Christmas cooking. Alice was relieved as there were only about 9 weeks left before Miriam was due. Both Thomas and Derry had speaking engagements and interviews about their researches past and future. Thomas managed to look up the Native American who ran a Christian Community. In his book 'Shalom and the Community of Creation', the author had used the Jewish passages to explain a deeper and wider meaning to the word' shalom' which is usually taken to mean 'peace'. He also showed that many of the values of Native American tribes are the same as the Old Testament values for God's people and the kingdom of God.

"We must meet him. It would do us good to make a diversion, perhaps with Koda, to visit this Community of Creation."

Derry was thinking through this exciting link when he had an unexpected call from Jane and Jake in Cairns Uni.

"DB we are sending you the name and contact details of a remarkable writer. He was born in England but immigrated to the USA. He has not really moved in our circles but I found an article by him about the role of women in the British Empire. He deals with the English women who were in the colonies with their husbands as well as the indigenous women of India, Africa and SE Asia. His insights are surprising and his attitude is very different to that of most books on the Empire."

"Hi, Jake here. I investigated him and his main interest is applied theology. He begins with the Christian education system in the colonies. I know we have touched on that with Mission Schools and the Stolen Children, BUT, and listen to this, he has written of how we have not valued the indigenous spirituality of the locals. He has begun to study post-colonial theology and evolving spirituality in the USA.

"He has also had dealings with Africa. He is in touch with a couple who run Ancestral Voices, an organisation with DVDs and programs in the UK."

He took a breath.

“He is exactly what we need. We’ll get Thomas to make the first contact because of his prestige, title and experience but I will invite him to Oxford if he agrees to work with us”.

As Christmas and the New Year approached, joy overtook sorrow.

To everyone’s great relief Esther did not need chemotherapy. She was able to eat a small but usual turkey lunch. She gradually took on more of her habitual activities while Alice took on less. When she went shopping for baby clothes she thought of her trips with Maria in Cairns. However, Esther was able to accompany her to buy baby paraphernalia.

A parcel from Cairns arrived. Alice held up the little dresses that had been sent by the Meditation Group. She held up a little wine-coloured, velvet dress with a white lace collar. It would be too warm to be worn in Cairns with its little sleeves, but she looked at it and found it was somehow familiar. She began looking through some old photos of herself as a baby but did not find anything. She then looked at her mother’s photos of her family, now framed and hanging on a wall. There was baby Esther in her grandparent’s arms. It was black and white, but she was wearing a velvet dress with a white lace collar.

Before Miriam was born, the theologian agreed to come to Oxford to discuss the possibility of working on this exciting project. He was Dr Paul S Rockingham who lived in Minneapolis, Minnesota, not too far from Canada. He had been born and brought up in Sussex but when he was 13 his parents immigrated to America for his father’s work.

He had younger brothers and sisters who would have found it easier to fit into the American way of life than a boy just entering his teens.

At school in England he had been especially interested in History, not just the Romans and the Tudors but the Empire, the colonies and the Second World War.

Paul Simon had settled in and been able to pursue his interest in the war but from the American point of view. He enjoyed their perspective on the battles and the victories they had won to help out the Europeans.

He had been an able student and took courses in philosophy, psychology and theology. He soon found himself embroiled in arguments about how the white invaders had taken the lands of the tribes and forced them on death marches to round the survivors up into Reservations.

Paul was an angry young man; he was angry with how the white men had treated the natives in America but also in the other colonies. After his first degree in History, he studied Christian Theology and indigenous belief systems. On his thesis his name was printed as Paul S Rockingham. He noticed that it was a frequent habit in America to use just the initial of the middle name, rather like some of the presidents.

He presented himself at the door wearing a black leather jacket, a thick beige jumper and brown Chinos. On his feet were brown, leather slip-on shoes. His hair was cut all over about an inch from his head.

Alice recalled the French 'en brosse' for this convenient style.

He was thrilled to live in historic college rooms, but of course he was often a guest at the Hartley's. He was a single, dynamic young man. This project was just what he needed to give him a sense of direction. He loved the prospect of travel to Africa and Australia. Derry shared his last book and his thesis with him so he could understand their background.

"Thomas will probably take you to Nigeria first when Esther's health is out of danger. I will take you to Australia, perhaps with my wife and child, the following year. Another colleague lives in Canada, he is a First Nation Doctor in Winnipeg. He will meet you and introduce you to an art specialist living a few miles away."

"I really look forward to producing papers on the compare and contrast of indigenous belief systems. I have not spent any time on botany, science and medicine. We have so much to learn from the tribes."

"I am glad to hear you say that. Alice and I began our married life in Cairns. She made a valiant effort to fit in with life there. She worked and made lots of friends and she would love to take baby to see them. We have a house in town, it's Let to students right now."

"A new wife in tropical rainforest! Quite a challenge."

"I will have to talk to my Uni about any possible funding. I think I will invite the Canadian guy to come and meet my professors to give it a boost."

Thomas and Derry were sorry to see him go. He was their missing link. They would see if their own kitty might be stretched to him too.

"Koda will love him! They can be angry together about the same things."

Esther continued to make an excellent recovery. She was her usual smiling, kind self. She started doing more and more in the kitchen.

Alice sat in her armchair in the corner looking at Derry's book in place of honour on the shelf. She was a little worried about how they would manage with Miriam. They would take Daniel's bedroom as a nursery to start with. She found herself remembering events, people and places of the past few, very exciting years. "Do all expectant mothers do this?" She wondered. She remembered her shock proposal from Derry, the wedding and the honeymoon in Thala. What lovely people she had met; neighbours, Meditation Group, the Anthropology department. She had a longing to be there again soon.

Thomas came in, "I have things to say to you my dears. I have something to suggest to you and Derry. I know you need your own home and I will help you find one. First I have plan I have drawn up with an architect. It could be time to make some changes."

"You mean changing the house?"

"Yes, fundamentally and for the long term."

"That's brave, Dad."

"When I thought that Mum might die and leave me alone, I had a kind of brainwave. I might not have too long left either. I am way past retirement. I will show you the plans when Derry is here."

The four of them spread the plans onto the dining room table.

"Alice and Derry I am leaving you this house when I die but these plans show how you can live in it now and we can make extensions and inside changes to make living area for Esther and I until we die or are too sick to cope."

The drawings, so neat, so precise showed an extension along the outside wall of the study. Inside, the end wall of the lounge would be removed, leaving the bay window end intact. A new wall would be erected right across the entrance hall and the inner study wall would be moved inwards so the remaining space would be narrower but longer.

"I am giving the piano to Daniel and if he has room, he could take it as soon as he likes. The lounge would just be a lounge and the bay window is a feature worth keeping. Here you can see there is space for a double en suite bedroom for Mum and me, a small kitchen and a not so small lounge as we join the television lounge to our area which would back on to your kitchen."

Derry and Alice were stunned. They started walking around the rooms and visualising the changes.

"The downstairs rooms and all the upstairs room would be your home" Alice visualised the study extended on the left and chopped off on the right. "The bookshelf would have to move into the extension?"

"No, dear. It would change walls and move to the end. There is just room. The extension would be all in glass like a conservatory."

Could she bear that? Her special place moved? She had made a new one in Cairns. There would be light and space for desks for Thomas and Derry and another one for Alice, Esther or visitors.

Derry examined the plans carefully, the angles, the door positions, the small entrance hall and the way it would all come together.

"Thomas, don't you need your own study?"

"No, because after my trips to Africa with these new doctors I am going to retire. I want to talk to you about that, Derry when we have finished."

"It is a totally brilliant plan. We will need our own home and we can discuss how we can share other spaces with you. Alice needs her safe space, her base."

Esther had clearly been in on the plan. She was smiling as he talked and saw that her daughter seemed to accept and even enjoy the idea.

Thomas had been working on the project for some months and had even sought planning permission.

"Now, off you go, you two and talk it through. If you decide against it, I will still help you get a house of your own. This will come to you anyway in my Will."

This was a D and M that Derry and Alice had never wanted. They had to face that Thomas and Esther would not be healthy and active forever. This would mean they could stay in part of their house until they died or had to go to hospital. They would not have to house-hunt during the pregnancy. Was this an offer they could not refuse?

"You can carry on living with your white bookshelf," he smiled. "things will change but our world is changing. It will not be easy for them to give up the freedom of their whole house and it will not be easy for us to get used to living in your childhood home, possibly making changes to it. We have to think too about what will happen to the 'granny flat' after Thomas and Esther have died."

"As ever, timing will be important. The work will take a long time so we could try to have it done while we are in Cairns. Your parents might need to stay elsewhere for a while, or combine it with a trip to America or Canada."

"I love the thought of taking our baby to Cairns and living in our old house and then returning to our own home here."

"What a lot to work out. We'll need some sessions of dadirri."

On a beautiful, sunny day in March, the daffodils were out in the garden and the pink cherry blossoms hung from the little row of trees.

Derry stood at the bedside near the midwife when Miriam Esther Barnes came into the world. She announced her arrival loudly and held her thick black head of hair against her mother's breast for the first few minutes of her life in the world.

Derry was weeping gently as he held her in her white towel and stroked her face and tiny fingers.

How can new parents put words to their feelings as they stare at new life? Derry had prepared his blessing but he could not speak. Miriam was washed and had her first feed and was put into her cot.

He regained his voice;

May our daughter feel the wind through her hair May she feel the sun warm her face

May she hear the water of a running stream May she see the moon and stars in the night sky May she know that she is loved

May she hear birds sing and see the flowers bloom

And know that she belongs to them and they belong to her May she always value the presence of God

And appreciate the mystery of the Creator, whose Being and attributes are beyond our comprehension.

Alice noticed he used the oil from Thala to anoint her tiny head. Thomas gave Derry a few days to recover from his fatherhood reverie.

"I want to spell out my intentions for the next year. I will take Koda and Paul to Africa and follow up the links that Paul has with Africa.

"When I return I will officially retire and hand over the project to you.

"I will be ready to help, but I need to spend more time with Esther and be there if she becomes ill again."

He was trying to be realistic.

"You need to take Heinrich, Koda and Paul to the Outback in Australia. You must decide if you take them together or in two groups. Alice is longing to return to your first home in Cairns and show off her baby. She can stay there for a year or so while you dart around the world. The building work can be done when you have your long period in Queensland so Alice can return to a finished building."

"The good doctors can travel on their own. They can fly directly to Cairns and to America and Canada. I do hope the first visit of Koda to Paul in America goes well. A lot depends on their working relationship."

"While we are in Australia, you and Esther can come for a while to escape the builders. We shall start warning our house-sitting students to move before we arrive. Thomas, thank you so much for this brilliant and brave plan. You have really faced the inevitability of change."

"Derry, you must know you are headed for a professorship in the next few years. There are increasing numbers of young professors. One young man is only 45 now. Try to get yours in England!"

Derry walked around the daffodils with his head in a spin. He sat under the blossoms and enjoyed the thought of all the plans for the next few years. He was very pleased with his new team in three countries.

He saw Alice with Miriam in her arms through the study window. He walked in and sat with her in the corner by the bookshelf.

"Out of our comfort zones, my dear Alice. A new corner, a new house, a new team of colleagues and a new project, let alone a new baby."

"It's a perfect solution while we are still travelling and while my parents are alive and well. I am sure that you will get a professorship in a few years and that we could end up anywhere in the country."

"I can always refuse to go and wait until a suitable Chair is available in a place convenient for us!"

Derry spent the next day in college filling in his colleagues with the latest developments. He was pleased to see how enthusiastic they were about Dr Koda and Dr Paul. He wondered how Alice was feeling at home with Miriam and so much on her mind.

Alice strolled in the garden with Miriam until the baby fell asleep. She put her in her pram and sat under the blossoms. She fell into a strange dream-like state. Before her eyes she could see the faces and places in her life during the last two years. Images of Cairns and the Aborigines, then like a moving film strip, images of Thala, the restaurant and the beach. She saw her Queenslander and remembered the cyclone. Then the prairies of Canada, the flooded fields, the Homecoming, the beautiful sewing of Pearl followed the film strip.

She then remembered the large collage on the floor of the art shack, made by a recovering drug addict.

"I know what I am going to do for the study wall when it is finished, a huge collage of all these people and pictures of all these places."

Alice took Miriam into the study and sat down in her corner. Her reverie continued as she imagined Miriam in Cairns.

“This is a time of new beginnings for all of us.”

She then started wondering if a Hartleigh would come along to join them and if they would actually give him that name.

13 Kyle in Cairns

Dr Koda and Heinrich decided that they needed to spend a prolonged time examining the rock art in Australia. New discoveries had been made, dating the amazing art to about 60,000 years ago. Alice was feeling confident that her mother was making a good recovery from her cancer operation so she was happy to accompany Derry back to Cairns.

When the building work at their Oxford house was underway, she expected her parents to spend some time with them in Cairns. Thomas was making an initial trip to Africa with both Dr Koda and Dr Paul. He wanted to make this his final journey before his retirement.

Derry decided to spend some time with his sister before they left. Zara and Kyle had both left school. Zara had made some very happy friendships as she trained in floristry and no longer wanted to try to immigrate to Australia. She planned to save money for a longer holiday when her aunt and uncle were living there again. Kyle wanted to talk to his uncle Derry. He left school and joined a firm of builders and was pleased to learn such useful skills. He enjoyed the camaraderie of the work place and was beginning to build a social life within the clubbing environment. Madeleine and Roy had joined a lively evangelical church some years ago and were very involved in social and Christian activities. Kyle could not forget the beauty and excitement of his time in Queensland and was longing to return.

Derry went for long walks on Epsom Downs with Kyle as he realised he was troubled inside, restless and wanting to talk. They stood by the Grandstand looking over the panorama of London. It was a clear day so the Shard was visible, the Post Office Tower and other recognisable buildings so familiar to the Walkers. They walked down the hill and up the other side to reach the woodland. A group of model plane enthusiasts were on the top of the ridge flying their model aircraft. They stood with a little crowd watching the displays. Some of the planes were so well decorated and contained a visible pilot. Others were little more than gliders.

"I loved coming here when I was a kid. I really wanted a plane but they cost hundreds."

"You are spoilt for lovely walking areas in Epsom. Did you also go to Epsom Common and the pond there?"

"Oh, yes. We made camps in the woods and swam in the ponds. Dad would bring us here and teach us the names of some of the plants. We often had family picnics."

"Did you understand what your Mum was dealing with some years ago when your granddad Bob was alive?"

"Mum was very good at explaining why Grandpa had such depression and anger. We were old enough to understand but I felt it was so long ago and so little to do with us that we should not worry about it all."

"That's very good. Keep it that way. You have your whole life ahead of you and you do not need to be concerned about events two generations ago. Mum was very brave in making us all look the issues in the face and then put them behind us and move on. It helped my Dad a lot and his last years were his happiest."

"Gran did not last long after he died, did she? I think that often happens, close couples often die more or less at the same time."

"They had carried heavy burdens in their life and of course it affected me a lot. Alice helped your Mum to make me face the problems they were worried about. It really did make a difference and it helped Alice and I overcome our pasts and enabled us to get married."

"You have an aim in life and lots of interesting subjects to research. I am not sure what my aim is and it troubles me."

"You enjoy your building work?"

"Very much. I would like to use building to actually do some good in the world but half of me seeks adventure. I so loved Queensland but when I consider the social life I lead here, I am unsure what to do."

"What worries you about your social life?"

"The pressure to try drugs. They are so easily available. In the clubs it seems to be the thing to do. Wacky backy too!"

"Have you tried some?"

"Yes. A pill and a smoke of cannabis. But I was worried and frightened. I could see that I could develop a habit and get more and more drawn in. I have seen some heroin addicts and some TV documentaries. I do not want that for my life"

"Kyle, why don't you spend a while in Queensland and look around for building work? There are some charities which are wanting to build on the Aboriginal town ships where they live in poor conditions. There may be some openings there. Check with your firm if you could take a three-month break in Australia. See if they would keep your post open for you."

"That sounds great. Let me investigate. Could I stay with you?"

"Yes. We will make a nursery for Miriam but there are two other rooms. My doctor colleagues will stay at the University and we will invite them for meals sometimes. They are planning to travel up north to the new cave paintings so they will be away for long periods. So will I."

"Alice likes you very much so I think she will be pleased to have you there when I am in the outback."

The talk on the Downs proved to be life changing. Derry's parents had died the year before. They were both able to meet Miriam before strokes and heart attacks took them. Derry and Maddy had arranged the funerals in Brighton and then dealt with the ensuing paperwork and house clearance.

Derry explained to the Walkers that he was starting a new project in three countries and that Thomas was then due to retire. They would live in Queensland for about two years but would return to Oxford, to a refurbished house to take up the project in Canada.

Thomas prepared his Africa trip with Dr Paul Rockingham. They wanted to begin with spiritual rituals. Koda and Heinrich would make another trip to consider art and artefacts when they had finished their studies in Australia.

Alice suggested that when Thomas was in Africa, she would travel with her mother to Queensland and set up home with Miriam before Derry arrived with Kyle.

"I am longing to return and show Miriam to the Meditation Group. You will love them, Mum."

Daniel and Charles came for a long weekend to Oxford to wish them all well as they left for their next long period away.

"Perhaps we will come over to Thala next year. I will miss Miriam!" Daniel cuddled her. "Oh, please do. I shall miss you so much, Daniel."

Daniel and Charles took Thomas out for a special meal to celebrate his final trip before his retirement. He was starting with Dr Paul for four weeks in Nigeria looking at spiritual values, to be closely followed by Dr Koda and Heinrich considering the art and tribal law of that area. After returning home to their families the doctors were then aiming to join Derry, once again in two separate parties to research two different areas of their project. Dr Paul thought he would return to Nigeria the following year to spend a longer period when he hoped to be joined by Dr Koda so they could work on legal family matters.

"When you return Dad, where will you and Mum go while the house is being knocked about?"

"My cousin in Abingdon. We shall return as soon as the walls are down and rebuilt and then be there to oversee the decorating."

"Please come to London for a long weekend too. We'll get some theatre tickets for you, or a concert, whatever you prefer."

Alice and Esther packed carefully with bottles and toys and clothes for Miriam. Alice already had clothes in Cairns and Esther only needed light clothes for two months. The three of them flew to Brisbane and spent a couple of days in a hotel to recover from jetlag. They set off the day after Thomas and Paul left for Nigeria.

Alice, Esther and Miriam arrived in Cairns.

"I'm with you now, Miriam. We'll have some fun."

Esther wheeled Miriam through the airport in Cairns. Steve came to collect them. Alice hugged him, "How are you all?"

He poked Miriam who smiled.

"The students have done a good job," said Alice, "They have tidied up and cleaned up after them." They then made up all the beds and made up a room for Kyle. Alice discovered her red car had been cared for and so she took Esther and Maria to the shops to buy a cot for Miriam. Maria was overjoyed to see them and to meet Miriam.

"We can eat in the cafe and then buy some groceries. I am treating you, Maria."

"When is Derry coming?"

"In about two weeks. He is bringing his nephew to stay for a few months. He's trying to decide about moving permanently to Australia." Maria helped choose a playpen and some cushions. They found a highchair in the cafe for her to sit in.

After the shopping trip for the lovely little cot, Alice took Miriam to meet Frank and Susie and Zippy the dog.

"She seems to love the dog!" said Susie as Miriam stretched out her arm towards him.

"We will be here a while as Derry is working in Canada as well as Australia. He has some new colleagues to take up north."

"It is so good to see you again. Miriam is gorgeous. She will have to get used to the heat very soon."

Steve came to welcome her back. He and Jeannie arrived with their two children to meet the baby.

"I'll take Kyle to the township with me and to the Ngurra Charity. They could do with his help as they are hoping to build two new houses and a new school."

Alice took Esther and Miriam to the Meditation Group meeting and invited them all to a picnic in her garden. Esther was warmly welcomed and Sandrine came and sat with her. During the longed-for silence, Miriam woke up and Alice took her outside until she fell asleep. She returned for the last ten minutes. When they went through for refreshments, she was greeted by a table with 6-7 parcels.

"Congratulations! They are all for you."

They had bought clothes, bottles, plastic plates and spoons. She had tears in her eyes as she opened them.

"Thank you so very much. I have missed you. You were all so wonderful to me when I was here on my own when I had just got married."

Sandrine invited them to her art shack for an afternoon. "Have you ever tried art and craft, Esther?" she asked.

"Not much. There was always something to do for Thomas, my husband. Alice has the same life as me. Thomas specialised in Africa and I went with him until my firstborn arrived, Daniel. I will have more time soon so I would like to try collage or painting."

Alice added, "I am inspired to make a collage by the one that recovering addict made last time I was here."

"I am afraid that he died. He was clean but he had damaged his organs too much and he had liver problems and his heart just gave out."

"I am so sorry."

"When we come to you, would you like me to come and help you? I have trestle tables and I can make some canapés."

"That would be great, Sandrine. We will hold it when Derry and Kyle are here so Kyle can settle in and meet people. I need to research some building firms to see if he can get some experience."

"He cannot work on his visa, can he?"

"No. He will help at the township building project and ask for experience at a big company."

Alice asked Simon if she could bring her mother to his workshop. He said they could come and have a meal with Eugene and have a look at his latest works. "Kyle is welcome too. I have some Aboriginal heads and some goannas."

"My brother loved your birds. They are on his wall in his London flat."

Miriam developed a rash and Esther was uncomfortable as the temperatures began to rise. They all had sleepless nights until the cream started working for the baby.

Alice left her with Esther when she went to the airport to pick up Derry and Kyle.

After their loving greetings, Kyle strode out of the airport building and was stopped in his tracks as the heat hit him. Once he arrived home, Derry went straight out again to buy some air-conditioning units for his increasing number of guests.

Esther had held Miriam at the top of the steps when Derry leapt up.

"Miriam, darling, I have missed you!" She held on to his neck when he took her into his arms.

Susie arrived with Zippy to meet Kyle. Derry saw Miriam reach for the dog and smiled. "She loves that dog!"

Kyle wanted to shower and sleep as he was knocked out by the journey. He took three days to recover. His first trip was to Simon and Eugene. Derry remained to set up the air-conditioning units while Alice drove them all to the woodwork studio. Esther loved the heads and bought one to take home for her new lounge. Kyle bought a goanna.

"Mum and Dad will love him on the wall."

"You are following up the new buildings for the Aborigines?"

"Yes, for the charity. I cannot work but I am looking for some work experience. I have saved enough for my fare and for my months here. I may consider staying permanently."

Kyle took himself to some bars and to one of the church youth groups that Alice had discovered. He was not as shy as Derry had been at that age and was talkative like his mother. He was slim and fit with wavy, brown hair.

Sandrine arrived on a Friday with the tables and the ingredients for the canapés. She had the bases and some olives, anchovies and tomato to make them up fresh in the morning. There was only just enough room in the fridge. Alice had made fruit salad and some quiches.

Derry's colleagues were longing to see his daughter so he invited all four of them to join in. Steve arrived with boxes of beer and fruit juice. Miriam sat in her chair surrounded by admiring people.

"Well, little lady! Will you be an anthropologist too? Look at your dark hair, you could be a model!"

Steve then sought out Kyle and sat with him in the corner of the garden. They made a plan of action together.

"You will get tired in this heat. I'll collect you early in the morning and you can stop in the middle of the day. I will take you to the township and to the Ngurra Charity to look at the plans. You will need to rest in the afternoon."

The two groups mixed well. Jane was able to tell Sandrine and Fiona about her work with tribal women.

"Some are abused by their male partners, not always husbands. I am trying to form a foundation to support the women. Tell me about your meditation group."

Sandrine and Fiona explained their system which follows the WCCM system of silent meditation. Then Jake got into conversation with Kyle and encouraged him to work with Steve.

"He deals with ICE."

"What's that?"

"Crystal Meths. Very dangerous and too easy to get. He researches it along with medication at the Uni but in his own time he meets up with the local lads and organises football."

Kyle sat quietly alone, that evening. His head was buzzing with excitement. He was so glad he could be with people who could help the boys off drugs.

On Sunday, Derry took him to a church service where Alice had discovered a lively youth group. Derry introduced him to the minister and said he was interested in joining a youth group. He was amazed at how he was welcomed and given a list of meetings. There was a music group, a Bible Study Group and a social group each Friday evening. He decided to start with the social group where there were a variety of games, indoors and outdoors and even a disco dance.

"It's so like the group in Epsom." he told Alice. She tried to prepare him a little for what he would find when he went with Steve, but he could not possibly appreciate how different it would be from anything he had ever seen in Surrey.

He got out of the car and saw the broken bits of cars scattered around the dry field. Dogs barked and leapt towards him. He saw their ribs clearly showing. The shacks had no windows and broken bits hung from the roof.

They went to sit at the bar and some of the young came over to them.

"Hello. I'm Kyle." He said politely. Two of them said "Hi" and two others looked down and sat on the bench next to him.

"Get some drinks in." Steve passed one some notes. Two of them returned with cans of cokes. They drank without speaking.

"Can you show Kyle where the new houses are going?" Two of them got up and beckoned him over. They walked to where a foundation area had been dug out, near a copse of trees. Kyle looked down at their bare feet and torn clothes. His instinct was like that of Alice; he wanted to return with some clothes for them.

"Want to see the school?" asked one. "What's your name?"

"Jojo, and he's Lenny. Why are you here?"

"I'm a builder and I am going to help build here."

"We want to help too. I plan to mix water and concrete." said Lenny.

"I'm sure you will be able to help. I'll let you know when I have something to do."

"Do you do pills? Got any?" asked Jojo.

"No way! Far too dangerous." They walked past the wooded area and reached another field. The foundation was clearly marked out.

"Quite long." Said Kyle.

"For 3-4 classrooms. The young ones can't walk so far to the big school so this is for them."

Steve came and joined them.

"The charity is training some Aboriginal teachers. They begin at 6 years old and have three classes up to 10 then they go to big school."

"How old are you? I'm nearly 20."

"I'm 16 and Jojo is 15."

"Will you find work?"

"Probably not. We have a card from the social services as there's no work round here."

Kyle was quiet in the car.

"It's a shock, isn't it?" Steve glanced at Kyle.

"I cannot believe that people live like that!"

"You and Alice had the same reaction. She was planning to come and do some crafts and painting with the girls before she unexpectedly had to return to England and go to Canada with Derry. I am so pleased she is able to return for a while now that he is on a new project."

"She and Derry have hearts of gold." said Kyle.

"What are you aiming for?"

"Building qualifications, to use my skills to help others."

Kyle waited until he knew what he would be doing with the charity and then took courage to ask for an interview with a building company he had looked up on line.

His eagerness impressed the boss of the Blue Reef Construction company. He asked for the details of his present UK employer and sent an email for a reference. He was given a very good reference and so he was offered two days a week on the site of a new building.

"It is going to be an aquarium and will be a huge tourist attraction."

"I am really interested in pile driving and fitting the blocks in between. I am prepared to do anything you want. I want to learn. Please could I do two consecutive days as I am helping with a charity project as well?"

"I'll ring you when we have had our team meeting and we decide where it is safe to deploy you."

"Thank you. I am very grateful"

Kyle returned elated to the Queenslander.

"I am going to be so busy with the building and the youth group!" Derry continued his talk with Kyle.

"You will find that club life of Cairns is not very different. Drug use among young people is worldwide. We can find out the reputation of some of the clubs and get you the best place without the temptation of pills."

Connie offered to babysit so they could all go to the Meditation Group. Richard took the chance to talk to Derry.

"I am hoping that you would have time to lead one of our Days of Reflection before you go north. You would give three talks of about 30-40 minutes each so that they lead into a period of silent meditation. We all bring a picnic and the day starts about 10.00 and finishes about 3.30."

"I could do that, yes. Any particular aspects?"

"You could tell us about some of your research in the outback, then about the art and work of Mary Ruth in the Northern Territory and then anything else that is on your mind."

"Where do you hold the meetings?"

"I'm in the Roman Catholic Church in Edmonton. We get about 60-80 people but if they know it is all about Aboriginals there will probably be less."

"That sounds wonderful."

Alice jumped up and hugged him when she heard of the invitation.

"I guess some of the meditators are not too interested in Aboriginal life. I had better not make it too academic but I hope Richard can get some of his Aboriginal friends to come. I would like to interview them and teach about dadirri." This day was planned for four weeks' time before Derry met Koda and Heinrich and flew north with them. Derry spent a long time planning his talks. He chose Tribal Wisdom as his title, hoping that this too would be the title of the new book which would come out of their years of research together.

His first talk would be on Bush Medicine and how the tribes use it. The second session would introduce dadirri in its fullest sense. He would ask the Aborigine visitors to lead everyone into a session of silent listening. He planned to end with the work and art of Mary Ruth and the interviews of the visiting Elder and of Kyle if he would agree to it. They would end with some Aborigine music and a poem to lead into silent meditation.

Derry discussed his plans with Alice and Esther as he still lacked confidence when it came to doing something different. They gave him a few ideas to prevent his talks being only aimed at academics.

"Your plans sound just right but do bring a couple of copies of your book. You never know, there might be some academics there."

Derry took Kyle for a drink in town one evening so that he could talk to him about being interviewed. Kyle was not too pleased to be asked as he felt he lacked experience.

"I will give you the questions in advance so you can work out what to say. I think it will do them good to learn about what the charity is doing. You have time for a few more experiences with Steve before this day. You will have viewpoints, opinions and feelings to share. You have a few weeks yet to think about it."

"I will, uncle. Thank you for bringing me here."

Alice was very pleased. She was glad to see Miriam's rash clearing and that she seemed better now in the heat since the air conditioning had been installed. She planned to return to the translation company again after Esther had returned.

Connie baby sat while she and Derry went to the cinema in the central shopping Mall and ate in a French restaurant. She was so pleased to have time alone with Derry but was still a little nervous about leaving Miriam with Esther and Connie.

"It will be strange when Mum goes back and then when you go too. Just like the first time when we had just got married."

"Miriam is nearly crawling and standing. It won't be long before she is walking. She will keep you very busy. I won't be away so long. Once Koda and Heinrich reach the north and the Kimberleys, I can leave them with the elders. Then when Paul comes I will start off with him and then return. They are very capable colleagues and they really understand our project. We'll have a weekend at Thala when I get back."

Kyle spent an afternoon at the Ngurru HQ. He looked through the architectural plans.

They explained that they had money and materials for the houses but not yet enough for the school. Steve hoped that he could get help from the council.

At the Blue Reef Construction Company he mixed concrete and helped sink piles. They had very modern machinery. He was pleased to learn how to operate such high-quality machinery. After about 6 weeks he could help place the decorative tiles on the outside of the building.

He was fascinated to see the huge sheets of reinforced glass for the various aquariums manoeuvred by giant cranes into their places.

His experiences with Steve were very different. Lenny and Jojo turned up to help mix the concrete and lay the floors. They had hand held wooden slats to smooth it out and no machines of any kind. He helped put in the pipes and connect them to the tanks under the ground. The boys were quite helpful but after a few days they would turn up late or leave early or just down tools and go off somewhere.

One day as they got out of Steve's car, a police car screeched up behind them closely followed by a black van. The two police officers ran out to a shack near the trees. There was a lot of shouting and screaming from inside. Two women from the black van were told to wait outside. A young girl ran from the shack and started attacking the women. She punched and slapped at them and pulled their hair. A policeman rushed out and grabbed her. He pushed her to the ground and put on handcuffs. He held her there with a foot on her back. The other policeman emerged from the shack carrying a little boy of about 3. He was sobbing and calling "Mummy!"

The officer handed the child over to one of the women. The other one walked over to the distraught mother. She seemed to be comforting her and stroking her hair. The little boy was taken into the van. The young mother was pulled up and released but was firmly held by the social worker while the black van was closed.

Steve ran over to her and told the police he would look after her, "When will she see her boy again?" Kyle followed him.

"She has to go to court for drug offences and she may well go to prison. If she is clean she may get him back but he was born addicted to drugs. He doesn't stand a chance."

Kyle found he had tears running down his cheeks as they took the girl over to the bar for a drink while the black van drove off.

"Have you any family?" asked Steve.

"My partner is sometimes with me and my Mum lives not far away but she is usually on the bottle."

"How can they live like that?" Kyle had a weep in the bushes. Half an hour later he returned to the building. No one berated him. Everyone understood.

On Friday evening at the youth group he told them about this incident. Several said they felt helpless and did not have a clue how to help. Alice and Esther invited Kyle to have a free day on the beach. She was able to tell him how she had felt and how the baby just born had died that same week. He loved the beach and the swings for children.

On his next visit with Steve he worked hard with the pipes and flooring and asked after the girl. He wondered if she had been to court.

"I am afraid that she never got there. She took an overdose and killed herself." Steve explained. "I am trying to find out where she got the tablets. But somehow these desperate people manage to find someone with them who will sell them." Kyle was stunned.

He wept again with Alice and Derry.

He accompanied Alice to the airport with Esther when she went to get her plane back to England. Alice and Esther hugged for ages.

"Mum, I must tell you something. We are getting ready for Miriam's first birthday but I think I may be pregnant again."

"Darling. Congratulations! When you are sure and have a birth date, let me know, so I can come and help you. Dad will be retired well before then."

"I haven't told Derry yet. I want to be sure and not give him any worries as he has so much on for the next few months." As Alice and Kyle returned in the car Alice asked him not to say anything.

"That will be hard. I feel so close to him. I have a wonderful uncle."

"He has his Day of Reflection talks and then meets his colleagues from Winnipeg and travels north. I will go to the doctor tomorrow and I will tell you and you can let him know!"

He gave a hug to Alice and they went indoors to Derry and Miriam.

Derry took him to his building site early next morning so Alice went quickly to the doctor. It was the same one she had already seen.

"I have not yet had sickness but I have missed at least one period but it could have been when my Mum was recovering and preparing for her trip here."

"No one with you? I can give you a scan now."

"No. My mum has just left."

"I'll get a nurse." The young nurse came and played with Miriam who was quite content to hit her with her teddy.

"Yes. I reckon you are about 6 weeks. Come back in a couple of weeks to see if Miriam has a brother or a sister."

Alice could not wait to let Derry know. She took Miriam to the park and then at home sat down with her dates and worked out that baby would be due in September or October.

As she greeted her husband and nephew with Miriam at the door, she signalled to Kyle to come into the study.

"I am pregnant. You can announce it!"

"You mean it?"

She opened the door and stood watching Derry on the floor with Miriam, laughing and hitting him with the teddy. He was tickling her and then stood her up to see if she would stand at the chair. She held the chair and one of his hands.

"Look Alice! She is standing."

"Yes, she does. She's quite sturdy. Derry, Kyle has some news for you."

"Uncle Derry, you are going to be a father again. Congratulations."

"Thank you, Kyle. Congratulations my dearest Alice." They hugged each other.

"Scan in a few weeks to see if it is Hartleigh or a girl."

"Due date?"

"Not sure yet, possibly September/October." Kyle was smiling.

"What's that name?" Derry spelled it out.

"Are we really going with Hartleigh Thomas Barnes? No other ideas?"

Kyle was laughing, "A girl could have Zara, Madeleine or Alice as a second name."

"Rachel, Rebecca, Sarah. Another Jewish one for Mum." Alice added.

Kyle agreed to be interviewed as did one of the Aborigines. She was more used to public speaking. About 50 people had subscribed for the day. Connie booked in so she could help with Miriam and Jane had booked in to attend for the day.

In the first session he mentioned his PhD and said he would return to dadirri in the second session. He told them about the various medicines and the Aboriginal wisdom on land burning. There were several questions and comments before the silent meditation.

In the second session he showed some of the works of Mary Ruth and talked about her work in schools and in teaching about Aboriginal culture. Some people were aware of her work. The Aboriginal Elder then led everyone into a period of silent, attentive listening for half an hour. She explained the meaning of the word and how it fits into Aboriginal spirituality and suggested they might like to listen outside where they could hear the birds. Many of them did. Richard called them in with his huge Nepalese singing bowl.

After the picnic Alice handed Miriam to Connie. She had slept in the morning and now needed a little outing.

In the final session, Derry called on the Aboriginal elder who told her story through the questions. She was one of the stolen children and had been taken away from her family. She was educated in a mission school but tried very hard to find her family again. She pointed to the other women present and said that the same had happened to them but that they had been kidnapped. Many people were wiping a tear from their eyesKyle was then introduced as his nephew. Through the questions he was able to explain about the building project. He explained that his own family had had to overcome a terrible family trauma and that this made him sensitive to the needs of others. He mentioned that there was a lack of funds for the new school.

After thanking his speakers, Derry asked for some music to be played. The soft music pleased everyone and when the didgeridoo stopped he stood up and said he would lead them into the last Meditation of the day with a poem.

Dream Walk

Walkabout, walkabout, walk away
From the white man's world
Where proud imperialistic attitudes
Condemn the sacred dreamtime
As primitive; dismissed by cultured
Advanced technological minds.
Such minds have lost the sacred wisdom,
The sense of mystery in the passing stories.
Dotted paths, x-rayed goannas, kangaroos and serpents
In circles of coloured earth,
Red earth, red rock, glistening white bark
Hand prints, hunting figures, spears and boomerangs,
Depict the time of unity between a sustained environment
And walking tribes.

Walk away, walk away and walkabout
To the fierce sun over wild, forbidding landscapes.
Breathe in the magic, the silence, the awe,
A soaring bird, a scuttling species unknown elsewhere
Feel the ancestral spirits in trees and rocks
Breathe in the silence, the magic, the awe
The Great Spirit, Creator Spirit
Is everywhere but we fail to detect him
In the white man's world.
Walk away, walk away, walkabout The Dreamtime.

After the silence several people asked for a copy; Derry was prepared and had printed out a few.

"You are so poetic, my love." whispered Alice.

Kyle was awarded a beautiful book on Queensland by Blue Reef to thank him for his work. He was also given a reference for his employers in UK.

Steve gave him some photo frames to hang up his pictures at home. He was promised photos of the new baby. He had even spoken a farewell talk and thank you at the youth group.

He said he might return one day to see the completed aquarium. Strangely enough he had also bought a lovely silver photo frame for Alice and Derry's children.

14 The Professor's Farewell

Alice sat in her corner by the white bookshelf in Derry's study in number 42. Miriam was asleep so she could cogitate on the big changes about to happen in their lives. She could not imagine her father retiring. The bookshelf in Oxford was a symbol of his personality and his life's work. She greatly admired the way he had overcome his grief over the death of his older brother. He and Robert had spent hours swimming, doing sports, camping in the woods. As Thomas matured and studied anthropology, he felt that his life had been enriched by learning about tribal people. As he became a tutor he grew aware that some of the students had taken up anthropology in order to deal with some inner pain. He recognised in them what he had been through in himself. He discovered that it mattered to him. He wanted to reach out and befriend those intelligent, hardworking but emotionally troubled young men. Too many of his tutor groups were arrogant, entitled, forceful and dominant and often lacking in good manners towards women.

Thomas planned his final trip to Nigeria. For the first month Paul would be with him. He was noting the rituals and the art associated with them in order to compare this with Aboriginal art and rituals. He always considered the colonial influence because he was teaching Post Colonial Theology. Thomas found that Paul, although exhibiting a certain confidence did not dominate or show pride. He was driven to discover the past and use his post-colonial studies to find ways to redress a balance. He felt that it had already taken centuries to be seen as the racism that it is. As he met Nigerian leaders and tribal dignitaries, he made it clear that he struggled somewhat with the kind of synchronism that had developed.

"They want the best of both worlds. They want to hedge their bets." He was describing the way that some Nigerian Christians who had been educated in the faith, would attend church and sings hymns of worship and then, when the ancient rituals were being observed, they would be present at animal sacrifices and smear crushed plants mixed with blood onto statues to get protection and appease the evil spirits.

"There are centuries of traditions almost running in the veins of every tribal member.

"Fear is very deep indeed. You will see how modern life impinges deeply into the rituals but not deeply into the psyche. A modern woman with a TV and a computer will still go to the elders to complain that her neighbour has put a curse on her crops, her child or her animals."

"I observe great respect, a great effort to please the ancestors, to lead a good life with high standards and I see a powerful hatred and desire for revenge."

"Remember, Paul. Nigeria is not Africa. As you travel to different parts of this vast continent you will experience very different countries. There are similarities in the sacredness of nature and the appeasement of evil. But you will also find big differences."

"And modern life intrudes everywhere so some will hold on all the stronger to the ancient beliefs."

"There are also aspects which can instruct and influence our western mind-set. Have you heard of Ubuntu?"

Thomas had shared this concept with his family after their visit to Buchenwald.

"In the west we have lost this sense of community and wholeness. 'I am because we are.'

"The west is greedy for all the resources of Africa. Money is our god. Our familiar empires are crumbling and we are more and more aware of the danger that our planet is in, but our structures make it difficult for us to change our ways."

Thomas and Paul had a good look around the museums with some examples of the famous bronzes, dating back to before the Europeans arrived in Africa. At least one collection had been restored to the country while many others could be seen still in the British Museum.

Derry kept in touch with Thomas, keen to know how Paul was working with him. Alice was keen to have her scan for her second baby. At the appointment with her doctor, she discovered that she was indeed expecting a boy.

"A boy and a girl! How lovely!" She was so happy. "Dearest Derry, it's a boy." He smiled and gave her a kiss. "Are you really not happy with Hartleigh?"

"He could be called Leigh Barnes. I'd prefer Richard or a double syllable name to go with Thomas."

"You don't like Hartleigh Thomas Barnes?"

"Well actually, yes, I do. I suppose we cannot stop him becoming Leigh to others. How did you feel becoming DB or Derry?"

"One teacher thought I was from Ireland. Once DB was used I just got used to it."

"How's Dad?"

"He enjoyed Paul's visit. It all went well. Apparently Paul's visit to Koda was a great success. They are happy to work together when their fields of focus overlap."

"He must find it hard to face retirement."

"Professors never retire. He will always be researching something"

"Where are you meeting Paul?"

"Here. I want him to meet the team before we go north. We are going to Arnhemland and the Kimberleys before we see Mary Ruth."

Paul returned from Africa and stayed at home a couple of weeks to attend a conference at his University before he flew to Cairns.

"Welcome Paul to our Queenslander!" called Alice from the top of the steps where she stood holding Miriam.

"What a house! Old style but so charming and oozing with atmosphere."

"Dodgy in a cyclone." replied Alice.

"I was so pleased to meet a real Native American, or rather First Nation Canadian. I love the family names."

He and Derry discussed his time in Nigeria. "What an amazing, wise and elderly Professor!"

"Now a different scene for you. We are going first to Arnhemland and the Kimberleys to see the rock art and then we go back to Darwin to see Mary Ruth, the teacher and artist. There are some other places that Koda will want to see but you might be more interested in the general culture, the lecturers and other teachers."

"Heinrich is a mine of knowledge. They will love the art but Koda wants to deal with family law as well."

Alice knew that her father was soon to be with Koda and Heinrich. When he met Dr Koda he recognised a brilliant researcher who maintained an arrogance to combat the years of being put down and counted as a lesser human being.

"I wonder if they will come here too?" She hugged Derry and he kissed her and Miriam. "Does it ever get any easier?"

"Probably not, but it is not for so long. We'll have a weekend in Thala when I get back." Paul took a copy of Derry's books with him to read in the plane.

When Alice contacted her father to find out how the second visit was going, he explained that Koda and Heinrich had been overwhelmed by the famous bronzes.

They discussed them with Thomas, the expert.

"I must look up Ifé and see if the origins are clear. They were certainly not the work of the Portuguese or any other Europeans. It's a very special technique of 'lost wax'." Koda commented. "The bronzes are so fine, so detailed, and so beautiful."

Thomas added, "These Igwe people considered the rituals to be secret and sacred so it's hard to learn about them. They traded leather, ivory and bronzes long before the 16th Century.

"Their leader was considered a human god and so are his descendants now, although they no longer rule. As usual there is a horrible story of massacre and colonisation."

"I am amazed at the skill in metal work, and SO early."

"Wait till you see the caves in Australia, they are older than Stonehenge in the UK." Thomas informed them.

Koda and Heinrich took hundreds of photos and watched a DVD of the actual casting method used to form the bronzes. Thomas gave him a little advice on terminology.

"Like the Aborigines, these people rarely speak about their rituals. When you look into their religion avoid the word superstition, and animism and paganism. They are superficial and not at all accurate as you will discover. They see the sacred in nature and they have a Creator Being. They have been written off by western educated people."

"I shall call a chapter 'Written off' or 'Dismissed' and another 'X-Rays on Rocks'!" Koda smiled.

Thomas was pleased with his visitors and envied them their trip to Arnhemland. His colleagues in the University and the museum gave him a huge farewell feast. He knew that in a few months he would be having many farewell celebrations at Oxford.

"It has been a privilege to work with you even for a short time." said Koda, shaking his hand. "We wish you a very happy retirement!"

Thomas considered both visits very successful. Koda had managed to interview the African leaders about family law. He had only limited time to check on past researches on natural healing medicine. He knew that this comparison would depend mainly on the information already written by Thomas, Derry and the team in Cairns. He carried his own notes on Native American/Canadian tribal healing plants.

In the plane Thomas thought of his house. He loved the bookshelf as much as Alice did, but now it was all packed up awaiting the refurbishment. He imagined his new view from the bookshelf overlooking the conservatory window, the blossoms and the tennis court. He was certainly feeling very strange. In his 80s he admitted he was slowing down and no longer wished to jet around the world. He would keep up with Derry's work but would leave the report writing to him.

He was hoping the journeys would go smoothly. He would meet Esther on her return from Cairns and they would both stay a while with Daniel and Charles before spending the last few weeks with a cousin while his house was being decorated. He had heard of course, that there was a grandson on the way and he was thrilled to think that one day he could teach him about tribes.

Paul met the team in the University. Derry talked with Connie and Jake about the healing plants and the comparison with those of Africa and Canada. They all agreed that more field work was not required. Instead there would be hours of study reorganising the old notes.

Having decided on the exact categories they would keep aside for Paul any reference to the spiritual aspects so they would be a separate part of the comparison.

Derry enjoyed seeing the Kimberleys again.

"It is a historic record; you can find animals, mega-fauna which are now extinct." They were both deeply moved by the sight of the rocks covered and even recovered with painted animals and people. Thinking of the dates was unbelievable. They saw a little of Kakadu National Park before returning to Mary Ruth.

Paul got out his note book as she spoke. She explained that the Aboriginal brain was mainly right side dominated, whereas the western educated person is mainly left dominated.

"There is another way of looking at everything. We have tasks but no titles. We get respect from doing the task, not having a title. We do not keep a title for the whole of life."

"See this picture, you see the stars in the heaven and you see a man." She explained that one person belongs to all the other persons, and all the stars and planets and all the earth and the things on the earth. "Tribes have a law. We must keep the law but we don't have a boss." Paul tried to grasp the meaning of the words she was tossing out. He liked to listen to the stories they told using a picture. Nothing was simple or as expected. Nothing is logical, mystical beings can travel across the skies and change forms.

Mary Ruth began again, "We do not look to the past. We do not look to the future. It is different. We see now, only this moment now."

She then spoke about family life and crafts.

"We are beginning again now, many crafts, teaching the children. A lot has been lost, plant eating, basket making, canoe making. Now we see it is important. We were stolen, we were lost. Now we find our identity again."

Paul interviewed her about schools, drug use, alcohol and smoking. Derry left him to visit other reservations and the colleges in Darwin. He would arm his notebook for the next series of visits. He would look into dadirri with Mary Ruth and into the mysticism linked to the belief systems.

"I have a lot to learn and there is much valuable enrichment in this mine!" Paul would spend a few weeks on his own in Universities in the Northern Territory before returning to Cairns

Derry returned to see his family and to prepare for Koda and Heinrich's arrival.

Koda brought a lovely Native doll and a pair of moccasins for Miriam. They had supper at number 42 and flew to Darwin.

"Show me where we are going." Koda asked

Derry spread out the map of Australia. These are the different Aboriginal tribal areas. It is bigger than Europe and they all speak different languages, often unable to understand each other. We are going to the north, Arnhemland and the Kimberleys and then I have planned for you to go to three other places just for the rock art. You go first here to the North West coast to Mugurja then a plane ride south to the Koondula Cave on the coast. Finally you go to Sydney where you will see the oldest image of the human face in the world. You are booked into the Kakadu National Park for two nights, one night at the other stops. After

Sydney you could return to Cairns for a while if you wish. The team would love to meet you.

"Thanks, Derry. Are you returning to Cairns to write up the report?"

"Yes. I have all Thomas' notes from your visits and we have to return to the UK for a brief trip to celebrate his retirement in Oxford in a few months."

"Have you been to these places?"

"Yes, when I was preparing my PhD on dadirri and mysticism and so on. Be prepared to be surprised. The southern caves were hollowed out by tribes several thousands of years ago. We can get film of them as they have been well catalogued."

"Sorry to leave you. We will come to Cairns but Bright Star is missing me."

They called in briefly to Mary Ruth before visiting the Kimberleys. She was very happy to meet a Native Canadian who was interested in art and he found his interview very helpful in understanding about tribal laws, they sometimes had their own 'courts' and punishments.

When Derry returned to Cairns he immediately booked a weekend in Thala. Miriam seemed to know it was a special place. She took her first steps on the balcony. They had ordered a childproof balcony; netting to stop toddlers falling through. She loved standing and looking out to sea. In the restaurant she was much more interested in the humming birds than in the food. Alice let her chew on a rusk while they enjoyed their delicious sea-food meal.

Alice was five months pregnant when they flew back to England to celebrate Thomas' farewell with feast, and presentations. They had booked into a hotel. They could never miss such an occasion.

They saw the house in early disarray. Hired workers had helped them clear the rooms. Alice looked into the study. Empty, no chairs, no desk, no bookshelf.

"That's been my life. Now I have a new one!" Alice smiled.

15 Kyle's Way

Alice and Derry and Esther were so proud of Thomas as he received his accolades and honours. It was an intense and emotional time. Thomas was delighted that he was going to have a grandson. David and Charles attended all the ceremonies and celebrations and then took Thomas and Esther back to London with them for a brief holiday.

Before returning to Cairns, Derry drove to Epsom to see Madeleine and her family. He knew that Kyle had been doing some serious thinking and he wanted to see if he had reached any conclusions. They went back to Epsom Downs and sauntered across the race course.

"Derry, I want to tell you about something I have found out about."

"Are you OK? Any problems in your social circle?"

"I went to the church and joined the youth group there. One night we had some speakers who had been to Romania?"

"Romania?"

"It's only a couple of hours away but it is every bit as bad as the Aboriginal township."

Kyle unpacked the events of that evening and what he had since learned. This group had been visiting a town outside Bucharest for 3-4 years. They took clothing, medicines and money for poor families. Each family on the list had at least one child who was HIV positive or who had Aids.

Kyle asked questions and discovered that they had Aids through no fault of their own. The blood supplies in the hospitals contained contaminated blood. Ceausescu had not allowed the doctors to talk about it and forced them to carry on using the blood. If a doctor did speak up he found himself in prison.

"Some of the contaminated people sold their blood for money, cash in hand, therefore spreading the disease further."

"After the execution of Ceausescu and his wife, journalists and doctors were able to publish the truth." He had a very serious look on his face.

"We were shown slides of some hospital rooms called 'Dying Rooms'. We had seen on the BBC the dreadful orphanages a few years before but this was just as bad. They went to some houses with food and toys and clothes. I did not think that anything could be as bad as the Aboriginal area. They want strong people to carry cases and also people with building skills. I have a few more weeks before I qualify so I thought I would go on a trip and see what I could contribute."

"Well done, Kyle. That's wonderful."

Alice and Derry returned to Cairns. Alice decided not to take up translation work until after the baby was born. Miriam touched the baby bump and spoke in her baby language to her brother.

Kyle went with the church charity to Ploiesti in early September before the baby was due. "I'm a bit disappointed bruv," said Zara, "I hoped you would be settled in Cairns so I could come and see you."

"Could still happen. We'll see."

At 20 he had become more serious minded and kept in close touch with his uncle.

A group of ten people set off in a minibus with as much luggage as they could pack in. It was a long drive across France and Germany before they noticed the completely different scenery, buildings, houses, villages as they drove into the old iron curtain area, through Hungary to Romania. Most of the buildings looked old, broken, neglected and dull. It seemed worse once they had crossed into Romania. There was some beautiful mountain scenery in both lands.

The journey was quite an adventure as they sometimes slept rough, sometimes had a kind of YHA stop over or used the farmers' barns. Crossing the frontiers had not always been straightforward. This was no longer a Communist state but the guards did not seem to know; long waits, lots of questions and a very thorough examination of passports.

It was a relief to arrive at the church in Ploiesti. They had noticed the spires and the onion domes of churches as they drove through villages but this was a converted house.

They parked in the courtyard and got out with their luggage and went into the ground floor room. This was an open plan worship area with stacking chairs. On the end wall was a large wooden cross.

The Romanian Pastor spoke almost perfect English, which was a great relief to the young people who only knew a little French. They were soon organised. They sorted their own items from the charity goods which were piled up at the far end of the church.

"Tomorrow we will sort it into piles. Four boys will sleep here in the church and in the attic rooms above. Three girls will be in church families. There are two cars available to pick you up.

"Get a good night's sleep. The roads are terrible, lots of pot holes, very bumpy."

They had a prayer and sang a hymn in English before they went to their lodgings for a meal. Pastor Marcel introduced his wife, Rodica who had prepared a meal for the boys and one leader. There was a bathroom with a toilet off the church room and another up the ladder in the attic. In the corner was a small kitchen.

Next morning there was much comparing of notes about the food they had eaten. The three girls and two leaders were brought to the minibus. There were two jobs, sorting the clothes into relevant piles and buying groceries. Kyle joined the shopping group.

"As yet there are no supermarkets of the kind you know. They are being built out of town. We go to the market for fruit and vegetables and cheese and then Rodica will take some of you to the shop". Kyle went with Rodica and two of the girls. They were holding shopping bags, trolleys on wheels.

The shop was wide but dark. The baskets were very small so Kyle picked up two. A woman with a headscarf ran over to him, shouting. She grabbed a basket from his arm.

"You can only have one." said Rodica.

Kyle was angry, "How can I get pasta and milk in here?" His arm hurt where the thin wire handle had been pulled along his arm. Somehow they managed and took the groceries to the bus. Back at the church Marcel read out the lists with the numbers of children and after a prayer and a hymn, they set off.

"We are going to Mizil, the gypsy area first. We have 6 parcels."

It was a short drive out of town up the main road north towards the Carpathian Mountains. Mizil was off on the right. The main road had been bumpy in places but this road was rutted and unmade.

"We cannot leave the bus. Someone has to stay with it." That set the atmosphere. Untidy, unwashed people stood around watching them and then followed them. Marcel called out a name and various arms pointed to a house.

He knocked and shouted until a lady in colourful clothes came to the door. She lifted up her hands and thanked God for the visit.

"Dumnezeu. God." said Kyle, "I like it."

At each house it was similar, clothes and food were given and each family prayed for. They chatted and asked after the sick people in the household.

After three similar days, Kyle asked Marcel about the building needs.

"We can take you there, but on your own. We cannot take the bus there. It is in a poor village to the south."

"Thanks. I have done some building in Australia in an Aboriginal village. I am qualified now so I can help you."

"Thank you for that. We do need help but we have next to no tools."

Marcel drove him down winding roads, through maize fields and stopped at the side of the road near a few houses. One, very ramshackle building was set back in a field. A cat with four kittens was outside. A dog with a puppy emerged from the open door. A woman and three children came out.

"Father has gone abroad to work to earn money. They often do that but some don't come back."

The door led into a small room which had a bank of cooking apparatus along the back wall and a small sink piled high with metal dishes. Off to the left was a smaller room with blankets and mattresses on the floor.

"They all sleep here."

Kyle recalled the township shack. "This is worse!"

Marcel greeted them all and received hugs and kisses. "This is Kyle from England."

"Hello!" they chorused.

"Kyle, this is where we want to build." He stood at the end holding out his arms. "A bedroom with bunk beds and a shower."

"When will you start?"

"We have the beds and most materials but not the roofing and the lighting."

He was beginning to work out if he could arrange a longer trip to return for this task. Marcel left them a small bag of food.

"We'll call on another family while we are nearby. It's a tough one."

After about 15 minutes of very slow travelling through little paths, they turned into a farmyard. At least that was covered with concrete.

A very thin, dark-haired girl came out wearing a flowery dress and a torn cardigan. She stood awkwardly as an old lady joined her. She was wearing a scarf wrapped around her grey hair and was stooped and bent over. There were friendly greetings all around. The girl ran behind the haystack and returned with another limping and bent over lady.

"Ama." She introduced her mother.

Kyle soon understood that she was deaf and dumb. Her crooked arm could not make hand signs. The girl hugged her.

"No father?" asked Kyle.

"Sad story. This is Cristina. She was born disabled and her mother who is a widow still looks after her. She was raped by some village boys when she was younger and gave birth to this girl."

Cristina could wash clothes, hang up the washing and feed the cows but little else.

"What sorrows some people have!" He could not bear to imagine what would happen when the granny died.

On the final day, Marcel asked Kyle to come to his house for a talk. He drove to his house in town. It had once been an elegant building but, like most others, was in need of repair.

"What's that beam?" asked Kyle pointing a heavy beam jutting out from the front wall.

"We had an earthquake which damaged many houses in the town."

He also asked about the smell in the air and the brown colour on many walls like a fine dust. Marcel explained that oil was being drilled just outside the town. Kyle had noticed the nodding donkeys as they drove around.

"It will soon be stopped. It is very bad for our health and for the water system."

Inside the heavily decorated, dark dining room, Marcel gave him a beer and sat down with him.

"Young man, I have observed you this week and I want to tell you that you have a calling over your life. I want to pray for you and see how you react and ask God to show you what that calling is."

Kyle was taken aback. Soon he talked about his family and his deep desire to help those in need. He described his months with the Aborigines.

"I thought of immigrating there but it is so far away from my parents."

He was leaving to return to the church with a sense of duty that he could not put down and a deep contentment that he had a sense of direction. He had no idea how it could work out or how he could support himself. He was working his way past the large table when he saw an apparition. A girl with long, flowing blond hair wearing a flowery dress squeezed in to the room.

“Hello Adina, this is Kyle from the UK. He is just leaving.” She was slim and natural looking.

“Hello Kyle, sorry to miss you. See you next time.” She kissed her father and left.

At home in Epsom he heard that his uncle’s son had been born a little early and that he was still in hospital with Alice. He wondered why Esther had not gone out to her.

Derry explained that Esther was not well enough to travel. She had some eye problems and seemed to have some memory problems too. Thomas and Esther had been staying with a cousin and were due to move in when the decorating had been done.

“I’m sorry we cannot have a talk. I want to tell you about Romania. I am going back soon for a longer time to help with some building.”

“That’s great. Use Messenger, or write an email.”

Kyle consulted with his company and with his church leaders. He could not expect more time off so he realised he would have to resign then job hunt after the building work was over.

16 New Books for the Shelf

Hartleigh improved gradually and was able to leave hospital. Alice was weak and tearful that her mother was so unwell. She was worried that in her late 70s she was showing signs of dementia. She knew that she would have loved to be with her for the birth of her grandson.

Alice remembered that when they had last lived in 42 she had been obliged to leave in order to accompany Derry and her father to Canada to meet Dr Koda and set up the new project.

"Perhaps I'll have to return earlier than planned. The story of my life."

"Get stronger first. Enjoy your son and then we will decide when they move into their new home."

Thomas received copies of all the notes. The two doctors had put some chapters into folders as extracts to be read before the whole book could be published.

He supervised the removal of their books and the placing of them on the white bookshelf in its new position. He made an area for Derry's recent books and left a space for the new ones to come. When the pictures were hung and the furniture moved to the right place, he went to collect Esther from his cousin's and bring her into her new home. The bedroom and lounge were comfortable and spacious.

"Where am I?"

"I'll take you on the tour." He made it as fun as possible He showed her each room and ended in the kitchen where he had put her familiar and favourite cooking pots in the side.

"Do I live here?"

"Yes, dear. Next year Alice and the children, Miriam and Hartleigh will come and live in the big house."

"Who's Hartleigh?"

"Your grandson."

"I'm Hartley."

It was not long before the hospital recommended an interview with social services to see what care they could obtain. She was offered a nurse twice a day to wash and dress her. Thomas hired the cook again for a few days a week. Esther enjoyed walking around the house and garden and they managed quite well for about three months.

In Cairns, Derry anointed his son and said his prayers of blessing over him. Alice loved watching him hold up his son and then cradle him in his arms. They paid attention to Miriam and saw that she also had lots of games and cuddles.

Miriam touched her brother, stroked his smooth, light brown hair and played with his little fingers.

"I wonder when we shall see the first sign of jealousy." Alice smiled.

One night Derry was late returning from the Uni and Alice was holding Hartleigh while sitting in bed. Miriam was putting more and more words together.

"Mummy, baby down now. Read me a story."

Alice laughed. "Bring me the book you want and we will read it together."

The next six months were very busy. Daniel and Charles spent every second weekend in Oxford and saw how much harder it was to care for Esther. She had her good days but she was dressed in incontinence pads as she often forgot where the toilet was. The cook came every day. Another carer came to give Thomas respite care so he could go out for half a day.

Thomas walked her in the garden and round the big house. Sometimes he just sat with her holding her hand and talking to her about the past.

"I found you in Blackwells." He would begin. She spoke less and less.

Alice felt that she should be at home with her parents but the journey with two little ones troubled her. Derry was involved in organising his team. Heinrich returned to Canada as he was not involved in the writing up. Koda and Paul had remained to liaise with the team.

Derry called them all to a conference and they worked on organising the extracts into a formal report.

On the other side of the world, Kyle had decided to return to Romania. He knew that his uncle would be very busy but he let him know that he was returning to help build a house extension for a poor family. He wrote lengthy emails to Derry and to his parents.

This time he flew to Bucharest and was picked up by Marcel. He was offered the couch in the small front room, but he offered to stay in the church and give them space. He said he would cook for himself if they showed him how the stove worked.

"You will eat with us many days after work."

Adina came into the room. This time she was wearing jeans and a jumper and had her hair in a pony tail.

"Hello again. Welcome to Ploiesti, Kyle. Listen, some days I will cook you a meal as I work in a law office in town."

He was delighted to see her so soon and wondered how old she was and how she could speak such good English.

Over the next few weeks he saw her often and found they could chat quite easily. She told him about her school days in Communist times and about some of her Dad's adventures as a 'hidden' pastor. She had seen him flat on the ground with a gun pointed to his head.

"They did not always shoot but they wanted to show they could and that they were in charge."

They had to be very careful as a non-registered church. They met in a farm out of town and did theology studies. When there was one of the crackdowns, he took all his books down at two in the morning and hid them in a barn. There was a spy in the group. He suddenly stopped coming when the peace marches took place in Berlin and Leipzig and there was a sign that the Berlin Wall could be opened.

Kyle felt he was falling in love with this elegant, confident, intelligent and beautiful young lady. He had the idea of inviting her to come back to England with him for a holiday. He decided to talk it over with Marcel first.

While a new life was opening up for Kyle, his uncle was very stressed about Esther's health.

He knew that Alice would want to be with them in their declining years. One evening as he was cuddling her, he said, "Dearest Alice, I will come back with you and the children but I cannot stay. I need a few more months before I can coordinate all our work."

"I hate to leave you and I hate to leave my team too. The children might cheer up Thomas and Esther."

Derry had a few things to clear up after the conference. He told his colleagues he would be in Oxford for a couple of weeks due to family ill health. He would return to Cairns for a few more months.

The tickets were bought and Alice was packing when her father rang. It was very sad and unexpected news.

"Alice, my dear, I am sorry to tell you that your mother died this morning."

The shock waves were terrible. No one had thought she was near death; Alice had seen years of care ahead.

Thomas and Daniel organised the funeral for two days after Alice and family landed. Daniel and Alice wept on the phone and wept in each other's arms.

Miriam was very affected by her parents' tears. She had never seen them cry before. Hartleigh managed the heat well but had several days of not sleeping well. When he was fractious, Miriam used her few words to try to stop him crying.

This was the saddest journey of their lives. Alice could not believe she would never see her mother again. At the house, Thomas greeted them but could not speak. Miriam remembered him and happily hugged him. He loved to hold Hartleigh and stare and stare at him.

Somehow they got through it all. Daniel had done a very good job inviting the Messianic Jewish group and several of her friends.

Miriam loved running around the house and garden. Alice and Daniel were comforted to be together to mourn their mother. Alice looked through some drawers and found a large photo of her mother smiling outside the Stasi Museum.

"That's how I want to remember her. It's going in a frame and on to the lounge wall." They sat and shared some memories of their happy childhood.

"I don't know what to do. I cannot leave him here alone and go back for a few months to Cairns. I hate leaving my home and my life there with all my lovely friends."

"Stay for a while and see how it goes. We will come over regularly. Dad can keep the cook." Derry joined them.

"I have to go back but I think I could complete in Oxford. Koda and Paul could get home soon and then come to Oxford for the final stages."

Next morning, Thomas asked Derry to come into the study. They sat in the corner by the bookshelf.

"I'm sure your third book will be a great success but I have a suggestion. When it is finished, here is its place; I think you should rewrite all your studies for a different readership. There are so many treasures for everyone, not just anthropology students. Churches, New Agers, armchair theologians, the Greens, they all need this knowledge. Think about it. Your publishers will probably not want to deal with the new books, but there are many others to try. I can look around for you when you are in Queensland. You might even make a series and someone could possibly make a TV documentary."

"That sounds great. As ever, great ideas come from you." He told Thomas about his nephew in Romania. "That's your inspiration, Thomas. You inspired me and it has come down to him. He has been doing a grand job and will return for a holiday soon with Adina, the pastor's daughter who is now his girl-friend."

"I am very glad to hear that. Let's go and see the children. I am so sorry Esther did not see her grandson."

Alice told her father that she would stay and prepare the house for their permanent time of living there. She would let Derry go back alone and finish everything up. She would ask her dear friends to clear the house and put the baby things into the store under the house so students could rent it again.

Alice stopped to look at the house. It had been beautifully refurbished. The granny flat was roomy and bright. Someone would love to live here. The new walls looked as if they had always been there. In the lounge there was still room for Derry's Aboriginal painting. The settee and armchairs were now in the bay as the piano was with Daniel. The TV was at the far end near the door to the dining room.

She and Thomas took the children to the river to see the ducks and to the town to see the red buses.

"Too early for the Pitt Rivers." Thomas smiled. "I'll take them there one day."

When the children were asleep, Alice went to see her father. He was not in his flat which did not yet have a lock on it. She found him in the study on the leather chair in the new corner. "No man is an island."

"Pardon."

"No man is an island. John Donne."

"Yes." She was a little mystified.

"When I hear those words I envisage an island, a little one in blue sea with a man standing on it alone."

"Yet it means the opposite."

"Yes, but 'ubuntu' now, we see a group from the very start. We all belong. No isolation."

"How very true. That has been your life's work, Dad. Think of Kyle now in Romania all because of your work passed down to Derry"

“There will soon be new books on the shelf.” Thomas sat back with a large smile on his face.

Alice went out to the little ones. Derry made a visit to University before his departure. He came home longing to tell Thomas that Koda had completed several chapters on Sioux tribal family law in extracts for folders before the book could be completed. Paul would stay with him in Queensland to complete the chapters on art and family law in the Northern Territories.

He greeted his wife and children. The little ones were both content, not quite asleep.

“He’s in the study.” said Alice. Derry ran into the study and saw him slouching in the corner. “Thomas I have good news for you.” But he did not stir. Derry shook his shoulder but he stopped. He saw that Thomas was a yellow colour and that he was not breathing.

“Alice, come quickly!” he called up the stairs.

She came and knelt at his chair and lifted his head.

“He died smiling. You know his last words? No man is an island and ubuntu.”

They hugged while weeping and then Derry phoned for an ambulance and Alice phoned Daniel.

The funeral was arranged when Derry had changed his ticket. It was held at Marsden Chapel. Alice was feeling very lost. She hated leaving Derry but she decided to stay in the house until he returned. She would invite Abigail and other old friends to stay for some company. She would settle her children into a routine.

“I love his idea for the simpler books. You will do that really well, Derry. We shall invite Kyle and his girlfriend to stay, even if you are not back.

“It is a beautiful house, Alice. I am sure we shall find someone who needs an independent flat with access to Oxford.”

Derry left with a heavy heart after the funeral. He had so often found himself in this position, leaving his wife when she really needed him. He found it harder and harder and knew she would suffer terribly from the loss of her beloved parents. At the same time he was enthusiastic over his final sessions with his colleagues in Cairns. They had become real friends.

While he was still packing up the house and the college rooms, he received an unexpected communication. The letter from an Oxford College was inviting him to take the Chair of Anthropology. He was not offered Marsden because he was the son-in-law of the last professor. He was deeply moved and immediately rang Alice.

"So soon! A professor in his 40s. Congratulations my dearest."

"Alice, I have a suggestion. Now that Thomas has passed away, could we possibly refer to our son as Thomas?"

"Would we change the birth certificate?"

"No, no need. We would just call him Thomas and have to deal with paper work in officialdom. He is Hartleigh Thomas, addressed as Thomas."

"I love it!"

She tried to tell Miriam that her brother would be called Thomas after her grandpa.

Alice went into the study with the children. She put Miriam on the armchair, standing by the shelf. She held little Thomas.

"Here's our corner Miriam and Thomas. There are your grandpa's books. There are your Daddy's books. See this space; it is for his new books."

Miriam held up her favourite Teddy and put him in the space on the bookshelf. "Waiting for Daddy."

Part 2
The Hartley Barnes Foundation

The new Professor of Anthropology and his colleagues discover that their research in three countries lead them away from mere academic studies towards charity. Following in the footsteps of Professor Thomas Hartley, who was awarded for his charity foundation in Nigeria, they founded another charity to help tribal people. Their caring extends to people in Oxford as Derry uses his home to provide a Spiritual Healing Centre.

1 The Doll

"Miriam, Thomas, bath time." Alice swept up her son and guided Miriam to the bathroom. She tested the sudsy water and lifted Miriam into the bubbles. She held Thomas and passed him the yellow, plastic duck.

"Where's Daddy?"

"I'll take you to the study when we have finished and show you on our globe where he is right now. After all the happy splashing, she wrapped her children in bright, colourful towels and carried them downstairs. Miriam walked to the desk and stood on the footstool. Alice put Thomas in the armchair with his toys and pulled the globe to the corner. She turned on the light and spun the globe round to Australia. A rainbow light shone on to the walls. She put her finger on Queensland.

"Here is your dear Daddy. He is asleep right now in our house in Australia. He is finishing his book and talking with some important people from all over the world."

"Daddy, Daddy."

"He has a lot of work to do in the University. Shall we go up to bed now? Where's your Teddy?"

"On the shelf. He is waiting."

"For Daddy?"

"Yes."

Alice waited to see that they settled and slept and then went down to the flat which would have been her parent's. She sat on the bed and looked at the glass cabinet on the wall. She got up, opened the door and took out the doll which belonged to her late mother, Esther. She held the soft arms and sat it on her knees and began to weep. Her mother had passed away so unexpectedly when she was away in Queensland. Shortly after the funeral which the whole family had managed to attend, her father, Thomas had drifted into death.

Her husband was completing his last research project and working with Dr Paul and Dr Koda before they returned to America and Canada.

Suddenly alone in her large childhood home in Oxford, she was overcome by grief. She was still in shock and had not assimilated the two deaths, or her husband's departure. She had longings to be with him in their Cairns home. She was aware that she had no appetite and was living on fruit and soups. She sat hugging the doll. She had grown up a little afraid of what the doll symbolised. At the age of 5, Esther had grasped the doll when her parents had put her on a train in Leipzig to escape to England on the Kindertransport. The Berger parents and grandparents had made this sacrifice in 1938 to enable the little Jewish girl to have a chance of living. To little Alice this doll represented something dark, something sad that could not be spoken of. She greatly missed her beloved parents and gave in to sobbing on their bed. When she could weep no more, she tucked the doll under her arm and went to check on her children. All was well so she went into the study to phone her brother. She tried to modify her voice and sound normal.

"Daniel, when can you come to see us?"

"Alice, we'll come at the weekend. Alice, get one of your friends to come for a while. You should not be alone so much."

"Yes, I have mentioned it to Abigail from the London Meditation Group. I will ring her next."

"Listen to me Alice, if I were married to a woman you would not hesitate to let me take the children out and have them for a whole day. Miriam is old enough to stay with us even. Do let Charles and I take them out while we are with you."

"Oh, Daniel, of course I trust you to have them. I need them right now because I miss Mum and Dad so much."

"So do I! We are both grieving, Alice, and Derry is too. He loved them."

"I know. He is very busy completing his book and conferring with the two doctors. They need to return home before they work on the Oxford conference. He will return as soon as he can and make sure he has a break before he takes up his Professorship."

"Alice, let's talk every day until then, I will see you on Friday evening."

"I am holding her doll. I'm going to ring Abigail."

Alice took the doll into her corner in the armchair to talk with Abigail. They had been close friends before Alice had married Derry.

She was very pleased to hear from Alice and promised to spend most of the next half-term in Oxford.

"Alice, I have something to tell you. I have met a man; an artist and I really like him. He is called Justin."

"That's so lovely, Abigail. I cannot wait to hear all about him."

"But Alice, how are you coping?"

"Badly, grief is overwhelming me. The children keep me going and Derry will be away for a few more weeks."

Charles took Alice in his arms when he came through the door and hugged her, weeping with her.

"I see you have Esther's doll." he said.

"I like to hold her. She makes me feel comfortable."

Daniel hugged her, "Alice you know we love you. We have brought supper with us and tomorrow we are all going out."

They did a river walk as the children loved the ducks and the other birds in the trees. They ended up in the children's playground. Daniel bent down to Miriam. "We are coming here tomorrow with just you, all on your own." Miriam seemed quite happy with the idea until tomorrow came and Daniel put on their coats.

"Mummy, Thomas?"

"We are going to come back and tell them all about it." This was an important first step. They were out for just over an hour and returned with smiling faces. Miriam held an ice-cream in one hand and another for Thomas in her other hand.

"I went down the slide, Mummy".

"Well done darling." Alice picked her up and hugged her.

After they left on Sunday evening, Alice tried to get Derry on Skype. It was so good for them to see each other.

"What have you got there?"

"Mum's doll."

"Are you alright, Alice dear?"

"Not really. Such waves of sorrow, such tears."

"I'm so sorry I cannot be with you. It won't be long."

"Daniel and Charles came for the weekend and Abigail will be here for half term."

"Alice you need to talk. Can you share with Abigail?"

"Yes I can and I will. She has a man in her life and wants to tell me about him."

"That's good."

"Derry, dearest you must be in mourning too."

"Yes, I am. Paul and Koda are very good with me, they totally understand. It is all going well. We are going to try to get Mary Ruth and an Aboriginal Elder to come to the conference at my new college."

"What a great idea. Start with a bang. Will Heinrich come?"

"I hope so. We want Steve and a First Nation leader from the Rez."

Derry finished the call feeling a little anxious about his wife. In his study in number 42 he lit a candle and prayed that Alice would find help and support.

Koda was putting together his paper on tribes, clans, families and the law. Paul was linking up the belief systems of the tribes from Africa, Australia and Canada. Derry was writing a detailed summary on the spirit world, the supernatural and the mystical in the three tribes using Paul's notes with those of Thomas, the last he had ever written.

Derry decided on a short-term rental for the house as he planned to return for a holiday with his family before they sold up and moved their base to Oxford. Once Koda and Paul had left he would pack up and return to Oxford. He invited them both to a meal at Thala. He told his colleagues that he would return in the summer for a final holiday with his family and would organise a more formal celebration at Thala for them all.

"I know Alice will want to invite you to Oxford and we have room as long as you do not all come at one."

In the London art studio, Abigail kissed Justin goodbye and told him she would return for the last weekend of her break. He stood in paint-stained clothes at the studio door.

"I'll miss you, babe."

Abigail took a train and taxi to reach Alice who was delighted to see her. "How is the group?"

"All well. I have shared with them all about Justin."

"Well done. Have you got a picture?"

"On my phone."

"Oh, a typical artist!" Alice looked down at the dark, long haired young man with a beard. "What's that?"

"He is standing near one of his latest installations, a kind of Buddha with lights."

"We'll go to the Modern Art Gallery in Oxford tomorrow. The children will enjoy that."

Abigail crept in to see the sleeping children then they went down for some soup and snacks. "Alice what is that doll you are carrying?" Alice explained while tears ran down her face. "Alice, you have had a sudden double dose of grief and you are without your husband.

"While I am here, I am going to help you find a bereavement counsellor. You must have someone to listen to you and find out how you are dealing with your grief. Take as long as it takes. You cannot deal with it in your own."

Alice wiped her eyes, "Derry said something similar."

Abigail added that the Meditation Groups often had people who were trained counsellors and Spiritual Directors.

"What are they?"

"I will tell you later on. It is too long to go into now and right now, you need something else, a different kind of person in your life".

Alice showed Abigail around the house. She took the doll with her as they passed the large Aboriginal painting which Derry had given them several years ago.

"It's wonderful, powerful, colourful and totally symbolic. We sometimes get the children to copy the dot style of painting. They love doing crocodiles and snakes."

Abigail hugged her glass of wine and explained how she had met Justin in a Whitechapel Art Exhibition. One of his strange collages was on show there. Justin de Boyadere owns his own studio but it is not open to the public yet. It is a huge, empty warehouse. On the ground floor there are piles of messy canvases and various art materials stacked in heaps. There is a metal, spiral staircase leading up to the mezzanine floor. This is where he paints, glues or fabricates. He went to Art School and came out with a first-class degree but he wants to be a free spirit. He does not like to feel he is under anyone's influence. He does not like to adhere to the norms of society.

"I suppose he is a rebel, but he is gentle, peaceful and calm."

"How interesting and how different from you."

"We have Meditation in common but he uses the Hindu Ashram or the Buddhist system. He sometimes goes to a Thai temple."

Justin understood that Abigail's group was Christian but he felt that Meditation is valid without being attached to any particular religion.

Abigail explained that she had not met his parents and that he had not met hers either.

"I know that mine would not approve of Buddhism and free spirits. He told me about his parents. He has had a very tough time especially with his father."

"Not into art?"

"Absolutely not."

His father is 'something in the city', with pretentions of grandeur. He sent Justin to private school and refused to let him study art in spite of the advice of his teachers. He was forced to take Science, History and Economics for his A level subjects. No son of theirs would take Art. Justin's father had given him 'work experience' in the city where he had to wear a formal, dark suit and carry a specially bought briefcase.

"I felt sorry for him! He obediently took his subjects and achieved ABB, and then he rebelled. He refused to apply for a university course in one of his subjects and was determined to apply to an Art School.

Justin had a legacy from an uncle so he used that money to apply for a place in a modern art college. He made his point by leaving home and studying a short course in Paris. He put this on his application form and was able to get into a prestigious school in London. With his first-class degree and the rest of the legacy, he bought his own studio in the East End near the docks. He loved the atmosphere of the area; hippy like, liberal, cosmopolitan and laissez-faire.

"I can breathe here. I can be myself." he told Abigail as he walked with her to the studio from the tube station. He unlocked the metal door and ushered her into the vast, disorganised space. She looked up at a spiral, metal staircase.

"Do you live here?"

"Come up and see." They arrived at a mezzanine floor where he worked. She wondered how he got his canvases and furniture up to the top floor. Justin explained that the building had been a kind of warehouse and that there was a wooden door to a lift leading to containers for the boats. The lift had once worked with pulleys but now had electronic controls. Up on the last floor was an impressive open plan flat, bedroom, lounge, kitchen and shower. He had decorated it with little lights and huge canvases.

"It was attractive and beguiling. I had never seen anything like it. He likes sculptures with neon lights."

"So how do you feel about your relationship?"

"He says he loves me, that I am the love of his life…"

"But?"

"He has no links with a church, he does not believe in marriage. I am not sure he believes in commitment at all. I am falling in love with him but I am so insecure."

They enjoyed the next few days together with the children. They called in at the Church of England nearby and looked at the notices.

Abigail found what she was looking for; 'Bereaved? Want to talk?'

She wrote down the number. Alice noticed the Mother and Toddler poster and decided to give that a try.

Abigail made the initial phone call and the counsellor asked to speak directly to her friend. Abigail had to return to London before the counsellor arrived.

"Hello, I am Jean Bolton and I would be delighted to meet with you and see if I can be of help to you." Jean agreed to come to her house when she heard that she was alone at home with two small children.

She was a retired teacher who was warm and welcoming but not overwhelming. She played with the children before they went for a siesta.

Jean asked about Derry's work and when he would return. Alice began to relax and feel more at ease. She was asked to talk about her parents. Alice took hold of the doll and explained about her mother escaping the holocaust but losing all her family.

"She had a kind of dementia at the end and did not even see her grandson. I was in Queensland when he was born a bit early. She died unexpectedly so we all managed to get back to Oxford for the funeral and to settle my father into his new flat. Alice took Jean round the flat that her father had designed with an architect."

Back in the lounge, Jean took Alice's hands.

"Alice, of course you are feeling odd, strange and very sad. You have had a terrible time of the loss of both your parents and then the joy of a new baby all within a few weeks. Expect to feel strange for quite a time. People talk of the stages of grief but I do not believe the stages come in any special order. Everyone is different. Be patient and very kind to yourself. Allow yourself to weep, to be angry. Do not suppress your feelings, let them out."

Alice held her hands tightly.

"I will come regularly to talk with you, perhaps once a week to start with. We can probably make it less often once you have got used to opening up. You need gaps between the sessions in order to assimilate what we have talked about."

Alice gave a sob, "That's my father's word!"

"Start where you like but tell me how you have been coping with your grief these past few weeks."

Alice told her about her brother and his partner and her friend Abigail from London. "Otherwise I have found myself needing to cling to this doll and sit in the dark. I love my children and do not want them to see me sad. I think Miriam misses her grandparents as she spent a fair amount of time with them."

"Are you eating regularly? Try and eat with Miriam and let her see you eat."

Alice felt encouraged by this kind, wise mother figure and was ready to tell her what she was feeling. Jean made an appointment to return next week.

In the next few weeks, Alice took her round the house and to her corner by the white bookshelf in the study. She talked about her wonderful father and the deep pain in her mother. She was asked to talk about her husband. She explained that they had had a long friendship before he had proposed to her and that he was a wonderful husband and father and found the separation periods very hard.

"But he has been made Professor of Anthropology at St Marcus in the autumn so, like her own father, he would not have to travel so much."

Derry was so pleased to see Alice getting some regular support. He made sure that Paul and Koda would be able to attend the November conference with Mary Ruth. They were both enthusiastic about this and thought it would serve the book launch for Tribal Wisdom very well. Derry took them both to Thala for a thank you meal.

They loved the view and the humming birds as well as the unusual food. Paul leaned over towards them and thanked them both for their work with him.

"It has been immensely fulfilling for me and I have some news for you."

He explained that between the Africa and Australia sessions he had returned home and attended a conference at his university. It was a four-day conference on the Incas of Peru, Bolivia and Ecuador. He met Vivienne, a translator of Spanish who had such an interest in the Incas that she had spent two long periods in those countries. He was very attracted to this down to earth young lady and invited her to meet him after the conference. He was convinced that she was the girl for him and asked her to marry him before he left for Queensland. She had asked for a longer time to get to know each other but realised that she would not see him for some months. While he was in Queensland they spoke every day and he was feeling very hopeful that when he returned she would agree to get engaged to him.

Koda and Derry wished him all the best. He said he would bring her to Oxford during the conference and get her to attend some of the relevant lectures and presentations.

They left in their three different directions, glad that they would meet again within a few months. Derry was very tired when he prepared for his return to Oxford. He was given the hearty congratulations of his team when they learned about his professorship. He was longing to see his wife and children and to go to St Marcus and begin to prepare a conference.

When Derry returned, he was pleased to see Alice coping with her grief and seeing a counsellor. He lifted Miriam up, after getting a little hint from Alice and took her into the study into the corner by the bookshelf.

"What's teddy doing there?"

"He's waiting?"

"For me?"

"For the new books."

"Don't you want him in your bed to cuddle?"

"Yes, I want him."

"Well, you take him because he likes to cuddle you and the books will not be long now."

2 Happy Couples

Esther's doll was replaced in the cabinet. Derry spent a long time in the study putting the finishing touches to Tribal Wisdom. He was writing a long forward in tribute to Professor Thomas Hartley, mentioning especially his work in Nigeria. Being with Alice was like a second honeymoon. Daniel and Charles came for several days to look after the children so that they had time to themselves. They went to concerts and to outings to local beauty spots.

"Alice, I have planned a holiday for us all in Cairns this summer. We shall stay for a treat weekend in Thala but we shall pack up our home and have time to plan what to do with our furniture. I am also organising a farewell meal at Thala for all the colleagues, friends and neighbours."

"Another new beginning for us. I shall be sad to leave our first dear home but we have a new way forward for you at St Marcus."

Now they planned to host some happy couples. Kyle was returning to England to introduce Adina to his family and to make wedding plans.

Jean was very pleased to meet her client's husband and soon understood what a close and loving relationship they had. She checked out with him how he was dealing with his grief. "Don't let being busy stop your grief or enable to hide your pain. Walk through the pain with your wife and you will be stronger for it in the end."

One afternoon they had the house to themselves so they took the oils from Thala and decided to make love in the big bed in the flat. A strong emotion overwhelmed Derry as he lay in Alice's gentle embrace and he began to sob uncontrollably. She wept with him but realised that as usual he had held in his feelings, his grief at loss and his elation at his son's birth and his promotion.

"Weep. Let it out." she whispered. She felt that this was a holy moment. She had never felt so close to him and so able to share the depths of emotion with him. They were walking through grief but also had strong hope for the future. Derry fell asleep so she slipped out for a shower to be ready for the return of Daniel and Charles with the children.

By the time Kyle and Adina arrived they were feeling stronger and were able to focus on this happy young couple. Adina was gentle and quiet and let Kyle do most of the talking.

Everyone asked about their future plans.

"We will have a wedding in Ploiesti in our church and then come to England for another celebration and blessing with my parents before we go on honeymoon to the south coast, Dorset or Devon."

"Tell them about Florin and his ideas." Adina spoke up.

Kyle held a glass of beer and sat back to tell them what he had shared with his family in Epsom. Florin was Adina's childhood friend from school and church. They had grown up together. After the 1989 revolution he had gone to work in America where some friends had invited him to earn some money. On his return he married Marianna, whose grandmother owned a cottage outside the town. The old lady gave it to Marianna and Florin. After she had died, Florin wanted to turn in into an orphanage. They worked hard for two years to deal with the paperwork to get building permission, to buy the adjoining field and to get social service permission to take in children. They had already agreed to employ staff to cook and clean and others to care for the children. The state would pay for each child taken in to the home. It was a single storey cottage but an architect had drawn up a plan to build over the top of it. The new building would be a two-storey building with bedrooms, bathrooms and kitchen and dining room.

"They have begun and already fenced off the field for swings and playthings for the children. The far end will be a vegetable garden"

Kyle unfolded the plans

"What a wonderful idea. Where do you fit in?"

"They need a caretaker to live in and deal with building problems as they arrive so we will have the cottage and we can also follow our own jobs. Adina can go to town to her office and I can build elsewhere. Florin and Marianne have a flat in town for their own family, but he will come and work here with the other staff."

"Funding?" asked Derry.

"I have a visa and work permit so I can look for a building job with a company. The orphanage should pay for itself as the Social Services pay for the placements."

"Well, that is an amazing start for you both."

"I will have to learn to drive. There is a bus to town on the main road but it is quite a walk. Kyle will have to learn more Romanian and he already has a class to attend." Adina added.

"God was the first word I learned. Dumnezeu! Isn't that lovely?"

Adina put a hand on his shoulder. "Tell them what you have been doing."

Kyle showed how disturbed he was over his last job. Marcel had led a small group to Campina, a nearby town. They took a train and walked from the station up a steep hill. It could hardly be called a road although cars were parked outside some houses. Local people had taken wooden beams from railway siding and placed them across the road which was unmade, muddy and pitted.

On the left was a large shed and as they approached with the bags of groceries, a middle-aged woman came out to meet them. She had a strong face that had once been beautiful. She called her daughter, a pretty, slim girl, to take the bags and indicated to Marcel that she wanted a private word. She invited them to come into the shed. There was a wardrobe with clothing piled on the top and the floor was covered with mattresses. Pointing upwards she indicated the damage that a rain storm had done. One corner of the roof was peeled back, mouldy and dropping down. They had put sheets of plastic across but the blankets underneath had been damaged by the rain. Marcel pointed out that 7 of them slept there. Opposite the shed was a concrete foundation. There was space to build but no money. The broken-down house contained a kitchen where they cooked. Marcel promised that he would get funds to build and called on Florin to help. This is where he and Kyle bonded well.

"The mother, like so many other Romanian women is amazing. Her husband is often in prison. Her sons drink and have been in prison for short spells too. Her youngest, that daughter, has Aids because she had a blood transfusion for a liver complaint."

Adina gripped Kyle's hand. "He really wants to help people like that." Derry was delighted with their story.

"Kyle, I will buy you a car for a wedding present and pay for driving lessons."

Adina went around the shops with Alice to look at wedding dresses. She was horrified at the prices. She said that Kyle's parents had offered to buy her the dress. "I'll choose one in Epsom with Maddy and Zara."

Such happiness came into the house with this visit. Both Derry and Alice said they would like to visit the orphanage when their children were older.

"Florin is building up his numbers slowly so there will be rooms for Miriam and Thomas."

Within a month after their departure, Paul contacted Derry to ask if he could bring his new bride to Oxford before they went off on honeymoon. On his return to Minnesota, Paul was pleased that Vivienne was as keen to get married as he was. They announced their wedding to their families and chose a church near the university. Vivienne had a small flat but Paul had been a resident tutor so they needed to buy a bigger flat. Both sets of parents contributed a sum of money to the large, modern flat they bought in a tower block. They had decided on a honeymoon in Peru. Whereas Vivienne had studied the history of the extraordinary Inca Empire, Paul wanted to find out about their descendants, still called 'Indians' who were living in communities today. He knew a little Spanish and was pleased that his wife had learned some Quechua.

Derry and Alice invited them to stay in the flat. "One day I will take Vivienne to Thala." said Paul "You will love it," said Alice, "it is like paradise."

"How do you manage with a husband who is so often away?"

Alice explained that her father had been the same, so she had grown up with a father who was often abroad. I am used to Derry leading the same kind of life but I expect he will not be away so often now that he is going to be a Professor.

Derry wanted to know how Vivienne had become interested in the Incas. She explained that she had studied some Post-Colonial Theology.

"We learn about the British Empire but most of the focus is on the Portuguese and Spanish invasions of Latin America. It makes a change to feel shocked and ashamed of what these people have done, instead of thinking only of the evils of the British!"

Miriam came into the room. Vivienne bent down to say 'Hello' "Who is that? I'm Vivienne."

"Teddy." Miriam held him out to her.

"How sweet!" Vivienne took him, cuddled him and gave him back.

Vivienne was happy to go out with Alice and the children while Derry took Paul to his new college and future office. He introduced him to the members of staff who would be there when he began.

"You saw my historic building last time and now you have a modern building to work in. I think we could always include Latin America in future research."

"Has Koda seen it yet?"

"No, he'll see it at the November conference. Now, you must take Vivienne to see the Oxford Colleges and museums and take her on a river trip, a very suitable honeymoon activity."

Paul and Vivienne ate out some evenings, cooked for themselves or were invited by their hosts. Over that last meal, Derry asked them to choose a gift from the collection of Professor Thomas. They felt very privileged and chose an African mask.

"I can see it on the lounge wall." Vivienne held it up. "I hope we can get it through custom." said Paul.

"It has a certificate." Derry reassured him.

"I shall be using my experiences with Thomas in my papers at the conference." added Paul. Derry asked Vivienne about her experiences with the Indians.

"Some are descended from the Incas. Many hold on to their traditions and a few try to mix more and embrace modern life."

"Different religions?"

"Mostly Catholic but there are thousands of different religions and rituals and customs. There is a real mish-mash of religions, languages and nationalities."

"I am glad to hear that." said Paul.

"The scenery is breath-taking in more ways than one. High in the Andes, the air is very thin and some people need oxygen."

"We have underestimated how old the ruins are. Some roads and ruins found recently are pre-Columbian."

"Living conditions now?" asked the professor in planning mode.

"Often terrible. They sometimes have droughts and their growth of maize suffers. Lots of obvious poverty but they are proud of their country, their religion and their culture."

Paul and Vivienne enjoyed their visits to the old colleges and also had a day trip to Cambridge as Vivienne had never been to either city.

"I love the way there is a row of colleges along the river Cam. But I love them both."

Home alone, Alice spent time with Jean.

"Alice, I have a suggestion for you," she began differently that day. She always began by getting Alice to speak of her feelings. This time she had a different agenda. "Do you remember I mentioned Spiritual direction to you? I believe, Alice that you have the gifting to be an excellent Spiritual Director, but you need some training."

Jean explained that the roles of a counsellor, a listener and a Spiritual Director were all similar but with slightly different aims. A listener is trained to know how to listen, to really hear people and not interrupt or make comments, to hear what the person is feeling and what they are wanting. A counsellor listens but is ready to give advice and find ways to draw the person out and help them express their feelings.

"Being heard and totally listened to is very healing in this age of rapid living. A Spiritual Director trains for longer and their task carries more responsibility. The term 'director' can be misleading. I have heard it referred to as 'soul friend' or even 'midwife'. The director is not there to give solutions but to offer possible ways forward so the client chooses their own path and their own solutions with the help of the Holy Spirit. The director is gentle, not forceful, guiding and encouraging but not giving sure and certain answers."

Alice took it all in and felt encouraged and privileged to be asked.

She found out about the cost, the timing and the venue for the training and how it links to Meditation. Jean explained that she would have to attend the sessions at a church in town. Alice would need a baby-sitter for the three hours once a fortnight.

When Daniel was not available, Jean offered to ask in her Meditation Group. "When can I start?"

"You can do the summer term and then continue in autumn and spring next year."

"Thank you so much, Jean. You have been wonderful for me. If I do the course, we could finish with our regular sessions. We are going to Cairns as a family for two months in the summer. We have to pack up our house and sell it with our cars. We are going to be based in Oxford. Derry has a conference in November with the book launch."

Kyle and Adina had returned to organise their wedding at the church in Ploiesti. They returned in June for their English celebration. Alice really enjoyed choosing outfits for her children. The wine-coloured velvet dress was too small for Miriam so she hunted for another one. She chose a blue and white suit for Thomas. She wore her blue silk shalwa chemise and Derry wore his wedding suit.

Alice missed her friends in Queensland. She had made such an effort to make friends when she first arrived there. She missed the companionship of Sandrine and Connie so she decided to make more effort in Oxford and join the local Mother and Toddler Group.

Maddy was very pleased to see Alice again and see how the children had grown. “My grandchildren will be in Romania.” she said sadly.

“But it is not so far and they will come to England quite often I am sure.”

“Adina looks lovely in her dress. She is a beautiful girl. We bought it in a big store in Epsom.”

Alice agreed that Adina looked stunning as she walked down the aisle. The dress was in plain white silk with a long white lace skirt. It was off the shoulder with a sparkling tiara holding a veil right down to below the shoulders. She wore her long, blond hair loose.

The congregation sang rousing evangelical hymns and as the couple stood at the front by the cross, people clustered round them, laid hands on them and prayed extemporary prayers over them. The pastor raised his hands in blessing. Alice and Derry found it very moving.

The celebratory meal was held in a restaurant on top of Epsom Downs. Derry took his family across the Downs to see the model aircraft after the meal. Thomas was delighted, jumping and pointing and laughing. He arranged for his children to be photographed with Kyle and Adina. It was the end of a wonderful day.

Alice joined the Mother and Toddler Group and found a baby-sitter to help out with her SpirDir course as it was called. She was surprised to be learning about the Desert Fathers and Mothers and some medieval mystics, St Ignatius, St Francis, St Teresa of Avila and St John of the Cross and then the personality profile system called the Enneagram. She presumed it was modern psychology but was amazed to hear it had begun with the Desert Fathers and the Sufi Mystics in Syria and Egypt.

She completed the first term and thought she would soon be able to make some friends from the group but now she had to pack for the Australian holiday. As she was deciding what to take and what to leave she was aware of some familiar symptoms.

“I had better get a check with the doctor before we travel.” Once again she decided on saying nothing to Derry until she was sure.

“I wonder how long it will be before you go to South America with Paul.”

"I reckon within 18 months." He smiled and hugged her tightly to himself. She so nearly said something but stopped herself.

She took her children with her and armed with date charts she had a preliminary examination. "I am sure you are pregnant but you need a scan later."

"I can start my own play school soon." she laughed.

Derry was in the study when they got home. The cases were lined up by the bookshelf. She stood next to him at the desk and put her arms round him.

"Dearest Derry, sorry to disturb you." he turned round and sat her on his lap. "We are going to have a third baby."

He kissed her and held her head in his hands.

"My beloved Alice, I am so happy. I hope it won't be too much for you in Cairns, two little ones and another on the way."

"Now we start the name game! Miriam with two brothers or Miriam with a brother and a sister!"

3 Holiday in Cairns

"This is your captain speaking. I am sorry to inform you that there will be a slight delay in landing at Cairns Airport. There is a problem with a plane on the runway so we have to circle a few more times before we are cleared for landing."

The small plane from Brisbane had already flown over the Great Barrier Reef. Alice put Miriam on her lap so she could look down at the coast, the colours and the islands. She tolerated the first 5 circles and then wanted to sit on Derry. The many circles and the roar of the engine as the plane turned began to make everyone nervous. It took at least 20 minutes before the captain announced the descent.

Steve was waiting for them with his van.

"They gave no reason for the word 'delayed'. I was getting worried."

"So were we! Thank you so much for coming for us." Alice greeted him with a kiss. "I have put some food in the fridge and number 42 is clear of students."

"Steve, you are wonderful!" said Derry. They climbed the steps and Steve let them in. Miriam felt at home and ran around the rooms.

"Granny. Granny!" Derry and Alice looked at each other. Derry picked her up, "Darling, you remember Granny is in heaven with Grandpa." Miriam was quiet for a while and then she got down and checked every room.

"Isn't that strange?" said Alice, "She must remember being here with her in those weeks before she returned to meet Thomas from Africa."

Alice fetched her toys and she settled down in an armchair. Derry went down to the van to see Steve off.

"Steve, Alice is pregnant. The baby is probably due near Christmas."

"Congratulations! Miriam will have her work cut out if it is a boy!"

"She will want to come to the Aboriginal area. She is well and energetic! We shall have a party at Thala for everyone before we go. Before then, we shall talk through with you what we can do with our furniture. We shall have to sell the house."

"Ok. Time enough for all that. Come for a meal when you have settled in. Two- or three-days' time? We'll make it lunch so we can get the children to bed on time."

Maria did not take long to arrive and cuddle the children. Zippy was next as Susie followed him up the steps. Miriam rushed to him and he knocked her to the floor with his enthusiastic welcome. She loved it.

Alice explained that they had come for a holiday and to pack up and sell the house as Derry was based in Oxford for the future. They chatted away and caught up with the news.

"I shall miss it. I love it here, my first home and such dear friends."

Alice then rang Fiona and Richard and asked if they could hold the next Meditation in number 42. She explained that she was pregnant again. Fiona was happy to come but she insisted that Alice did not prepare refreshments. She promised to bring finger food and biscuits and drinks.

"Do you want to leave it a week to settle in?"

"Good idea. Thank you."

Jet lag meant that they did not sleep too well that first night. Alice stood on the balcony and looked at the stars and twinkling lights on the hills. Fortunately, Miriam and Thomas slept well.

"We'll take it in turns to sleep tomorrow." suggested Derry.

Alice sat in the study and talked to her third child. If you are a boy, you will be Robert in the middle after your Granddad Bob. First you will have a Jewish name for Esther, your other Granny.

"Shall I go to see my colleagues at the University?"

"Perhaps after we have been to Steve. You need to tell them about our party and find out who is able to attend your conference. Goodness, baby three will be with us soon after the conference."

The Meditation Group members rang to welcome them back. They were all happy to come to their house next week. Connie rang to offer her baby-sitting services. She was not sure if she would be able to attend the conference.

They had an enjoyable BBQ with Steve, Jeannie and their children who had grown taller. They were old enough to play with Miriam and Thomas in the sand pit and pool.

"We'll come to the township with you and see Kyle's work. You know he has just got married and gone to live in Romania"

Derry was pleased to tell him their story, their romance, their weddings and their work in Ploiesti.

Alice called to Steve, "You know there has been another wedding? Dr Paul has married Vivienne an American girl and they spent their honeymoon in South America."

Derry added, "We could well end up on another project in Peru in a year or two."

Before the Meditation Group meeting they all went to see their friends at the university. They talked about the party and the conference and made a few plans for the future once Derry had got used to being a professor.

"Jane and Jake are in the bush working on recipes and medicines with the women. They will be back in about a month."

"Good. They will not miss our party. I want to give you all a formal invitation to the conference and book launch. We hope Mary Ruth and an Elder will join us, and I have high hopes that the African who worked with my father-in-law will be able to come."

"This is a holiday! Unwind, Derry. Have fun. Go to the zoo and go up Skyrail. I will come with you to help with the children." Connie insisted.

"You know we are expecting a third child at the end of the year?"

"Steve told me. Congratulations! You will need more help. Do let me come, I love it! Are you having a scan soon?"

"Yes, in a couple of weeks."

Derry hugged her, "You are so good to us."

Eugene joined Simon on the Meditation evening. Sandrine came with Richard and Fiona.

"I hope you will have time to come to the workshop with your little ones." said Eugene, "I love children."

Alice said that Miriam would be very interested and that Thomas loved anything that moved.

Derry placed a small table in the middle and lit a candle. He put on a CD and they all sat quietly for a few minutes.

"I have the reading," said Richard and he read out a passage about how, if we look silently into ourselves, we find God. The half hour of silence was only broken once by Thomas crying for drink. Alice put him back to sleep in Miriam's room. They all chatted on the balcony and in the living room over the lovely food which Fiona had prepared.

Derry called them all together before they left. He invited them to the leaving party at Thala. "We want to thank you for your friendship and all your love and care for us. We also want to offer you Open House in Oxford. We can put up 2-3 of you and you will be very welcome to have a holiday with us in Oxford. Just not all at once."

Alice caught up with Sandrine. She told her about her friend Abigail and her artist boyfriend. "He has his own studio and I would love to go there with you. Do consider coming to us after the November conference."

"It would have to be school holidays. How thoughtful of you."

"Baby three is due towards the end of December. Could you come at the beginning of the month? I might be able to book my brother to have the children so we can spend a day and night in London."

Alice was exhausted so Derry gave her a perfumed oil massage to help her sleep.

The next week baby three was referred to as a second boy.

"Let's use Robert as a middle name for your Dad. I hope you are not going to suggest Elimelech or something similar for a Jewish first name." she smiled.

"I have just been reading the amazing story of Joseph. What ups and downs he had, injustices and hardships before he became famous. Joseph Robert Barnes sounds good."

"I love it."

The Barnes family thoroughly enjoyed their holiday. They had to confirm the numbers and the menu for the party with the staff at Thala.

"Alice, would you like to choose the food with the caterers? I think you would be better at it than me. Count all the university staff and Meditation Group.

"And our neighbours." added Alice.

"Ok. I will take the children to the esplanade and you can go to Thala. Buffet or sit-down meal?"

"Buffet, better for circulating. Is our weekend booked?"

"Yes." She saw him off with the children. On the esplanade were fountains, swings, houses to climb in, and cars to ride in. They all got thoroughly soaked but the ever-prepared Derry had put a pile of towels on the back seat between the car seats.

Alice looked through the menus and made her choices. The buffet was every bit as good as the main menus. She chose a 5pm start so they could enjoy the sunset over the sea.

Derry decided to put the house on the market in case he could meet the new owners before they left. They thought that Steve would have people in need of furniture among his Aboriginal friends.

At the township, people came to see the children and Alice asked after the boys. They were doing better at school since they had 'helped' Kyle with the building. The infant school was now open and both houses were occupied. They admired the work he had completed.

"He is doing the same in Romania now. He has got married to a Romanian girl." In the bar, Alice spotted the football, muddy and deflated. Steve could feel the atmosphere and tried to lift it.

"We have started building a clinic and a baby centre," He saw the ball. "We keep trying. We'll get a new ball."

"What about our furniture? Can it be used here?"

"Some, certainly but you could also give it to Social Services and they distribute it to clients in need."

Clients, thought Alice. *Social Work clients, counselling clients and Spider clients, all with such different needs.*

She had learned much from her fist term of training and saw that Silent Meditation was a door to many other aspects of life. Some days her baby played football inside her.

When they arrived at Simon's workshop they were greeted by Eugene holding out a little wooden plane with moving wings and wheels for Thomas. Simon stood behind with a beautiful baby bird pecking at the earth for Miriam.

"You have gone to such trouble!"

"The good Lord did not enable us to be fathers so we can be adoptive grandfathers instead." Eugene smiled as he watched Thomas roll his plane along and fly it around his head.

Connie asked them if they would like her to baby sit for the Thala weekend. Alice and Derry were very reluctant.

"They will love the beach and the rockpools. But I have an idea. Perhaps you could have them one afternoon and night in our house and then we will come and get them in the morning." It was agreed. It turned out to be a very good idea. Alice knew that Derry was not good at holidays and that his mind was already turning to plans for autumn.

Without the children they could totally relax and enjoy a perfumed oil massage together. Derry massaged the unborn Joseph and spoke to him. They slept a long, satisfying sleep. Derry awoke and kissed Alice awake. "Let's get Miriam and Thomas." After a Thala breakfast they returned home. Connie heard the car and carried Thomas down the steps while Miriam tried on her own one at a time.

"Mummy. Daddy!"

"They have been so happy and so good." said Connie. "We have tried some games, sung some nursery rhymes and danced. We even tried hide and seek."

"Connie, thank you so much. Do try to come to Oxford and stay with us even if you cannot make the conference. They will miss you."

"I am waiting for Jane and Jake. I will have plants to study when they get back. But thanks, I would love to come sometime."

She kissed both children. "Off you go to Thala. Enjoy! Remember what Esther said, 'No tribes and no research'!"

It was the evening of the Aboriginal presentation. Miriam amused everyone by going to the front and stamping her feet along with the dancers.

After Thala, Alice and Derry took it in turns to attend the Meditation Group. When Alice went she told them about the Spider course. Some had heard of it but not experienced it. Alice urged them to consider bereavement counselling if they ever lost someone close.

"Within about a month both parents died and I had a new baby. I was especially sad that my mother did not meet her grandson, Hartleigh Thomas Barnes and that my children will never know their wonderful grandparents."

There were three people interested in buying the house. Derry showed them round but there were no firm offers. Then Steve turned up one evening.

"Would you consider selling your house to the university as a student hostel?"

"What a wonderful idea. Who do I see?"

"Me. I often look after student accommodation and I am sure that I can persuade the bursar that it is a bargain with the furniture and air con."

"We can sell the double bed so you can buy two single ones."

"I will buy your bed. Ours is very old."

"$10 to you!"

It was a great relief to take down the For Sale sign and know that there was no more to do. Alice was overwhelmed with sadness and insecurity as she faced spending the last days in number 42. It was her first marital home; both her parents and Miriam had lived there and Thomas had been born there. She felt very, very weepy and needy. She remembered what she had learned in the counselling. "What is all this about? I should speak it out."

She sat on the sofa with Derry and cuddled him. "Derry, my love, I am feeling very strange. Could you bear it to spend some time just giving me your love? I am feeling insecure and a bit lost."

"Bear it? It will be my delight. Do you know why you are feeling insecure?"

"This was my first home with you and I put so much effort into making it mine and to belong to it. It hurts to leave and know that we are not coming back."

"I can understand that. And you were alone here for nearly three months. You dealt with your stress by working so hard to make a life for us here."

Alice felt tears run down her cheeks. He held her and caressed her. "Perhaps because I am pregnant too."

"Alice, I love you more than my own life. I love Miriam and Thomas and Joseph. God loves you. He was with you through all the difficult and sad times. He is with you now and he will be with you as we start again in Oxford with three little ones and a new post."

"I never want you to let me go." She clung to him until they both fell asleep.

Awaking, Alice took a deep breath and let it out slowly. She leaned over and kissed Derry awake. He sat up and held her securely against him.

"Do you remember the first time you ever held me?"

"I'll never forget. Outside the RFH by the river."

"Nor will I. My heart was bursting."

Alice put on her nightgown and went to the children. They were both waking up slowly. Derry bent down to speak to them, "It is party night. Mummy must rest today, and you and I will go to the park." Derry enjoyed playing with his children.

"You will be three one day when we are back in England. Your baby brother Joseph will be born."

The party was a very happy occasion tinged with sadness. It was clear that the university colleagues thought very highly of Derry. They gave tributes to him in their speeches and presented him with gifts suitable for hand luggage including mother of pearl handled knife and pens, cuff links and a leather desk set. Connie stayed with the children so Alice could stand with him. She had already helped her feed them. The different groups had mingled very well. Jane and Jake gave them all a big hug and started some informal dancing.

The sunset had been mainly a thick purple streak across the sky with a narrow, bright yellow streak playing on the water. Alice remembered the brilliant sunset in the bush, three years earlier.

She found Sandrine as the dear friends gradually dwindled away. "Don't forget. Oxford in early December."

"I will book it soon. Don't you go and have your baby too soon like Hartleigh Thomas." She hugged Alice and went out of the dining room.

4 St Marcus Conference

The Thala goodbyes were tearful all round. It was clear that Derry and Alice were loved and appreciated. The university colleagues made it clear that they would invite Derry for a lecture tour in Australia within the next two years. Alice had a look at the aquarium that Kyle had been building. A lot of progress had been made and it was due to open in the next few months.

They had a last look out of the plane windows as they flew to Brisbane. They lovingly watched the coast, the rainforest, the islands and the blue sea.

With renewed energy they took up their Oxford life. Derry reorganised his new office and shared with his colleagues in the Anthropology Department. They were enthusiastic about the conference and his idea for future research in Peru. He organised rooms for the guest speakers as they booked in. The delegates would use some of the halls of residence.

Alice re-established a routine with her children and picked up the second term of her SpirDir training and her attendance at Mother and Toddler Group at the local church. There were times when she was aware of missing her parents and asked for a session with Jean.

"How are you finding your SpirDir course?"

"Very interesting. I am amazed that such ancient teachers and mystics are so relevant to today. I am looking forward to Jung and the Enneagram work. My Director is Jeff, a retired teacher and psychology writer."

"Are you working on any particular aspects?"

"We are looking at the Psalms which express loss, sorrow or regrets. I am including leaving Cairns in the bereavement process."

"Have you read 'A Grief Observed.' by C S Lewis?"

"Not yet. I am a bit afraid of stirring up the uncertainty I experienced when I left my first home in Cairns."

"That's alright. Wait until you really want to have a look at all that."

Jean checked out when the third baby was due and advised Alice to get plenty of rest for herself. Alice mentioned that she was so looking forward to the visit of Sandrine from Cairns between the conference and the birth of Joseph.

Derry was relieved when his colleagues booked in. Koda, Heinrich, Steve, Mary Ruth, an Aboriginal Elder called Jeremiah whom they had met in the Outback teaching the old skills to the younger generation. Paul and Vivienne had also booked in. She was not intending to go to all the talks but hoped to spend some time with Alice and the children. It was a very special delight when two of the Nigerian doctors who had worked with Thomas agreed to come.

They were Dr Oluwale and Dr Idunnola. They had both met Koda and Paul.

The conference would begin with an introduction of Tribal Wisdom, a tribute to Professor Thomas Hartley and a brief book launch by Professor Derwent Barnes. He planned to follow up the main presentations with smaller 'interest' groups for discussions in the teaching rooms. He also offered two afternoon outings, a river trip and a visit to the Pitt Rivers Museum. The groups included Tribal Law and Laws of the Land, Creativity and Spirituality and the Respect and use of nature for food and healing.

Alice wanted to hear the talks on Australia and Peru. She could look back on what she had learned and look forward to the new direction in Derry's work.

In the church group, Alice had found a reliable lady with a little girl the same age as Miriam. She was glad of the extra cash and was happy to babysit for a couple of hours so Alice could attend some of the meetings.

The opening papers were on Nigeria. Koda headed his talk 'The Importance of Blacksmiths.' Beginning with the Guild of Bronze Castors still functioning today, he traced the use of this special skill back to pre-colonial times. He told how archaeologists had found evidence of trade routes with other areas such as Mali, even before Benin. There were overlapping kingdoms with decorative pottery well before the Europeans and Islam arrived. Bronze making was a sacred and secret skill. In spite of videos showing the workers making bronzes and brasses today, there are still secrets kept by the Guild. The magnificent bronzes had not been made for sale and tourism but for ritual, story-telling, festivals and telling about the culture. He admitted that most of the work done today was for tourism.

Paul mentioned that the delegates should all visit the British Museum where there were many beautiful examples of the Benin Bronzes. They had been scattered all over the world by the various empires but that now there was an effort being made to return at least some of them to their country of origin. He went on to mention his post-Colonial studies and the harmful results of the competing Empires in the Niger, Nigeria and Chad area. Britain, France and

Germany all had massacres and atrocities on their record. He ended by showing how the religions had mingled. Islamic greetings were addressed to the tree spirits and Christian festivals mixed with animistic rituals.

Paul introduced Dr Wale and Dr Idunnu, using the shortened forms of their names. They spoke of how Professor Thomas had encouraged them in establishing a museum and helped them overcome the long-held prejudice among the European colonisers that Africans could not possibly have made such intricate bronze work. Dr Idunnu could remember his great grandfather who had had relatives killed by a French Army Captain. Whole families and whole villages were wiped out just within the memory of his antecedents. Professor Thomas had set up a foundation to provide housing and schooling to some of those regions. Alice was so touched to hear of her father's achievements. Both doctors pointed out that many of the modern problems were due to the mining of Uranium which was often used for manufacturing in Europe. The discussion groups were able to see the comparison with the same mining in the Outback of Australia.

Mary Ruth and Elder Jeremiah dealt with art and spirituality. Mary showed some of her canvases which showed respect for ancestors and for the sacred land. She ended her session by getting everyone to have 15 minutes of dadirri.

Koda's paper on the First Nation Laws came before Steve's presentation about the Reserves in Australia. In this way it was easier to make comparisons and analyse the resulting problems for the indigenous people today.

Koda gave some examples of how the law of the land sometimes contradicted the Sioux tribal law. Women had specific roles in the tribe with some limitations. Interfering with the actions of a young male was forbidden unless an Elder gave permission. This led to a family tragedy. A woman saw her son throw a rope over a branch and as there was no one about she had to watch him make a noose and hang himself. She later found herself in Canadian Court. He tried to explain the very different culture which allowed young men to make their own decisions, good or bad.

Before Heinrich gave a paper on Canadian Rock Art, comparing it with the art of the Australian caves, Koda described the immense deprivation, drug and alcohol addiction on the Rez. He ended with some signs of hope. Some residents of the Rez had become film makers and, on show in the city cinemas were their films depicting their lifestyle with humour but also with the uncomfortable truth.

The discussion groups were extremely lively and began to move in a different direction. This was even more obvious after Steve's presentation on drug use in the Aboriginal urban area. He began by referring to the research on medicines completed by his department under Derry. He mentioned the work of the Botanist, Connie and the bush research by Jane and Jake. They were beginning to produce some medication to help addicts get off Crack Cocaine and Crystal Meths. He told them some of the tragic stories of those he had been involved with. His presentation had a big impact on the delegates. They were used to dealing with academic studies and theories but he challenged them with the facts of daily life for many of the indigenous people. From the discussion groups came the proposal that Derry could establish a foundation like the one Thomas had made in Nigeria. Paul saw that such a foundation would be Post-Colonial Theology in operation; it could actually bring about some solutions. Derry called all the speakers together so the conference could end with a proposal and a list of delegates willing to be involved.

"The Hartley Barnes Foundation." suggested Koda.

Before Derry's closing address he had asked Paul to say a little about anthropology in Peru. He headed his paper 'Anthropology or Archaeology'. He explained that he had recently spent his honeymoon in Peru because his wife had pursued her interest in the Incas over several years. They had naturally been to Machu Pichu and seen the bones of the Inca burials in other areas. The Incas were of course finally destroyed by the Spanish and some other indigenous tribes who wanted to see an end of their domination over such a vast empire. Paul wanted to look at the descendants of such peoples and observe how they were living today. The obvious place to start was Cuzco and the islands on Lake Titicaca.

"We move from archaeology to anthropology. We are dealing with living people who try hard to keep up their ancient traditions and yet suffer bad living conditions in our modern age."

Paul showed that nevertheless, archaeologists were still making new discoveries today. They had found advanced roads, aqueducts and ramparts which pre date the Incas. The religious beliefs were often revealed by the examination of tombs and rock art. Some of the original designs are still used in the popular weavings for tourists. Ponchos, and hats were hung up in all the markets along with wall hangings. He was not surprised to see that ancient goddesses were depicted and included in rituals for harvest and fertility. Tribal people, still referred to as Indians often lived in close communities, supporting each other with the old skills of fishing, weaving and llama herding. He was surprised to find a real mix of nationalities which had come about from the trading within the local countries and with peoples who travelled to the Pacific coast. He discovered some mixed-race descendants of the Chinese labourers who were brought over in the 19th century.

"There is research to be done in the future. There is repentance by the old Empires and restoration to be done for the sake of the people who still pay the price today."

Derry reminded everyone of the books on their research of the past three to five years, He set out their proposal to make the Hartley Barnes Foundation to provide benefits for indigenous people living in poverty and deprivation and to bring healing both medicinal and spiritual to those in need. He received a standing ovation and a welcome as a new professor to the college. They brought the conference to a close with a drinks and canapés party so that delegates would feel free to depart for their trains and planes. Derry felt emotional as he bade farewell to the colleagues who had worked with him for so long. He was exhausted and took some days off to spend time with Alice. He was relieved that Daniel was coming for a week while Sandrine was visiting so that they could travel to London together for a day.

He was overwhelmed by the response to the foundation. He knew that many would not follow up nor be able to give the degree of time and effort required but there would still be a good number to administer the support work. As soon as possible he started producing the Conference Report. His other colleagues had taken on the task of a book launch in their own countries.

He brought three copies of the book home to place on the bookshelf. They were very heavy tomes indeed.

5 The Art Studio

Sandrine arrived at Heathrow and took trains to Oxford to avoid pressurising her busy hosts. Abigail rang to say that she was longing to share with them as she found herself in a very difficult situation. Sandrine wondered if the two of them would prefer time alone but Abigail felt comfortable sharing with another member of a Meditation Group.

Alice settled her children with Daniel. He was on his own as Charles had been asked to play a few concerts with an orchestra he often worked for. Alice drove Sandrine to Abigail's flat where they spent some time getting to know each other before calling on Justin. Sandrine told her about her teaching and about the Art Shack for Art Therapy.

"What a wonderful idea," responded Abigail, "I'd love to be involved with something like that."

"Could Justin's studio be used?"

Abigail explained her dilemma. She was the leader of a Christian Meditation Group but had been brought up by strict Evangelical parents. They did not really approve of such groups. Over the past year she had become very attached to Justin who seemed to love her and want her in his life. He, however, valued being a 'free spirit' very highly. He was reacting to a domineering father and had gone against his wishes to study art and become a full-time artist.

"So you are in conflict with your parents?"

"Both with my parents and my boyfriend. My parents refuse to see me until I give him up and he wants me to move in with him without getting married."

"Your parents have thrown you out?"

"Sort of. They believe I am disobeying God and being unfaithful to Jesus by having a close relationship with someone who is not a born again Christian."

"That sounds like a very narrow minded and judgemental attitude to me!" Sandrine sounded adamant.

"It's a matter of how we interpret the Bible. Is it the unerring Word of God whose rule is relevant to us today? Do we have no say about the rules?" Alice added.

"My parents and their church believe it is the Word of God and that we should obey it without question."

Alice thought of Daniel's experience in his student days.

"I've seen what such opinions can do to people. You are asked to choose between parents and lover. It's heart breaking. I am sorry, Abigail. Will they not compromise at all? If you decide to stay with Justin will they really reject you?"

"Yes. Justin cannot understand how loving parents can treat their daughter like that."

"Nor can I."

Abigail mentioned some Bible verses she had been quoted about being unequally yoked, light mixing with darkness. Alice used some of her SpirDir training, "Those words were written over 2000 years ago to a very different society. We need to see who they were written for and why they were written. Our culture is totally different now. The meaning of such identity and distinguishing behaviour of tribes at that time is no longer relevant to us today."

"Justin is kind, considerate and serious minded where spirituality is concerned. He has broken free from the tradition of his father and their rather nominal church affiliation. He has searched out a path along New Age lines and become comfortable with the Buddhist and Hindu ways of meditation."

Sandrine was finding it difficult to grasp. "And your parents think that is wrong?"

"Absolutely. But it worries me that Justin does not feel that marriage is necessary or even valid in our society. He feels that a couple should just live together without ceremony and vows. He quotes all the examples of the rich and famous that spend thousands on a wedding and then break up and are unfaithful after a couple of years." They easily thought of the examples of celebrities and the Royal Family. His view was easy to understand but it put Abigail in a difficult situation.

"Would you feel any better if he married you? He would still not come up to your parents' expectations."

"Are you encouraging me to go ahead regardless?"

"Have you talked to him about how you feel?"

"A little."

Sandrine said that she thought a loving relationship was very important and not to be rejected lightly in spite of a different creed and religion.

At the art studio, Alice and Sandrine were delighted at this unusual place and with Justin himself. He welcomed them and offered to show them round. He kissed Abigail who noticed that there were some new pictures hanging up. They were photographs in black and white of various parts of the human body taken from strange angles so that it was not always clear what they were. A message both attractive and unsettling seemed to be shouting out and Alice was stunned by their power. Sandrine told him about her Art Shack for therapy and asked him if he could see his studio being used for healing therapy?

"It is certainly that for me. Let me think about it. I feel very drawn to that thought." He responded.

Knowing that she would probably not see him again, Sandrine spoke boldly to him. "Abigail has told me what she would lose if she were to live with you. What do you think of that?"

"I cannot understand how parents can be so harsh. I had to disobey my father and reject his values in order to feel free. Abigail can only decide herself if she is willing to do the same. I am sorry it would come to that. I really want her with me. She is the love of my life."

"It is a very hard decision for her, especially because of her family background. Someone has to compromise if your love relationship is worthwhile."

Justin was clearly embarrassed and so were Alice and Abigail.

"God bless you both and find you a way forward." added Sandrine.

They ate together on the third level of the studio in Justin's open-plan flat then they looked through his art work. Justin went to the easel and using a sponge and a narrow piece of wood he began smearing different colours over the canvas. Using smaller pieces of wood and sponge he began moving the paint around, allowing it to drip. Gradually the head of a flower appeared. With fine brushes he shaped the petals and added stalks, insects and more colours.

"This is amazing, Justin, you are very talented and you have a powerful message. Show it, use it, and open a gallery to the public."

They all hugged when they separated. Alice and Sandrine drove back to Oxford, leaving Abigail to make her decision. Sandrine was still there when Abigail rang to say that sadly and reluctantly she had decided that she could not stay with Justin. Vows and commitment were important to her. His free spirit meant more to him than Abigail's peace of mind. They were both very sad about it.

Sandrine enjoyed talking to Daniel who remained a little longer so they could visit the Modern Art Gallery and other parts of Oxford.

Alice sat with her in the study and told her about the immense changes her father had made to the house so that they could all have a home there. The phone rang and an animated Abigail spoke loudly, "Alice, Sandrine, Justin has made an amazing decision. Instead of accepting that I had left him, he came to see me. He really loves me and said that it is much more important that I should have a commitment and a ceremony than that he should feel like a free spirit.

"He said he is not free without me. I mean so much to him that he is willing to get married."

"And so he should!" said Sandrine.

"Yes, he should value your feelings above everything else." Alice was thinking of Derry and his total devotion to her.

"It does not alter my parent's views but at least they know I will not just be co-habiting."

"You are both welcome to come to Cairns at any time."

"I wish you all the best, Abigail. After my boy is born please bring Justin to us for a weekend."

"Those parents do not know what they are missing, Let's hope they have a change of heart in the future. I will keep in touch with Abigail and Justin."

"It's been great to have you Sandrine. Give my love to the group. I hope some others will come in the next few years."

Daniel had several concerts leading up to Christmas so Alice was pleased when Maddy offered to come and help out when Joseph was home. She was so aware that there were no longer any grandparents.

Derry took up running and visiting the gym to get fit after his prolonged period of academic activity. He was running along the river side when the phone rang.

"Hello, Maddy."

"I am on my way to you. Alice needs to get to hospital as she is having regular contractions."

"On my way back now." he rang Alice.

"I have asked Jean to come as I think Joseph is coming now."

"Early like Thomas?"

"Not quite so early. I hope he will not need intensive care."

Miriam understood that her new brother was coming and she bounced around with Jean as she was so excited. Derry took Alice to the maternity ward. The labour was not so long and Joseph was born before midnight. The nurse noticed the marks on his head as he emerged even before he was cleaned. She placed him on Alice's breast. Alice looked down at the tiny head and saw the red marks.

"What's that?"

"Your baby has some birthmarks. This one on his head and two on his legs. You will be given some advice about them later on."

Derry stroked his little head.

"Alice, he has birthmarks which neither of the others had but we will love him just the same and teach him to cope with whatever reactions he gets as he grows up. Both parents kissed their son and helped wash him. He had two red streaks across the right side of his forehead leading to a bigger red patch over his ear.

"Like Gorbachev." said Alice. She felt sadness for the teasing he would have to endure. She looked down at him and said to Derry, "Actually, he is very beautiful."

Maddy and Zara arrived at the hospital.

"We've got sleeping bags. We'll help you with meals and cleaning."

Joseph was thoroughly checked and allowed to go home. On that first evening Miriam and Thomas came to kiss and hug their new brother.

Derry told them he had a special mark which he would grow up with. They did not seem to notice. They held his hands, played with his fingers and kissed his face over and over again. Derry lit a candle and read out his blessing. He added some phrases for Joseph.

"God has given Joseph a special mark so we pray that he will know he is a special child. God protect him from the ignorant comments and cruel teasing he might get over the years. Fill him with confidence that he is loved by his family and by God. Show him how to use his markings to bring blessings to others."

6 Spiritual Direction – A Case Study

Alice recovered quite quickly with the help of all her relatives and friends. Joseph was a calm baby and responded wonderfully when Miriam and Thomas touched him and spoke to him.

Maddy and Zara were a great help for the first ten days. Alice wrote to Connie to tell her that Joseph was waiting for her visit. Abigail sent some baby clothes and a wedding invitation. Her Meditation Group offered to help her with the catering and the flowers. Her Anglican church allowed her to have the ceremony there with the use of the hall for the Reception. Unconventional Justin had gone with Abigail to Camden Market to choose a wedding dress. They chose a long flowery dress with huge coloured petals.

Alice was feeling unsure that they could attend with three little children of 4, 2 and newborn. Maddy suggested that they drove down and stayed the night after the wedding in their Epsom house. They could squash into the lounge on the settee and camping beds. They agreed that this was the best idea. Abigail made a crown of cream flowers for her long hair. The Buddha's Words on Loving Kindness, the Karaniya Metta Sutta were read out with the Lord's Prayer and Psalm 23. The only sadness for the couple was that Abigail's parents had not come. Justin had not expected his parents to come but was happy to see that his mother came and was very sweet and friendly to his new wife.

The Barnes family survived the journey and the over-night stay. Maddy and Roy were so pleased to have the children there.

"I wonder when Kyle will be a father!" It was obvious that she was longing to be a Granny. "Zara might be first. She seems to have a steady boyfriend."

Alice completed the final months of her training and was being prepared for her first client. She asked Jeff to delay this as she wanted to focus on her new baby for a few months. In the Enneagram studies, Alice was discovered to be a 6 with leanings towards 5 and she felt sure that Derry was a 5 with leaning towards 6, but he was not inclined to take much notice of that kind of profiling, He preferred Myers Briggs where he was INFJ.

Jeff explained about the feedback group and Supervision. They would often hear very sad stories from their clients and find some situations difficult to handle. The bi-monthly feedback session was for the Directors to share their experiences and get advice from each other. If the problem was very personal or even gory, they should make an appointment with the Supervisor.

"I think I have found the right lady for you, Alice. She is a retired, professional widow who has held down very responsible jobs over many years. She has a long association of church membership and has been actively involved all her life. She asked for a SpirDir to help her work through some events in her life."

"An easy one for me as a beginner. Can she come to me? I have people to baby sit. Could I perhaps meet her and explain that I need a bit longer to get used to my baby?"

On the day that the new client was due to arrive, Alice saw Miriam go into the bedroom with a flannel. She crept in behind her and saw her rub soap on the corner and go to rub Joseph's face.

"No, darling. We cannot wash off the mark. Remember the prayer that Daddy read?"

She wiped off the soap and sat down putting Miriam on her lap and Joseph on Miriam's lap. She explained that he would get some special cream when he is bigger.

"What do they look like?"

"A snake. A lizard."

She read out the prayer again and Miriam kissed her brother over his mark.

Soon Miriam could begin Nursery School and Thomas could go to Play School. Joseph was a delight. He lay on his back waving his arms and kicking his legs. They were very happy to play with him when he lay on his special pad on the floor. They were very upset when he cried and were happy to watch him feed from his mother's breast.

Louisa Greenfield arrived at the front door and Alice let her in and led her to the study. Her children were upstairs with the baby sitter.

Alice made coffee and they sat near the bookshelf in the study. "What interesting books!"

"My father and my husband have both written books on anthropology and they have both spent long periods abroad with indigenous peoples." Alice explained

"How fascinating. I have just begun to look at some other religions. I have been rather traditional and narrow minded."

Alice asked Louisa to tell her something about her life and family. She had attended several very different churches in her life and was now used to living alone as her husband had died three years earlier after 40 years of marriage. She explained that she had changed her opinions and her theology a great deal during the past 25 years and was rethinking some of the events of her past. She decided to ask for the help of a soul friend to walk through them with her.

"I will be very pleased to accompany you on this path, Louisa. Can you return in about three weeks when I have my baby sitting organised?"

"Have you anything for me to read?"

"I have 'Falling Upwards' by a Franciscan, Richard Rohr, all about dealing with the second half of life."

"Second half, more like 4/5 for me." She asked if she could meet the children before she left.

Miriam obliged her with her name, Thomas just stared at her and she noticed Joseph's birthmark.

"How beautiful. He has a special mark. Does it resemble anything?"

"Miriam says a snake or a lizard."

"Thank you very much for taking me on when you have your hands so full with 3 little ones."

Alice looked forward to beginning the sessions with Louisa and could not have imagined what a challenge this kindly, elderly lady would bring her. She made a special corner in the study. She put a vase of flowers on the side table, a candle on a small coffee table and drew two chairs into the corner. She left the globe light on and had gentle music playing when Louisa came in.

"This is a holy time and we are together in the presence of the Holy Spirit. What would you like to begin with?"

"The Rohr book was helpful. He spoke of disappointments we face in the later years of life and past events we have to face. I have over many years made some serious decisions about my life based on what I understood to be the teaching of the church and the leading of the Holy Spirit. Some of those decisions led me into real difficulties. I am feeling as if I failed because what I thought I was called to do came to nothing in the end."

Alice could not imagine what she was referring to.

"Do you think you made mistakes in some of your decisions?"

"When I look back and see how things turned out it would be logical to say that I had made a mistake but when you see the events that led up to the decision; the Bible verses, the spiritual leadings, the prayers and the context of the church I was in, it is not so straightforward."

"I think it would help me understand if you could give me an example."

"I think it is a matter of interpretation and presumption."

Louisa and Reg had belonged to a large, successful free church for many years. Louisa had a kind of dream, word of knowledge experience one evening when she felt God ask them to change to a smaller church in the village. At the same time she had the impression that God was asking her to be involved in Christian work in Hungary. She discussed her experience with her new pastor and discovered that the church had already made some links with a small free church in a village outside Budapest. Louisa made an effort to read about the history of the country and even to learn the rather difficult language. She spent time and money on this project and was encouraged to join the next group trip to Hungary. She enjoyed meeting the people who had survived Communism in the land since the war. She loved the different culture and the sewing and embroidery skills of the ladies. She found that many of the young people could speak English and seemed pleased to hold conversations even with an older English lady. Reg could not go on the trips because of his work but helped entertain the Hungarian visitors. Louisa was surprised that God had led them to a new church without knowing they had a connection to Hungary. This motivated her to continue for three or four years even though she was not at ease with the extreme version of evangelicalism they held. The church contacts seemed to fade as they moved more in the direction of caring for the under privileged people in their own area. It all seemed to lead to nothing and Louisa felt like a failure.

She gave Alice a further example when she recounted that in a session of 'praying in tongues' she found some strange sounds in her head and wrote them down. She had no understanding what they were for but wrote the very definite sounds down, putting them aside until one trip to Hungary she read them out to a young man and asked if they meant anything to him.

"It sounds like two boys' names and a message for them to call on God."

"Was it from God? Why did He lead me there? Did I fail in some way?"

Alice did not really know how to respond. She decided to write notes and save them for a session with the Supervisor. She had some readings and Psalms ready to end the sessions. They had decided on weekly sessions to begin with.

Alice's training had shown her that she should not talk about her own experiences in Germany but should draw out Louisa to express what else was bothering her. She asked her to talk about her husband and his death in the following session. She had spoken of the interpretation of the mystical kind of leadings she had in her prayer times and her presumption that something definite would result.

Alice felt overwhelmed and unable to find ways to encourage Louisa and get her away from feeling a failure.

The next session was even harder to cope with and moved Alice deeply to hear of the suffering that this lady had gone through in her life.

Louisa saw Joseph in his cot, kicking and gurgling.

"Not a lizard but a peninsula and a Pacific Island on his head."

Alice rather liked that; maps of islands like those on the Great Barrier Reef. Thomas walked over to her and held her hand. She was smiling as they went downstairs.

"Thank you for the lovely corner you have made for us. I am sorry that for a first client you have someone with such complications as me."

"You have been through a lot, Louisa. Your years of the Hungarian project is only part of it, I am sure. Tell me about Reginald Greenfield today."

"Before I was married I was LLL! What do parents think of? Louisa Lily Lambert. I was glad to change my initials. We were unable to have a normal marriage."

Alice swallowed. What was coming?

"I met Reg when he was a volunteer youth leader at the local church. It was another bizarre experience which I have often contemplated and yelled out 'God what were you doing?'" Louisa had been at the prayer meeting for Revival in the 1960s. Her head was full of the recorded stories of Revivals in England such as those under Wesley and Whitfield. As she made her way home she felt led by an inner voice to take a different route and to go down a street she had never been down before. She found herself at the end of an alley so she walked down it. Some youths were leaving a hall and someone was walking in the bushes next to the alley. She stopped to read the youth Club notice board. The boys explained that the club was closed but if she wanted information a youth leader was walking his dog nearby. Reginald Greenfield had come over to see if he could help. She asked about the club and its activities. The conversation led to an invitation to coffee and inside the flat she noticed that the bookshelf contained Christian books. They discussed the churches they belonged to. This was a modern Anglican church but she belonged to a free church in a different part of the village. It was very evangelistic and also fundamentalist; evolution was eschewed for a young earth theory and the Genesis flood was considered an historical event. God had made everything in 6 days.

She brought some friends to meet Reg and invited him to join the prayer meetings for Revival and they promised to pray for the youth of the club. Reg came to her flat one day with a letter for her. He wrote that he could not attend the meetings because he had just given up being a Christian because he could not be both gay and Christian. He was about to resign from the club.

Alice breathed in deeply, recalling her brother's experience when he was a student. Her training showed her that she should not mention her own life and experiences.

Louisa felt she had been called to help this man. She suggested he spoke to her pastor. The next part of her story bore some resemblance to Daniel's experience of prayer to become heterosexual. Louisa offered to be a volunteer leader at the club and for several months she worked with him, admired him and the way he worked. He seemed to enjoy having her there and included her in outings and activities. She grew fond of him although he showed no interest in her as a woman. Eventually he decided to leave the church and the club and change jobs. Although they moved in different directions, they kept in touch. She felt she loved him but she was held in the friendship by the strange way she had met him. He decided to join another church and helped with Scouts. After nearly 10 years of keeping in touch in this way, she decided to tell him about her fall from grace several years previously. When Reg had left she had not met any other young men who interested her. Within the church there were some tensions and splits began to happen between some of the leaders. She had shared her heartache with one of the leaders after Reg had left. This leader was stressed by the church splits and told Louisa he was in love with her. He was married but had himself come from a difficult family background and had emotional problems. He seduced Louisa into an affair with him. No one ever knew. They succeeded in keeping it totally secret. Sad over the lack of relationship with Reg she had been unable to resist. As the church was falling apart she managed to break away from her lover and live a busy single life.

During this sharing time Reg told her that he hated being gay and wanted a wife and children. He had used the ads in Gay times to find other men but he was eaten up by guilt.

Alice said that she was very sorry she had been so broken. Both Louisa and Reg suffered from extreme guilt and as they shared they felt that they should get married, have a marriage of convenience without the sexual side.

"Next time I will tell you how we managed to stay together for 40 years!"

Alice tried to take in the facts. She lived with a husband she loved without any physical love for 40 years. She was punishing herself for her sinful affair. Alice decided to see Jeff for Supervision before their next meeting. Louisa had held a tissue and dabbed her eyes a few times and was obviously finding it difficult to tell her tale.

"Louisa, shall we leave it for two weeks? I think you need to recover from speaking out so bravely and openly. Does that suit you?"

"Yes, I have very rarely shared my story, only bits of it to encourage other people."

Jeff was very surprised. He was sorry that he had thrown a beginner in at the deep end. He expected it to be a gentle and undemanding walk-through spiritual paths to closeness to God. "So she feels a failure because of the Hungary project and I bet she feels a failure about her marriage. With her evangelical background I wonder if she also hoped that God would miraculously 'heal' him."

Alice took a note to find out her hopes and beliefs when she got married. Jeff had further words of warning.

"I guess there is more to come, possibly worse to come. If after the next session you feel it is too much for you, be honest. Tell her you are upset and inexperienced and that we will find her a counsellor."

"I would hate to do that but I do fear that her story is so sad that I won't be able to help her with her change of theology and the decisions she made when she had a different belief system."

Jeff asked her to find out what support she had had and who was in her life now to help her through widowhood.

After the break Alice felt afraid of what would be revealed next but she felt full of compassion for Louisa.

"Louisa, how do you want to begin today? Has God been speaking to you?"

"My mind is a muddle because I would like to understand why God led me on such an impossible path."

"Did you ever seek counsel or prayer?"

Louisa had turned to the church leader after Reg had left. He took a hard line and told her to serve God as a single person. He was the same leader who had told Louisa he loved her a few years later and seduced her.

Louisa described the prophetic words and prayers which led them to agree to marry. They both had elderly parents and they knew this would please them. Her parents liked Reg very much. She wanted to hear from God that He had led them to be married. She wanted to be clear that she had not chosen that path for wrong reasons, selfish reasons or sinful reasons. Was she now facing that her motivation had been wrong?

Alice was feeling sad. She asked about friends and support. Louisa spoke highly of her several friends in England and in Hungary who had been a real support for her.

"Some of them have had problems and two have given up on God. Having been strong Christians all their lives they cannot reconcile the all-powerful God who can do anything with the suffering in the world. 'It's a fallen world' is no longer an adequate answer. The beautiful world of nature is also a cruel world. Disasters happen mainly to the poor in volcanoes, tsunamis, mud slides and so on. Man can be so cruel to man. Where is the God of unconditional love? I don't know how to answer them"

Louisa had not given up on God. She had known the presence and love of God many, many times throughout her life but she was stuck in incomprehension.

"In the first few years of marriage I prayed and prayed that God would 'heal' Reg. One of the churches we attended called gay people forward for prayer. He had to go for prayer in the week and the elders called for me to come too. They prayed over him and we were told to ensure that we had a normal marriage because God would heal him from homosexuality. He even went through exorcism."

Alice could hardly contain herself but she managed not to talk about Daniel.

"That was a terrible time. I was full of hope and Reg was full of fear. There was no change at all. In order to cope we had to accept that we would have a celibate relationship with no pressure on Reg to perform. Praying friends did help us through that. I am Catholic now and I love the liturgy. I belong to the Meditation group in my village."

Alice was longing to identify with Louisa about her brother and Meditation and prayers for gay men but she held back and tried to move the story on.

Louisa and Reg had a lovely house in a village with a large garden and a conservatory. They decided to use their house for hospitality to people in need, to youth with problems. They had many of the Hungarians to stay.

"We were getting on well; good companions and a good team together. We were well liked in our fellowship. When I came home from work one day I found police officers on my doorstep."

They had been married for nearly 20 years when Reg was arrested. They said that letters and photographs from Reg had been found in the London flat of a known paedophile. He was at the Police Station for questioning and they had come with a search warrant for the house.

Alice felt glad that Jeff had warned her. Worse was certainly to come.

Louisa was shaken and shocked. The search revealed a folder of photos of naked men but also of some boys in pornographic poses. The police asked her what she knew of them. She said that she knew nothing except that her husband was a gay man. She had no idea that he had photos or had written letters.

The investigation lasted for weeks because the officers were convinced that Reg was part of a Paedophile ring with access to boys through the church club. Such a ring groomed boys through choirs, youth clubs and took photos to send to other paedophiles.

Louisa discovered that Reg was a very clever liar and had fooled her all those years. Reg swore to her that he had never abused or even groomed a child but that he had only corresponded and swopped photos with men through Gay Times. When he had been in London for 'work' he had really been going to Soho to see films, buy DVDs and magazines and meet men for impersonal sex.

Alice spoke out, "This was your reward for your sacrifice and your faithfulness. Why didn't you leave him?"

"Several friends thought I should leave him but most church friends thought I should stay and keep my vows."

Alice was weeping now.

"Why did I stay? I was so gripped by the way God led me to meet him just when he had given up being a Christian. The upheaval of separation after so many years of good companionship played a big role. I loved him and felt sorry for him. I was angry with him of course and a part of me did want to leave him."

The police had found no evidence of a ring but had arrested his correspondent in London. His letters were fantasy; the fictional description of encounters with boys. Louisa saw the secret, dark side of this man. He was given a one-year prison sentence. Reg lost his job and they lost their home. Louisa was able to apply for promotion and they downsized to a small terraced house in another village.

"My church got me through. They supported me and regularly visited Reg in prison. He asked to see the chaplain and joined in the church services. He wrote to Louisa to say how God was blessing him and helping him.

"I didn't want to know. I did not want to hear of his blessings. I wanted to hear about his repentance and his determination never to behave like that again. I felt I counted for nothing."

"That does not surprise me. What was God doing in your life?"

Louisa felt God's presence and protection. She felt He was helping her survive. By then the whole family knew and the whole church knew. Shame, humility, brokenness were Louisa's life for months. She felt humiliation every time she queued up with the women who were used to this life style waiting outside the prison door.

"I wondered what else I did not know. What had he not told me?"

"Between his arrest and his trial, I tried hard to get him to tell me what else he had been involved with."

Reg had made trips abroad for 'work conferences' but in truth he had gone to Amsterdam to meet his correspondent and attend the easily available porn films in the city. Louisa knew she would never trust him nor believe him again.

When he was released he came to the new house and tried to find work. He was never able to work again but he did permit voluntary work for friends and did many good things for many people.

"Louisa you are wonderful. You got through this trauma and still supported this man in spite of how he treated you. God helped you through and God is still with you. Everything is a mystery. We often cannot grasp what God is doing in our lives but, Louisa, He loves you." Alice read the Psalm and they hugged as they parted. She saw Jeff again before the next session.

"How ever did she get through that? She must have been worried sick about what he was doing and where he was going."

"She has been under immense stress for a very long time. She must be strong. Get her to go over the positive and good things in their marriage. She mentioned that she is Catholic and that she attends a Meditation Group. I wonder how that happened."

Alice decided that she would not take on any more Spiritual Direction in the immediate future but she did not want to reject Louisa. She wanted to reach some kind of closure with her. Between sessions she had to block her out in order to give proper attention to Derry and her children. They were her delight. Derry was enjoying his new post and co-ordinating the teaching in his department. He even had time to begin simplifying his books for a different publisher. He remembered Thomas's offer to search for one for him.

Joseph was progressing well. No teddy for him; he chose a soft rubber pterodactyl from the Science Museum. He cuddled it, slept with it and flew it above his head. Hartleigh Thomas was speaking well and loved being read to. Miriam was very interested in letters and sounds. The bright coloured alphabet and pictures were all round the kitchen.

Derry decided to plan a holiday in England for the whole family. He chose Dorset as he recalled the family holidays he had loved as a child in spite of the fact that his father had been so hard on him.

Abigail and Justin were due to come for a week to stay with them. Kyle and Adina decided to save money by staying in Romania. They planned a trip to the Carpathian Mountains and the castles including Bran, the Castle of Dracula. Paul had worked hard on the book launch and had travelled to several Canadian Universities with Koda. He was getting in touch with other anthropologists in Peru and neighbouring countries to build up a team of researchers.

Alice was looking forward to the Dorset holiday. Derry had looked for camp sites with self-catering lodges near the cliffs. He had really overcome the memories of his father's harsh treatment which almost broke his spirit because he understood the reasons for the problems, the fears he lived with. He was ready to see Durdle Door and Lulworth Cove again and let his children enjoy them.

Alice had a cry and a prayer before Louisa arrived for the next session.

"Positive aspects. In spite of everything, there were many. He was a lovely man, kind and helpful to others. We had many lovely outings and holidays together. He was very domesticated and helped with all the housework and shopping as I was working full time to pay the mortgage. He did voluntary work and took good care of our elderly parents, the finances, the medicines and their placing in care homes when they were ill with dementia." After serving half of the sentence Reg was released but had to attend a Sex Offenders course at the probation office. This helped him understand that the boys in the 'no harm to anyone' photos were real boys having their lives ruined. Louisa was hopeful that the past was the past and not the present for Reg. Unfortunately that was not the case.

"I think I could write a book about dopamine and addiction. God really did bless us with my job and our church activities. I expect I was rather complacent sometimes. I had been very naive and ignorant about what homosexuality was. It was the same with addictions."

Reg discovered the internet and the Gay Chat lines. He continued to go to towns where he could access porn films and DVDs. Normal behaviour for gay men seeking a partner was very dangerous for him because he went to houses where there could be boys being groomed. As far as she knew this had never happened and he met up only with other lonely men. She wanted to believe him when he said that he never met children but underneath the sense of panic never left her.

She felt rather cross with God in that He found ways of alerting her and letting her know that Reg was in trouble. She did not understand why God did not deal directly with him. She took to searching through drawers and cupboards. Once it was after a bizarre dream showing Reg dressing up in odd clothing. Another time it was a phrase in a book she was reading by an ancient mystic. It stood out on the page; 'the man who deliberately puts himself in the path of evil'.

She just knew both times that Reg was again indulging in dangerous activity. She challenged him and he confessed. Something broke in her and she announced to him and friends and family that she could not carry on. She was going to leave him. He felt that he should leave her in the house and move but he was very sorry and pleaded with her to stay. After long talks and many tears, she did stay.

Reg was diagnosed with bone cancer in his mid-seventies. After radiotherapy he recovered and went into remission. After a couple of years the cancer returned and spread. Louisa had some serious hospital treatment herself and they were both grateful for the care and support of church friends while they were both ill with life threatening conditions. Louisa had keyhole surgery on her bowel cancer but then suffered a broken heart valve. Both operations were totally successful.

When she was able to drive again and stand and cook, Reg sank. His chemotherapy was stopped as his body could not tolerate it and he became bedridden. On palliative care the morphine caused him to lose the ordinary function of his mind. It was a very sad, slow decline and he died in hospital.

"My first reaction was relief. It was dreadful to see him suffer so much. Then came all the difficulties of paper work, insurances and so on."

After three years she began to feel sad and confused because her past prayers seemed to have achieved nothing. She became aware of a return of energy in her own body and mind as she no longer had such a terrible weight to bear; living in fear of Reg's secret double life. She stopped her routine of prayer and Bible study and took up Meditation instead. What could she make of her past? She had sacrificed human love and motherhood and been rewarded by lies and betrayal. Why?

Alice ended her Case Notes here. She did not know what to say to Louisa. She had no answers. She did think that perhaps Louisa's sacrifice had prevented Reg getting into even worse scenarios. The press had revealed terrible abuse by paedophile rings and some well-known celebrities. Could Reg have gone down that path with the strangers he had met? Did his marriage to Louisa prevent all that?

Her final SpirDir session became the beginning of a new relationship. Alice moved her chair so that she could take Louisa's hand.

She told her that although she was laying down SpirDir for the time being, she would like Louisa to be her soul friend, her prayer partner for the years ahead.

"It has been a great privilege to share your life, your pain and your doubts. I want to share some of my experiences with you. Would you see me regularly and share our lives together?" Louisa burst into tears.

"You may need to see a trained counsellor as well and Jeff will help you find one, but I do not want to lose you. You have gone through loneliness, trauma, stress, lack of sex, lack of love, and lack of children. Please agree to stay in my life."

The Case History ended and a loving relationship of mutual support began. They decided on fortnightly meeting to begin with. Louisa was invited to Sunday lunch to meet Derry. They went to the swings with the children and a walk by the river. Alice began to tell her of the links which resonated with her as Louisa recounted her story. She started by telling her about her Jewish mother with German origins and her escape from the Nazis.

Next time she told her about her gay brother and his partner.

"That's when I began to change my theology." Alice mentioned how she had to rethink science and evolution and the meaning of the Bible today. Over the months she mentioned her nephew in Romania.

She heard about Louisa's move to the Catholic Church. She had read John Henry Newman's life story and was familiar with his hymns and other writings so she visited the Oxford Oratory and his old home, now a museum and retreat centre just outside Oxford. She discovered silent Meditation, Centring Prayer and found a group to attend.

"When society opened up to gay people and the church began to do the same I really did offer Reg his freedom to make healthy relationships. I did really mean it. He was not capable of forming relationships as such. He did not want to go down that path because he was in the grip of addiction to porn."

Louisa talked about her hobbies of art and craft and poetry writing. "You must come when my artist friend is here with his wife."

Louisa's life was transformed. She was more and more accepted by Derry and the children and they called her 'Granny Lou,' Alice went to the Oratory with her and recalled the Mass she had been to in Cairns cathedral. She really appreciated the beauty of the Mass and started to read Newman.

Joseph became 'the boy with the map on his head' in the family and at Mother and Toddler Group. Alice and Derry took a look at an Atlas of Australia to see if any of the island shapes was a match to his birthmark. The peninsula at Yarrabah bore a resemblance but they would have to look elsewhere for the elongated island.

Alice and Derry had a D and M in the lounge one evening. She wanted to tell him about Louisa because she had kept the confidentiality rules and not shared anything with him while she was in SpirDir role.

"She is amazing. She has come through such terrible pain but she has not given up on God. She wants answers so she asked for Spiritual Direction to get help in her confusion and to seek a closer relationship with God. Prayers do not remain unanswered. God is always doing something else. We just find it hard to come to an understanding. It is hard to accept mystery but that is what we have to do while trusting a great God who is beyond what our mind can grasp"

"Alice dear, she had found God in finding you. You care for her; you want to include her in your life after her years of rejection. You have found so much to share. The children have taken to her. She has such a lovely way with them. I think we adopt her as a Granny."

Alice told him that she would include her when Abigail and Justin came as she was interested in art.

"Bring some of your art work when Abigail is here. Justin's are huge, so I doubt he will bring any. They will have photos though.

"How would you feel about a trip to his gallery in London one day?"

"With three children?"

"Not that visit. I have baby sitters and Derry is often at home working and I have a lovely brother who comes often to look after his niece and nephews. You will meet him first and hear his story. He is a musician."

"That sounds wonderful. I'd love to do that. I do go to London sometimes as I love the galleries and museums. I love the music of Eric Whitacre and I have twice been to a concert of his. I drive down to London and use a Park and Ride." Louisa said. "I could also baby sit for you sometimes once the children have got to know me and I understand their little ways."

"Please come Friday week and eat with Abigail and Justin and we can arrange the London trip."

Louisa left her feeling as if she were walking on air. This wonderful family had adopted her as a Granny.

"From Case Study to Grandma." Alice told Jeff who quite understood that Alice needed to wait a few months or years before she could become a regular Spiritual Director.

7 Granny Lou

Large painted pebbles, greetings cards and a few framed acrylics were spread out on the coffee table in the lounge. Louisa produced mainly abstract designs. There were colourful geometric patterns in the frames, birds, flowers and letters of the alphabet on the pebbles and the cards were abstract, bold coloured streaks framed by the cut-out card frames. A few were collages in themes of animals or flowers.

She chatted with Justin about his own abstracts and his unusual photographs which she saw on his iPad.

"You have a real gift," she said, "I am looking forward to visiting you and your studio with Alice. I can see real potential here. Do you ever work with themes of thoughts and titles or do they come later?"

Justin could hardly believe that and elderly, retired, professional lady would show interest in his works.

"It does change," he began, "it is like therapy for me as I found it so hard to deal with my father and my emotional reaction to him. I needed to express anger and frustration. Later when I was able to exhibit in galleries I needed to express freedom and boldness. They were general ideas but gradually as I worked, thoughts and titles developed as the sculptures or collages developed. On rare occasions a word or phrase grabbed my attention and I tried to find ways of expressing these thoughts.

"It is just a hobby for me but it is also a therapy. It is relaxing to paint. I am not very good at representational art but usually ideas for titles come second. I sell them in charity shops and use them as presents."

"What are your recent works dealing with?"

"My lovely wife. I cannot do her justice but I am trying a portrait and she models for photos. Look at her wedding dress." He enlarged the little photo. "I want to do a series with those flowers. I must find a way to express love and also gratitude that she was willing to marry me." Justin was very at ease with Louisa. Derry did Daddy duty while the four of them went to the Oxford Art Galleries.

On their return, Derry was feeding his daughter and sons. They sat round the garden table. He was very capable of handling his three little ones at the same time.

"What's this?" Louisa picked up the pterodactyl. "It's Joseph's teddy substitute." laughed Derry.

"What's Derry short for?" she had never thought of it before. "Derwent. I was named after a river!"

"He's Professor Derwent Barnes." added Alice.

She went to prepare a meal for the adults and Abigail joined her. Louisa sat with the children and spoke to them.

"Miriam, do you like painting"

"Yes. I use my fingers."

"What do you like painting?"

"Flowers and a house. I want a dog."

Derry looked up, "Do you darling? You mean a real dog?"

"I want a dog to play with."

"We'll think about it, Miriam, when we come back from holiday." He remembered how she loved Zippy in Cairns. He knew he would probably have a trip to Peru in the next year and he wondered about leaving Alice with three children and a dog.

He next asked Louisa about her Meditation Group. She explained that about 4-6 people met in her village and they used the John Main approach with a mantra or anchor word.

"I lead sometimes."

"That's what we did in Cairns. I hear you write poetry."

"I have written some poetic meditations in the past when I was going through hard times. It was my way of calling out to God."

"Could I read some?"

"I will bring some after your holiday. Do you write too?"

"Not exactly poems. I have written some prayers for the children and some for my family when they had to face some problems. I did write one for our Day of Reflection in Cairns."

"Can I see that one?"

"Swop when we next meet."

Louisa found a large card and typed out a couple of her 'Songs from God' section which had given her blessing in traumas. She prepared it for her visit in about a month's time.

Derry and Alice realised they needed something like a people carrier with three children and room for luggage. He mentioned the dog to Alice.

"She has talked about a dog a few times. It is so good for children to grow up with a dog. She remembers Zippy. I'd love one but perhaps when Joseph is walking. End of the year perhaps."

Justin and Abigail had related well to both Louisa and Derry. Justin felt rather overawed to be speaking with a professor.

"My Dad would be proud of me." he smiled.

They returned to their studio home and he had more inspiration for his exhibition on Loving or Lovers. He remembered Sandrine's words and decided to put on an exhibition together on his ground floor.

The Barnes family squeezed everyone into the car and drove to Dorset. He had booked a large lodge with three bedrooms and a deck with a table. It was in a camp on the cliff top near Durdle Door.

The site had a swimming pool and plenty of activities for children; swings, climbing ropes and roundabouts. Miriam and Thomas ran to the park and squealed with delight. Derry stood at the top of the cliff to watch the sunset. Alice did not have to cook every day as there was a restaurant on site, wonderfully appointed for families. They walked on the sand, played in the sea and visited Swanage, Monkey World and the Tank museum. Thomas thought he was in seventh heaven with the tanks.

Towards the end of the second week, Alice was a little concerned. When their little ones were sleeping she sat with Derry on the deck. She placed a candle and some wine on the table. He came and put his arms round her. She kissed him.

"Dearest, my period was due this week and it has not come. It could just be late."

"Joseph will be one in December so if you are pregnant now the baby will be due in spring."

"Well I am happy to have a big family but I am a little surprised that they have come so quickly. I feel we need a longer gap."

"If you are not pregnant this time we must certainly do that!"

“We must make a nursery for them. Two of each would be convenient. But otherwise it will be one for Miriam and three to share.”

“I usually wait until I am sure before I tell you but this time I did not take a note of dates because I was so concentrating on sessions with Louisa.”

“Our first night here, one night when Justin and Abigail were with us, the night when you were so upset over Louisa’s story.”

“Isn’t it great how she related to Justin? I am looking forward to her meeting Daniel and Charles too. I must tell her about them before they meet.”

Derry had babies and dogs on his mind as he packed the car. He would look for a new one as soon as they got back and before he started his writing.

Justin had given a few suggestions of dates for their trip to the gallery. Daniel and Charles had been to Leipzig for concerts and then went for a two-week holiday in the Black Forest. They were experienced walkers so they followed the many paths through the forest and hills. Alice gave them the suggested dates to see if they could come for a few days so she and Louisa could go to the Art Studio. They chose a Thursday towards the end of August. They would arrive on the Wednesday and stay until Saturday.

Alice had no period when she came home. She then started being sick in the morning. She was sure then so she made a date to see the doctor with her estimated date chart.

Louisa arrived with a card and poems for Derry. He said he would go and read them in the study. The children greeted her gladly. Joseph was happy to be picked up by her and to play with his pterodactyl with her.

“Shall I bring some pebbles one day for Miriam to paint?”

“What paints do you use?”

“Acrylic but they are not suitable for children. You cannot get them out of clothes and they dry very quickly.”

“I will get some more children’s paints for her. She will love to paint pebbles.”

“How was your holiday? Thank you for the postcard.”

“Wonderful. We loved it. Derry has bought a new vehicle as it was such a squash to get in. We are considering getting a dog and, big news…I think I am pregnant again.”

“How lovely, Alice, I am so pleased for you.”

“You’ll have four grandchildren next year and Joseph will only be one!”

"If it's a boy I will help you buy a train set to go round the house. If it is a girl, you will need a doll's house."

"My brother Daniel is coming towards the end of the month. He will come with his partner, Charles."

"A gay couple?"

"They have been together since the early 80s. They are musicians, they play piano mainly as soloists, duettists and as part of an orchestra."

"We have shared so many things in our lives, Alice."

They arranged for them to meet Alice on the Thursday over supper. She said she would cook a meal for the 5 adults.

"Do you all like curry?" They did so she planned to make a chicken Balti with rice and other dishes and keep it in the freezer.

Derry came out to the garden where they were supervising the children in the sandpit. He drew up a chair near Louisa.

"Thank you for this beautiful card. It makes me think of outer space."

"I often try to depict the vastness of the galaxies, the universe and the greatness of the Creator and how small we are."

"And Louisa your poems are so moving. I really love them. 'Sometimes' and 'I know you' come as if from God."

"I often felt I heard from God but not all of the words became poems. Some became actions and decisions, not necessarily wise ones." She smiled and the tension and agony seemed to have come out of her.

"Here, Alice, go and have a read. I'll stay here."

Alice took the card and poems into the study. She read two of the poems that she had written when she was struggling with understanding God's will, God's leading in her life.

Sometime, sometimes
I break into your life.
Sometimes, sometimes
I bring my love and light
When you are not seeking me.
Sometimes, sometimes
I come to you
When you are not expecting me.

Sometimes, sometimes,
You ask and seek and knock
And you hear nothing
You receive no open door.
Sometimes, sometimes
The sky seems as brass
And you think I am not there.

When you ask
When you seek
When you knock
I am with you.
When you do not know
When you do not feel
I am there
I am working in you
I am purifying your heart
I am sifting out your mind
I am helping you die to self,
Yield all to me.

Sometimes, sometimes
You seek and do not find.
Then I am with you in your seeking
I am with you when you do not find
I am changing your heart and mind.

I know you.

I know you; I know you.
I know your heart, the way you feel
The way you feel about yourself
The things you hate about yourself
The colours of your emotions.

I know your mind

The way you think
I know the questions never shared
The questions quietly asked
The doubts you try to fight
The whirling darkness of your thoughts
I know them all.

I know the hidden things pushed down so far
You think they're hidden
Even from yourself
I know your fear,
Your very real fear
The primal pain of bringing up and bringing out
Those deep, deep hidden things.
I know you better than you know yourself.

I see you and I ask you
To bring them all to me
I know you and I love you
Let me in to every part
Open every hidden depth to me
I alone bring light to heal
I see you and I know you and I love you
I am everywhere
You can find me anywhere
Spend time with me
I know you and I love you and I want you
In my company
I want you to be with me.

Alice felt tears running down her cheeks because she knew what they represented. But there was so much love to and from God that she was stirred emotionally. She felt so blessed that she had such a loving husband and four children to bring up. She really wanted to reach out more and share her blessings with people in need. She rejoined the garden group.

"Do you ever use them for other people?"

"I kept them in a book for years and never thought of them as poetry. In more recent years as I was introduced to Meditation and saw the poems of other people I realised I could use them, sometimes as an introduction to our Meditation."

"Louisa, do use them. Get them into categories and print them out. One day we will have Days of Reflection again and we can sell them there. Derry said he would help her as he already had contacts with some printers. She was happy to edit them and had already put some into categories. One section was about becoming a new Catholic. She had read a lot and studied the old sticking points; the Virgin Mary, the Saints and the Sacraments. She could almost produce a whole book but she preferred to make smaller collections, perhaps with some explanations.

"Derry you have not given me your poem yet."

"Here we are. It was part of the Day of Reflection in Queensland when we were considering Aboriginal Spirituality. We had an Aboriginal artist who gave us some of her canvases, we had some designs and crafts by Sandrine who was here last year and we learned about dadirri, the silent listening of the Aborigines. The day finished with a meditation introduced by Dreamwalk."

"Does it mean anything?"

"The Dreaming is the word for the tribal belief system, nothing to do with dreams in our culture. It is about the importance of the ancestors, of nature and of the sacred land."

Louisa read it through slowly. "So the colonials do not think much of the tribals. We need to find out more and see that we have something to learn from them."

"That's exactly it!"

"Dreamwalk would go well with a painting. I might have a try with those depictions of people and animals using dots, I think."

Louisa drove over with the food on Thursday morning and found Daniel and Charles having breakfast with the children. She unloaded the food in the kitchen.

"We are so pleased to meet you, Louisa, or Granny Lou. Thank you for befriending Alice." They got up and she went to shake their hand but they both hugged her.

"Have a lovely day in London. We must go to the studio one day. It is not too far from us." Alice kissed her babies. "Be good for your uncles and Daddy. He is busy but he will have lunch with you. See you tonight but I think you will be in bed when Granny Lou and I come home."

"The roads are not too busy so we will park at the docks."

Abigail and Justin gave them coffee and cakes on the third floor. They took the lift and admired the living space. Justin had taken notice of the comments made to him and had started to clear the ground floor. He built a tall, narrow bank of lockers to store the art materials. He moved as much as he could to the second floor where he worked. He planned to clean and paint the walls and turn it into an exhibition space. He would start with small exhibitions but then later do some larger shows for which he would charge.

In her late 70s Louise could not cope with the artistic and atmospheric spiral staircase. She used the lift.

"Make it a feature," she said. "Some people would love to go up but use it as a feature. Hang things on it. Use it for something you make."

"I will. I have good friends who will help me paint and clean."

Louisa wondered what they would do about children if they lived on the third floor, open plan with a drop to the ground floor.

"If I have a baby we could probably manage for about a year. Tricky if we have two. We are waiting for some time though. We are using the pill like you did, Alice."

"Take a seat, Abigail. I have news. I am expecting a fourth baby in about March."

"Four babies! Congratulations dear Alice. We might have to get a bigger flat later and you will need a bigger vehicle."

"Derry ordered a people carrier as soon as we got back from holiday in Dorset."

"Our honeymoon was in Dorset! Great place." said Justin. Louisa studied the canvases and the sketch pads and photos and colour plans.

"I'm planning an exhibition about Love or lovers. I won't charge for that but I shall see how it is received. I shall put up posters and advertise in art galleries, art schools and universities."

"Why not make a small charge to get people in. Art Galleries are so expensive. No one will mind spending £5."

"I'll call it Abigail de Boyadere Gallery."

"How about naming the exhibition 'Lifted by Love'?"

Abigail and Justin looked at each other. "I love it." said Alice.

"Sounds amazing!" Justin responded. "It says exactly what I want to express. The wedding dress will stand in the middle. Canvases on one wall, photos on another or hanging on the spiral stairs, sculptures dotted on stands leaving room for drinks and nibbles on tables near the door."

They went for lunch in a local pub. The area was Bohemian, friendly and colourful.

"I'll get you all lunch. Louisa and I are eating this evening, a meal she has prepared so we will have a snack. Please have a meal if you like." Over lunch Justin told them that his mother had made contact. She was prepared to disobey her husband and see her son and his gallery and his wife. They were all very pleased. She was hoping to change her husband's attitude but they did not have much hope. She had made it clear that she was going to have her son in her life whatever he might think.

On the way home to Oxford Alice told Louisa a little of Daniel's experiences in a church as a student. She said she had totally understood what Reg had been subjected to.

"I expect he was given the same kind of booklets with testimonies of ex-gay people who had been healed."

"Oh yes. We later saw some TV documentaries and read that most of the men had not been changed. Some had married and had children but returned to men, others had stayed in compromised marriages but many had joined an ex-ex-gay movement."

Derry and Daniel had prepared the table for their meal. Charles had put the children to bed and sung and read to them until they fell asleep. At the table Daniel and Charles spoke about music and no one wanted or needed to talk about the past stories. Louisa asked them if they knew the music of Eric Whitacre. They had heard of him but did not know his works. They had heard of similar modern composers like Einaudi but they mainly lived with the well know Classics. More recently they had looked at Gorecki and Arvo Pärt. Daniel was especially interested in the Symphony of Sorrowful songs by Gorecki because they were about people in Nazi Concentration camps and the composer had been unable to perform in Poland because he was Christian until after the Berlin Wall had come down.

Louisa had twice gone to London to hear Eric Whitacre and see him conduct. "He has pop star looks but his music is so moving."

Louisa was very tired after the driving and left after the meal. She was invited to return for their final supper on Friday.

"I do salmon with a pesto sauce. Is that OK?" asked Charles. It was.

"How do you divide the housework?" asked Louisa as she went to the door. "We share the cooking; we both enjoy that. We work around our concerts and commitments. We have a cleaner as it is a large flat and she often does the washing and ironing. We are very lucky."

After she left Alice wanted to ask Daniel how he had recovered from the loss of their parents. He said that Charles had been a brilliant listener and support to him. He did have a few sessions with a counsellor but it was very expensive. Nevertheless they had helped him come to terms with the powerful emotions he sometimes experienced and the way he often felt like weeping.

"And I have some news for you, Daniel and Charles. We are expecting a fourth baby for you to look after"

"Goodness me, Alice, when?"

"I have a scan soon but I think about March."

"I can see you are very happy. Congratulations dear sister. I am sorry they will not know their grandparents."

"We are very happy. Derry has bought a bigger vehicle. Miriam wants a dog too. It's good for children to have a dog but I was hoping to wait until Joseph could walk. You know Mum wanted more children. She told me she was disappointed when she had no more after me but she decided to accept it and just love us both."

Abigail rang to thank them for their stay and to say that Sandrine had invited them to stay with her in Cairns and to visit the Therapy Art Shack to see how it worked; they were delighted with the invitation.

"I will definitely make a small charge and we will go after the Lifted by Love show. I am very interested in using the studio for therapy."

Derry had a call from Paul. He and Vivienne were going on a trip to Peru in summer with some anthropology colleagues.

"It is a non-Inca but sons of Inca trip!" he laughed. "Derry I am asking if you can be our leader. You will not have to be there more than say three weeks. We will gain much more prestige if a professor is heading it up and is with us in the jungle. I have some other tribes to look up near the border areas."

"That is exactly what I want to do!" Derry spoke excitedly. "Can I tell you that Alice is expecting a baby in about March so I shall see she has help while I am away."

"Well done! Congratulations to Derry and Alice. I hope the same will happen for us soon. I would like to be a father before I am 37 and Vivienne is 32 so we both want a baby as soon as possible."

"Let me know any news of a baby Rockingham on the way. All the very best. You have a wide choice of names with your Spanish and Inca connections."

Derry trusted him to choose the most relevant areas of research to enable them to form their charity foundation in the next few years.

On Friday evening they all enjoyed Charles' cooking. Louisa mentioned that she often took herself to London for concerts and said she would like to attend one of theirs.

"The next one is a recital with piano solos and duets and a piece when I accompany a friend on the flute."

"I am not very familiar with recitals, but that sounds lovely."

"Granny Lou, you are like our aunty so we will send you a ticket and a programme in the post."

"How very kind." A tired, happy old lady drove home.

Alice talked to the children about their new baby the next time Louisa was present. Miriam and Thomas understood and were very excited.

"I do hope there are no surprise birthmarks. A few months after the birth, Derry will be in the South American jungle for 3-4 weeks with the American Theologian. He recently married and is hoping to be a father quite soon. They are both in their 30s. If she gets pregnant soon, she will not be able to go to the jungle."

Alice told Louisa that she and Derry would like to hold a weekly meditation group in their home. They had found it impossible to get to one as it was too far to go in the evening with three children and Derry's work schedule.

"Would it be feasible to invite your group to us?"

"I'll see what they say but most of them walk to the meeting in the village. I do not think they would like a 15 to 20-minute drive in the dark. You could just start a new one and ask in the local churches and at the Oratory."

"Two small ones could work."

"If you ask in the Oratory it will not be that small. People living nearer to you might be pleased to come to you instead of the town centre. You might even have to limit numbers. How many could you comfortably fit in?"

"There are 6-7 seats in the lounge already and we could get some stacking chairs. I reckon about 10." She was feeling really positive about making new invitations.

"Louisa please consider joining us if we get a new group and will you also have a think about the time when Derry is away. It is not until summer next year. Please think about coming to stay for that period but please say no if it is too tiring for you. We could reach a compromise and you could just come for odd days to be with the children."

Louisa promised to have a think about all that. At her age she recognised that she had limitations to her energy. She knew that Alice had other baby sitters so she could help out in a team.

Alice went for her scan in late August. The doctor told her that her little girl was already 9-10 weeks on so that she would be born in early February. She was very surprised and had to go back to the calendar and try to remember. She could look at her reports for Jeff which would have been dated.

"My little girl. A sister for Miriam. How wonderful."

She went to a cafe and sat quietly with a coffee to take in the news. *I am assimilating it*, she thought remembering her father.

She had guessed wrongly at the date when she had wept and felt so terrible after her session with Louisa. Derry knew that she was not permitted to tell him the story of a client. He had comforted her with his wonderful massage. She had encouraged him to make love to her as she took oil to caress him too. She remembered saying to him, "Derry, your love is so powerful. You always find new ways to show me your love. I have to feed Joseph now but I don't think he will like the oil so I must have a wash."

She recalled that lovely time together as she sat in the cafe. That must have been April or May. *My new little girl needs a name to express that.* She thought of the Lifted by Love Exhibition that Justin was preparing. She remembered a Bible reading and the name Bethany came into her mind. She went home to Jean who was baby-sitting while Derry worked in the study.

She knocked on the door and went to Derry leaning over his desk. "My dearest, Bethany will be born in February!"

"Bethany! Beautiful." He got up and held her. "I think she was conceived that night when you comforted me with a massage when I was so upset about Louisa's story. Joseph was only 4-5 months old and was in his cot in our room."

"I remember." He held her head, pushed his hands through her thick black hair and kissed her gently.

"Choose a middle name."

"Sarah. Bethany Sarah Barnes."

"You have already had a think! I love it!"

"Did you have a boy's name ready too?"

"No. I just felt you were expecting a girl."

Alice went and thanked Jean and told her the news.

"I so want to use my home and my family and my friendship groups to help others in need"

8 A Year of Babies, a Dog and the Sons of Incas

Christmas drew near and the Barnes Children became very excited. A new baby in February was nothing compared to the puppy coming for Christmas. Joseph was tottering and nearly walking. His older brother and sister were sweet and kind with him most of the time. Alice sat looking at them. Miriam was the only one with the thick, black curly hair that Esther had passed down to her. The others had straight, brown hair like Derry's. Granny Lou went with the family to choose a dog. Miriam wanted all of them. They found a litter too young to be separated from the mother. The owners picked out six little brown and white Springer spaniels and let them run around the coop. Thomas and Miriam were lifted in. They bent down and one puppy constantly came up to them. Granny Lou picked it up and saw it tagged for them.

It was difficult for Alice to explain why they could not take him home that day but in the end they accepted that they would come back just before Christmas to collect him. She distracted them by taking them to the shop to choose a collar and lead, a bed and some toys. She held Joseph and let him stroke the puppy in Granny Lou's arms. He smiled and stroked rather roughly in the wrong direction.

"The next task is to agree on a name. More difficult than for a baby! We'll wait till we get him home and see what Miriam and Thomas come up with."

Alice was making posters and adverts for the new Meditation Group starting in January. She mentioned that numbers would be limited to 10. Louisa said she would join them if there were enough spaces but that she would also continue with her own village group.

"Have you ever had a massage?" Alice asked her. "Once or twice."

"I am going to look into healing massages and I am thinking of ways we could serve people."

"Healing massage? Sounds interesting. I am going to see your brother next week at his recital. It clashes with Meditation so I will miss that week."

"That's lovely. I hope you enjoy it!"

"I shall go for the day and visit a museum first." She had been trying to paint a picture to go with Dreamwalk and discovered that the dot work was not as easy as it looked. She had bought some books and searched for ideas on the internet.

Derry and Paul were using Skype to plan the trip to Peru. Paul had discovered a people whose ancestors pre-dated the Incas. The descendants of the Aymara people lived near Bolivia and tried to live in communities which kept up their old traditions. The more he looked, the more he found. He asked the local anthropologists to identify some tribes for him. Near the Amazon border he heard of the Matis tribe.

In October Paul phoned Derry to tell him that Vivienne was pregnant and so he would have to change his planning. No way could a new born be taken to the rain forest. Just before Christmas he phoned again.

"It's not about the trip, Derry. Vivienne is expecting twins."

"Congratulations. It will be a year of babies. Do you know the sex yet?"

"Not exactly. One is a boy but we cannot see the other clearly enough."

"Alice will be pleased. Do get Vivienne to ring her."

Vivienne giggled down the phone, "We were keen to start a family soon and now we have a ready-made one already. Our parents are delighted." Alice thought about Abigail and Justin both estranged from their parents to some degree.

On the day of the Recital, Louisa drove to the north London Park and Ride and spent the day in the British Museum. She rested in a park, had a pub lunch and then went to the church for the concert. She found her seat in the middle, two rows back. She felt so proud when the three performers came up on stage and bowed. The flautist sat to one side for the solos and duets. The last piece before the interval was very haunting flute music, unfamiliar to Louisa. The second half began with a lively duet followed by a long, meditative piano piece played by Daniel. The flute finished it all.

There was a standing ovation with cheers which surprised Louisa. Daniel stepped down from the stage, picked up a posy and walked to Louisa.

"You are the nearest person to a much-loved relative. Thank you for coming." he said softly.

"Is he your son?" asked her neighbour.

"More like an adopted nephew." she replied. She lovingly shielded her posy on the train back to the P and R bus. She was tired of course but she was overwhelmed by joy when she looked back on her tentative steps in Spiritual

Direction, feeling like a failure and crushed by confusion at the sadness in her life. This step had led her to be given this lovely family to accompany her during her last years of life.

Two days before Christmas Louisa accompanied them to pick up the puppy.

"What shall we call him?" asked Alice. Miriam looked down at him in his new blue collar. Thomas bent and stroked him, "Hello doggy. You are our doggy." he said.

"What's your name?" Alice asked the puppy.

"Is he perhaps Hunter? He will hunt balls and toys if you hide them from him." suggested Louisa.

"He is Hunter Barnes, Miriam." Alice looked at her. "He cannot be Zippy, can he?"

"We already know a Zippy. He can't be Zippy. Try calling him."

Alice led him away and the little girl's high-pitched voice called the puppy as she bent down. Fortunately, he obliged by leaping towards her.

The Barnes decided to have a quiet Christmas as Alice was so large and so tired. Louisa usually spent the day with old friends and did the same that year. In spite of the Christmas activities, Alice was still preoccupied with ideas she could initiate to bring healing, hope and support to people. The Meditation Group was top of her list. Six strangers had booked in for the first meeting in January. Derry was leading with music and a reading but he felt it was important to explain what this silent prayer time was all about for any people who were not familiar with it. Louisa agreed to take turns in leading especially after Bethany was born.

Alice and Derry strolled around the garden one evening.

"I suppose we will make use of the tennis court when the children are older and can invite friends round. We still have a lot of space after the children's play area."

"What are you thinking of?"

"A building as a spiritual centre for Meditation, counselling, massage and other therapies."

"That sounds like a wonderful idea. We would need a lot of help with planning permission, trained therapists and so on. Perhaps rather too much to take on with a new baby, a dog and three toddlers."

Alice knew that now was not the time and that she would not be able to cope with it for several months. Derry was a born project manager.

“We could call on the same architect and he could draw a plan, cost it and investigate planning permission. It overlooks woodland and would block no one’s view. There is enough garden space around the house.”

“You are getting carried away.”

“He will be doing all the work. You can sit and give him commands, the number of small group room, the size of the main meeting hall.”

“I’ve lit the fire and you will rocket off now!”

“I must get back to Paul and Koda for the final plans for our trip. We need to check on accessibility to the new tribe. It is a vast subject, far too much for us so we must prioritise. Koda wants to look at how the communities function now, what rights they have. Paul wants to look at the religions and the post-colonial influences. Paul has a linguist on his American team.” Derry explained that they would have to get injections and take medication and creams with them as they were venturing into the rain forest.

Hunter ran around the grounds with them. “He’s gorgeous!” said Alice.

The first Meditation went well. There were 4 women and 2 men from Anglican and Catholic churches. Derry explained that the first meditation would only be for 15-20 minutes because he needed to tell them what to do and what not to do.

“Do not try to think about things. John Main’s method of getting us to draw close to God was for us to choose a mantra or prayer word. We say this in silence over and over in our heads to stop us thinking about anything else but to concentrate on the Presence of God.” Over coffee they chatted and shared a little about themselves, their churches and their prayer experiences.

“We shall start promptly and end promptly and we shall not take too long over refreshments as we have three, soon four sleeping children upstairs. Fortunately we have reliable baby sitters.”

It was February 14th when Alice went into labour.

“A Valentine girl.” she said but the labour lasted for a long time and Bethany was not born until the morning of the 15th. Louisa stayed in the Granny flat for the first week but then returned home and joined in with the team of helpers. Bethany had no birthmarks on her face but two small ones on her leg and one on her upper arm. The other children stood round the cot as Derry anointed her and prayed over her. She did not have the black, curly hair but her brown hair was quite thick and not totally straight.

Two nurseries had been made, a large one where all four could play and a smaller one where the two girls could sleep. Alice prepared for the visits of Maddy and family and Daniel and Charles to meet Bethany. Louisa investigated doll's houses and train sets for future birthdays.

"I like the idea of a building in your grounds. Will it be part of the charity Foundation?"

"It could be, that's beyond me, and Derry will work it out with his University colleagues.

"He has a long list of interested supporters."

Paul learned what it was like to leave loved ones behind. In June, Vivienne gave birth to twin boys. They were tempted by indigenous names but they felt it would not be fair on the boys as they grew up.

They named them Nicholas and Victor after ancestors in the Rockingham family. Koda flew to Minnesota to see Vivienne and the twins and both of them flew to Lima with a Peruvian specialist, a linguist and two other colleagues. The six of them were booked into a Lima hotel where Derry joined them the next day. He found it heart breaking to leave his family this time. He was due to set the research in motion near the Bolivian border, spend two weeks with the Aymara tribe and then one week in the rainforest on the Amazon border with the Matis tribe. From there he would fly home leaving his colleagues to complete the studies.

The Aymara people lived in extended family groups and used the ancient Ayllu system of mutual assistance which extended to every aspect of their lives. Their crops were quinoa, beans and potatoes like many other tribes. They added fish and llama to their stews. Some groups lived on floating islands. The linguist used Quechua and Spanish and explained that these people were unusually willing to answer questions and talk about their rituals.

Back in England Alice regretted that she could not get to the Lifted by Love exhibition at de Boyadere Gallery. Louisa, Daniel and Charles met up there and went for a meal together.

People paid the small entrance fee and came in their dozens every day. A reporter wrote a positive article with photos and made a double page spread. 'Lifted to Paradise by Love' was the headline. It was a spectacular show with bright colours. There were paintings of flowers, hand-made paper flowers and a wall of real flowers. The dress was in the centre near the spiral stairs. Hangings from those rails were huge, close-up photographs of bees' wings, legs, butterflies and parts of flowers. A journalist from ITV arrived and interviewed Justin. His photo was in the papers, on the news bulletin and in a documentary on art.

Abigail rang Alice so she could watch the coverage and they wondered if their parents would see it. Daniel took a video to show Alice and Derry.

She was coping well with the support of Louisa, the baby sitters, Jean and her brother.

"One more week and Daddy will be home." Alice lit up the globe and showed them where he was. The guide took them to the more inaccessible tribes. They sailed up a river with camping gear. They were putting up the tents when Paul and Derry both yelled.

"I've been bitten!"

"Something has bitten me!"

"I saw a yellow, furry caterpillar." said Derry. Their pain was like nothing they had ever experienced. Out came the creams and the disinfectant.

"What did you see?" asked the guide.

"A yellow, fluffy thing, quite big, a few centimetres long." They both noticed red dots swelling up in the bite area.

"It looks like a little shoe imprint!" said Paul.

"I am sorry you are going to feel unwell for a few days. You will need anti-itch cream but it will go quite soon." They certainly felt unwell. Paul was robust and seemed to cope with the pain but after two days Derry was pale and vomited frequently. He looked near to collapse and the team decided he should go to hospital. Paul felt he should go with him. They made a stretcher using the tent and rowed back to the last little town. Paul called for an air ambulance and they flew to Lima hospital. Alice was in the study when the call came.

"Alice, listen I am sorry but Derry is in Lima hospital. He has suffered an allergic reaction to a bite. I had the same bite, hell on earth, but I am OK. He is getting the treatment he needs and usually people recover in time. Here is the number if you want to call the ward."

"Can I talk to him?"

"Not yet. He is semi-conscious and sick." What agonies they all went through. Alice told the children that Daddy would be delayed but did not tell them he was so ill.

His doctor was concerned about his breathing. He was put onto oxygen.

"It was not a bite but the toxin in little tubes in the hairs of the Southern Flannel Moth or the Furry Puss Moth. It is painful and not usually serious but this man has had an allergic reaction. He will get better."

St Marcus sent out their medical advisor so Paul could return for the last few days to his team and the professor could be brought home.

Alice was extremely grateful. Paul rejoined his team and Derry was flown to a London hospital. Abigail and Daniel went to see him. Alice arranged to come to London as Louisa and Jean looked after the four children. Alice had a pounding heart on the train journey and tried some meditation to calm down. She was still shocked to see him, the tubes, the colour of his skin and the red swellings on his arm.

Alice held his hand and spoke softly to him. He opened his eyes and moved his mask. "So sorry, dearest. Something bit me. I will be better soon."

"Paul was wonderful. He stayed with you and took you to Lima by air ambulance."

"Where am I?"

"London, tropical diseases. You need help to breathe and you are on medication."

"Alice, do not come. I have enough carers. Stay at home, rest and enjoy our babies. We can Skype every day. What a terrible fuss I am causing." He replaced the mask and took some breaths.

Abigail and Justin, Daniel and Charles were regular visitors. Maddy and Zara came up from Epsom. The red swellings went down and he managed to drink a little soup and eat a little toast and keep it down.

The specialist told him about the Flannel Moth and said they were taking samples from his body for their records as he had such a bad reaction.

"I have never felt so ill in all my life, Are there any long-term effects"

"You will be weak for a few weeks and you will not have much appetite. You will gradually recover as the toxins work their way out of your body. We will have you back for a thorough check after you have been home for a month.

"I have four babies at home. One was born in February." It took two more weeks before he was released. He was told to check in with his GP. Paul went home to Vivienne but phoned Derry every 2-3 days and so did Koda. Daniel collected him and drove him to Oxford. He said he would take him down again in a month for the check-up.

"Stay away from caterpillars!"

He was able to walk from the car and hug all his children. He was told to take two days bed rest but he needed an arm to help him get up the stairs. Louisa showed him Daniel's video of the exhibition and Alice sat on the bed to watch it with him.

"Stunning. Absolutely marvellous!"

"They are off to Cairns soon to stay with Sandrine."

"I will pay for them to have a weekend at Thala. Can you arrange that Alice?"

"Of course. I will send a bank transfer to Sandrine and she can sort it out."

At meditation Alice gave prayers of thanks for Derry's return before leading into the 30 minutes of silence.

She sometimes put Bethany in the cot with Joseph. They seemed to enjoy being together and Bethany began taking an interest in the pterodactyl. Her cries for food were louder than the others and her giggling was also some decibels louder, making the others laugh.

Louisa finished the painting of dancing figures, seated groups among rivers and paths. She decided to give it to Derry when he could come downstairs. Once the London hospital had sent the details to the Oxford GP, Derry had an appointment. Alice drove him to the surgery.

"You have four little children and you risk your life in the rain forest." The doctor sounded annoyed. It hit Derry like a blow in the stomach. Alice was not sure of her reaction but she longed for him never to be in danger again.

Derry got up and came down every day but he was not yet able to function normally. He could not read for very long, losing concentration after about quarter of an hour. He made sure he spent time with each child every day. He had a walk in the garden with Hunter each day. Alice was concerned to see him in such a weak state but she was pleased with all the support he got. The meditation group was her anchor, her haven of rest and the members were pleased to see Derry join them. Louisa came to take Hunter out and play with him in the garden. Derry loved her canvas and promised to hang it when he was stronger. Colleagues from St Marcus visited him and made plans for the new term if he was still unable to resume his duties.

Charles and Louisa stayed with the children. The health check took hours and was very thorough, blood, liver, muscles, brain, heart and lungs and breathing.

"Professor Derwent you have had a nasty shock. You are recovering but you will not feel stronger for several months. You could work some of the time but you will need plenty of rest. What have you got coming up?"

"The new term will not start until late September. I have a day conference soon after that. Now I have the report for my caterpillar trip, some departmental planning and some writing."

"Good, mostly sedentary. No trips?"

"A lecture tour in Australia next year."

"Something to aim for. We'll check you again in 6 months."

Derry was relieved but realised he and Alice needed a serious talk about the next few months. They found Hunter rushing around the lawn with Miriam and Thomas. Joseph was in the sand pit and Bethany was drinking a bottle in Charles' arms. Derry shared the outline of his results with them.

"I must be patient and not expect too much too soon but at least I am in the clear."

The Meditation Group was a real help to him. His anxiety level went down and he had some hope restored to him. He decided to hold the first meeting to set up the Foundation early in the term but he thought that Paul and Koda should not make the effort to come to that one. He would get the basics agreed on and then they could attend the next formal meeting with the lawyer. He invited Paul to come to take some lectures on the Aymara and Matis peoples, possible around the time of the charity foundation being legally set up.

Alice booked Derry in for a healing massage in a parlour in town.

"I agree that these massages are very helpful. It would be a good service to offer. Let's get the architect back with his plans now my drama is nearly over."

"You will pace yourself, Derry dear. Let me know when you need a rest."

"You remember we talked about contraception so we could leave bigger gaps between babies? Well this is the best contraception so far. I hope it will not last too long."

"We need to change our life style, our priorities. You must get better first. When we can make love again I shall offer you a celebratory treat of your choice."

9 The Hartley Barnes Foundation

The Aboriginal picture by Louisa was framed with Dreamwalk and hung on the wall on the staircase. Louisa was thinking ahead to her 80th birthday. She thought she might hire the back rooms of the Eagle and Child and have a C S Lewis themed party in the late autumn.

She made friends with the new meditation group members. They were mainly consistent attenders. One lady dropped out but a new man from the Oratory joined as he lived nearer to the house.

The flat was used for various visitors, Maddy and Roy, Zara and a boyfriend and Kyle booked it for a week in autumn.

Paul and Vivienne sent lovely photos of their twins.

"I think they are identical. I was expecting Inca names but they chose traditional names in the end." Derry added.

"A mother can always tell the difference, I gather." Alice smiled.

In August the architect brought his plans for them to see. Alice had talked him through her plans for various rooms and for one main meeting room. The plans themselves cost several hundred pounds and the planning permission was still to come. Alice listed the activities, healing or spiritual massage, counselling, Art Therapy, Spiritual Direction training and small retreats so a few single bedrooms could be included. The large meeting room would have glass walls with blinds, two small toilet blocks with showers and basins, a kitchen with two hobs and a large oven with wall cupboards for crockery. Derry sat with him to draw up the Planning Application. The stimulation helped him feel better.

When the inspector and technicians came, Derry walked around the grounds with them. Mr Bowden took many photographs from all angles and he walked outside the grounds to see the impact the building would have. He walked through the woodland where there were some public footpaths. The single storey building would hardly be seen. He sent the technicians with various instruments to make measurements.

"You have no neighbours except trees. You are lucky. Your drive goes nowhere except to your house. What about parking?"

“You see on the plan, behind the building there are spaces and we have at least 10 spaces around the house.”

“Your privacy?”

“We are not building for ourselves or for profit. It will be part of a charitable foundation.”

“Oh, which one is that?”

“It is in the early stages of being formed by St Marcus College.”

“What’s it for?”

“We are anthropologists and we travel widely and see deprivation and poverty among the indigenous people. Our charity is to support them with building clinics, homes, schools.”

“What kind of people?”

“Tribes and natives. But this building here is for the poor and needy in the UK.”

“All very interesting. OK, Sir and Madam I will take the information back to the committee. They meet towards the end of December.”

They thanked him and saw them all off. Louisa was inside with the children. She had found a train set and a doll’s house for them. Miriam loved the train set as well as Thomas. Joseph loved playing with the tiny furniture from the doll’s house. They were both a great success with the little Barnes.

Derry was able to get down so some writing not for ‘the man in the street’ but for the ‘reader in the pew’. Louisa, Alice and Daniel tried them out for him. Hunter was totally a member of the family. They often walked him in the woods and threw balls for him on the lawn.

“He won’t like losing his lawn.” said Derry.

“And he will give the builders a hard time. He’ll bark like mad when they start.”

Louisa and Daniel met again at de Boyadere Gallery. Abigail and Justin contacted Alice to thank her for the Thala weekend. They sent a huge thank-you card with clothes for the children. Justin had loved the Art Therapy Shack.

“He was thrilled by it and he is finding out how he can make space in his studio. If he has a show on there will be no room. Lifted by Love was such a success he wants to do others with an entrance fee. He is contacting the Mental Health Services and any other providers to find out what the take up might be.” Abigail was so excited she could hardly stop talking. Justin had been contacted by other journalists and had appeared on another documentary. He had even had a haircut and a beard trim but that was the only concession to the norms of society. Abigail asked after Derry's health.

"He is improving slowly. We are waiting for the green light for our building project. Did we tell you we are planning to add Art Therapy to the services on offer? We have a week's holiday in Dorset before he returns to the university. He cannot make love yet but I am going back on the pill to prevent another quick pregnancy when he does."

"Have you seen a doctor?"

"Yes. His own GP is monitoring him and wants to wait a while longer before using medication. His body took a severe beating."

In Dorset, their sleeping babies allowed them to sit on the deck and watch the sunset.

"In Peru, when we sailed down a river we rounded a bend where the river opened out to a wide stretch. There was the most gorgeous sunset. I wish you could have seen it. I was not able to film as we were passing the territory of a tribe for whom we had no filming permission. The top of the sky was like black cloud, then a dark purple streak. Underneath was the bright setting sun and pink streaks reflected in the river. I thought of you and then we soon landed in caterpillar land."

"Derry, I am back on the pill so that I do not get pregnant so quickly when you can make love."

The check-up was due before Louisa's birthday. All went well and the tests revealed that there were no problems with his organs and blood. His impotence, he was told, was a normal reaction to toxic shock and allergy.

"I do not want to try and fail."

"Would your wife cope if you tried and nothing happened?"

"I think so."

"We can give you something to help you both. Here is a pamphlet to read."

Derry was grateful but really hoped he could avoid medication and aids. He showed the pamphlet to Alice and they both agreed to wait while there were so many events to deal with; Louisa's birthday and the launch of the charity Foundation.

Alice went with Louisa to choose the menu and ensure there was space for about 25 people. Each guest had to bring a quotation from C S Lewis. This was a popular idea and the party went very well. Miriam and Thomas came for the first half hour with the distribution of presents. Derry took them home to where Jean was baby-sitting and they swopped roles as she went to join the party.

Derry had contacted all the volunteers on his lists and was pleased to see that just over 80 people turned up. He had invited a lawyer and a member of the Charity Commission. Notes were handed to everyone. He listed the areas of their concern; support for the building of homes, schools and clinics in the urban areas and reservations in First Nation Canada, Aboriginal Australia, a tribal area of Nigeria and the tribal areas of Peru and Bolivia. Second came the staff to be appointed; a group with a leader for each geographical area. They would receive travel expenses. Third he wanted a team of fund raisers with inspirational ideas. The final page was headed 'Charity begins at Home' He described how he and his wife wished to donate land and a building to open a healing centre as a service to the local people in Oxford. He explained that this was dependant on them getting planning permission. He listed the group of activities that they had given to the inspector. The Meditation Group will be affiliated to the WCCM. He asked for general comments and questions before people broke into various groups.

"What did Art Therapy entail? How would the building relate to the charity foundation at the university? How would the anthropology department be involved?"

"Art Therapy. I am no expert but we saw one in operation in Queensland and the artist de Boyadere is about to start one in East London. The therapy will be for anyone struggling with depression, mental problems, stress and so on.

"The building will be set up to be self-funding and the services offered will undercut those of the private and commercial world. It is 'watch this space'. The charity foundation can function without the building if necessary.

"The anthropology department will continue its normal research. We shall contact the departments in the countries we are involved with and contact the departments in other UK universities. I already have quite a team in three countries. My colleagues can be as involved or separate from the charity as they wish."

A long-haired woman in hippy style clothes stood up.

"I love your work so far. I was at your conference and I was in Queensland when you did the presentations with Mary Ruth. I am from the Anthropology Department at Norwich University and I would like to offer to lead this group. First, though, I would like to congratulate you on this initiative. Well done Professor Barnes. Especially as I gather that your wife has just given birth to a baby and that you have recently recovered from a toxic bite in the rainforest." There was a burst of applause. "It is a privilege to know you. We need more like you." She sat down to more applause.

"Thank you very much, Doctor, please give your details in at the group. First will those interested in being attached to a geographical area please meet my colleague Caroline at the back of the hall. Second, in the first small group room, please will all those interested in fund raising meet Bronwyn in the second small group room. All the other volunteers who would be happy to be called on for making adverts, posters or distributing them or making any other specific offers of help, talk with Aziz in the other front corner. Aziz had lists headed printing, distributing, advertising, legal issues or total blanks.

"Finally, anyone with ideas or actual contacts to help provide staff for the Foundation House, please see me at the front of the hall. Please reconvene in 45 minutes."

Derry reminded his group that he did not yet have planning permission. He explained that it was mainly his wife's inspiration but that she could not accompany him on trips as the baby born in February was one of four babies under five. I am young for a professor but I plan for my colleagues to do most of the travelling. We cannot start recruiting until we know we have permission. All we have is the advice of a lawyer, a bereavement counsellor and a leader of Spiritual Direction. We clearly need staff with expertise.

"I will canvas the known practitioners and see if any would be ready to offer an hour or so each week." she added.

"I have qualified people in my family who I know would offer some massage."

"Would you include Reiki and other alternatives?"

"Not initially but we are open to adding other kinds eventually."

"I'm an artist and would be pleased to take a group once a week. Would you include evenings?"

"I should think so for nearly all the groups. We will appoint a manager and a care taker, salaried posts, but it is too early to advertise yet. We need the foundations down at least."

Most groups returned after an hour. The leaders tidied up their lists and handed them to Derry.

"Thank you for coming today and for signing up. I will repeat that we shall appoint a manager and care taker for the building once we know we have got one! For the countries, I suggest you get together and choose a leader for each one. Queensland is taken. Fundraisers please do the same. I am very encouraged by this start. I will call you all together even if we do not get permission to build because we need to establish the charity foundation at the university. We are calling it the Hartley Barnes Foundation."

Derry walked to the group choosing leaders for each country. The Norwich Doctor had four other people prepared to work for the Queensland charity. There was soon a leader for each area with at least two other people.

"I will send you the names of my colleagues heading each area. There is Dr Paul Simon Rockingham in the USA leading the Peruvian and Bolivian tribal areas. In Winnipeg is Dr Koda Keith Blackhill, in Nigeria we have Dr Oluwale and Dr Innundola and I am over the Queensland group. Anyone who prays, please pray for the Oxford Council to agree with our building." He managed to go over to the Dr from Norwich and asked her name.

She said she was Dr Beate von Friedland.

"Your English is perfect but your name is German."

She explained that she was from Frankfurt am Rhine but that she was brought to England by her mother in the 70s when she was a baby.

"My grandfather was a famous Nazi and in the 60s and 70s the Baader Meinhof Gang were hunting Nazis who were still in good jobs in Germany and had never been punished. My father's colleague was murdered. My mother was able to settle with some other relatives in Norfolk."

"My wife will be delighted to meet you. Her mother was also German and you will have a lot to share."

"I would like that Herr Professor."

The best Christmas present was a letter granting the planning permission for the Hartley Barnes Foundation Spiritual Healing Centre. Miriam was attending the first class of the local school so the headmistress has picked up the gossip that the Barnes were going to build on their land. She phoned Alice one day.

"I have been looking for a building which my year 6 could observe. It is a project for them to visit a building site every week and note the progress, the stages of building, and the machinery. They draw, write notes and take photos for the school project wall. They work in pairs or in little groups.

"That is a brilliant idea. They could walk to us. We'd have to consider health and safety with the builders. How many?"

“There would be 25 if they all came at the same time. We could divide them into two groups.”

“I need to speak to my husband. I’ll ring you back.”

“That’s free advertising for our charity!” said Derry.

As if that were not enough to deal with, Kyle rang to say that he and Adina were coming to the UK for a month because they were expecting their first baby.

“It really has been a year of babies. Bethany, Victor and Nicholas and now a Romanian baby. How lovely.” Alice laughed aloud.

“Do we know when baby is due?”

Derry held her in his arms, “Our great nephew is due in May.”

They felt so happy to see so much life opening out before them; The Hartley Barnes Foundation, the Healing Centre, the simplified books, the lecture tour in Australia, the art therapy in Justin’s studio, Dr Paul’s lectures on Peru, the school children’s project on their building and the new life coming to the Barnes family in Epsom and Romania.

“I have a five-year plan like the communists once had,” Alice announced, “When our youngest is 5 we shall have a holiday in a lodge in Queensland with a long weekend in Thala.”

“I like that idea.” He kissed her, “Do you remember the first time we gave each other a perfumed oil massage in Thala?”

“How could I ever forget? Come on then, and do not worry if it still does not work.”

“When I close my eyes I can see that Peruvian sunset.”

They awoke still covered in oil. Alice quickly checked all the children.

Miriam and Thomas were awake but reading their books in bed. Joseph and Bethany were still asleep.

“Stay a little bit longer and we shall all have a pancake breakfast together.” She found Derry just coming to consciousness. She kissed him awake.

“It’s a good job I am on the pill.” She smiled and joined him on the bed and they made love again.

“I promised you a treat. What will it be?”

“Invite Dr Beate von Friedland from Norwich to come for a day or two and treat her to a meal.” Alice was surprised. “She is a German who grew up in England and has quite a story to tell. She is heading up the Queensland Foundation work. She escaped with her mother in the late 70s because the Baader Meinhof Gang were hunting and killing some Nazis who were in powerful companies and had never been punished. One of her father's colleagues was murdered."

"Hanns Martin Schleyer!"

"I know you will have a lot to talk about. She was at the conference and in Australia at our presentation with Mary Ruth. How about that?"

"I'm speechless! Who was the Nazi in her family?"

"Her grandfather was notorious but possibly her father also. She comes from Frankfurt where the Gang bombed a department store."

"It's all in my thesis."

Kyle and Adina arrived in Epsom. His father let him have the car to drive to Oxford. They all hugged and kissed and let their happy visitors meet Bethany and see the other children.

"He is Liviu Barnes." said Adina patting her baby bump. "Liviu, what an attractive name." Alice put an arm round her, "No middle name, that one will be enough for English people."

"I love it!" Alice smiled to see their joy and aware of her own joy that Derry had recovered from his toxic shock without the help of medication"

10 The Inspiration of Doctor Beate

Alice held her glass of crisp, dry, white wine as she sat in her armchair by the white bookshelf. She took sips as she looked over the new books on the shelf. She was amused to see the tiny Peruvian figures standing in front of the books. She had asked Paul to bring back colourful ponchos for Justin and Abigail and he had also squashed in four shawls for the Barnes children and a row of little sewn figures.

He had flown in with Koda and Heinrich and stayed an extra few days to spend time with Dr Beate von Friedland.

Sometimes a person comes into the life of one or two people with an indefinable power, spiritual or psychological, mystical or mysterious; a power which resonates with the deepest parts of their lives. Such was the influence and inspiration which came to the lives of the Barnes through Beate.

Alice had had this experience when she met Louisa. There were resonances with Germany, Romania and gay people in churches. It was Derry who picked up the vibes with Beate. She had been in his meetings twice but he had not noticed her or even been aware of her presence. In St Marcus she had stood up and made offers of support and somehow he knew she would become significant in the work of the Foundation.

Alice sat with her in the study on her first visit to their home. Before she arrived Alice had asked if she would enjoy a German style meal; Rindfleisch mit Senf und Sahne.

"Mrs Barnes, if you had asked me that a few years ago I would have tried to hide my reaction of abhorrence and would have refused as politely as I could manage."

"Please call me Alice. You now have a more positive reaction?"

"Yes. I would be delighted. I shall explain when I meet you."

Alice got Miriam to help her make the cream and mustard sauce.

Beate arrived in a long, ethnic style olive green skirt and a lovely lacy blouse, with a woven bag slung over a shoulder and her long auburn hair with ginger streaks held back by a green, bejewelled headband.

"You look so lovely!" said Alice as she opened the door.

"Thank you. I am so pleased to meet you. I am so grateful that you allow your husband such freedom to travel and to do research in faraway places."

"I am used to it. My father was Professor Thomas Hartley. Have you heard of him?"

"You are the daughter of Professor Hartley! I read his works on Nigerian indigenous spirituality when I was studying and I heard him speak at Marsden some years ago. He was dealing with art and artefacts as an expression of tribal belief systems."

"Come and meet the children. Derry will be back soon. We both want to hear your story."

"He is such a special man." Alice wondered if she were perhaps too fond of Derry. He certainly seemed drawn to her. Beate proved very popular in her exotic clothes with Miriam and Hartleigh Thomas. Joseph and Bethany did not mind being picked up and admired by her.

"I have probably left it too late but seeing such gorgeous little ones makes me want one! But it would not suit my lifestyle."

"Do you have a partner?"

"Yes, but she is a girl. We have been together four years now and we are a little bit activist for women's rights." Alice smiled.

"I think we have Germany in common." said Beate.

"Yes, my mother was a German Jew rescued from the Nazis just before the war and brought up in England."

"You are Jewish!" Beate's eyes filled with tears and she hugged Alice.

"My mother was adopted by Anglicans so she became a Christian. Later in life she joined the Messianic Jews and worshipped with them a few years before she died."

"When Professor Derwent is here I will explain."

"Call him Derry. Hardly anyone uses Derwent."

Alice prepared a three-course meal as a treat for Derry and Beate; melon starters, asparagus and pureed potatoes with the meat followed by a variety of ice creams. The children enjoyed the sauce but were not too enthusiastic about the tender roast beef. After supper she settled her children in bed and read to them. Derry took Beate to see the progress of the Healing Centre. Hunter was glad of the run and sniffed every tool and machine and lifted his leg against the few bricks that were the start of a wall.

“You cannot believe how I feel about your plans to include counselling for depression and trauma. I would not be here if I had not had such counselling when I was younger. It is so expensive so to offer it as a service is so important.

“We’ll share in stages, Beate. It is exhausting to share deep and painful things. You can tell us tonight about your German background and I think that will be enough. Tomorrow I would like to hear about how you became interested in Australian Aborigines when in Norfolk.” Alice admired his sensitivity and prepared herself to hear some hard things.

“Coffee or wine?”

Alice and Beate both chose wine. Derry sat and poured the wine. “Blessed. What a lovely name.” Derry said.

Blessed is not what this young woman felt when she was in her teens. She grew up with her mother who spoke English with a German accent in a single parent family. They lived with Maria, her mother’s much older sister and her English husband. Maria had married her English man long before the war and had settled in Norfolk. Maria and Johanna Kreus had had a brother between them and were both very upset when he joined the German army and was killed in the war. Johanna married Volker von Friedland and lived in a beautiful, large house with her in-laws. She was proud to live in such an ancient and admired house in grounds like the aristocracy. They were away from the town and the bombing. Volker and his father Dietrich had joined the Nazi Party when Hitler came to power, convinced that there would be ‘new times’ and a stronger, more powerful Vaterland. Volker joined his father’s company after he completed his education and then joined Siemens, remaining with this company during and after the war.

Johanna did not realise that they were both involved in another activity. They joined the Nazis who rounded up the Jews from rich houses, sent them to camps or ghettos and stole the art works, silver, ceramics and any other valuables from the houses which were then taken over by the Nazi soldiers. She was suspicious when she saw lorries drive around the back and parcels were unloaded into the cellar, a huge space under the whole house.

Father and son escaped investigation in 1945-6. Dietrich retired at 62 and Volker continued to deal in stolen goods, hiding, selling and passing on the Jewish loot. In 1968 rebellion and demonstrations broke out in both France and Germany. The Red Army Faction and the Baader Meinhof Gang emerged as terrorists. They were left wing, pro Russia and anti, just about everything else in Germany. Intelligent, well educated, some the sons and daughters of ministers of religion, young people lived in communes and formed terrorist groups which kidnapped and killed enemies and bombed places symbolic of capitalism. They believed in a new world order. They especially hunted any prominent business men who had been Nazis and remained unpunished. Johanna had her daughter Beate in 1975. The terrorism came close to home in the next few years. Dietrich and Volker were exposed as thieves of Jewish property. The house was searched and they were put on trial. When Hanns Martin Schleyer of Siemens was murdered. Johanna felt she and Beate were in danger. She was very shaken when she learned what her prestigious family with a 'von' had been doing.

"No different from burglars and common thieves. I am divorcing you." She did not care if they went to prison. She decided to come to England and change her name. Maria and her husband took them in. Beate heard some German as she grew up but after a while they spoke mainly in English. Johanna told Beate that she was divorced from her father and never intended to return to Germany. Beate had no memory of either her father or her grandfather. She thought of herself as English. As they settled Johanna contemplated changing her name but in the end she did not think it was worth the trouble as they were perfectly integrated.

In senior school Beate learned about the war in her history lessons. She became increasingly upset when she read the books and saw the videos of the rise of the Nazis and their atrocities. The next few years were very traumatic for Beate. She became quiet and depressed and took on the whole Nazi guilt upon herself. She hated anything German; names, food, newspaper headlines, school holiday trips and German language lessons. She chose French and Spanish and avoided anything to do with her country of origin. She hated anything to do with the place she thought of as a hell. If she heard mention of the Jews she had a shaking fit. She cried and often had outbursts of screaming and shaking. This was not only at night. She was a broken child. She had friends around her with fathers and grandfathers of whom they spoke with affection and pride. She was ashamed of hers and ashamed that she had their name. She asked her mother what they had done and why she had divorced her father.

Johanna thought it was best to tell the truth as she feared that Beate might think that they had been guilty of the Holocaust and had actually killed Jews themselves. Her truth was bad enough but it could have been worse. Johanna did not know where to turn to help her traumatised daughter. Her behaviour at school was erratic and when she had her outbursts she was taken to a quiet room with a trained school counsellor until she calmed down. This intelligent, high performing student was overwhelmed by her negative emotions.

The school discovered there was a waiting list for counselling so Johanna consulted her GP. She was given a list of possible counsellors for children in crisis.

"This saved my life." Beate wiped her eyes. Instead of seeing her life and its opportunities open out before her, she wanted to die. She was eaten up with anger and hatred for her country, the Nazis, her father and grandfather. She could understand the left-wing terrorists. She wanted to do the same as they had done and kill ex-Nazis and the von Friedlands. She longed to meet Jews and say 'Sorry'.

Sadness filled her thoughts much of the time. She thought about various ways to kill herself. "It took the psychiatrist, Dr John a long time to break through this overwhelming ocean of emotion. He was a patient man. It took about three years before I lost the desire to kill myself. The intensity of anger, hatred and shame gradually lessened as he taught me to value my mother and her bravery in giving up her comfortable life to keep me from danger. He used art. He sent me to a therapist once a week to use art and creativity to help me confront my dread and hatred of all things German. The therapist introduced me to different styles of art. We looked at Stalinist communist style as well as the primitive people of the world.

"That's when I first saw Aboriginal art."

Before the therapy certain things would trigger her violent reactions, screaming and tearing up her work, banging her hands on the desk and her head on the wall. Dr John advised the school on the triggers and so she could miss certain history lessons. She was bright and loved academic challenges. She threw herself into her studies and always achieved good results.

She did not meet any Jews until she reached University and by then she realised that there was no point in making a personal apology.

Alice and Derry sat in silence as Beate wiped her eyes.

"Thank you Beate. We really do understand. Derry had to go through shame and dread over some events with his grandfather. I was able to help him through that trauma, so we both sympathise. We will never say 'We know what you are going through.' You have come through amazingly well and you will be able to sympathise with others and help them too." Alice held her hands gently.

"Dr John was private and very expensive. My mother managed to get the fees from my father. She used the case for justice for her daughter because his crimes had caused her problems. Your centre here will rescue people and save their lives and change them for the better."

"Would you like to see some TV or listen to some music before you go to bed?"

"I saw some Australian music CDs in the study. I would love to listen to that before I sleep."

"Coffee?"

"Yes, please." They went to the kitchen and changed wine glasses for coffee cups. They both gave Beate a hug and she took her coffee and music to her room.

"Tomorrow, Aborigine time." Derry said.

"Well done, Beate, I'll show you a video of an art exhibition tomorrow. The artist is thinking of starting an Art Therapy group in his studio."

Hunter led the whole family into the woods after breakfast. Beate appeared perfectly relaxed with them all. With the older ones in school and the younger ones having a siesta, Beate was able to explain how she ended up studying anthropology. She had enjoyed learning about the iconic designs of Aboriginal art and saw their own sadness depicted as through the coming of the white man they lost their land and way of life. She escaped when she learned about The Dreaming and the Songlines. She studied Geography as one of her A levels and on a 'taster' day at Norwich she found a brochure on anthropology and took it away with her.

When she applied she was asked about her experience of travelling. As she had none she decided to back-pack in Australia. She got a job to earn money for the fare and for food and any travels in Australia. Johanna was reluctant to let her go but saw that she now seemed in control of her emotions. The psychiatric therapy had taught her that German did not mean Nazi. She met up with some German young people in the hostels and coped well. She asked advice and managed to get into the Bush to some tourist centres where Aborigines gave demonstrations and told stories. She decided that this would be her special study. For her first degree she included New Zealand and the South Pacific Islands. She spent time in Māori areas and on Vanuatu.

At University she had both boyfriends and girlfriends and decided she was probably bisexual. She remained a student for an MA and her PhD and was invited to stay and teach as she was considered so able and well organised.

"I was in the Northern Territories when you were there with a First Nation Canadian and Mary Ruth."

"Dr Koda. You will meet him when he comes for the inauguration of the charity Hartley Barns Foundation. He will have Heinrich with him, another German who speaks 'Gothic German.' And you will also see Dr Paul Rockingham again, a theologian."

"I remember those names from the conference and the books."

"When I go on the lecture tour in Australia, I would like you to meet me when I am in Cairns University. You should meet the team. Their names are in the book too. This has been my base for many years."

"We started our married life there. I miss it and I love it. Hartleigh Thomas was born there. We will go back for a holiday when Bethany is five."

"Thank you for asking me. My studies were my escape and I loved the Aborigines and their culture."

"You are a great encouragement to us, Beate. Thank you for coming and do call in again when you come for the inauguration of the charity. We'll, probably have Koda and Paul too. Do you get to London much?"

"My partner's parents live in London so we go quite often. They live in Brixton so we take advantage of the museums and galleries when we see them. Her father is Ugandan and her mother is Hindi. They fell in love about the time when the Asians were expelled from Uganda. Mixed race couple with a mixed-race child, they needed to get out and escape Amin. Her name is Sushilla. She is very exotic but she works in a travel agency. My mother would have preferred me to have a boyfriend but she has accepted Sushilla and is very kind to us both. She is so relieved that I have recovered."

Alice had her coffee in the study and looked at the shelf where she hoped she would see some of Beate's books one day. Her story had so inspired them to prioritise in art therapy and counselling when the building was completed. She decided to contact Justin and arrange for Beate to visit his studio. She researched art therapy groups in Oxford and discovered one was functioning at Oxford Prison. She planned to attend their next exhibition.

Beate's inspiration extended to Justin. She and Sushilla called in at the studio and she pressed him to make the therapy group a priority.

"You will help so many people, maybe save some from suicide, like me."

Justin and Abigail looked more seriously for a bigger flat where they could start their own family. This meant that the third floor would be the therapy room, leaving the ground floor free for the exhibitions.

When Beate attended the formal opening of the Foundation, she met Koda, Heinrich and Paul.

"I saw you in Australia with Derry and Mary Ruth."

"How amazing. Pleased to meet you. I am, afraid I was fully preoccupied and did not see you."

"How come that you have such a German name?" Heinrich asked. They exchanged some snippets of information about their German backgrounds.

"You are an art specialist. Have you ever encouraged the natives on the reservations to try some art?"

"I am not a teacher."

"You could be."

"It would be a good idea. Koda encourages them to try many activities. They could learn how to make little totem poles or how to decorate the wigwams."

"They so need it, Heinrich. Art is a great healer. Please look into how you could do it. There must be artists around. I would not be here if it were not for counselling and art."

When she had her talk with Paul, she asked after his family. He told her about his wife who had an interest in the Inca and how he had searched out their descendants and those of other ancient, less well-known tribes. He told her about his identical boys.

"Where are your studies going?"

"I am speaking in the UK soon about the Peruvian tribes and I am still doing Post-Colonial Theology in the States."

"I read your papers in Tribal Wisdom. This is such a vital subject. Do consider making it more accessible to non-academics. I think Derry has started doing something similar but it is a neglected subject. We are so ignorant of what our countries did in the lands we conquered; atrocities by all European occupiers."

Paul was taken aback a little.

"Thank you, Beate. I shall work with Derry on making the Peru report more straightforward."

"And even consider documentaries. People watch rather than read about anthropology."

"You are making me a map for my way ahead." he smiled.

Derry's next task was the lecture tour in Australia. He was due to go to universities in the south, in the west as well as Northern Territories and Queensland. Beate flew to Cairns and met his team. Her visit was like an encouraging light to both Jane and Steve.

"Could I work with you sometime? I could bring some of my students." she asked Jane. Jane was so delighted to meet a women anthropologist with an interest in women's roles and rights.

Steve took her to the township where he was working with the drug squad to combat the prevalent use of ICE among the young people. She was moved of course by what she saw but she asked Steve why he had not completed his doctorate.

"I was married with two young children and then this voluntary work took time and energy. It is so worthwhile."

"ICE and young people in trouble will still be here is 2-3 years' time. You must not miss out. Take a few years out. Other doors will open for you if you are a doctor. The drugs will still be there when you have finished. What would you research?"

Steve felt moved that a comparative stranger could collar him in this way. She was an encourager because she herself had been encouraged and healed after she had been broken.

"I am most interested in medicines created from the roots, leaves and fruits of the rain forest. I could major on that."

"You have written a brilliant chapter on it. You are not a beginner. Would your Uni support you?"

"I hope so. Derry would back me."

Derry took her to meet Sandrine and visit the Art Therapy Shack. Beate praised all that she saw there and met three of the clients. She watched what they were doing and asked them about their work.

"Well done, Sandrine. You are a real gift to these people. Derry and others are setting up something similar in Oxford and London."

Beate seemed to have been a uniting factor of all the strands of Derry's work. She had spoken up at the Foundation meeting when the lawyer and the Charity Commissioner had spoken. They read out the familiar list of needed buildings. She raised her hand and stood up.

"Dr Beate von Friedland, University of Norwich. I am sorry to interrupt but I think we have all missed something. Even without buildings we could identify some individuals who could be trained to train others to educate, train to build or to provide other therapies. If this is at the top of the list, the natives would train others and begin to accept responsibility."

"Thank you Dr Beate. We shall consider that seriously. We would need a venue for training but we could hire something. Trained builders would indeed be invaluable when the building starts. It is certainly worth putting that at the top of our support list."

On the last night of her stay in Oxford, she met Louisa. Alice brought out some photos of her mother.

"You are so like your mother." said Beate. She looked through the little pile and found Esther as a baby with her parents. She was silent for a long time and Louisa saw that she was moved to tears. She put her arm round her.

"Their legacy lives on for good through Alice."

"And you have your own legacy. You have overcome and you have put into motion so many good things for other people. You have brought good out of evil and your name will be blessed like your Christian name." Alice added. Beate wept softly and let Louisa hold her. As she left for Norwich the next morning Beate said to Alice, "You have a wonderful family. I hope you will have even more little ones."

When everyone had left, Alice picked up Bethany and wrapped her in the Peruvian shawl and sat with her in the study in her corner.

"Here is your legacy, my little Bethany. This is your start in life, brothers and a sister, a Mum and Dad who love you. What will you become? I do hope you will not have painful traumas. However I have met so many people who have overcome trauma, sadness and disadvantage yet turned their lives into a blessing for others."

Derry returned and crept in to join them. "Are you here for a reason?"

"It all began here with this bookshelf. From my early years I loved this corner, the masks, and the big books with strange pictures from all over the world. I want them all to love it and be inspired by it too."

"Alice, I used to sit here with your Dad and tell him about my problems with my Dad, So long ago!"

"Beate was amazing. She told me she is considering asking Sushilla to have a Civil Partnership with her. Like a proposal."

"And Daniel and Charles. Do you think they will do the same?" asked Derry.

"I reckon they will. They did not meet Beate so they did not have the irresistible challenge. Did you hear the challenge she gave me?"

"I can guess. Don't let Bethany be the last baby."

"How did you know that?"

"Things she said. Not directly, about how lovely our children were and what a privileged start in life they had had."

"We could wait until the healing centre is up."

"We could. We will be very busy recruiting staff in the first year. Do we wait until then?"

"And my five-year plan? We must find someone to take Hunter while we make our trip."

"We do not have to wait for that as by then Bethany would not be the youngest." They were laughing.

"Our decisions made by the bookshelf have had a tendency to come to fruition." Derry picked up the sleeping Bethany and called Hunter for a walk.

Part 3
Songlines for Professor Barnes

With a growing family, new anthropology researches and a flourishing charity, Professor Barnes and his colleagues make some family plans which have unexpected repercussions. Academic research led them to charity work and to genuine, life-long friendship which sustains him as they cope with tragedy. Following the mythic Songlines he has taught, he tries to find a positive way through the desert tracks of life.

1 Celebrations and a Farewell

Derry and Alice were preparing to celebrate their tenth wedding anniversary. Earlier in the year Nathaniel, their third son and fifth child had been born. Alice was looking back over ten years. In 1992 she had prepared herself for life as a single woman. She worked as a translator of German and did voluntary work teaching English to Muslim ladies. After a sad experience during her university studies she found herself unable to trust men, to trust relationships and could never had imagined that within ten years she would be the wife of a Professor of Anthropology and the mother of five children.

In June 2003 they would celebrate their tenth wedding anniversary.

She sat in the garden while three of her little ones enjoyed the sandpit and paddling pool. Bethany and Nathaniel were asleep in their prams.

From her advantage point she looked over the Spiritual Healing Centre, the low building nestling in the trees at the end of the garden.

A row of cars was parked at the back and inside as she looked on, an Art Therapy Session was taking place. A small group of 4 or 5 people were being inspired and encouraged by a trained tutor. In one of the small rooms another client was receiving bereavement counselling. Tomorrow a massage specialist would arrive and give healing, spiritual massage to a mental health patient. The centre was in use nearly every day.

This was the fruit of her husband's efforts to turn his anthropology research into a charity. Her father had done the same years before during his work researching Nigerian art works and spirituality. He focussed on the bronzes of Benin and the ongoing bronze and brass work of modern times. He had encouraged his team to open museums and teach about the incredibly beautiful and skilful art works. As he studied the past he was moved by the needs of the tribal people in the present. He formed a charity foundation with his colleagues. His last researches when he was already in his eighties passed the work on to an American, a Canadian and his own son-in-law. Professor Derwent Barnes had formed a team with Dr Koda, a First Nation Canadian heading up anthropology in Winnipeg and Dr Paul Rockingham, an American theologian now teaching

Post Colonial Theology and researching indigenous spirituality in Minnesota. Alice had met both of them with their wives and children. They had become close friends.

Alice began her married life in Cairns and along with her neighbours she became good friends with Derry's colleagues at the University.

She has a special bond with Queensland as she had been so well befriended during the early years when she had just two children.

Family life and professional life were intertwined but she also had some precious friends who were not connected to Derry's work.

Her best friend, Abigail married an artist, a modern abstract artist with a studio in East London. They used one floor of the studio as an Art Therapy venue. They were starting a family and moved to a flat overlooking the river as the studio was not a safe place for children.

Granny Lou had been adopted by the family as a grandma for the first four children. She had initially been a client for Spiritual Direction but Alice was moved by her painful life and her qualities of friendship, kindness and encouragements. The result was that Alice stopped her own efforts at direction and adopted her as Granny instead.

Derry's nephew Kyle and his Romanian wife were also close but they lived in Romania with their children. They made the trip to see his family in England whereas Derry was not free to make trips to Romania because of all his other travels.

Several of the Cairns colleagues visited their Oxford home; Connie the botanist and faithful baby sitter, Steve, researching drugs, now Dr Steve Hampton and his family. From the Cairns Meditation group, Sandrine, Simon and Eugene all made trips to see them.

Derry had confined his efforts to local researching and charity work as he recovered from an allergic reaction to a toxic caterpillar in the Peruvian rainforest. He did not want to put his life in danger when he had so many very young children. Dr Beate from Norwich had taken on a lot of responsibility for the Hartley Barnes Foundation. After Bethany was born she had encouraged them to have more children. Nathaniel was the result, born as they approached their tenth anniversary.

Dr Beate had followed Derry's career, conferences and charity over several years and took an inspirational role in the Queensland section of the charity. She had lived for a few years with a lesbian partner but when she had suggested they make it a Civil Partnership the relationship had broken down. Instead of a public commitment their discussions became disagreements and the exotic half-Indian, half African Sushilla decided she would rather be a free spirit with an open relationship. Beate needed to recover from the sadness and sense of failure so she took on more work with Jane in Cairns. Jane was researching the role of Aboriginal women. Beate had considered herself as 'bi' rather than Lesbian and decided to try dating some men.

Alice's brother Daniel and his Civil Partner Charles continued to flourish in the classical music world. They often stayed in the Oxford house to dog sit for Hunter the Spaniel when the family went away.

As Alice sat contemplating the past ten years, she could not have imagined how the next ten years would impact the lives and friendships of their children as they related to Koda and Paul across the world. Derry was well known for his books on dadirri, the Aboriginal way of meditation. After the next ten years he would also be known for his books on Songlines.

Derry had booked the Randolph for the celebratory meal. Alice had asked Paul to bring some Peruvian artefacts back as a gift for Derry. She managed to hide the beautiful feather ornaments he had chosen for him to add to his display in the study at home.

Abigail and her husband Justin were able to celebrate with them, bringing their son Marlow, nearly 2 with her second baby on the way. Justin's happiness as husband and father inspired him to open more exhibitions and he planned to open the Art Therapy group on a daily basis after the birth of their daughter.

During the past five years Derry and Alice had travelled a lot less. Derry had some short lecture tours in Canada, Australia and America but Alice was very pleased to have a more settled existence for the start of her children's education. She maintained her dream of returning to Australia for a prolonged stay. Derry had found her a beautiful bracelet of coral and Reef pearls as an anniversary present. She was so delighted that both Connie and Steve from Cairns had been able to be with them. Steve was booked to lecture at St Marcus and Connie was invited to spend time in the anthropology department after the party.

Daniel and Charles managed to smuggle an electronic keyboard into the Randolph without being seen. Neither Derry nor Alice had played a musical instrument since childhood but Daniel had looked for a state-of-the-art keyboard with headphones so that their children could learn and practice at home. They had noted that both Thomas and Joseph took an active interest in their grand piano at home. Miriam was more interested in cooking and swimming but they hoped that little Bethany would also show an interest as she grew up. Granny Lou had some photographs enlarged and framed, Hunter the dog with each one of the children.

She was pleased with them and hoped to see them hung in the corridor near the bedrooms. Derry and Alice took the opportunity to change some of the furniture in the 'granny flat. They sold the big double bed meant for her parents and bought a double bed settee and a single bed to make it easier for single guests. They changed the guest rooms in the attic and were able to offer a room to each of the five children. The photos with Hunter could even end up in the bedrooms.

The celebration at the Randolph ended with a recital by Daniel and Charles. As they stepped out onto the street, Derry and Alice ushered their little ones towards the car. They were filled with gratitude for the blessings of the past ten years. They thought of the years ahead and had decided to include their children in more of the foreign trips. Neither of them imagined what a complicated network would be built up as they travelled and made deeper relationships with the other families.

As June came to an end and the visitors left, Alice decided to make more time to spend with Granny Lou. She was approaching her mid-80s and was suffering from high blood pressure, palpitations and heart problems. The four oldest children were in school or nursery so she took Nathaniel and Hunter to see Louisa. She noticed that the house was not cleaned to the usual standard and the fridge had too many out-of-date items of food.

"I'll come and clear up for you each week, Louisa. I might be able to find you a helper from AgeUK for the garden."

"I am seriously considering moving into a sheltered flat. I can't cope anymore."

"I'll help you look. We can take the little ones with us."

"Alice, I have written out some notes for you and Derry in case I collapse. In the drawer there is my Will and papers to be signed by my solicitor to make one of you my Attorney."

"You are wise and sensible, Louisa. Derry and I have prepared papers too in case he gets a worse bite in the jungle!"

"Your healing centre has worked wonderfully, Alice. Wasn't it hard work to find the right staff!"

Alice said she could never forget those first three years. The prison art tutor had applied to take a group once a week on a voluntary basis for the first year. She had been with prisoners so long that she had trouble adapting to being with people who did not steal the equipment. She was used to collecting things in, counting them and locking them up. Her first clients had been sent by NHS Mental health services and were amused at her 'over the top' treatment of scissors, brushes and glue. She soon settled in and offered two days a week and recruited another tutor.

"And what about Serena?" Louisa laughed. Alice soon laughed with her as they both recalled this woman who arrived for her interview in a gold lame bikini top and shorts. She had misread the advert, believing the Healing Centre was some kind of alternative massage parlour. She had worked in the sex industry and presumed that this centre was a cover for such activities. She shook her head of blond, Marilyn Monroe-style hair. jangling her sparkly dress jewellery. Louisa and Alice were convulsed with laughter when they remembered how Derry had handled her. In his polite, academic manner he explained to her about spiritual healing. She quite quickly withdrew and tottered up the stony path in her high heels.

"Then there was that eccentric applicant for the manager job! I am so glad that Peter was eventually found." Peter had been a teacher who had left because of the stress of disruptive pupils. Capable and calm he had organised the timetable, booking system and finances, all with a gentle smile.

Peter had liaised well with Ken, the caretaker, builder and general factotum. The eccentric applicant had arrived at the centre for his interview at the same time as Ken, who had come through the double doors and went to walk down the corridor and nearly fell over the long-haired young man sitting cross legged in the middle of the walkway, hands held out, eyes closed and chanting 'Om'. While he was getting in touch with the vibes of the building, Ken was being asked about his previous experience. The guru figure did not move even when invited into the office. A couple of Derry's team from university had been asked to join the interview panel. The guru was unable to answer any questions about his organisational experience so they persuaded him to sit in the hall while other candidates were interviewed. They felt they had returned to sanity when Peter came in to the panel.

"Derry and I went in to sit with him on the floor. Derry explained the ethos, aims and funding of the Centre. He raised his eyes once, lifted his hands and chanted more loudly. We left him sitting there until the end of the day while we appointed Peter."

"Jeff soon organised a Spiritual Direction Training course and Jean brought in other counsellors for the bereaved and depressed."

In those first few years there was just one serious attempted break-in. Derry, Peter and Ken got advice and installed an alarm system with lights and sirens.

Peter and Derry organised some Days of Reflection when a group of about 25 attended a day of meditation built around a theme. Derry had done Dadirri and Aboriginal Spirituality, Justin talked about the healing power of creativity and let people try out making some art or plaster sculptures, Daniel gave a day on healing and meditation through music and Dr Beate spoke about forgiveness and dealing with the past.

They had enjoyed reminiscing about the opening of the centre. Alice left her, promising to call again with Joseph. Granny Lou was specially drawn to the little boy with the visible birthmarks and so was Daniel who took a great interest in him as he showed an aptitude for music. In Daniel's flat Joseph had quickly pressed the keys on the grand piano.

Derry made sure that he organised a family holiday each summer. They usually hired a lodge, a chalet or tried camping. They went to Yorkshire, Wales, Scotland and the South Coast.

They needed a break from their busy lives surrounded by other people. Derry also made sure that Alice had time to herself, time to see friends. She loved being a mother and spent time teaching her children some German and letting them paint and draw. In the woodland with Hunter, they collected and identified leaves and plants.

A few weeks later they had to say farewell to Granny Lou who died peacefully in her sleep just before she was due to move into a care home. Alice and Derry wept with their three older children to lose such a precious, loving grandma. Her solicitor, who was her Executor, arranged to see them before they had a date for the funeral. They wept again when they read her Will. She had asked for the house to be sold and all the proceeds to be given to the Healing Centre after each of the Barnes children had received £5000. Even after tax that large sum of money would be a great boost to the work of the charity. This would enable them to give grants to some clients for free treatment and to afford to pay more staff.

Alice decided to spend time with one of the bereavement counsellors for a few weeks. She had suffered the loss of her parents with great difficulty and losing Louisa meant she had lost the nearest person to a relative. The funeral was held at the Oratory where Daniel played the organ and led the choir. Justin and Abigail came to Oxford especially to attend. It was a beautiful service of thanksgiving for Louisa's life and for the way she had fought to overcome the traumas and trials, to keep her faith and to reach out constantly to others in need.

2 The Growth of the Barnes Clan

"Nathaniel will be our last child." Alice and Derry agreed.
Now their other four children were getting older it became more and more complicated to fit schoolwork, extra-curricular activities including sports around Derry's trips away and his work at the University.

Both Thomas and Joseph had welcomed their baby brother, Nathaniel. Miriam had become quite bossy and she and Bethany developed a kind of rivalry with their brothers. She insisted on playing with the train set and refused to allow the play room to be just for boys. However, the doll's house was in her room and she only just about allowed Joseph in to play with it. He was fascinated by the miniature furniture and loved changing all the rooms round.

Bethany and Joseph both adored Nathaniel. He had been born during the cold spell in the second year of the new millennium. He was a little older than Paul and Vivienne's third child, Cristina.

In the next few years the personalities of each child, their likes and dislikes became more and more evident.

Miriam was gifted at languages and aimed at taking three at GCSE. She loved cooking, reading recipe books and trying out new dishes. She was an enthusiastic swimmer and attended lessons after school every week.

Thomas gradually realised that his first name was unusual. He introduced himself as Hartleigh when he started Junior School. He loved all sports and joined both football and tennis teams at school.

From the age of three it was clear that he was also gifted at making music. His uncles taught him piano and violin but he pleaded for a guitar. On his tenth birthday he had his wish. He was interested in IT and spent far too long staring at screens. In his early teens he let his thick hair grow long and wore a man bun. He took an intelligent interest in his father's work. He read through the books, asked about every trip, found out where it was on the map and asked searching questions.

Joseph had developed witty ripostes to anyone who dared try to tease him about his birthmarks. He was also fanatical about music. He borrowed Thomas' guitar and asked for some wind instruments. He was often found dancing and jigging around to jazz and pop music. His teachers recommended that he follow a career in music as his abilities were obvious. He had perfect pitch, could play on several different instruments and had a very musical ear, able to pick up melodies very easily.

Bethany did not like being called the baby of the family. She did not have to wait very long before she had a baby brother. She sat with Miriam and read her school books and tried the Spanish words when she was doing her homework. She was also developing an interest in languages.

Nathaniel was spoilt by all his older siblings for the first five years of his life. He loved sport, especially swimming but showed no interest in music. Instead Alice noticed that he would often take a sheet of white paper and go and sit alone to draw some of the objects around him. He also copied other pictures from books and from the items decorating his home.

Kyle and Adina's family grew quite quickly. Within six years they had Liviu, Annamaria and Catalin. Kyle had regular paid employment with a German firm of builders. On the road between Bucharest and Ploiesti there were houses, factories, shops and office blocks being built. They continued to live in the cottage attached to the orphanage and often helped out in the large house. They let their own children play with the orphans in the well-equipped playground. They had learned to be careful, however. Some of the orphans had been traumatised in their early years and relating to other children in a friendly way had not been part of their upbringing. They could be aggressive and violent. One or two very disturbed children would self-harm; some twisted their hair and pulled out little tufts, others scratched their arms or smeared excrement on to their faces. The staff had a very challenging job. One brother and sister were admitted and shown into a bedroom. They were 4 and 6 but looked much younger and under developed, thin, under nourished with big dead, staring eyes. The carer gave them a bag each and suggested they unpacked their clothes and put them in the cupboard. They opened the small door and both of them climbed in and curled up together. They held each other until they fell asleep. Florin explained that the cupboard at home was the only place where they felt safe. They had been badly beaten and abused. It took the caring, patient staff about four months to coax them out of the cupboard at night and to discover the comfort of a bed.

Kyle's parents, Maddy and Roy went to Romania for a holiday to celebrate their silver wedding. The cottage was too small so they stayed in a hotel on the edge of town. Their grandchildren loved visiting them in their large rooms. Kyle talked with Marcel, his father-in-law and with Florin about the possibility of building on to the cottage. With two boys and a girl he could foresee problems as they grew older and needed their own rooms. He consulted his uncle Derry who had experience of architects.

Derry gave lectures tours several times during those early 'noughties'. Koda became Professor Koda so Derry attended the ceremony. He noted how his son had grown up. He was 7 when he first met him and was insisting on being called Wayne. Now at 15 he reverted to his given name of Little Bear. Derry did not discover the Sioux pronunciation of these names. The girls had never wanted white man's names. Silver Star at 12 was becoming a beautiful young lady. Bright Star was nearly 6, a pretty little child taking after her mother, Shining Star.

There was nothing little about Little Bear. He was tall like his father and worked out for his arm muscles and chest. He wore his long shiny, black hair in a plait down his back. Derry and Koda discussed the possibilities of their two families spending time together.

"We could overlap our research and teaching times with the summer holidays and meet up to go camping. Would Shining Star agree?"

"Oh, yes. I am sure she would just love that. It is really hard to be a family man and have to work in faraway places."

"Have you linked up with Paul's family?"

"I have, but not my wife and children. We tend to meet in each other's homes and then travel together."

"You have met the twins?"

"And baby Cristina."

"We could also meet in Oxford. We have good camping places in the UK."

This little chat was the first step on a new path. The academics had visualised ways that their families could spend time enjoying each other's company, combining their professional lives with leisure time, but they had not analysed it like a research study plan. They had not identified the possible outcomes of their idea. This was a solution to a present situation so the researchers into tribal culture, did not visualise the Dreaming tracks which would develop.

Dreaming tracks twist and turn and change direction and cope with topographical features to find other tribes or water holes. The anthropologists thought of their children swimming, playing, camping, walking and laughing. They did not see what topographical features could occur as the years went by.

Derry, Koda and Paul and their wives and children had become like an extended family. The three groups of children would become like cousins until the years of higher education when they would go their separate ways and make new friends and take on new commitments.

Derry had written about the Aboriginal Songlines and caused them to be understood and appreciated anew. They were a positive aspect of spirituality; a mythic interpretation which nevertheless had a practical use, helping tribes over hundreds of years to find other tribes and find their way across miles of desert to water holes and trees.

The first indication that there were aspects which had been overlooked by the focussed academics was not seen until after the first ten years of the Millennium.

The Barnes clan grew again when Zara was married. She had been living with her boyfriend for about two years. She discovered she was pregnant and they decided to get married. Her parents were thrilled.

Carson was a trainee policeman and Zara still worked in a florists. Kyle and Adina had two little ones when the wedding took place but Derry and Alice brought all 5 of theirs. It was a happy, relaxed occasion at the same restaurant on the Downs in Epsom.

Derry spoke to Kyle about a possible extension for his cottage.

"One day we will come and see you but it is difficult with 5 children and all the other travels I have to make."

"It has worked out well. We are very happy, Uncle. Adina's family are very kind and helpful to us. They love their grandchildren!"

"When you next come over, do come and stay. We can run a children's holiday camp. I am glad you can get home so often."

"When do you next travel?"

"Canada for a brief lecture schedule and I am taking our oldest three to be with Koda's family. Alice is not coming because she prefers to stay with Bethany and Nathaniel and spend time with an English friend. It just makes life that much easier. Our American and his wife will join us for a week with his three little ones. We are still hoping to spend some time in Cairns when Nathaniel is older. A big part of Alice's heart has remained in Cairns."

"Ten years! So much has happened in these last ten years!" Kyle exclaimed.

3 The Growth of Anthropology Research

In those early 'noughties' not only did the Barnes family grow. There were new initiatives and projects in the anthropology departments. The main inspiration for the new project was Dr Beate of course. She used Cairns as her base where she worked with Jane. She was, however, happy to jet around the world. She wanted other tribal women to be involved as she planned a lecture tour or a conference. She wanted a tribal woman from Nigeria to join Jane, a First Nation Canadian to join Koda and a South American woman to work with Paul.

"Brilliant idea! Hard work to set up. I'll investigate and get back to you."

Derry talked to Koda about this aspect of their work which had been somewhat neglected. Koda said that his wife would have very relevant things to say after her nursing experiences. He was sure she would be in touch with other women who could contribute to the academic world. Shining Star had already recorded her experiences of nursing training and her struggles to rise up the promotional ladder, all before she left to have her first child. She had been a fiery activist at University and was still in touch with her fellow activists. Koda was pleased to set up a new project with Beate and Jane.

"Jane is from Nigeria. She is married to a very successful business man and they have a family living with them in Cairns. She was recruited through Professor Thomas' early work in her country." Derry explained that she had already begun to work well with Dr Beate in Australia and that this would be a development to her chapter in the last book, Tribal Wisdom.

"If Jane in Cairns is Nigerian, then surely we could include a Nigerian researcher in the project." Shining Star said as Derry realised that the project was getting bigger by the hour. He reported back to Dr Beate who immediately began to co-ordinate. She planned to make a film report of her three weeks with Jane and then Jane would go to Nigeria with Koda to recruit some women known to Dr Idunnu. He had found some women who had tried to restore wedding ceremonies which had been forbidden by Boko Harum.

Koda took his whole family to Nigeria to meet Jane and be introduced to Aduka. He then brought them all to Oxford where his son and daughters enjoyed being in the large house, sharing the rooms with the younger Barnes. This was the first attempt at a work/holiday period to take place in Oxford. Miriam proved to be a good hostess to the two little Stars.

Shining Star was delighted to be involved. She soon offered the names of three women to be approached. Shining Star introduced Red Dawn to her husband. When she interviewed her she felt convinced that she would fit right in with the project. She planned to elucidate on the tribal view of the role of women in contrast with the law of the land. She too had a record of her experiences of working in hospital administration.

Beate's communications with Red Dawn, Shining Star and Jane revealed to her that although the Canadians were more advanced politically, all the tribal women held their spirituality in high regard, allowing it to dominate their decisions and their behaviour in daily life.

Derry next took his whole family to the USA for a work/holiday time. Paul had felt that he would not have much to contribute but when he heard of the strong ties to spirituality he agreed that he could research the roles of women in the Peruvian tribes. He even got the anthropology department of his university to hold the conference on women's roles. Beate drew the strands together and was greatly praised for the papers and the two-day conference on Conflicts and Challenges for Modern Tribal Women. It was first held in Cairns and also Darwin, (to include Mary Ruth,) then they went on to Oxford, Norwich and London, Nigeria, Lima and Winnipeg.

Derry praised Beate for this amazing effort and was grateful that she had coped with it all so well without him having to travel much. After the demanding months he invited her to stay a weekend in Oxford.

She spoke to them both about her break up with Sushilla. "How are you managing now?" asked Alice.

"I think I am 'bi' rather than just Lesbian so I have been dating some guys. I have met some interesting guys but none that I would want to live with. After I recover from this marathon tour, I think I will go back to girls."

"How do you date?" asked Alice.

"I do internet dating but I also go to gay venues as I really prefer to see people face to face."

This was beyond Alice's experience and she found it hard to imagine living in this way. She hated the basic insecurity of internet dating, aware of certain obvious dangers that she had read about in the Press reports. This life style was beyond Derry's comprehension. He did not try to get involved but just wished her well in whichever partner she found. He was just grateful for her inspiration in women's studies and was glad to have new projects for the future.

It had been Beate's idea that training should be the priority rather than buildings for the charity foundation. Dr Steve was the first to initiate a training program for young Aborigines. They used the new school building to gather girls for childcare and cookery lessons. The boys were learning construction skills. It soon became clear that they could not continue sharing the building with the infants and so the first building to go up was a training centre.

In Canada, Koda encouraged Heinrich to share his artistic abilities with a group of Rez boys. Girls arrived in the class and were welcomed, overcoming some traditional attitudes. He also recruited tutors in IT and construction.

Dr Beate joined Paul for a 'taster' visit in Peru.

"Sons of Incas! I want daughters of Incas!" she laughed. "What about Lima University?"

"They gave us some experts, a linguist, a translator for our first trip. We must talk to the whole team and ask about women's studies. I want to research more about their religious belief systems. It is a very confusing picture. The spiritual traditions are vitally important to women. They seem to lead the rituals for good harvests, good crops, adequate rain and protection from diseases."

In Lima, they met Professor Margarita de Santos. In herself she was an example of what Paul had noted; the total mix and muddle of ancient, native spirituality and Catholicism. The native religions were not consistent as there had been a mingling of various systems followed by different tribes after the upheaval of colonialism.

Professor Margarita had been raised in a southern tribe, educated in a Catholic School and had studied at a university in America.

They decided to start with the Matis people near the Bolivian border. Margarita spoke two of the local languages as well as fluent Spanish and English. She gave them a copy of her thesis on Ancient Skills of Tribal Women and went with them to where Paul and Derry had already been. The thesis was very well illustrated and showed Paul that weaving, feather decorations and pottery were all closely linked to beliefs and also were influenced by colonial occupation. Professor Margarita took up the challenge of the 'tribal women' projects.

Paul skyped Vivienne each day and was concerned to hear that both Nicholas and Cristina were unwell with similar symptoms. So far Victor had not shown any signs of sickness. After two days he decided to return home early. Both children were in hospital and Victor was with Vivienne's mother.

"I am so sorry Paul. They are both on drips and I am staying with them." Vivienne informed him.

Beate stayed with Margarita and took many notes on the spirituality of the women and then flew to Paul's home. She knew that both little ones were home again and on anti-biotics.

They had both lost weight. Somehow Victor had not eaten the same food which gave them gastro-enteritis. Over the next year Cristina seemed to have recovered completely but Nicholas was always a fussy eater and was often sick or had diarrhoea. He ate mainly vegetarian food with some fish but had a very small appetite.

From Minnesota, Beate flew to Canada and spent time with Koda's wife and Red Dawn. Their old activist leanings came to the fore as they shared together, reported on the present situation and made proposals for the future.

Derry kept in daily touch with Paul during this difficult time.

Beate gave her notes to Paul who was able to produce a paper. He invited his students to choose one of the tribes and investigate the lasting influences of the colonial power.

The death of a dog set the families on a new stage of their journeys. It was 10 years into the Millenium.

Hunter had been adored by the whole Barnes family, by Daniel and Granny Lou. He was about 11 when he began to have health problems; his eyes clouded over and his back legs kept collapsing. He became incontinent and was diagnosed with liver problems. The Spaniel was lying on his duvet on the kitchen floor as each child came to stroke him, kiss him, cuddle him and say goodbye while weeping.

Derry lit a candle on the coffee table and encouraged his children to sit in silence for a few minutes. He then suggested that they all draw and write about Hunter to make a book to remember him by.

He then picked him up in his duvet and carried him to the car. Alice wept and said her goodbyes to him then sat with her children while Hunter had his final injection. A few days later she picked up a casket of ashes from the vet and they buried him in the flower bed near the tennis court.

Over supper one night Alice suggested that this could be a good year to spend summer in Cairns. Their plan began. Richard and Fiona did a reccy for them and told them of a huge block of luxury holiday flats in the town centre, which overlooked the sea. Derry told Koda and Paul and suggested that they might like to attempt a joint holiday for a couple of weeks. He and Alice would travel there in early July. He hoped that the two families could agree a period when they could hire flats in the same block and spend some time together. August would be winter but with temperatures between 20-27 degrees it would feel like English summer. This was the first time that all 11 children would be together. They had met each other in different combinations over several years. Nathaniel and Cristina would be the youngest aged 7. Little Bear was an adult of 23 but decided to come for the experience as he was finishing his social work studies. His sisters were 20 and 16 but loved being with the twins and the Barnes. The Barnes ranged from 15 to 7. The twins were just the right age to play with Joseph and Bethany. This time together in Cairns extended the Songlines and sent them in at least two different directions.

4 Songlines Start

For Koda and Paul it was easier to get together for holidays. Derry had once joined then without Alice and the two youngest children. On the occasions when the families came to Oxford, one family at a time, there was great happiness as the flat bound children ran around the house. The death of Hunter, the Spaniel encouraged them all to go on a holiday all together in Cairns.

The anthropological cousins had spent these weeks together and gradually they sorted out who they liked, who they disliked, who they could have fun playing with and who they were in competition with. Koda's children, being older were really above it all. Bright Star was 16 when the eleven got together but she had previously got on well with the twins and Joseph and Miriam who was only a year younger. Vivienne had taught her children Spanish so Miriam was able to use her Spanish with them. Little Bear kept himself a little apart over these three years but he was happy to spend time with Thomas who sought out older company.

Little Bear had chosen a Social Work Degree and had studied his native Lakota Sioux. He was aiming to find a post where he could work with First Nation Peoples. He had decided to join all the families as this was his last chance before he took on the responsibility of a job. They had managed to book three holiday flats in the same hotel overlooking the sea.

Miriam heard Little Bear teach some words to Thomas and the twins. Her linguistic trained ears pricked up and she sat with the group and asked lots of questions about this strange language.

"My mother learned Urdu, the alphabet as well. Can you show us some writing?" Little Bear said he would bring some from the flat next day. The 'cousins' intermingled for meals when they did not have BBQs and picnics on the beach. Poor Nicholas wanted to stay with his parents as there were so many foods he did not like. He tended to be vegetarian on the whole but would eat fish. There was always fish at the BBQ thanks to Vivienne.

Alice arranged a joint visit to the aquarium, now completed and open and truly spectacular. They all went to the swimming pool and competed with each other to do lengths and dives. Derry led them all in a meditation session, squashed into their flat. He lit candles and they all remembered Hunter the dog. He read out some 'Thank-you' prayers and invited them to suggest things they were thankful for. Little voices added thank-yous for friends abroad, for sport, for music, for the Great Barrier Reef, for their parents and for the joy of other languages. Derry put on a CD of Aborigine relaxation music and they all sat in silence for 15 minutes. It was moving for all of them.

Holy magic. thought Alice remembering her mother's phrases.

They had one free family day and then Alice and Vivienne took the younger ones to the cinema and Silver Star organised a trip to the Reef. Miriam sat next to Little Bear and annoyed him by asking the names of things in Sioux.

"We don't have corals in Winnipeg."

"Leave him alone. You're being a pain." Thomas spoke roughly to her. On Green Island they put on snorkels and plunged into the sea.

Miriam's long black hair floated behind her. Little Bear chased her and pulled her hair. His plait was still intact so she tried to pull that too. Out of the water he commented on her thick, wavy hair and his own dead straight hair. As they touched each other's hair their eyes met. She smiled and the annoying school girl was transformed into femme fatale. Thomas caught the moment and seethed with anger and jealousy. He strode over to them, "What do you think you are doing?" Everyone looked round and everything stopped.

"Nothing!" said Miriam and plunged back into the sea. Shining Star would never rebuke her adult son in front of strangers. She observed but said nothing. Alice tried to find out why Thomas was upset but he just said that Miriam was annoying him.

Anyone observing would have seen the signs but no one was observing except Shining Star and Thomas. When Little Bear appeared Thomas came alive and sought out opportunities to stand near him or to stare at him from afar. Little Bear and Miriam were joined by an invisible thread and sought out every opportunity to be near each other. All the others were enjoying the beach and the Cairns esplanade. Three large holiday apartments gave the determined pair the opportunity to be alone and unseen. Miriam gave an excuse to go back to the hotel and lingered in the lobby until she saw Little Bear approach. He took her hand and led her to the Blackhill apartment. Once inside he shook out her hair and untied his own.

They caressed each other.

“I love you, Miriam.” he whispered into her ear.

“I love you Little Bear.” She was nervous but it all felt so natural and so right. She could not imagine that it could be wrong. He was experienced to some degree at the age of 23. She had never experienced such joy.

“This is sex. You are my first, Miriam; I have never gone all the way before. I love you, Miriam.”

She was silenced by his deep mouth kisses. They caressed and kissed until he felt they should wash and dress in case someone came back.

“This is our secret for now. We can try again tomorrow.”

“I never want to leave you. I want to stay with you. I never want to let you go.” For four days they managed to repeat the secret, sexual encounter. They were very comfortable together and chatted freely between the love-making.

“We’ll have to work out a way to be together.”

“We’ll find a way.”

“How old are you?”

“Nearly 16.”

“I’ve broken the law.”

“You are an old man over 20!” she laughed.

The next day there was a family picnic further up the coast towards Palm Cove. It was not so easy to get together. They wandered off to a rocky area and Little Bear sat on a rock while Miriam knelt in front of him and unravelled his plait and combed his hair with her fingers.

This is what Alice saw when she wandered through the palm trees. Little Bear sat on a rock while someone was combing through his hair and caressing him. She could only see the arms and hands at first but as any mother would know, she recognised her daughter’s arms and hands.

She went through a few scenarios in her head; yelling, confronting, walking away or making a noise to disturb them. She chose to walk away and deal with it later with Derry because she could see the level of their intimacy and knew they had already made love. Shining Star was watching for Little Bear’s return and noted how Miriam returned some minutes later from a different direction. She also noted that Thomas went towards Little Bear as he strode down the beach. The thirteen-year-old was besotted by him and hated seeing the signs of affection between him and Miriam. At the end of the day, nearly their last day all together, Alice told Derry she needed to talk to him.

“D and M needed.” She smiled but he could tell she was worried.

Miriam was reading in her bed while Bethany slept.

"Derry, Miriam and Little Bear have been having a sexual relationship."

"What! How? When?"

"Remember the times they were missing. Did you notice? I didn't at first but I came across them this afternoon, kissing and caressing in a very intimate way in a secluded part of the rocks and palms. There is no mistaking. I did not let them see me and I have said nothing yet."

"He's over 20 and she is 15. It is illegal!"

"She will be 16 soon and many girls in the tribes are married by then, even sexually active at 14. We should not be so shocked."

"I am so shocked and upset. Our dear little Miriam! What if she gets pregnant?"

"We need to know if he used a condom. We need to talk to her and to him."

"It never entered my mind when we arranged these holidays that our own children would fall in love. We've done all the talks about sex but it was impersonal and not a reality to them. It just did not occur to me."

Shining Star was having a similar talk with Koda. She had picked up the signs and observed. A native mother does not interfere with her adult son, but there was a very young girl involved, an under-age girl.

She shared with Koda what she had observed and knew he would be very angry with his son. "We must speak with Derry and Alice and decide how to handle the situation. It will not be like Romeo and Juliet with us forbidding them to see each other but it concerns two families and two countries."

Derry invited them to the bar downstairs. "It's not an academic plan." he added. The years of friendship and mutual respect made it easier.

"Our two oldest children have formed a sexual attachment."

"I have only just discovered. Shining Star was aware before me."

"I think he is really in love with her. I don't think he plays around." said the mother, "We have not spoken with him yet."

"Miriam is only 15 and she will be broken hearted to leave him when you go."

"Let's talk to them now. We can sit outside."

"I'll get Miriam." Alice got up.

"I'll get Little Bear." Koda left the bar.

Miriam was sick with anxiety when her mother came to fetch her.

"Darling, we love you. We need to work out the next steps for you and Little Bear." Little Bear's immediate reaction was to spoil for a fight.

"No argument, Little Bear my son. We all have decisions to make." Miriam and Little Bear stared at each other and then held hands.

"You have fallen in love. That's not a crime. You have had sex and that, strictly speaking is a crime as Miriam is only 15. We would all have preferred you to wait but it is too late. It is done. Now we have decisions to make." Derry spoke first.

The young pair shuffled uneasily.

"I love Little Bear and I want to be with him." said Miriam, gripping his hand. "Ok, you are 15 and you have exams coming up. Do you want to abandon them?"

"I don't know. I can marry at 16."

Little Bear looked down with his shoulders hunched. Alice stated the obvious, "If Miriam is pregnant there will be even more decisions to make. Where will she bring up her baby?" Little Bear straightened himself and stared at Miriam.

"Did you consider you could make her pregnant?" asked Koda. "No, Dad. I just fell in love with her and wanted her."

"Couldn't you have waited? You have led a disciplined life all through your studies and you are about to begin your career. You did not consider what a wife and child would mean for you?"

Little Bear put his arms around Miriam. "I am sorry. I only thought of the now and not the future. She was so keen to love me too."

"We love you both. We will all help you whatever you decide," Alice said. "If Miriam is not expecting a baby and returns to school, you still need to decide what you want to do in the future."

"Miriam, if you feel you cannot live without Little Bear you would be welcome to come and live with us but you would miss your wonderful family."

Koda added, "We will not try to separate you but 16 is very young. We have wisdom and experience and we realise that you are still getting to know who you are. You will change over the years. You will have to learn how to get to know each other and how to tolerate each other."

Miriam began to weep. She was realising for the first time that she might soon have to leave her family. She knew from school lessons on sexual relationships that there would be difficulties to overcome. She thought of her school friends who would call her a 'slag' if she told them she was pregnant.

"What happens next?" asked Little Bear. "Do we go home as planned and wait to see if Miriam is pregnant?"

"Probably that would be best. Miriam will not want to leave her family so soon and come to Canada." Shining Star said.

"I will soon be finding a Social Work post in or near Winnipeg. I will save money and find a home for us both. I agree that she should not leave her family so soon. We can skype every day."

Koda addressed the lovers, "Tomorrow, spend some time together and address your issues. Tell each other the truth and then let us know what you decide."

"We are sad and disappointed in you both. Not because you have fallen in love but because you have acted irresponsibly and thoughtlessly, possibly jeopardising your future studies and careers. We would love to have Little Bear as a son-in-law. We love you, but it is all a bit too soon." Derry said as Koda joined in, "Yes, I love Miriam too but I feel angry with my son.

"He has let himself down and let Miriam down."

"Mum, when will I know if I am pregnant?"

"We'll work it out from your last period. We shall certainly know in two months, maybe sooner."

None of them slept well that night. The last day together was a local beach day for all the children. Thomas noted Little Bear's absence and began to sulk. Alice tried to distract him so he ended up playing crazy golf with Joseph, the twins and Bethany. It helped.

Alice spoke to Derry, "Dearest, I think we may have to address another issue. Thomas is only 13 but he is obsessed by Little Bear and very jealous of Miriam's relationship with him. He could be going through a phase but he could also be gay."

"Well, we will support him as he grows up and be ready for anything. He is very intelligent and has good career prospects ahead of him. Let's wait and see before we speak to him."

"Of course. We could see him turn to girls in a couple of years."

Shining Star wanted to talk to Alice and be reassured that their friendship would continue. "We both love the lovers!" responded Alice.

Paul was aware that something had happened but wanted to say nothing in front of his children. He was pleased to see how Nicholas had joined in and seemed to eat better. Derry found a time to talk to him and Vivienne together.

"Something unexpected has happened and we have been rather distracted for the last couple of days. Our two oldest children have fallen in love and are declaring undying love to each other."

"Goodness. Little Bear is an adult and Miriam is still a child."

"That's the problem."

"How likely is it that a marriage at 16 would last?"

"Sorry guys! We'll have that problem to deal with one day!" Paul smiled.

"We have dealt with it calmly and we remain very good friends. Don't worry; we will continue to work together."

At the beach the children were happily playing in the pools. Shining Star came over to Alice and whispered, "Come over here for a minute and see this."

They quietly stepped nearer the pool where Joseph was sitting with Bright Star. She was drawing in the sand, trying to copy the design of his birthmark. She traced the shape with her finger on his head and then went back to the sand.

"It's like a map," she said, "I think this one is like an island in the Lake of the Woods. Have you been there?"

"We went to a lake when Dad took us to Canada but I don't remember the name."

"Where did you stay?"

"Kenora."

"That's on the Lake of the Woods. Next time you come we will look at a map."

"I was told that this one is like the peninsula in Cairns and that this one is a Pacific Island." They rubbed out the drawing in the sand and plunged into the pool.

"Isn't that sweet?" said Alice. "He has coped really well with his birthmarks."

"He has. He is nearly 12 and Bright Star is 16. Is this the shape of things to come?" Little Bear and Miriam kissed and cuddled and walked along the front.

"One last time before we go?" he suggested. "Where?" Miriam thought the flat might not be free.

"The flat. They are all here on the beach. They told us to talk together and make decisions."

They found the flat empty and went in to his room and began to undress. Miriam felt uneasy. She thought of pregnancy and of her parent's words. She was not relaxed but a very passionate and forceful young man kissed her into submission.

"It's already too late. This will be the last time for ages." she told herself as she gave herself willingly to him.

She wept in his arms when he had finished.

"Go home with your parents and finish your schooling. You could have the baby at home and then come to Canada."

"What if I am not pregnant?"

"The same. Finish your exams and then come."

Miriam sensed that he was more distant and was preparing to return home but he was not pleading with her to stay with him.

Derry took her to the airport to see them off as they caught the plane to Brisbane. Derry hugged them all and Miriam clung to Little Bear weeping and sobbing. He seemed unable to handle the situation. Derry held his sobbing daughter as they went through the gates.

He drove her back to the flat.

The next day Paul and family were flying back to America. The young ones hugged each other as did the adults.

"See you soon, possibly with Beate in Peru." said Derry.

"Sir, it has been an honour to know you and your family. I am so pleased to be with you all." Nicholas held out his hand. Everyone was taken aback and smiled. "I'd like to be like you when I grow up and travel to the tribes in the world." Nicholas picked up his rucksack and went through the gates as Paul ruffled his hair.

5 Topography of the Dreaming Tracks

Alice and Derry spent their final weeks with Steve, Connie, Sandrine, Simon and Eugene. They started by driving to number 42. Both Thomas and Miriam remembered the house. Outside were mopeds, bikes and cars. They did not try to find out how the students were living inside. Zippy had died and Susie and her husband had moved. Maria was still living on the other side. They were all pleased to see each other again.

Next they met Steve in the township. Nathaniel played football with the children on the rough ground. Bethany tried to befriend the dogs. One puppy obliged and was pleased to play with her.

"We are so privileged, Miriam. Look how some people have to live."

"I'd live in a shack with Little Bear."

"I'm sure you would. You must get to know each other; understand how you think and what is important to you. He is just beginning his career. He got a good degree in Social Work and now has to join a team and train. He could be dealing with drugs, drink, broken families, old people. It's a hard but worthwhile job."

"I could help him."

"You will when you become his wife."

"It's old-fashioned. Today people just live together like Zara did."

Both Derry and Alice had talks with Miriam, acknowledging that times had changed and that teenagers were having sex a lot earlier without even thinking about love and marriage.

Derry found Alice weeping in the bedroom before they were due to leave. She wondered what their Cairns friends would say if they knew Miriam might be pregnant. "I am afraid she has messed up her chances for higher education. I visualise her learning Lakota Sioux and living with him in Canada. That's the best outcome but I am afraid that Little Bear might break her heart and leave her as a single mother."

"That's my fear too." He acknowledged that he was a good-looking young man and his long native hair was an added attraction.

"I doubt that Miriam was the first girl he has been with." Alice said.

"He told her that she was the first. He said he had not gone all the way before."

"I wish I could believe him."

Alice took Miriam to the beach with a calendar and they sat and worked out the dates of her last two periods. The next one was due in roughly two and a half weeks.

"We'll be home by then." said Alice.

"Miriam you are very beautiful and attractive to boys. I cannot understand after all our love for you and our talks about sex that you could not stop him making love to you."

"It was so wonderful. Once he looked at me and touched me I would have done anything for him."

"You have really fallen in love with him and you want to trust that he feels the same about you."

"He does. I know he does but he is better at waiting than me. I pleaded with him not to leave me but he told me I should go back with you all until I know about the baby. He did not plead with me to go with him."

"Did you think about your exams?"

"Mum, I feel I am pregnant. I know I am. I can't think of anything else."

"How did your talk with him go? Did he reassure you?"

"We didn't talk much. He really wanted to make love one last time. I said I wanted to stay with him but he said it was impossible until I was 16."

"I am sorry to hear that."

"He really persuaded me because I thought we shouldn't have done it any more after our talk with you all. He loved me so much and I could not stop him. In the end it was so lovely."

"It is lovely. It is such a powerful force in our life. That's why we should treat it with care and respect. It can also be a destructive force. If you have a baby it will affect everyone in the family. It will affect the lives of all your brothers and sister to have a new baby in the house."

"I'll be in Canada by then."

Alice was stunned at her attitude and conviction. There was no sign of regret. She thought Miriam would be very disappointed if she were not pregnant.

On their return to Oxford they wanted to make life as normal as possible. They restarted sports and music lessons and helped Thomas decide on his GCSE options. At school he was now known as Hartleigh by his friends and most teachers.

There came an unexpected shock during the first week of term; a topographical feature along the path. The Headmistress asked Derry and Alice to come and see her.

"We are going to speak with your daughter but before we do we wanted to check the facts with you. Is she pregnant?"

"She could be. What's happened?" asked Derry.

The head told them that Miriam and a group of girls had been chatting in the changing room after PE. The teacher stopped by the lockers when she heard their conversation. Miriam was showing photos on her phone and was boasting that she had had sex in Australia with a long-haired Indian. They did not believe her until they saw the pictures. How likely was that? Sex with an Indian in Australia!

The head could tell by the faces of the parents that it was in fact true.

"I'm afraid that it is true. She had sex with an older young man, the son of a professor from Canada. They are First Nation People. We were all on holiday together in Australia. He is 23 and about to begin his career. They managed to fool us, escaping while we were with all the other children on the beach. They fell in love and Miriam is convinced she is pregnant. We shall know if she misses a period in a couple of weeks." Derry explained.

"We are very upset and we did not know about any photos. I am afraid we have been very naive." Alice added.

"I hope you can see that we cannot allow that kind of boasting giving the girls the impression that it is alright to be sexually active at that age."

"Of course. We have had many talks with her. She is besotted by the man and convinced they will marry when she is 16."

When the head spoke to Miriam she was much angrier and stricter than her parents. She spoke of immorality and ruined careers. She said that if pregnancy were confirmed she might be asked to leave the school.

"I'm going to Canada." was her response.

"You are not to show your photos. It will encourage the girls to think it's OK to have sex at this young age."

"My boyfriend took them of me and sent then to me. I took some of him too. We skype every day." Miriam was equally belligerent with her parents. "Everyone takes photos and shares them. What's wrong with that?"

Miriam's period did not come. Her visit to the doctor proved nothing. She was told it could just be a late or missed period and that she should come back in a month for a scan.

"I know it's a baby." said Miriam.

The scan proved she was right. She was then about seven weeks pregnant. She was so excited to tell Little Bear and to start planning names.

"I'll be 16 when it is born and we can come straight to Canada. I want a Sioux name."

"Send me some photos of your body as the baby grows. I have three job interviews next week."

"My love, my love. I miss you so much! Good luck. Tell me how you get on." She sent an immediate photo of her tummy so he could watch the progress.

The next unexpected topography also involved an overhearing. Miriam was boasting but so was Little Bear.

Koda left his study to walk to the bathroom, passing Little Bear's room. His friend was with him and they had left the door ajar. Who could hear them?

Koda stopped in his tracks when he heard his son's voice.

"I've got this English girl pregnant. She is a professor's daughter."

"However do you get them to have sex? How do you do it"

"Tell them you love them and sound as if you mean it. When she gives in tell her she's the first one."

"She believed you? She let you?"

"She loved it. She played with my hair and boy, was she good at it. Look at this." He opened his phone.

"She let you film her actually doing it?"

"She's sent me photos of her swelling tummy. She's gorgeous, a slim body and long black hair. She's gagging for it. I had her 6 or seven times in Australia."

Koda was thunderstruck. His son was a promiscuous cad. "How come she got pregnant?"

"I didn't take condoms on a family holiday. I was not likely to meet a girl to shag, was I?"

"But you did. Didn't you care?"

"No, I didn't care. I wanted her so badly and I knew she was up for it."

"What will you do?"

"Don't know yet. She thinks she is coming here with the baby and that we will marry. But she's not 16 yet."

"What! She's 15, a kid. You are impossible. You have broken the law. How many others have you got on the go?"

"Just the two regulars. They just enjoy it and don't want anything in return."

"I'm going. You are a paedophile; a pervert and you don't care. Don't call me, you pervert!"

Koda was stuck in the corridor as the friend rushed out, brushing past him without speaking, Koda went in to his son's room.

"I believed you! I believed you were in love. I am very angry and very hurt for Miriam and her family. You are what your friend called you, a paedophile and a pervert and a promiscuous, heartless, selfish, uncaring cad. You will leave this house to pursue your chosen lifestyle as soon as possible but before then you will set up a bank debit to pay a sum to Miriam each month for her baby for at least five years. I cannot tolerate such a selfish lifestyle. She is a 15-year-old school girl and you seduced her. I will get the money going straight away. She needs to know sooner rather than later. You can take over all the payments as soon as you start earning. Who have you had sex with in the last few weeks? You are a sex addict and you need help."

He took his son down to his mother and told her the sorry tale. She was weeping. His father's anger was easier to cope with.

He felt humiliated, unveiled, discovered. He knew his father would contact Derry and Alice. He could not face Miriam so he felt let off the hook. They would tell her. He had no intention of marrying her or being with her long term and bringing up a child.

He bore the brunt of his parent's anger and hurt. They had no idea of the secret life of their son.

He texted Miriam, "Do not send me any more photos." He turned off his iPad. Koda phoned Derry and poured it all out.

"I am so sorry my son is a sex addict, heartless and selfish. He took pornographic photos and I made him delete them. Miriam also has some on her phone. She needs to delete them. I have arranged for him to send a monthly sum of money to Miriam for the baby for the first 5 years."

Derry called Alice, "Dearest, the worst has happened." Together they went to Miriam and told her about Koda's phone call.

She screamed and shook. "I don't believe it. It can't be true. I must speak to him."

"Try." Derry passed her the iPad. She entered the name and found no picture and no connection. "You must delete the photos. He has deleted all of his. You have been seduced by a very handsome and sexually experienced man. He is a heartless con man and a paedophile." Derry hugged her and stroked her hair while she sobbed. Alice remembered how her father had done the same for her when she had been broken when she was 18. They let her go to bed with some cocoa but they knew she would ring and skype all night. Bethany heard her weeping and crept in and snuggled with her.

Thomas asked his Mum what was wrong.

"Darling, I am sorry but Miriam is in trouble. She has been fooled into thinking that Little Bear was in love with her. She feels she is in love…"

"And they have had sex!" he yelled it out. "Yes and she is pregnant."

"I hate her!"

"No, you don't. You are hurt and upset because you really liked him but he has behaved like a selfish, unkind, uncaring man. He has broken her. Please be as kind as you can to her." Poor Joseph and Nathaniel understood nothing. They played together and ignored their sisters and Thomas.

Derry and Alice decided on a meditation prayer with Miriam for her baby. In her room they lit a candle and sat with her on the bed. He anointed her with oil and let her rub it on her baby bump.

"God bless this new Barnes baby. Let him or her know they are loved by their mother and by the whole family. Give this baby joy in his or her heart. Bless Miriam as a young mother and help her heal up her broken heart. Bless Little Bear, the father and help him become a better man and live a better life. Help him succeed in his career and learn to respect women. I ask you to fill Miriam and her baby with peace and joy and hope for the future. In the name of the Father and the Son and the Holy Spirit."

Miriam hugged them both and they left their weeping daughter to try to sleep. Alice leaned to Derry, "How about we buy a new puppy?"

6 Baby Dreaming Tracks

Miriam was allowed at school until she was 6 months pregnant. At home Alice schooled her and she was allowed five hours a week home tuition. Vivienne took to skype to speak Spanish with her every week. Nicholas and Victor kept in touch with Bethany and Nathaniel. Miriam asked if she could speak with Koda's daughters, the two Stars as she wanted a Sioux name for her little girl. Little Bear had started work and no longer lived at home.

"Another Star?" asked Bright Start "Perhaps. Is there a Dawn Star?"

"Yes and it has a special meaning. You can see the star sometimes after the sun has risen in the blue sky."

"Please send me the Sioux meanings."

"I like Dawn Star Barnes."

Her 16th birthday came just before the baby was due. Her family spoilt her with gifts for herself. Baby gifts would come later. This was her day. She was a woman now. She asked Silver Star if she could send her a photo of the baby to send to Little Bear.

"I don't see him much. He is working outside town and lives away from home."

"He should still see his daughter."

"Are you getting the money? He sends it via the bank every month?"

"Yes, thanks."

In Epsom, Zara had a little boy. She called him Michael as her husband Carson wanted the name to honour his father who was quite ill and did not have long to live. He was Michael Chadd.

Abigail's little girl was named Marilla, to go with Marlow their son of two. Alice wondered where she had heard that name before. One evening she was reading to Bethany who still enjoyed being read to at nights when she found the name in her book. Marilla was the name of the lady who had adopted Anne of Green Gables.

"What a lovely choice." Alice told Bethany.

Thomas was a deep-thinking young man. He was 14 when his niece was born. He had not said much to his sister as he was still fighting his own jealousy. As the nine months passed, the reality of what she was going through hit him. He made her a card, drawing some flowers and writing out 'The Lord is my Shepherd' underneath his bouquet. Inside he wrote, 'I am sorry. God bless you and your baby.'

Love from Hartleigh Thomas. Miriam was very moved and so was Alice. Great uncles Daniel and Charles came to see them all.

"We love the name and we look forward to meeting her. We are going to write a piece of music for her. Joe and Thomas, perhaps you can help. Twiddle on the keys and flute and see if you can come up with some pretty new bars for your little niece."

Derry and Alice were thrilled with the intervention. Charles found some North American Tribal music which included a well-known song, Spirit of the Redman.

"Let's build around this tune. They sat at the piano with Thomas on the keyboard and Joseph with his flute."

Daniel found Alice in the kitchen.

"A granny. Alice a grandma!" he gave her a hug. "I can hardly believe it."

"We are going to take Miriam into town to let her choose a buggy."

"That's a great idea. Thank you dear. It's been such an ordeal. I'm thinking of getting another puppy. She is so low and thinks so badly of herself for being so fooled."

"A puppy, good idea! The others will love that too. You know you have two very musical sons. Joseph will study it I am sure; Thomas has his mind on other things. He is fascinated by Derry's work."

"Do you think he is gay?" Charles looked surprised.

"I do. He is finding his way." said Daniel. "When did you last have some time alone with Derry?"

"Can't remember."

"Find a long weekend and we will come and be strict uncles before puppy and baby arrive."

"End of term perhaps. But puppy may well be here before then."

"We'll manage!"

"Sounds lovely. We have been so upset. Young people lead such different lives today. Attitudes have changed a lot. A break sounds wonderful."

End of the spring term Derry could find a long weekend. “We need sun.” He said as he booked a weekend on a Greek Island.

Alice took all the children to the kennel where they had bought Hunter. She let them look around the available dogs.

“Do we want the same as Hunter or different?” she asked them.

“Different.” came several voices. A black puppy caught their attention. He was lifted out of the pen and was wiggling his body, wagging his tail and looking up at them.

“He is jet black!” said Thomas.

“Jet, that’s a good name.” Alice picked him up and they all approached to stroke his head. “We are allowed to take him home today.”

In the shop Nathaniel chose a red lead and collar. Joseph chose a bed and Thomas, Bethany and Miriam selected toys. The happy Barnes longed to show their Dad.

“Welcome, Jet.” said Derry as he bent down and Jet responded by doing a big puddle on the hall floor to the children’s delight.

“Can he sleep with me tonight?” asked Joseph.

“Yes, you can take it in turns for the first few nights and then he must learn to sleep in his bed in the kitchen or on the landing.”

Jet explored the garden, the Healing Centre and the car park but was not yet allowed into the woods as he had a few more injections to come. Derry was preparing the next forum for the charity foundation and was glad to have a break in Greece.

Alone in their hotel room, looking out over the Mediterranean they admitted their deep sadness over their daughter and could talk of their pain. They found it hard to think of making more trips with Paul and Koda and families. A cloud had descended over them. Derry told Alice about Songlines in his earlier book. He said he would show her one of the maps he had printed out. They are also called Dreaming Tracks. You will see how they twist and turn and overlap and take different directions. They are always positive in the end. They lead to hills and water holes. We will grieve the future that Miriam might have had and look positively at the future she actually has. They were eventually able to relax and resume their loving intimacy.

Jet seriously needed some house training. He had weed in several places and chewed some cushions. Miriam took on the training, showing him how to bark to go out and to wee only in the garden. She played with him with the new toys. Daniel and Charles were worn out by the end of the weekend.

One evening, Joseph came down holding a paper.

"Look, Bright Star has found my island." He had got help from Thomas to take a photo of his forehead as she had not kept the drawing she had made in Australia. She drew out the shape and then opened the map of the Lake of the Woods and looked around for a similar shape in the thousands of islands. There was a large one which was a tourist attraction with a hotel. She compared it carefully and traced it out. She put both shapes together and sent the photo to Joseph. He printed it out to show his family.

"When you come again we will go there. Heinrich can take us on his boat."

"It's so close, nearly the same shape. Can we go there?"

"I'm sure we shall go to Canada before too long. That's remarkable, so alike." Derry answered.

Miriam looked over both sketches. "Joseph island." She smiled.

Miriam was experiencing some discomfort and the doctor suggested some blood tests and swabs.

"Miriam, I am sorry but you have a touch of venereal disease. You need to have treatment quickly and your boyfriend will also need treatment urgently. Can you let him know?"

"My baby?"

"There could be some problems but I hope we have caught it in time. "What will happen?"

"We do not want to scare you unnecessarily. There could be some effects on the baby but she could also be OK." If Miriam needed proof that Little Bear had been promiscuous, this was proof enough. She was terrified. Derry phoned Koda and gave him the medical names for the disease and explained that he needed to get treatment immediately.

"I think my son may pay a heavy price for his lifestyle."

"We are praying for Miriam and Dawn Star."

There were tension and tears during the final weeks of the pregnancy. Fortunately Jet helped lighten the mood. He had grown quickly from a podgy puppy to a sleek, happy, well-behaved Labrador. All the children loved taking him into the woods and playing with him on the lawn. Miriam had a long and difficult labour. Alice stayed with her in hospital when Caesarean section was being proposed. The baby started coming naturally after nearly two days. Miriam was given stitches after a rough time of struggling and crying at the birth. She held her black haired baby and examined each part of her.

"Is she alright?"

"Yes, Miss. We have some more checks to do. She was weighed and washed. Each orifice was swabbed and her eyes were wiped. Yellow puss stopped her opening her eyes.

"She will need drops for a long times, several times a day and you must continue with the pills you have been given." Alice spent two days with her in the hospital. Miriam was very scared about coming home and looking after Dawn Star without the nursing staff.

Derry rang Koda. Shining Star rang Alice. Little Bear was getting treatment. He had admitted having unprotected sex with more women than he could remember. He was told to contact all of them and tell them to get treated. He understood that he could be so diseased that he would become impotent. He had agreed to get some treatment also for sex addiction.

Miriam let all her brothers and sister and Jet meet Dawn Star. Jet seemed to adore sitting near the baby. Derry held her, remembering baby Miriam. She had a head of black hair, straighter than Miriam's. They were all relieved when after three weeks the puss seemed to clear up and the baby looked around with her black eyes.

The headmistress invited Miriam to come back to finish the summer term and take her examination. She was not sure she could cope.

"Try, Miriam. You can always retake next year."

She did try. There was no more boasting. She told her friends about the VD and said she was not sure if her baby's eyes would be affected long term.

The anthropological 'cousins' all sent cards and gifts to Miriam.

Silver Star was very angry with her brother and said so in her card. Miriam was very touched to get cards from them all and to see that Cristina had signed the card with Victor and Nicholas.

7 The Worst Track

Everything seemed to settle into a happier routine. Alice had persuaded Miriam to take her GCSEs. She passed them all but instead of the straight As she would normally have achieved she had a mixture of Bs and a C except for A in Spanish. She nevertheless had a place in the Sixth Form to take three Languages and English. Alice assured her that she would happily look after her granddaughter.

Thomas and Joseph often played music together and Thomas applied himself well to his studies. He had chosen Music as a GCSE but he was aiming to take Geology, Geography and Science at A level. It was obvious that he was a gay young man and began to date boys. He was aiming to apply for a place to study Anthropology at Marsden, following in his father's footsteps.

Joseph joined music groups and played jazz in the school group. He had astonished the whole family with his flute playing for the musical welcome for Dawn Star. He corresponded regularly with Bright Star and the four years of age difference made no difference to the depth of their friendship.

Bethany was in constant contact with the twins. Derry was planning a trip to the USA for Bethany, Joseph and Nathaniel, leaving Alice at home with Miriam and Dawn Star and Thomas who wanted to spend time with his friends.

Nathaniel was a gifted artist. He was a good all-rounder in sport and in his studies, but he even spoke about Art School when he was not yet ten.

Paul worked well with Beate on the spiritual aspect of women's studies and was preparing a conference. He travelled less and was delighted with the progress of his children. Nicholas started to eat more and put on weight. Victor made sure he spoke to Bethany every week and Cristina shared art with Nathaniel but was more interested in language studies.

Koda and Shining Star had great emotional pain over their son. They were shocked that they had known and understood him so little. He had kept up a double life for years, sleeping with as many girls as he could. He had been severely chastened by the virulent strain of VD he had contracted and passed on to others. He applied for a social work role with a court on the outskirts of Winnipeg where he would work with the residents of a Reservation known for deprivation. This was his punishment to himself. Keeping it secret from his work colleagues, he joined a 'sex addiction' course. He was desperate to get help as he realised that his behaviour had not been normal. He was embarrassed to tell the group that he had a STD which could affect his child and had infected several women. He gradually was made to understand why he needed the 'high' of seducing women. He realised that he had never loved and yet he had witnessed the love between his parents. He learned that the drive was partially there because of the struggles he had when his parents had to deal with racism, being put down, being treated like the lowest of the low and worthless, destined for alcoholism.

He tried to write a letter of apology to Miriam. He did not want to re-ignite her love for him if she still felt it, but he wanted her to know he was learning to be a better person. It took him months to write and another few weeks to post it but at least he sent it before he reached his 25th birthday. His treatment was embarrassing and uncomfortable. He wore special dressings, put on cream and feared that he might remain impotent. He did not explain that to Miriam.

Jet was the delight of everyone. Alice coped well with the baby while Miriam was at school and she had to learn how to hand her over to the young mother. She tried games with Dawn Star and tried to get her to follow a light. She feared that her sight was not normal. The baby smiled when Miriam held her up or when Jet came to her but Alice was convinced she had a problem.

She accompanied Miriam to the next check up and asked if her sight could be tested. They were given an appointment with a specialist and given some aids to help the baby follow the movement of a colour or a light.

"What can she see?"

"We will know more later but she certainly has some sight. It is too soon to try some lenses on her."

Miriam wept herself to sleep. After a few days Little Bear's letter arrived. She left it unopened for hours. Alone in her room she opened it, read it and wept. She got pen and paper and replied immediately.

"I am trying to forgive you. Your daughter has damaged eyesight because of the disease you gave her and me. You have possibly ruined our lives forever. Are you proud of yourself boasting about seducing a professor's daughter? I do hope you learn your lesson and behave better in the future." She took Dawn Star in the buggy to the Post Office to send it off.

Dawn Star was a happy and contented baby. She drank her mother's milk and took her bottle in the day time. Bethany took time to play with her and helped her begin to sit up. She could also stand while being held upright on a lap.

"She's progressing well darling," said Alice, "We'll work together to help her eyesight."

"Look, Mum," she handed Little Bear's letter to her mother. Alice read through.

"That's real repentance. He is not trying to seduce you. He is asking for forgiveness."

"I've written back but I did not forgive him. There is no hope of any love. He does not know what it is. I will let him know how his daughter is doing as she grows up but I do not want him in her life at all."

"Give it time."

Derry was planning a trip in 2013 for Joseph, Bethany and Nathaniel to meet the Blackhill girls at the Lake of the Woods. Paul and family might join them for part of the time. That year would be their 20th wedding anniversary. Alice suggested that they celebrate in 2018, their Silver Wedding as the clouds over the family were still too big. Derry agreed that Miriam and Dawn Star could not be left alone but that in a couple of years they could once again come on foreign trips. Miriam was depressed to hear them planning to go to the Lake of the Woods and she realised that her mother was limited because of her presence and that she would never leave her alone with her small baby.

Zara and Carson, Abigail and Justin all tried to spend time with her. She was invited for weekends but, although she was grateful, she did not feel confident enough to take her baby on trips yet. They brought their children to play with Dawn Star in Oxford. Nathaniel was invited to the de Boyadere art studio.

Derry let Beate take the lead with the women's studies and travelled as little as possible. He was thinking ahead to the 2018 celebration and wondered how to celebrate it with Alice.

Thomas would be 21, Joseph would be 19, Bethany 17 and Nathaniel 15. Normally he would not have hesitated and organised a trip to Thala. Somehow a black cloud hung over Queensland. Now and then he mentioned ideas to Alice but she was too preoccupied to make any decisions or have any ideas.

Miriam was planning to return to full time in the sixth form but she asked for time off to go to the clinic with her baby. She explained that she needed tests and treatment for her eyes.

"Is that because of the venereal disease?" the Head of Sixth Form snapped. Miriam was struck dumb and hung her head. "You should tell your sexy friends about it. They might just think of controlling themselves." Miriam burst into tears and sobbed. She said she was going home as she could not face classes today. She walked out and ran down the corridor sobbing loudly. She did not go home but walked along the canal, sat on a bench and watched the swans and ducks. She arrived home at the normal time. Alice could see she had been crying. She did not ask but waited for her to speak. She hugged her broken daughter.

The next appointment was a long one so Miriam did not attend school at all that day. They sat amazed at all the technology used to check a child's eyesight. Dawn Star was quite happy to have lights shone into her eyes, a contraption placed on her head with various lenses. She played with the soft toys, kicked her legs and giggled.

"She's a happy baby." said the nurse. They were asked to sit in a waiting room until the specialist could come and speak to them.

Miriam felt sick. Her private parts, still fighting the disease seemed to react to stress and she felt very sore and uncomfortable.

They were called into a smart office with a large desk. The male specialist in a white coat sat behind it.

"Please take a seat." They did.

"What a lovely little girl. Is she mixed race?"

"Her father is a native Canadian or Indian." responded Miriam.

"That explains the black hair and black eyes. Mrs Barnes, Miss Barnes I am very sorry to say that your daughter is almost totally blind. She has no sight in her left eye and very little in her right. She can respond to light but she will never be able to read. She will need to attend a school where she can learn Braille and to move around by touch."

The volcano exploded in Miriam's head. "Blind?" she whispered. Alice put her arms around her shoulders.

"There is much more we can do these days. There are many more aids, not just a white stick. We will be with you all the way, helping with aids and tests, checking on her regularly. She is a delightful, happy baby and I think she is a fighter. She will make the best of her little bit of sight. I am going to arrange for you to visit a special school so you can see what the children can achieve."

"That's very helpful. Thank you." said Alice. Miriam was trembling and cuddling Dawn Star.

"She will need your love and patience. I will also send a physiotherapist to your home to go round all the rooms with you, she will provide stair gates and door stops for when she can walk. The kitchen is the essential place to make her aware of danger. I am sorry they did not catch the disease in time." He looked at his notes. "They did not discover it until you started to mention pain towards the end of your pregnancy. It was too late by then."

"The father has also been quite ill and is still on strong anti-biotics. He is in Canada."

"He will probably be impotent. It is a terrible type he had contracted."

Miriam was weeping softly.

"Is there anything else? I think Miriam needs to go home. It is a lot to take in."

"I will put it all in writing. Do go now. I am very sorry indeed and I wish you the very best with your lovely daughter." He put his hand on her shoulder as they all stood up.

Alice recalled Granny Lou. "How could she bear this?" Now she was overwhelmed but determined to encourage Miriam to be as positive as possible and take it all day by day.

In the car park Miriam broke down and screamed, "How much more? What else? My poor baby!" Baby started crying too as she had never heard her mother scream.

"I'll take her for a walk. Sit in the car for a bit and try to calm down. We all love you both my darling." Alice did not go far and watched Miriam bang on the window with her fists as she screamed until she was hoarse. She held her head in her hands. Her eyes could hardly open. Alice put the sleeping Dawn Star into her baby seat and sat and held her broken daughter.

"We'll get through this." She was also weeping so it was an hour before she could drive. "Leave Dawn Star with me and go and lie down for a bit. Do you want to tell Dad or shall I?"

"Please tell him."

Dawn Star was happily swinging in her bouncy chair. The stricken Derry wept with Alice and went up to Miriam's room. She was sobbing on every breath as she slept. He stroked her head and held her hands.

"We'll get through this. She is so lovely. We'll go and see how the other children get on in the school." He kissed her burning forehead.

"Do you want a drink?"

"Yes, please." He brought her favourite milk drink. He then got the other children together. "Listen, my dear children. I have some sad news to tell you. Dawn Star saw the specialist today and they told us that she is nearly totally blind. We'll all have to be very careful with her, especially when she starts walking. We'll get a lot of help from the doctors. We will all work together to help her."

Bethany burst into tears. "Can I see Miriam?"

"Yes, she might be asleep." Bethany jumped into her bed and cuddled her. The boys asked questions and wondered how she would get around the house.

"She will go to a special school and learn Braille. We will get some and all learn it with her. We'll put on some music tonight or Thomas and Joseph would you like to play something?" Jet bounded into the room. "Please take him out. Mum and Miriam have been out all day." They were glad to go into the woods.

The next day Alice rang the school to say that Miriam would not be in for a few days after getting bad news from the hospital. Bethany skyped Victor and Joseph skyped Bright Star. There were so many messages of support. Alice and Derry were waiting for a few days before talking to Paul and Koda.

Miriam asked Alice to look after her baby because she wanted time alone.

Alice was not happy to leave her alone for too long so she persuaded her down for lunch. She could not eat. Towards the end of the afternoon Miriam came down fully dressed.

"I think I'll take Dawn Star for a little walk in her buggy. What's for supper?"

"I'm roasting some vegetables. You will enjoy them."

"Yes, I love them. I think I can manage some of those." She picked up her baby and strapped her in.

She walked to the road and started down the Woodstock Road. When a bus came along she got on and quite confidently stored the buggy in the designated place. In the town centre she walked to the Fordco Centre and walked her baby around the shops. She took the lift to the third balcony and walked around it, looking in the windows. She looked down at the mothers and children, the groups of youths and waited until nearly closing time. She took her baby out of the buggy and climbed onto the railings. She tipped forward and jumped, falling head first. She held Dawn Star upside down and they both hit the ground. People screamed as she fell and those at the bottom were traumatised to see the bodies. They also screamed. Some went over to see if they were dead. Black blood oozed from the long black hair and the lifeless baby had her head smashed in.

The security staff rushed over and called the police and ambulance. The people were asked to leave the centre. Many did so weeping. An officer found her phone in her bag.

"She planned this, poor girl. She had left her phone open and there is her home number." It was Derry who answered.

"Please sir, can you tell me your address, some officers are coming to see you. We have some bad news for you."

"Have you got my daughter and granddaughter? They are unusually late coming home?"

"Yes, sir. Is your wife with you?"

"Yes and I have four children at home. Can you tell me what has happened?" He gave his address. "Are they alright?"

"No, sir, I am afraid they are not. Our officers are on their way and will be with you in about ten minutes." He asked the children to stay in the play rooms while he spoke to the police. Alice saw his white face and shaking hands. She went to the door when the bell rang and they answered it together. Two officers stood at the door, a man and a woman.

"Mr and Mrs Barnes?"

"Yes, do come in." Derry let them through. "Our children are upstairs. Can we talk in the lounge?"

Jet barked at them and Derry calmed him down, put him on the lead and got him to sit at his feet.

"We are so sorry to tell you that your daughter and granddaughter jumped from the third balcony at the Fordco Centre and they both died immediately. We are so very sorry."

Alice and Derry were both weeping. Alice spoke first, "She had some bad news from the hospital and was told that her baby was blind. She spent the day in bed and I thought it was good when she wanted to take her out for a walk in the buggy. How did she get to town?"

Derry asked if they could see them.

"Yes, sir, we need you to identify the bodies. Can you get someone to stay with the children?"

Alice rang Jean and told her there was an emergency and they needed to go to the hospital. Jean agreed to come over. Derry went up to see the children.

"My dear children we have to go to the hospital to see Miriam and Dawn Star. Jean is coming to stay with you. If you are hungry please help yourselves in the kitchen and please feed Jet." They knew it was bad news because their father was so white, weeping and shaking. They did not dare ask. Before Jean arrived Alice went into Miriam's room and found her diary and a letter on the bed. She picked them up and brought them down to Derry. He opened the letter and read her suicide note.

Sorry dearest Mum and Dad, I am not brave. Dawn Star cannot be blind. It is better if we die. I cannot live after what I have done to her. I love you all and I am very sorry.

They wept together and with Jean when she arrived. The trained officers knew how to handle the situation. The lady officer held Alice and then gave them both a glass of water.

"Jean, please do not tell the children, they only know that Miriam is in hospital. We shall tell them when we return. Thank you so much for coming. Please encourage them to eat and walk the dog while we are out."

They could not stop crying as they got into the police car. They held each other and felt unreal as they walked into the hospital and followed the police lady to the mortuary. Both bodies had been cleaned up and covered in a sheet. There was dried blood in Miriam's hair and Dawn Star's head was covered in a white shroud to hide the smashed skull. They could only kiss their foreheads and cheeks and hold their hands. Alice visualised little Miriam climbing the steps to the Queenslander calling 'Granny, Granny' after her mother had died. Derry saw little Miriam take her teddy from the bookshelf where she had put it to wait for him to return from his trip.

The lady police office spoke to Alice. "I will stay with you tonight. You have had a terrible shock, Are there any relatives to come to you?"

"From tomorrow onwards, my brother and my sister-in-law."

She drove them home and went into the house with them. All four children ran to their weeping parents. Derry took them into the study and sat Alice on the leather chair. They all sat on the floor around her. Jet leapt onto her lap and snuggled with her. He knew.

The white-faced children sat in silence. "What happened?" asked Thomas.

"Dear children, this is the worst day of my life. I am sorry to tell you that our dear Miriam and Dawn Star are both dead." He let them take it in. Bethany wept and Joseph cuddled her. Nathaniel put himself on Thomas' lap.

"She was so upset about Dawn Star being blind. She thought it was her fault. She jumped with her from the highest balcony in the Fordco. She left us a note.

Here it is." he passed it to Thomas. He started to read it but could not finish it for weeping.

"Did anyone see them in the Fordco?" asked Joseph.

"Yes, I am afraid they did. We shall take some flowers there."

They could only sip water. They thanked Jean very much for coming and offered a drink to the policewoman.

"I'm Susan. Please call me Susan. Is there anyone else you would like me to contact?" The next two days were a blur. Death certificates, police questions, finding the buggy, planning the funeral, the coroner, the autopsy and telling others. Daniel and Charles, Maddy and Roy, Abigail and Justin arrived. Susan contacted Koda and Paul and Steve and the Cairns Meditation Group. The house was soon filled with flowers. Huge displays arrived from all over the world. Derry called Beate and the Nigerian doctors. Beate left it a few days before visiting. The Headmistress arrived at the door with a huge display from the school.

"The Head of Year told me of her last conversation with Miriam and she is feeling sorry and very guilty."

"We knew nothing about it. Miriam did not tell us."

"Miriam was a very bright girl and passed all her exams even though the grades were lowered by her emotional state."

Thomas spent the time speaking with Daniel and Charles.

"Can we make a book for them like we did for Hunter?" asked Nathaniel. "Of course we can, dear little Nathaniel." Alice hugged him.

Derry and Alice took a display of flowers to the Fordco. They went to the top where the buggy was found. They looked over and saw how easy it was to climb up and jump. They went to the bottom and noticed some bunches of flowers left by the artificial grass area. It had all been cleaned up and replaced. They placed their basket of pink roses at the side with the little card *In memory of Miriam and Dawn Star.*

"I am sorry for the people who witnessed it. What a terrible thing to see." Derry put the buggy in Miriam's room and sat and drafted a letter to the management of the Fordco. He explained that his beloved daughter had been given the news that her baby was blind and was so upset that she decided to kill herself with her baby. He apologised that she had chosen the Centre and had caused further trauma to other people.

The invitation to the special school arrived. They had forgotten to inform the hospital ophthalmic department.

Derry and Alice took time to cuddle all their children; they all took time out from school. Beate said they could delay their trip to Peru. Derry said he would decide after the funeral.

The bodies had not been released yet because there had to be a full autopsy in case drugs were involved.

The Press got hold of the letter to the Fordco.

Tragedy at the shopping centre.

Tragic teen kills herself with her baby at the Fordco. Professor apologises for daughter's suicide.

Teen kills blind baby and herself.

Journalists turned up at their front door. Alice came out and spoke to them as the TV cameras rolled.

"This is the worst time of our life. We have lost a beautiful daughter and granddaughter. We are in a state of shock and bereavement. We cannot speak. We have not even had her funeral. Now is not the time to speak. Later we will speak and we will try to help other people who have to cope with similar situations. Please respect our time of bereavement and wait for interviews."

Some were heartless and yelled out. "Isn't your husband a Professor?"

"Did you support your daughter's illegitimate baby?"

"How many children have you got?"

Two approached her and left their cards. They invited her to contact them when she was ready to speak.

The next ordeal was the coroner's report.

"This young lady had no sign of drugs in her body. She had a virulent strain of venereal disease which would have caused her to be infertile for the rest of her life. She had planned her suicide and had jumped headfirst and was clearly intent on suicide and on murdering her baby. She left a suicide note for her family. In a depressed state and while the balance of her mind was disturbed, she took her own life and that of her blind baby."

Alice and Derry learned how not to weep in public after so many terrible experiences. Ashen and drawn they responded to the questions. They had no idea of her intentions because she had cleverly asked what the supper was and told them she would look forward to it.

When she had not returned after an hour they tried her phone. It rang but was not answered. It was soon with the police.

Daniel had taken a portrait of her on her 16th birthday and had it enlarged and framed. It was a beautiful memory of her.

Daniel played at her funeral and with the two brothers they performed the tribal song they had composed. Charles arranged to have a copy made and recorded.

Connie had flown in from Cairns. She had so loved Miriam and Thomas in those early years when she babysat in the Queenslander.

She and Beate stayed in the granny flat. Daniel invited the whole family to come to a concert in London and stay in their flat for the weekend.

Alice returned to bereavement counselling and suggested that Derry did the same instead of keeping all his pain inside. This time he agreed.

Koda phoned and told them that Little Bear had not returned to work after the compassionate leave but had sunk into depression. Knowing that he was impotent was bad enough but knowing that Miriam and his daughter had died was too much to bear. He spent some weeks being treated for depression in a mental institution.

"So many ruined lives." Koda added sadly.

"We are going to use it for good. We have agreed to be interviewed. I told them I would answer questions when I was able to speak. We shall deal with promiscuity, teen sex, loveless sex and the dangers. We shall also provoke interest in dealing with blind and disabled babies. People need to be aware." Alice explained.

"Wonderful." Koda was amazed at her strength.

After the funeral Derry took them all with Jet for a holiday in Dorset. It did them all good. On their return Alice rang the journalists. One had lost interest but the other came to their house. Derry wanted to be present in case the questions were not appropriate. He spoke firmly at the beginning, "We are not here to sell your papers. No salacious gossip. We want to give out warnings to young people about sexual activity, loveless sex and we want to bring up the issue of dealing with blind and other disabled babies."

The journalist asked if he could film as there was a possibility that there would be a documentary on teen suicides. The journalist was very surprised to learn about the Spiritual Healing Centre which they had built and run at their own expense.

Mother of tragic teen suicide speaks out.

There was a double page article with a photo of Miriam and Dawn Star. On the whole they were pleased with the article which included at the end, an introduction to and information on the Healing Centre.

The amount of interest surprised them. There were donations, offers of help and applications for joining the various counselling courses.

Derry and Alice knew they would never get over their loss. They started reading about the mystery of suffering and tragedy. Nevertheless they still wanted to keep up the trips with Koda and Paul. The one to Lake of the Woods was planned without Thomas who had his own set of friends and his own agenda. Paul and family would join them at some point. Koda would just bring Bright Star as his oldest daughter was now working and had her own group of friends.

Derry made up his mind to spend time with Little Bear during the trip.

8 Accept the Mystery

'*Accept the mystery.*' These words were written on one of the many cards they had received. There were hundreds which Alice kept to read through later. She chose to do this at Christmas, always a sensitive time for bereaved families.

The children all made their contributions to the Remembering Miriam and Dawn Star book. Nathaniel produced a drawing of them along with other decorations to ornament other pages. They pooled their photographs to choose the best ones together and they all sat and wrote their memories of their sister. The hardest part was reading her diary where she had poured out her love and desire for Little Bear, her sense of guilt and her despair. She even wrote that she was aware that other people would be affected badly by witnessing her fall. She had purposely gone at the end of the day so there would be fewer people.

She planned how to jump without hitting anyone else.

Alice recalled her Spiritual Direction training. The director should not imagine that he or she could solve problems and give answers to the client. The task was to accompany the client on their journey and to encourage him or her. She had done that for Louisa. In giving up direction and adopting her as a granny for her children, she had given her a happy end of life.

Who would help her? She and Derry both went to bereavement counselling separately, but they spent a great deal of time talking to each other.

'Why?' loomed large in their thinking and they knew there was no answer. Could they have prevented it? Possibly, but only with hindsight. They had been willing and determined to support Miriam and Dawn Star through the process of growing up with a blind baby.

Now they had been left with a new kind of freedom. Alice would be able to accompany Derry and the children on their trips with Koda and Paul. Instead of directly celebrating their 20th wedding anniversary, they decided to make their trip to the Lake of the Woods with Koda, Shining Star and Bright Star their treat for the year. Paul, Vivienne and their children planned to join them for 10 days.

Daniel and Charles dog sat for Jet for three weeks. Derry arranged with Koda to spend time with Little Bear.

"I would like to see him on my own. We shall have a hire car so I can drive back to Winnipeg and leave Alice and the children with you and Paul. Alice wrote to Curt and Pearl in Amaranth to share the sad news and explained that they were spending time at Lake of the Woods in the summer. She hoped they could call in on them. She said they would have three of their children with them. During the winter months it helped them all to dream of the lake in the summer. Right now it would be under six foot of ice and Heinrich would be crossing it on his skidoo. She asked them if there were a place to stay for a couple of nights.

"Our cellar, if it does not rain." was the answer.

Planning, dreaming, thinking of the amazing beauty of the lake and of Amaranth restored a sense of hope. Derry had postponed his own trip to Peru but encouraged Paul to go with Beate. They thought of inviting Jake and Connie from Cairns. These plans were afoot as the year came to an end.

Daniel and Charles joined them for Christmas Day. They had concerts in London and Leipzig in the New Year so Alice took Thomas and Joseph to hear their uncles play and to see the old East Germany. They both enjoyed the experience of attending a concert at the Gewandhaus but Joseph made it clear that he preferred modern music.

They especially enjoyed seeing the remains of the old Berlin Wall and the No-Man's Land on the old border with West Germany not far outside Leipzig.

As the new year began Alice and Derry realised how mature their children had become. They remembered their older sister but they did not collapse into weeping. They all had school friends who came to the house and went out, mainly for sport, with them. They did not seem interested by the clubbing culture.

Derry and Alice had talks with them about the sex and drugs scene.

Alice took Nathaniel to London to see the de Boyadere studio. It moved and inspired him. He sat through an Art Therapy session and answered the questions of the clients trying out their skills. He told them he loved drawing but was not yet confident using colours. He enjoyed making collages.

Bethany took up Spanish Conversation with Vivienne.

The loss of Miriam dominated both Alice and Derry and they had to make a conscious effort not to let it affect their love and relationships with their other children. They recorded their memories of her growing up in Cairns and Oxford and added them to the family book.

Nearly a year passed before they decided to tackle Miriam's room. Bethany said she would help with the clothes and baby things. They distributed them to various charities.

"Would anyone like to swop rooms and take Miriam's old room?"

No one wanted to do that. They decided to redecorate it and use it as a guest room for their friends. Alice had chosen one dress and one pair of shoes and Bethany chose some jewellery to keep. Thomas said he would help decorate. He cleaned the walls and painted them white and pale grey. He gave it a very sophisticated look. They gave the bed away and put in two single beds for guests. The bedding was pale grey and white. On the window wall they hung the portrait of Miriam with Hunter and the one of her on her 16th birthday.

"Nathaniel would you like to make a collage for the new guest room?"

"Yes, but not flowers, can I have wild animals?" They all helped him look through magazines and second-hand books for suitable pictures. He enjoyed his project and it looked very good once framed.

The Meditation Group had restarted a month after the funeral and Thomas and Bethany both joined in. The members were sensitive to the loss and sorrow but participated with music, prayers and readings before the silence. They all knew that Derry and Alice were struggling with their pain. Alice sometimes found Derry in tears and Derry sometimes found Alice in tears. Something had triggered a memory of Miriam; her wet hair as she ran in from swimming, her favourite teddy, her love for Zippy the dog, then Hunter and then Jet, when she made such an effort to train him. Jet showed that he was aware of her absence. He would go to her room, sniff around the area where Dawn Star had her hanging, bouncy chair. He soon attached himself to Thomas who seemed to love taking him out, sometimes accompanied by Derry when he returned from the University.

As the trip to the Lake of the Woods drew near, Curt and Pearl said they there would be a room for the parents and one for Bethany. Would the boys mind being in the cellar? Koda, Shining Star and Bright Star called in on them before they drove east. Paul and Vivienne hired a large camper van so they did not need a hotel. Derry hired a car and drove west from Winnipeg to Portage and Amaranth.

It was a happy reunion although Pearl could see that Alice and Derry were pale and had lost weight. Joseph and Nathaniel thought it would be an adventure to sleep in a cellar but were pleasantly surprised to see how well furnished and decorated it was. They loved the animals, the small holding, the little village and the huge Lake Manitoba.

"Miriam was possibly conceived in Canada," said Alice, "I found out I was pregnant just before we went home."

After a few happy days together Derry drove east to Winnipeg, Kenora and Sioux Narrows. Heinrich met them and took them to a lodge by the lakeside. Koda and family were in a chalet nearby. Paul parked his van on their drive. During the ten days in Sioux Narrows the children mixed and matched. They were happy to see each other and they never decided where to sleep until the evening came. Heinrich took Joseph, Bright Star and Derry out to see Joseph Island. They all enjoyed seeing the very similar coast line to his birthmark.

Bright Star sat on a rock and told Joseph about her course in music and theatre, dance, singing and acting. They spent a long time sharing what they liked and disliked in styles of music. Joseph said he was going to look for a modern music and jazz course rather than classical.

Bethany was glad to have Cristina's company. She missed Miriam very much but she was at ease with the twins. There were very few squabbles as they went swimming, boating, fishing and hiking.

Derry talked to Koda about his visit to Little Bear. They decided to swop cars so the larger one could stay with Alice for outings. Koda arranged insurance and Derry left the three families with Alice's blessing. It took over five hours to reach the Rez outside Winnipeg. He had written to Little Bear, a peaceful, considerate letter of reconciliation so Little Bear, although he dreaded the meeting, was not feeling in danger of being shouted at and abused. He was surprised to see his father's car turn up at the Court House. Derry noted immediately that Little Bear had shaved his head.

"We swopped vehicles. I am here with Alice and three children so ours is bigger. Paul has a camper van for his three."

Little Bear took him to a bar and they sat with a beer in the garden. "Will you let it grow again?"

"Perhaps. Derry, I am a different man now. I have had a lot of therapy and I have learned what caused me to be a heartless cad. I am trying hard to treat women differently."

"How is your health?"

"Not good. I have ruined my own body. The specialist has told me that there may be a drug I can try to restore me but even if that works I shall be infertile."

"So was Miriam. She would never have been able to have another baby and she was still on pills after the birth of Dawn Star."

"How can you bear to see me?"

"I love you as I love all of your family. I understand that you had an addiction problem and were a damaged young man. Miriam really loved you but she was immature and unable to understand what relationships entail. She did trust you and of course she was broken hearted when she learned the truth."

"I got her note. She did not forgive me."

"It takes time. Dawn Star was absolutely lovely. She was happy and peaceful and I think she would have flourished as a blind child. We were all ready to learn Braille to help her."

"I've been depressed so I understand that Miriam was so desperate that she killed herself and our baby. I felt like doing the same."

"Tell me something, your women, were any of them native?"

"No, never, always white girls."

"Have you worked out why?"

"I think it's linked with the way I fought back when I was treated like I was nothing. In my course I faced that when white girls found me attractive I was not just flattered but I was getting my own back! I felt so good, so powerful each time. I was a winner."

"Ok."

"I felt like a conqueror. I could not handle the fact that I was attractive to white girls. I took advantage to feel good about myself."

"How did you get the disease?"

"I didn't use prostitutes. They usually have tests and keep themselves clean. I was used to shagging 3-4 girls a week. Some became regulars. Some girls acted like me, picking up guys in bars all the time."

"You don't know who had this virulent strain?"

"No but it must have been just before I met Miriam as I had had no symptoms until afterwards.

"Did you have to contact the women?"

"Yes, the doctor ordered me to list them and tell them but I had no idea who many of them were."

"When you boasted that you had got the daughter of an English professor pregnant, did you overlook the fact that you were the son of a Professor?"

"Boasting was part of the act. I had to look good to other men too."

“Thank you for being so open and honest with me, Little Bear. Miriam was adored by all of us and we will never recover from her death. What Alice and I are determined to do is bring good out of evil and use this tragedy to help others. We have four other lovely children whom we love dearly. They loved Miriam and they are also in grief. You heard about our Healing Centre? We already have bereavement counselling. When we are stronger we will find ways to help other teenagers.”

“I’d like to help.”

“How is your writing?”

“Not bad. I got a good degree.”

“Could you begin by writing about your life, your experiences of racism growing up and how it led you into sex addiction?”

“What for?”

“We also work on Post-Colonial Theology. This is led by Paul, the Theologian. We deal with racism, women’s issues and the lasting influence of the colonial occupation.”

“I’ll write it up for you especially if it will help.”

“Thank you, Little Bear. I will keep in touch. I see you have been broken too but I am sure you can bring good out of this tragedy. Your court work will help a lot of your fellow natives.”

They stood up and the shaven headed man offered his hand. Derry ignored it and hugged him as he was weeping.

“You are part of our lives; Little Bear and you are a link with Miriam.”

Derry felt this was a step towards healing. He drove to Amaranth and spent the night with Curt and Pearl. In his room that night he remembered his first visit there with Alice.

He drove back to Sioux Narrows and arranged to have a talk with Koda and Shining Star with Alice. Paul and Vivienne took all the children on a picnic. Derry told them of his talk with Little Bear and reassured his parents that through his illness, his breakdown and his course he was on a path to healing. He explained a little of the reasons which led to the sex addiction and that Little Bear was going to do some writing for his research with Paul. The four parents were all suffering deeply and three of them could not take in the meaning and implications of what Derry was saying. They knew they were on a good path, a Songline leading to inner healing.

Alice got out the card she carried with her. “Accept the mystery, that’s what we are doing. We always ask ‘Why?’ We accept that we don’t know. There is no answer. It is a mystery. If we fight and wrestle we get nowhere. If we give in to anger and bitterness and disappointment, we do not become stronger. Accepting means trusting without understanding.”

They heard Paul’s van return and smiling faces greeted them as they decided where they were going to sleep that night. Alice and Derry had the twins and Bright Star, Paul had Bethany and Cristina, Koda had Joseph and Nathaniel; another successful mix and match.

Going out on the lake was a wonderful experience for them all. Watching the loons with their fluffy chicks on their backs, the clouds of cormorants swooping in and out of the water and the white pelicans elegantly moving round the boat gave them all a sense of joy.

9 Songlines to the Silver Wedding

In the five years leading to Derry and Alice's Silver Wedding, the studies and future careers of the children became clearer. The criss-cross songlines of their lives continued.

Little Bear wrote a clear and articulate report which was used in a paper by Paul as part of the ongoing influence of colonial occupation. It tied in with the TV documentary, where the interview with the grieving parents was shown in a program about teenage suicide. Derry and Alice kept in touch with Little Bear and were pleased to see his real reconciliation with his parents over the years.

Thomas was accepted at the Oxford College for Anthropology but kept up his music with Joseph, composing and performing and in college he joined a modern group. He met another gay student in college and although he was not interested in music, they became close friends in his first year.

Joseph applied to study music in Manchester University where he could find a jazz group, a musical theatre group and could study modern composition. When he was 20 and the four-year age difference with Bright Star became irrelevant, they announced their intention to marry. Bright Star would live with him in the UK and follow her own musical theatre and dance career. The year before the Silver Wedding, Joseph escaped being hurt by the terrorist bomb at the Ariana Grande concert. He did not attend the concert but was close enough at the station to hear the explosion.

Bethany and Victor fell in love. She was studying European languages and training to teach English as a foreign language and they planned to live in the USA. Alice was sorry that her only daughter would be so far away.

Nathaniel went to art school but did not want to have a studio. He was going to find out how best to use his skills.

Vivienne and Alice wondered if Cristina and Nathaniel would also form an attachment but it was too early to tell.

Derry's work continued to flourish. He made short trips with Koda, Paul and Beate. He wondered if Alice would like a trip to Thala to celebrate their anniversary. They were both very tired. All her life Alice had longed to return to

Cairns but she could not make her mind up. Somehow the black cloud was still over Queensland. One night she remembered how Miriam had taken her first steps on the balcony of the Thala lodge. She had an outburst of weeping. She suggested that they go instead to Romania and visit Kyle and Adina and their growing family.

They had a party in Oxford with Daniel, Charles, Maddy, Roy and all their friends and then flew to Bucharest. They stayed in a Ploiesti hotel and hired a car for trips to the orphanage and extended cottage. They spent some time in the Carpathians and enjoyed the spectacular scenery. It did them good to see Kyle and his family together.

At home, joyfully welcomed by Jet, Derry experienced some pains in his chest. He was examined and tested and advised to take early retirement. He was given some medication but he still had a heart attack. He survived and slowly recovered but he was warned that he should slow right down and stop working.

It was a shock of course but something happened inside both Alice and Derry. They sat in the study by the white bookshelf and felt that they could actually be free. The bookshelf had for Alice become a symbol of stability, of a privileged life and of a duty to use knowledge and wisdom to do good to others. It was also a symbol of love as Alice had dearly loved her parents. After her marriage to Derry she had longed to have her own home but instead was compelled by circumstances to stay in her childhood home, even after her parents had died one after the other. She now experienced a longing to be free of this symbol and make a different life for herself and Derry as he took care of his health.

"Alice, I have a radical suggestion. Let's sell this house and the centre and move to Cairns and spend our last years there where we spent our first months of marriage. We shall talk to all the children. Any who want to join us are welcome and we will see that those who stay here or go abroad are well provided for. I will hand over all the work to my colleagues including the running of the Hartley Barnes Foundation and the Healing Centre."

"When you are stronger I will go to Cairns, perhaps with Nathaniel and look for a suitable house. A Queenslander will be no good for a sick man. We must also find out what we need to do to take Jet with us. He has a few years of life in him yet. I cannot leave him. Most of the children will be in their studies and will not want to cope with him."

Derry accepted that he was ill and was in danger of other heart attacks. He needed to check that Alice could cope in Cairns; that the black cloud had gone.

"We will never forget what happened, but the worst happened in Oxford. We can rest and enjoy Cairns although many of our friends will have changed and even moved. It is a special place for us. The white bookshelf gave stability and a drive to duty. It is over. We need to rest. You have been the most wonderful husband. We have been a good team. We have wonderful children and just look how your work has put them on paths all over the world. We need to buy them a home, especially Thomas and Joseph and let them know they are always welcome in our new home in Cairns."

There was a big family get together with Daniel and Charles, Maddy and Roy and the four young Barnes. They understood the situation and felt somewhat insecure at the idea of losing their home. As Derry explained the plan to provide for them all until they could get their own home or settle abroad, they began to see the advantages and they all wanted their father to live as long as possible.

"We need to be free of this house and the Centre. Dad needs to be away from Oxford and learn to live a new life without all the stress and responsibility." Daniel said how much he would miss them, the dog and the house but they looked forward to visits to Cairns and Thala.

Nathaniel wondered if he would be able to study Art in Cairns. He would miss his sister and brothers but they would also be scattered around America and England.

They researched houses on the internet and found some modern housing on a new estate near Palm Cove. There was hardly any garden and the houses were all newly decorated. They were single storey with very large rooms and several bedrooms. Derry was still able to cope with the finances and began the deals to get homes for his children wherever they wanted them. He had an experienced estate agent who could organise the sale of the house with or without the Centre as going concern. He hoped it could continue but it was a lot to ask of a new owner to live with a busy centre at the bottom of the garden. He wanted to safeguard the jobs of all the tutors. The house with an internal separate flat was advertised along with the information on the Healing Centre. He invited all the staff into his house to talk to them about their plans. "If I stay and continue working, I will not live long then I am no good to anyone!"

There was sadness and insecurity all round. Nathaniel decided to travel with Alice and look at the houses and at college possibilities.

They started applying for emigration, knowing that the proceeds from the large house would provide the finances needed and Derry's standing at the University would assist their application.

The new houses were on a little estate of similar houses. Some of the houses overlooked the coast. They were near transport into the town centre and also near one of the large shopping centres familiar to Alice. Alice noted that they would be much nearer to neighbours.

Nathaniel loved the idea of being in a house that no one else had lived in. He rushed from room to room.

"This is mine!" he claimed one. "The big one is yours and Dads. I can have Jet in with me." He was very excited.

"Where's the study?" Alice walked across the huge open plan room, found the kitchen and noticed a big alcove on one wall leading to the corridor for the bedrooms.

"Perhaps in this corner. We could put in another door."

Once the finances had been agreed and the house was bought, the whole family travelled together to look at the new family base. They all loved it. Thomas, Bethany and Joseph were travelling back together and staying with Daniel until their moves to their new homes. They all said they would visit as often as they could from the other parts of the world. Joseph and Bright Star said they would have their honeymoon in Thala. Derry told Alice that she should go the Bethany's wedding in America, if indeed she had one. Long journeys were finished for him.

It took months to get sorted out of course. Deciding which furniture to take, what to sell, what to leave, was a terrible ordeal for them. It took some weeks to get Jet with his dog passport accepted.

Derry was given special attention on the flight and had a wheelchair at each stop and transfer. He decided to get his own wheelchair for future use. He had always thought ahead and planned and provided.

To fit along the modern wall, the bookshelf had to be cut down by one shelf. They would not keep all the books now he was retired. They chose their favourites before the University took the rest.

Nathaniel helped choose the curtains and blinds and the first pictures to go up were the portraits of Miriam with Hunter and on her 16th birthday, Nathaniel's wild animal collage joined them. He was looking forward to visiting the Art Schools and the University.

It was not long before visitors from Canada, America, Norwich, London and Oxford arrived. The colleagues in Cairns were not the same. Steve and others had also reached retirement age, nevertheless both Alice and Derry felt happy, relieved and ready to change, to slow down. From their front garden they could see the waves lapping at the islands.

The best part of the amazing decision was that the new owners of their house in Oxford were happy to allow the Healing Centre to function in their garden. This was the greatest blessing for them. The new owners almost immediately said that they would call in architects to change the internal granny flat and enlarge the study and lounge. Alice did not suffer insecurity this time but she sensed a new freedom and a new life. Jet missed the garden but he had the beach. He went crazy the first time he plunged into the sea and rushed up the sand.

Derry recovered enough to explore other walks for the dog. He visited the University, caught up with Steve and Jeannie who now had grandchildren. Some of the Meditation group had died. Simon had lost Eugene but kept on the workshop. Sandrine was retiring from the Art Therapy Shack but others were taking over. Her old neighbour Maria and her husband had moved into a Care Home because of their mobility problems. Alice was able to find them and visit them.

Alice and Derry had never dreamed that their Silver Wedding would also be the end of one phase of life. Miriam's death had taken a huge toll on them both. Derry's heart had not withstood the stress and pain. His father had died of a heart attack when he was in his 60s. Derry opened out his earlier book on Aboriginal Spirituality and looked at the diagrams and chapters on Songlines.

"Always a positive ending."

Alice and Derry sat in their new home. They speculated on their future grandchildren. Bright Star and Joseph would bring theirs up in England. Bethany and Victor would bring theirs up in America. They thought that Thomas, even with a stable partner would not venture into having children with the methods available in these modern times.

"I am so surprised that you are so content not to be working on a project. I am pleased as I know you need to avoid stress. I am just amazed that you have adapted so willingly." Alice sat holding his hands.

"I am peaceful inside. I have nothing to prove. My body is telling me to step back. I hope I still have some time to spend with you, my dear Alice. Where better could we spend our last years? I am so grateful that you have been my wife and I am so sorry that my work brought such tragedy into our lives."

"It was not your fault. And Little Bear has turned his life around and is helping others. The pain of Miriam will never go. I dream about her. I see her sometimes. I am very happy to be here. This is where we began our married life."

"We have been blessed. We must constantly accept the mystery of our tragedy. Meditating on the beach helps. You have coped so well, my love."

"If she had not died we would be reading Braille with our granddaughter now. Miriam was so beautiful and so bright, our first little girl. She was so loving and sweet."

"I shall write when I feel stronger; recollections of the wild places I have been to, the tribes I have seen, a memoir of Miriam, a tribute to you."

"I love you, Derry."

"I love you, Alice." They hugged and kissed.

The Silver Wedding was not their last; Derry's weakened heart allowed him to live for three more years. He did not achieve all his planned writing. In that final year all their children, close relatives and friends came to visit.

There was a white bookshelf, but no corner. Alice loved walking past and observing the books and the artefacts. Nathaniel had helped her make a photo collage of Derry starting with him holding his babies, then in his University, his PhD robes, in the bush with Steve, in the rainforest with Paul and Beate, in Amaranth and Winnipeg with Koda. It was a wonderful tribute to the professor who died too young but who had touched many lives by his brilliant mind, innovative projects and most of all, his unceasing love and care.

Part 4
The Widow of Sundale Court

This final part follows the remaining family members all dealing with the family tragedy in their own way, caring for each other but often living in different countries. Alice is the widow left living in Australia while most of her children live abroad. This part shows how she deals with her grief, learns to live a new life, meets new people and faces big decisions for her future. She is given another chance of happiness in life from the most unexpected quarter.

She keeps in close touch with her children and is delighted to become a grandmother. She also looks for opportunities to use her skills and gifts for the good of others.

1 The Professor's Widow

Sundale Court is the name of the new estate on the edges of Palm Cove, near Cairns. The Barnes Family had moved in just over five years ago when Professor Derwent had taken early retirement due to ill health following a heart attack in Oxford.

Nathaniel, their youngest son had travelled with his mother, Alice, to help choose the new house and had decided to stay with his parents. Derry had lived there for three years with Alice. She had to care for him and their aging Labrador who had been allowed to join them. To celebrate their Silver Wedding anniversary they had gone to Romania to enjoy the mountain scenery and to spend time with Kyle, their nephew and his Romanian wife and children. The journey had proved too much for Derry, who suffered a heart attack soon after returning home.

Sundale Court was very convenient for them. It was a large bungalow with 5 rooms off a corridor which led to two bathrooms and an open plan area. The kitchen was at one end and could be shut off by a screen. The rest was for the lounge and the dining area. The front window looked out to the Palm Cove coast. It was idyllic.

Alice did not fear loneliness when Derry died because she had so many good friends in Cairns, many dating back nearly 30 years. All her children, her brother Daniel with his partner, Charles, her best friend Abigail and family all came to visit her. She decided not to downsize as she had so many visitors each year.

After the funeral of Professor Derwent Barnes, the Sundale neighbours were left in no doubt about who Alice was. The University took on a lot of the responsibility for the funeral and arranged a memorial service a few months later, with a series of tributes. His colleagues of many years were able to attend; Professor Koda from Winnipeg, Dr Paul Rockingham from Minnesota, the staff of the Anthropology Department of St Marcus College, Oxford and Dr Beate von Friedland from Norwich University. The Barnes children and their partners, her brother, her sister-in-law, Maddy, and best friend Abigail were all able to join. This was a life time of friendships and relationships, 'The Songlines or Dreaming

Tracks', as Derry would have called them. There were several reports in the Press about the life and death of the Professor.

Alice was so proud to see her oldest son, Hartleigh Thomas give the family Eulogy. He was completing his Anthropology Degree at Marsden College and planning to do a Masters and a PhD, just like his father had done. He owned a small flat in Oxford which his father had bought when he sold up the large Oxford family house.

His brother Joseph moved back to the Oxford area after completing music studies in Manchester. He was about to marry Bright Star, the youngest daughter of Professor Koda Blackhill, a First Nation Canadian. She was a performer in dance and musical theatre. Joseph and Hartleigh Thomas often met, practiced music together and sometimes did 'gigs' together in a pub.

Bethany, their sister lived in Minnesota with Victor, one of the twin sons of Dr Paul Rockingham. She taught Spanish in schools and English as a Foreign Language in a private language school. Victor was also studying theology like his father. The twin brother, Nicholas, was following a career in IT but was also interested in anthropology. Their younger sister Cristina communicated regularly with Derry's youngest son, Nathaniel but although they were close in age and were like cousins, they found romance closer to home. They were both dating friends from their colleges.

When Derry died, Nathaniel continued to study art in Cairns but he soon had an opportunity to go to a more prestigious college in Brisbane. Alice did not want him to miss out on such a good career move. They noticed that the two-hour flight to Brisbane was treated more like a two-hour commute to London by train.

Alice was eventually alone in the big house with Jet, the aging Labrador. She had felt loved and supported by University Colleagues and members of the Christian Meditation Group they belonged to. One of those members, Simon, a retired teacher and woodworker was a frequent visitor. His partner, Eugene, a retired surgeon, had died not long before. He kept their workshop and continued to produce artistic carvings, mainly for the tourist trade.

Simon enjoyed Alice's company and he greatly admired her for the way she had coped with the tragic death of her daughter as well as Derry's death. Alice felt safe and relaxed with Simon. As a gay man he had no ulterior motive in befriending her.

Alice and Derry had enjoyed a close, loving and caring relationship. She missed him terribly. Although he was a professor who had to travel to tribes in other countries several times a year and he wrote several books, he never neglected his five children. He made sure he made time for each one. There were few conflicts, even when they were teenagers and every child had a good relationship with him. They never feared to approach him and discuss their lives with him. Their eldest daughter who had so tragically died was never forgotten. He generously provided a home for each of the four before he bought the retirement house in Queensland.

There is a whirl of activity, necessary but demanding and stressful after a death and a funeral. It is impossible to cope totally rationally during those months. Alice realised it was far too early to make decisions about the rest of her life.

"Recover first then weigh up my options." She had been a translator of German and a teacher of English to Muslim women and she felt she could pick up either again.

She would visit her children in America and Oxford while she still had her health. She decided on a recovery plan for herself. Instead of bereavement counselling which she had already been through twice she planned to ask for a Spiritual Director to give her some sessions when all the paper work, the Will, the insurances had been dealt with.

During the three years in their new home, Alice had made an effort to get to know her neighbours, although she was mainly preoccupied with caring for Derry who became gradually weaker.

Most of the new houses were owned by young couples with children. On her left were David and Carol with Carl and Milo. They were 6 and 8 and loved playing football in their long garden. They were often noisy and very active, but she was pleased to talk with them, offered them homemade cakes and biscuits. On the right, set back a little from the coast road were young teachers Tony and Wanda with their baby Perry. David and Carol had BBQs with friends and invited Alice and Derry when he was well enough. They worked long hours and came home late quite often. A relative looked after the boys. Tony and Wanda were quieter and took more interest in Derry's work. They had meals together in the first year before Derry had to remain mainly in bed or in a wheelchair.

Alice regularly visited Maria Benetti who had lived in the old Queenslander next to her and had been a good companion when Alice had to shop for furniture and decorating materials. Maria was widowed and lived in a Care Home as she had mobility problems.

Alice kept close to Sandrine the artist, Steve and Jeannie who were now grandparents and Connie, the University botanist who had loved babysitting for them when the children were little. This had been the beginning of their married life. Alice had so loved the place and the people that all through their years in Oxford, she had longed to return to Cairns. Now she was alone in Cairns with three of her children scattered round the world she had no idea what she wanted to do with her remaining years.

Sometimes she thought she should write a memoir but as she had never written in a consistent way she lacked confidence in her ability.

There was much of Australia she had never seen and although she was interested in travelling, she knew she was not ready to do so just yet and she would prefer to go with others rather than alone.

She invited Abigail and Justin and their two little ones, Marlow and Marilla to come for a holiday before she ventured abroad. Her beloved Jet had to be put down just before they arrived. Nathaniel came back from Brisbane to be with his mother when she took him to the Vet. He wanted to say his own goodbye to the beloved member of the family who had helped them through the painful months when Miriam and her baby were dealing with tragic news and then after their deaths, Jet had been a comfort and a treasure for them all.

Alice loved having Abigail's children running around. Justin had also become part of her life. They had seen each other through some difficult times.

Abigail wanted to know why Alice was planning to see the young man who had been the cause of Miriam's tragic death.

"Derry spent time with Little Bear on our last trip and saw that he was truly sorry for what he had done and through illness and therapy he had turned his life round."

"And it is his youngest sister who has married Joseph?"

"Isn't it extraordinary? They have been very good friends for many years. Bethany is living with the son of the other colleague in America. Did you hear Derry talk about overlapping Dreaming Tracks? That is what has happened. I shall visit Bethany and then it is not far to fly to Winnipeg and see Koda's family, including the oldest son."

"You are amazing. You have an incredible capacity to forgive."

Abigail's family visit helped Alice on her path to recovery and it was about two years after Derry's death that she felt able to accept invitations to see her children and to visit Curt and Pearl in Amaranth. Her tour started in Oxford where she arrived for the wedding of her son Joseph and Bright Star. She booked rooms in a hotel for Bright Star's parents, Koda and Shining Star. Their two older children had not been able to make the journey but Little Bear, their oldest son send a lovely message to his new brother-in-law, looking forward to seeing them when they came to Canada.

The wedding was in a Registry Office followed by a reception in an Oxford restaurant. Many of Joseph's school friends and music group colleagues and their present musical and theatrical friends all helped make it a very entertaining occasion. Bright Star had discussed with Joseph and had decided to wear a traditional Sioux jingle dress.

They had said they would travel to Thala for their honeymoon. Alice flew back to Cairns with them. She was so happy to see her son who had been born with red birthmarks across his forehead. He had become a confident young man who had stood up to teasing at school and showing great musical ability chose a career that meant he was often on show to the public.

He had won over everyone so that the marks were hardly noticed. He had tried growing a fringe but it did not cover the marks so he went back to the shorter style he thought suited him. The childhood friendship between the children of the anthropologists and theologian, who so often worked on projects together, meant that they became like cousins but with three of them it had grown into a love match. Bright Star had always taken an interest in Joseph's mark and had even found an island in the Canadian Lake of the Woods which closely resembled the shape. At the airport in Cairns they took a taxi and then Alice drove them to Thala, the Ecotourist Centre where she had Derry had spent their own honeymoon.

"I remember picking you up in your home when you were not even two. You were not happy to come to me at first but later you let me hold you."

"I don't remember that."

"If you want to go out of Thala, you can have my car. Just give me a call. There are days when I don't use it at all."

"Thank-you so much. When is Nathaniel coming?"

Nathaniel was due to ring to arrange to come from Brisbane to see his brother.

As Alice drove home her head was full of happy memories. She and Derry had often returned for short holidays at Thala, her parents had spent time there before they became ill and died in their eighties.

Her brother and partner had stayed there and so had her sister-in-law. It was a very precious place to her. Miriam had taken her first steps on the lodge balcony.

Nathaniel arrived and went to Thala to have a meal with Joseph and Bright Star. He hugged his brother and his wife. They happily shared their lives together. Nathaniel explained that although he was in frequent contact with Cristina, they both had friends in their colleges.

Nathaniel told them a little about his girlfriend in Brisbane. Alice gave them a celebratory meal at home and introduced them to her neighbours. Tony and Wanda, the teachers, invited them all to a BBQ.

When the honeymoon came to an end, Alice saw them off at the airport. The happy couple caught the same plane as Nathaniel to Brisbane and then flew to England.

Several months later her tour continued. Bethany and Victor had invited her to their flat in Minnesota. Just before she left, Joseph told her that Bright Star was pregnant. She flew to America feeling overjoyed that she was to have a grandchild. She had so loved her first granddaughter, Miriam's baby and she still grieved for her.

At Minnesota airport her daughter Bethany threw her arms around her neck and held her.

"Mum, I am expecting a baby!"

"What, two grandchildren at about the same time. Amazing! Congratulations my dearest girl."

"You know about Joseph and Bright Star?"

"Only just! You keep in close touch with each other?"

"I do miss him, and Thomas and Nathaniel. We are so far apart but we use Skype."

"We have already decided that Bright Star and I will fly to Queensland when our babies are old enough, in about one year and we will all come and stay with you!"

"What a fantastic idea."

"Mum, now we are going to be parents we have decided to get married. Victor's parents are so happy. We have arranged to have a small wedding in their church while you are here. We have booked a restaurant near the river. You need not wear anything special. I am not getting an expensive dress."

Alice went shopping with Vivienne and Bethany to choose the kind of dress she could wear again. In the end it was rather like the flowery dress that Abigail had worn.

"My friend Abigail, do you remember, she had a flowery dress and her husband mounted a beautiful exhibition called Lifted by Love with his art works, photography and the dress in the middle. I think you saw Daniel's video."

"Vic will not be doing anything like that!" Alice was delighted with the simple church wedding with just a few friends present. She had time to visit the city with Paul and Vivienne before she took the plane to Winnipeg.

"I have made this flight so often to see Koda," said Paul.

"They were such good years when we all worked together."

Shining Star met Alice at the airport and drove her to their flat. Alice could not forget the first time she had been there when Little Bear called himself Wayne and the other two girls were four and nearly two. Now the flat was empty. Shining Star had her own office for the paper work involved in the women's project with Dr Beate and Jane from Cairns.

"Alice you look so much better. I am sorry we have all lost Derry. It was wonderful to be with you all."

Little Bear took some days off work. He offered to drive Alice to Amaranth for her visit to Curt and Pearl. She and Derry had stayed with them in the prairie hamlet on their first trip to the Native Reservation. She was very pleased to see them again. The journey was several hours on the straight road west and she accepted the offer of a lift with relief. She had not wanted to drive and planned to take the bus. Little Bear had remained single and had his own home near a Rez and a Court House where he worked with young people on the fringes of a criminal life. He was dedicated and determined after his ghastly past.

Curt and Pearl lived in an isolated small holding outside Amaranth.

It was an interesting experience to see the way of life of people who live so far from a town and have dramatic weather conditions to deal with. Alice had never seen it in the snow but had been sent photographs of six-foot-deep snow covering the roads, filling the ditches. She had experienced something of a flood on her visit.

Curt and Pearl would not hear of Little Bear driving to a hotel in the little town.

"We have rooms and you are very welcome." Pearl showed him into a sweet bedroom with wall hangings which she had embroidered.

"Can I go and get you some groceries?" he asked. "We have no need of anything, Little Bear."

He went with them to visit the Rez where his father had worked with the youth. The new training sessions were going well with building skills, woodwork, artistic woodwork, sewing and art work going on in the hew cabins

"Derry's legacy." said Alice. Everyone nodded and smiled.

Little Bear left them to have time together and went for a drive. Alice and Pearl returned to the Haberdashery and chatted about the loss of Miriam and Derry. Alice was able to reassure her that she was recovering and had the support of very good friends in Cairns.

"I love being in Cairns where we began out married life. Nathaniel still lives with me but he studies in Brisbane. My friends are like my family. I do miss my children but I think they are all working at getting over the loss of their Dad in their own way. They had such a terrible time recovering from Miriam's death. They are all very close and use modern technology to stay in touch."

"It is so good to see you. You have lost weight. Not surprising. They were good days when Koda brought you all to see us."

On the long drive back to Winnipeg, Alice had the thought that she could have been visiting Miriam and Little Bear in their home near here. No marriage, no home, only illness and death. She wanted to engage him in conversation and find out about his life.

"Derry told me that you had shaved off all your long hair. I am glad you have let it grow a bit. It really suits you. Tell me how you are managing."

Little Bear explained that a drug had restored his potency so he could marry. He had dated some native girls but none of them were willing to marry knowing that they would never have children. He was infertile after contracting the terrible sexually transmitted disease which had so damaged Miriam and their daughter.

"I really hope that you find a loving companion, Little Bear."

"And you are a widow in Cairns, Australia. How are you getting on?"

"I love most of it. It is early days. It is hard to get over Derry."

"You are still young and healthy. I hope you find a new husband."

"I have good friends and I am not at all interested in a new husband."

She was pleased to communicate with this pained young man whom she had once really loved like a son.

2 Two Widowers

Two grandchildren on the way, Alice was feeling rather sad that she would probably not be with her daughter for the birth. She knew Vivienne would be there to see her through. She knew that she had some months to think and talk about it before asking if she could be with Bethany as she had been with Miriam. She suspected that Shining Star may be feeling the same about her grandchild being born in Oxford.

Alice decided to take a course of Spiritual Direction instead of bereavement counselling. She wrote to Jeff in Oxford who had set up the training course in their Spiritual Healing Centre.

Dear Jeff,

I have just begun Spiritual Direction with my new director. He reminds me of you. I am glad that all continues to go well at the Healing Centre and that although retired, you can call in from time to time. I have been given the Rev. Philip Browne who is a retired Anglican Vicar. He is an experienced director and put me at ease in the very first session. His wife, who sounds like a typical caring and efficient Vicar's wife, died about five years ago. He lives in town with a married daughter and family.

He knows his Bible well and also has many other books and poetry which he likes to use. I did not want to go through the same process of bereavement that I have done twice because I want to focus on my spiritual life, to dig deeper and try to understand how to overcome the loss of Miriam, Dawn Star and dear Derry in his early 60s, how to unravel my emotions. I am looking forward to working through with him and finding out what to do with the rest of my life. I have health and restored energy. All my children are doing well and I will soon be the grandmother of two little girls, Bethany and Joseph's wife are both expecting girls.

Alice signed off and prepared for her next session with Philip.

She loved walking into the large Catholic Church and seeing the stained-glass windows and the reflected colours on the floor.

Philip had lit a candle and placed it on a little round table between the two low armchairs. He was playing some gentle music as she sat quietly gathering her thoughts. He opened with a brief prayer.

He asked her which writers she had found helpful in the past so she reeled off the familiar titles, The Cloud of Unknowing, St Teresa of Avila, Richard Rohr, Thomas Merton, C S Lewis.

"Do you feel drawn to any particular book?"

"I am greatly challenged by the first two. They are so dedicated and only seem to think about their relationship with God."

"Does anything trouble you about being a widow?"

"How to deal with the heartache and what to do with the rest of my life. I could work, translate or teach or help at the Aborigine charity centre. Life is before me like a blank sheet of paper, or rather I feel I am walking in a forest with 6 or 7 paths in front of me and I don't know which one to take."

"The presence, or rather your awareness of the presence of Jesus with you can help with the heartache. Tell me of any time you recall when you have felt comforted by God, the Father, the Son and the Holy Spirit."

She could remember 'magic' times as her mother had called them when she sensed that she was loved; walking into Cairns Catholic Cathedral, watching the birds on the Lake of the Woods, seeing a sunset and mostly during silent meditation. She mentioned the prayers that Derry had written and the times of silence he had led when each baby was on the way and again when they were born.

"He sounds like a very special man."

"He was indeed. I miss him terribly."

"I am going to pray for you and send you away with a couple of chapters from the books you mentioned because I think you need to make a real effort to spend time with God and shut out everything else except the awareness of His presence with you, just you as a person."

She felt secure with this experienced, gentle man and felt free to tell him that her dog had died. She found tears falling down her cheeks.

As she left the church she looked in at the hall where Derry had taken The Day of Reflection. She was delighted to see his meditative poem, Dreamwalk, framed and hung on a wall.

"Will you get another dog?" Nathaniel asked Alice when he came for a weekend.

"Perhaps but not yet. I will wait until after my trip with your uncles. They have suggested a trip to Uluru and Alice Springs. You should come with us and use it for your art work."

"I'd love to Mum. When are you going?"

"I am waiting to hear from Daniel. You remember what it's like working around their concerts."

"I'll send you my term dates so you can choose a couple of weeks when I can be with you." She hugged her son.

"That would be wonderful."

Alice made dates with Philip about every three weeks. She did not want to be overwhelmed by her emotions. She had a session with him before the trip to Uluru was arranged.

"My emotions are all over the place." She announced as she sat down with Philip. "I am content on my own but I do miss my children. I am worried that my daughter will have her baby without me being there for her. I think Joseph's wife will have her mother with her. I am asking why Derry had to get so sick and die so soon. The heartache is still there but the attacks are less frequent."

"How did you get on with the reading from St Teresa? Did it help you feel closer to God?"

"I could see that she was close to God. She only had thoughts about being one with God. That's not me. It is a challenge but I do want to be closer to God and feel His love for me." She explained that she wrestled so much when she tried to pray that she tried to meditate in silence more often. She would often find peace of mind in the stillness.

"I was wrestling with my daughter's suicide and the heart attack brought on by the stress."

"Can you tell me more about your daughter?"

She gave the outline that at 15 she had had a sexual relationship with a Native Canadian, the son of a colleague with whom they all were on holiday. He had seduced her and made her pregnant without realising he had contracted a serious disease. He had been very promiscuous over many years. Miriam had a baby girl but she was blind because of the disease and Miriam was infertile. Although they had supported her and were willing to help her with her blind baby she had jumped off a high place with her baby and killed them both.

Philip seemed disturbed and Alice thought he looked just like she had done when a Spiritual Direction Client, Louisa, had told her of a devastating trauma in her life. She had been overwhelmed and that is how he looked.

"You have had a major tragedy. How long ago was this?"

"A few years ago. Miriam was loved by everyone. The whole family has suffered."

"I last saw the boyfriend on my trip to Canada and there was reconciliation and forgiveness. He has suffered and he has turned his life around. He is doing good for others." She pulled out one of the cards she carried. It was the one made by Hartleigh Thomas with his drawings of flowers and the verse, The Lord is my Shepherd. "I treasure this greatly."

"That is so precious," said Philip, "You are dealing with much more than a family bereavement."

"My husband was a wonderful man and my children are amazing. We are all close in spite of the distance."

"That's good. You 're going to Uluru soon with your brother, I think you said."

"Yes, my brother and his partner. They are musicians."

"Partner? In a music group?" Alice felt sure that Philip would not approve of gay partnerships but she did not want to lie.

"They are Civil Partners. They have been together since the 1980s."

He was experienced and respectful enough not to express his personal opinions. He said he would like to give her some short Meditations that she could use each day on her trip.

"I do hope that Uluru turns out to be another place where you feel the presence of God."

"Thank-you, Philip. I will see you after the trip."

He ended the session with a prayer and handed her the little booklet of John Main Meditations.

In all the years she had known Steve and Jeannie, they had never talked about their extended family. They had supper with her one evening and somehow, sitting under the new gazebo, watching the waves, Jeannie started speaking about her two brothers.

"I thought of them because they are both coming here soon with their families. They live in Townsville so we don't meet very often. We are having a big family party because we are both 65 soon. Our kids said, 'Why wait until the big 70?' They have organised a celebration in a big restaurant near the Botanical Gardens. We are planning to send you and Connie, Jane and Jake an invitation."

"Oh, that's lovely. Thank you so much. Tell me about your family."

She had not met their son and daughter since they had married and moved away. As children they had played in Alice's house, number 42. Now, they each had two children to keep their grandparents busy. They lived quite nearby. Alice remembered Jeannie telling her that her mother had been one of the 'lost generation', 'a stolen child'.

Her mother had lived in a tribe in the Queensland Outback. Ngala was one of the hundreds of children, stolen by the Anglican Church and placed in a Mission School. She had last seen her parents when they had screamed and cried as her children were pushed into a bus. She and the other children had wept as they were driven away. Alice thought of her own mother who had also been given away by her parents when she was five, to save her life in the Holocaust. Ngala was an attractive girl and was groomed to become a maid to a rich white family. She settled down to her studies and training. She learned a good level of English, cooking and sewing, laying and clearing a table and she could curtsey and say 'Yes, Ma'am' in a very charming way. She wore silk bows in her hair. Ngala was given the name Nina when she joined the O'Neill family. They also trained her to make beds and do the laundry. A young Aboriginal boy had been hired to clean the shoes and work in the garden. Ngala looked after him as he was so thin and sad.

The O'Neills treated her kindly and fed her well but never thought of letting her further her education. There were four children in the household, all immaculately dressed. Ngala learned to bow her head to them too. She was only a few years older than the oldest daughter. Their uncle Frederick was coming on a visit and they were all very excited because he was young and fun, unlike their father. This much younger brother was a student and was just 20. He had floppy blond hair, was slim and sporty and liked to tease his nieces and nephews and make them laugh. He shocked them all when he spoke to Nina.

Most guests ignored her totally as she cleared the table. He thanked her and asked her name. "Ngala." she almost whispered.

"That's Nina. Don't bother with her." said one son.

She was then a very pretty girl of 18. Somehow Uncle Frederick O'Neill had a completely different attitude to Aborigines and to servants in general. He automatically treated them with respect and understanding. Over the next two years the family tried to limit the visits of Frederick but he was in demand by the children. Each time he came he made sure he spoke to Ngala and used her native name.

One evening he announced that he was going to invite her for a walk.

The walks became a regular occurrence and Frederick decided he wanted to marry her. He had to consider his own father. Would he be cut off? Probably. Could he finish his studies and get a job and rent a place for them to live without family money? He would have to. He spoke to his father and older brother and as expected, they were very disapproving, if not horrified. Frederick took Ngala for a walk and asked her to marry him. He told her he would not be rich but he would have a job in the city and enough money to rent a small home.

He told Ngala that he loved her, did not care that she was Aboriginal. She agreed to marry him as she had grown to love him and thought she might end up as his mistress. She had never dreamed he would marry her.

He was surprised when she said she had no family but explained what had happened to her. Frederick did a lot of research to discover the dates she was in school and which tribe she came from. For their honeymoon he took her to find them. She was reunited with her parents but had no news of her brothers and sisters. What weeping and hugging there was. She introduced her white husband and promised to come and see them at least once a month.

Frederick and Ngala had a very happy marriage. His father had given him an allowance but said he would leave him nothing in his Will and no property. Frederick had a good, reliable job in a big company in the city and could provide for his family. They had three children, James, Jeannie and Jonathan.

Alice was thrilled to hear the story.

"So you were Jeannie O'Neill. That's an Irish name. People thought Derry was Irish when he shortened his name."

"They are bringing their families so you will meet a whole bunch of mixed-race people." Alice went to the shops to find a suitable present. She chose a huge wall clock with moving sun and planets and lights which indicated scientific facts including the positions of the planets and stars. It was too big to hide so she arranged for it to be delivered on the morning of the party.

She found a smart fitted party dress that she had not worn for years. It was one of Derry's favourites but on the whole he was not interested in mundane things like fashion, outfits, styles. She was not aware that she looked very beautiful in the pale yellow, sleeveless dress which contrasted with her black, wavy hair, now shortened to her shoulders. Streaks of grey were just showing.

As she entered the large restaurant garden, several friends uttered a 'Wow!' to let her know how good she looked.

Steve came up and thanked her for the clock which had arrived at their home that morning. "We love it! It's going in the lounge in all its glory."

Jake and Connie came over to see it. "We thought of something similar but in the end the department chose a wrought iron table and chairs for their garden."

The drinks were on a side table and Jeannie came over to offer some Prosecco.

"Meet my brothers." Alice met James and his wife and their grown-up son and daughter. James was very like Jeannie in colour and size.

"There's a town like you!" said a rich, plumy voice behind her. She turned and found herself facing a very dark-skinned man.

"I'm Jonathan, pleased to meet you." As they shook hands Alice found it hard to believe that this very dark-skinned man was the younger brother of Jeannie and James. His dark hair, cut very short was greying at the sides and he was more formally dressed than most of the other men. He wore a pale blue suit with an open neck, white shirt. Alice looked round for his wife and family.

"Your family?" asked Alice.

"Out of sight at the moment." He looked all around him. "I'll introduce you to them later. As I was saying, there's a town like you." He smiled.

"I'm going there soon with my brother. I have read the book."

"I've seen a film version and read his other books but I think this one is best. I hated 'In the Wet', why did he turn to dreams and fantasy?"

"I don't know his others. I stuck to the classics and Fennimore Cooper and Hemmingway."

"Quite a mix, did you do English too?"

"Only to A level, I did French and German at University. I was a translator until I married. I also did a little EFL."

"Ah, here's Lisa, my daughter and my son is just over there." Alice hesitated to ask about his wife.

"Are your children here?" Jonathan asked.

"My daughter is married in the USA; I have two sons in Oxford and two grandchildren on the way. My youngest son is in Brisbane. Quite a list scattered around."

"You had 4 children?"

"Actually, we had 5. Our eldest daughter died in her teens."

"I'm sorry. My wife died ten years ago when my children were in their teens. She had cancer. We have both had ordeals to go through; someone mentioned you were also widowed."

"I am so sorry. Yes, my husband died nearly 3 years ago. I'm still recovering from the terrible loss."

"You don't really recover. You learn to live with loss, grief, pain and you make life go on."

"That's so true. How did your children cope?"

"They had some counselling through their school. They had seen Helen suffer for about three years so they were expecting her death. They helped her through chemo and hair loss and all that goes with it. They were very upset when after a long remission the cancer returned and she sank quite quickly. What did your husband do?"

"He was Professor of Anthropology in Oxford but he very often worked with Cairns University. We started our married life here.

"When we knew he only had a few years left to live, we sold up and decided to spend our last years here as well."

"That's moving. I hope you find a fulfilling life here. Two years is not long. I expect you are still in grief."

"Yes, so true, but I have so many very good friends here, more like extended family. Your sister and Steve have been wonderful over nearly 30 years. Other Uni colleagues are also close friends. Several are here tonight and I have another bunch from the Christian Meditation Group in town."

"Meditation? I am not familiar with that. Do you sit and chant 'Om'?"

"We once met a man who did! We are from different denominations and we have music and readings and 30 minutes silent meditation. It does me a lot of good. It was very important to my husband."

"I'd like to know more. You can tell me one day because I am moving to Cairns as Lisa and Anthony have partners, not married but living together and they have both moved away from home. I wanted to be near Jeannie because I felt rather alone in the big house. I've always loved Cairns."

"Do you know where you will live?"

"I have bought an old Queenslander in a street near the Catholic Cathedral. I am a DIY aficionado so I am doing it up."

"Oh, really! We lived in an old Queenslander near there for many years. I loved it but we sold it to the university when Derry became a professor and had to live in Oxford."

"Not number 42?"

"Yes. How did you know that?"

"I am moving to 63, almost opposite and I have noted the many students going in and out, celebrating and so on. I am staying with Jeannie while it is being brought up to date and redecorated."

"We had to have a single storey building for Derry as he was so ill. I hope you settle in alright."

Food was being handed round.

"Ah, here they are. Lisa's partner Joe."

"Is Joe a Joseph? I have a son called Joseph."

Lisa pulled her brother over. "This is Anthony and his partner Liz. That causes some confusing fun." Anthony and Liz shook hands.

"Hello, Alice, you are the widow of the well-known Professor Derwent Barnes, aren't you? Did you spend your life traipsing through the outback with him?"

"I spent my life waiting for him to return from the outbacks and jungles of the world. I went with him a few times but our children were too many and too small for me to go."

"I am sorry for your loss," said Liz, "we read about his funeral in one of the Queensland newspapers. Did you keep the articles?"

"Yes. He had a wonderful send off and lots of tributes. I have one son with me in Australia but my others are scattered in USA and UK."

"I considered anthropology at one time so I followed his work a little but I chose IT instead. I loved my studies and work for a big foreign company in Townsville, however, I have half an eye on what's happening in anthropology. My uncle Steve sends me updates from Cairns." Alice warmed to Anthony and Liz and felt warm inside to hear people talk about Derry's work.

"Was that your discipline too?"

"Not at all. I was a linguist, mainly French and German and a little Urdu."

"Urdu? Pakistan?"

"I did not go to the land but I taught Muslim ladies in London before I married." They balanced their food plates and moved to include others in their circle. Jonathan had stood with his daughter all through that conversation. Alice noticed that his son and daughter were both lighter skinned. Their mother had been a white lady.

Lisa looked at Alice, "You do not look old enough to have so many grown-up children."

"Well thank-you. I shall soon be a grandmother. Both my daughter in America and my son in England are expecting girls." Joseph is the father of the one in England. Lisa still found it hard to believe.

"You will see Dad again as he is not leaving with us. He is moving to Cairns."

"So I gather. Your aunty was wonderful to us when we first moved here. I was a young bride and after an idyllic honeymoon he left me in our house to go into the Outback. He was finishing a book for his last project. He worked very hard and was dedicated and focused."

"I'd like babies one day. Dad would love to be a granddad." Lisa smiled. "He's been dedicated and focused too. He looked after Mum and then brought us up while he was teaching. Jeannie helped a lot but she had her own children to care for. She moved to Cairns for Steve's work at the Uni."

"I'll have to write down all your names tonight. So many to remember."

The party ended with some congratulations from Steve and Jeannie's son. He told a few amusing stories but most of all he praised his father for his charity work.

"To Dr Steve Hampton and Mrs Jeannie Hampton. To Mum and Dad."

3 Alice Springs and Uluru

Before Daniel and Charles arrived, Alice decided to move out of the master bedroom so it could be a guest room and she put herself in one of the smaller rooms. Even the smaller rooms were a very good size with room for two beds or a double. Alice had a washbasin in her room and made the second bathroom her shower and toilet. Nathaniel kept the room he had chosen and used the master room in suite if there were no guests. She took into her new room the portrait of Miriam with Hunter and hung the other on her 16th birthday next to the collage of Derry in the lounge.

Alice had prepared for the trip by reading a book called 'Tracks' and watching the film based on the true story of a young woman who trained to lead camels and did a long trek across the desert with them, mainly on her own, to recover from a broken heart. Alice Springs was her starting place. She also read about the Dingo baby scandal at Uluru, where Lindy Chamberlain had spent about 5 years in prison, accused of killing her baby. In the end there was evidence found that dingoes had taken the baby and eaten her. A recent documentary revealed that the Aborigines had found dingo tracks right at the beginning of the faulty investigation.

Daniel and Charles warmly embraced mother and son. They had walks by the sea and a couple of good night's sleep to recover from jet lag before they flew to Alice Springs. Steve had agreed to take them to the airport but it was Jonathan who got out of the van.

"Sorry, he sent me! He's got to get to Court with one of his Reserve School kids." Alice introduced him to the others.

"How is your house getting on?"

"Slower than I hoped. I am having storm protection put on the roof and a strong garage built underneath."

"What are you doing yourself?"

"Painting, decorating, new windows, new air con, new cooker. Actually that is being put in for me. I can't do electrics well. I love painting."

"Are you having a study?"

“Yes. Computer screen and files and some cupboards for paper work. I have not bought the desk yet.” Alice told him about the shop where she bought her desk and bookshelf. She could not be sure it was still there as there had been so many changes to the town. She had used another shop with Derry for the furniture they did not bring from Oxford.

“Have a good trip everyone.”

“Thanks, Jon for taking time out to transport us. Very kind of you.” said Charles. They piled out of the van to wait for their plane over the Red Centre.

This flight reminded them of the vastness of Australia. There were thin lines across the wilderness and tiny blobs which were small towns. Alice was thinking that this view helped put life into a new perspective. When they landed they would go to a hotel and then next day take a bus for the journey across the desert, a distance of over 400km, to Uluru. Daniel took lots of photos on the descent and Nathaniel was very excited to see people and buildings coming towards them after the stretches of red sand.

Alice’s father and mother had visited this place in the year that she married Derry. They had wanted a real holiday, “No tribes and no research.” Esther had said. She needed to recover from the emotions of the trip to Leipzig and the Concentration Camp where her family had died.

“Derry would have understood this place, the tribes, the history and its importance to the Aborigines.” Alice said.

“A lot has changed. I have been reading,” said Daniel, “in the book that Dad brought back for me that the government gradually made changes to show more respect to the natives.

“Since then there have been other changes.”

He described how in typical colonial style; the area had been taken over as a tourist centre although the natives considered it a sacred place. Alice was relieved to hear that motels, hotels, a runway even and main roads had been moved away from the rock. It stood in the National Park and for some years, the right to climb was fought over.

The ban was only imposed in recent years.

Alice remembered the Green Ants film she had seen with Jeannie many years ago where local tribes were sitting in front of diggers to stop mining on their sacred ground.

They joined the walking group around the base of this mighty structure. Nathaniel read from his granddad’s book that it was like an iceberg in that what we could see was only the tip and that most of the granite rock was underground. On the walk they saw the different kinds and colours of rock, the crevices, the boulders, the deep, smooth round holes from water action and the almost parallel lines which streaked down from top to bottom. It had immense power. The thin trees, the clumps of spiky grass and the wild flowers added to the sense of strangeness. The earth really was red. The sky was bright blue and the rock was golden in the sunset. On the second day they took another walk along the modern, metallic board walk which led over the pools of water, more like lakes of water. In the early morning, the rock had looked almost white as the sun rose. Different shapes and colours of boulders reflected in the still water.

"We need to compose a piece." said Charles, "We can try it out with Hartleigh and Joe when we get home."

"What a wonderful idea." Alice took her brother's arm. "I am so glad you take such interest in them. I am grateful that you are both in London and not too far from them.

"Jonathan looked like an interesting man but I find it hard to believe he is Jeannie's brother. He is so dark in comparison. It must be a matter of genetics."

"Yes, their other brother is as pale as Jeannie. Both of his children have white partners and both the children resemble Jeannie, not him. He speaks such educated English; I could not believe it when I first met him."

"So he has two grown up children and is a widower?"

"His wife died ten years ago leaving him with two teenagers to bring up. Sad story. He was an English teacher and specialised in literature to the older students."

"And he will be a close neighbour for you."

"Daniel, don't. I am happy as I am. After our trip and when my granddaughters have visited I am going to help in the Aboriginal charity and look for some translation and possibly some English to Foreigners work. I want to do something useful."

"Of course you do, but don't shut the door on new friendships."

They stood looking up at the rock which had once been called Ayers Rock after a local white official. Alice thought that Paul should see it as part of his Post-Colonial Theology studies.

The mystery, the atmosphere, the myths associated with it, all fascinated Alice. She decided to read some of them. It was indeed a place where she felt the presence of God. This sandstone heap was unexplained and there were still many theories about how it came about.

The Pitjantjatjara people named it and owned it. They were like the guardians of a sacred place. It was a major culture clash when the Europeans arrived.

Alice was walking past a sign to a spring called Mutitjula. She said she wanted some time alone to meditate so she walked around the still water and pulled out the booklet of meditations given by Philip. She looked up to see little white puffs of cloud against the bright blue sky.

She read the words 'My refuge and my stronghold, my God in whom I put my trust.'

Her mind went first to the Anangu, the name of local tribes. She had read about their beliefs in ancestral beings who had created the rock, the creatures and the plants. She closed her eyes and let her mind wander back to the thousands of years when native peoples had lived in the land, living off the land in a sustainable way. Although the Europeans had taken away land and culture from the native people, and had developed the rainforest and wilderness into mines and cities, the ancient peoples still exist and maintain as much of their culture as possible. She thought of the God who is our stronghold and remembered that He was the creator of this amazing place and also of the whole universe. Images of outer space filled her mind, breath-taking and mind-blowing. No image on a stained-glass window can depict such a God and such a mystery. Yet Alice was not aware of fear or dread. She was aware that this source of power beyond human comprehension was a power of love. She opened her eyes and read the words of the Psalm again.

"He loves me and He is with me. He is all I need. Solo Dios Basta, God alone suffices." She quoted the words of St Teresa of Avila. As she stood smiling she looked around the water hole. Walking along the banks she saw Miriam. Her long, dark hair was wet as if she had just come out of the water. She was wearing her flowing, white party dress which she had worn for her 15th birthday. Her hand brushed the grasses as she walked. Alice was staring, numb, silent. She stretched out her hands towards Miriam who was now smiling. She then seemed to walk into the rock and she disappeared.

"Where's Dawn Star? Where's Derry?" she said aloud, "Miriam, where are you?" She was aware of deep inner calm and peace but she still wanted to understand why the others had not appeared.

Nathaniel came up to her, “Isn’t it amazing?” he said. “Yes, darling. What can you see?”

“See? The colours, the reflection, the stillness of the water.” He took more photos on his phone. In a way she was relieved that he had not seen Miriam. That vision had been just for her.

“Did you see the eagle?” asked Daniel as they joined her. “No, where?”

“Near the crevice there, high up. It’s a wedge tailed eagle. Look!” He showed her the shot on his phone.

“How fantastic. Spiritual magic. Do compose some music.”

Suddenly the sound of strange music reached their ears. Over to the left, at the base of the rock was an Aborigine playing the didgeridoo. Next to him stood another nearly naked native with clap sticks. Soon he began to sing out a mournful tone; up, down, high, low a chant in time to the rhythm of the sticks.

They all stood transfixed.

4 Claire and Esther

The power of Uluru remained with them for several days. They returned to Cairns to spend time with Alice and then went back to London and Brisbane. Nathaniel started some oil painting in Brisbane. Daniel and Charles began composing some piano tunes in their home and invited Hartleigh Thomas and Joseph to bring a guitar and flute to add to the new composition. Joseph could only spare a couple of days because he was now a father. His new daughter was Claire Dawn Barnes and he was besotted by her. She had black hair like her mother and no birthmarks anywhere. He had feared that she might inherit the birthmarks he had on his forehead. Bright Star was pleased with the Sioux name to match the other family names and she knew that Claire would be acceptable in England.

Their flat in Oxford was adequate but small. It had been enough for a single musician who had used the second bedroom for his instruments. Claire was sleeping in their room so he was hoping to move to a bigger place. He knew that Bright Star was missing the open spaces of Canada and was planning a holiday at the Lake of the Woods sometime after the mother and baby trip to Alice.

Hartleigh Thomas was soon being sent abroad for his studies. Alice gave him a full account of their visit to Uluru and encouraged him to go there. His father and grandfather had spent many years researching Aboriginal tribes, culture and spirituality but there were still tribes in the Northern Territory and North Queensland which had never been researched. He said he would spend some days in Cairns to see his sister and sister-in-law and his new nieces on his way to New Zealand and the Pacific Islands.

Alice was thrilled that she would have three of her children in the house at the same time. Bethany and Esther travelled from America to England and spent a few days with Hartleigh, whose flat was bigger. He had a sibling meal with Bethany and Joseph had a sibling meal while Bright Star cared for the babies.

"Lovely choice of name," said Hartleigh, "after Miriam and granny?"

"Yes, of course." Bethany answered. "I do miss you all. I loved it when we were all together in Mum and Dad's new house. It's a wonderful place for her and for us to stay."

After a couple of days Joseph drove them to Heathrow and felt bereft when they disappeared through the gates. He returned for an evening with Hartleigh.

"When do you join them?"

"In ten days and then after four days I fly to New Zealand, Christchurch University for a briefing before we go to the Islands. Dad used to talk of the 'Sons of Incas' and we are looking at the 'Sons of Maoris'. We are preparing a documentary on how they keep up their culture and belief systems."

"Are you working on the Uluru melody?"

"Yes, guitar mainly."

"I have several concerts while Bright Star is away. It's good for me to keep busy."

"I wonder how Victor is managing. I'll contact him soon on Messenger."

Alice went to Cairns airport with a thumping heart, feeling breathless and giddy. She wanted to show off her granddaughters to everyone.

She saw Bethany first and then Bright Star both pushing their buggies with a porter behind them pushing their trolley of luggage.

Alice and Bethany both wept as they hugged. Alice then hugged Bright Star who was smiling broadly.

"I miss you so much." Bethany wiped her eyes.

"Joseph misses you too and I miss my family but it is much nearer for me to go and see them." Bright Star smiled.

"Meet Esther." Bethany took her out of the buggy and handed her to Alice. She held up the sleepy child and kissed her several times. She noted her thick, dark brown hair, her blue eyes and her little plump body.

"Hello darling Esther. And now Claire Dawn." They swopped the babies over. She was thinner and had black hair but also the blue eyes of Joseph and the long limbs of Bright Star.

"Hello darling Claire." Claire opened her eyes and looked at Alice with staring eyes. "Aren't they both just perfect? Do they relate to each other?"

"When they met for the first time we put them on a duvet on the floor. They each had a toy but they were fascinated by each other and seemed to stretch out their arms to reach each other."

"I have borrowed two cots from Steve and Jeannie's children. Now we have beds in all the rooms."

"Great."

"Well done, Mum."

She drove them to Sundale Court and showed them their rooms. Claire and Esther were on a duvet on the lounge floor.

"Tomorrow I have invited Steve and Jeannie and her brother Jonathan for a buffet supper in the garden.

"Uncle Daniel mentioned that you had met a widower. I'm looking forward to meeting him. Oh, it's so good to be here. You are such a wonderful mother!" Bethany hugged her.

"Yes, you are, Alice, thank-you for coping with us all."

"I miss Dad." Alice wiped her eyes.

"Of course you do but you must make a new life for yourself. Are you going to do those jobs you mentioned?"

"I hope so. After you leave I shall start looking."

Both young Mums needed to sleep. Alice delighted in sitting with her granddaughters and seeing the baby food containers in the kitchen. They woke up with headaches so Alice provided water and pills.

"We'll go to the beach but you can't take buggies in the sand."

"We both have baby carriers." They looked very professional as they strapped their babies to their chests. There was an idyllic sunset across the islands. A few surfers were still active in the waves. Purple and gold streaked the waters.

"No wonder you love it here." said Bethany.

They returned for a hot meal and to watch some television before their first night's sleep. In the kitchen they chopped and sliced and heated and chatted.

"Tell me about Silver Star, how is she?"

"She has married a native man and she works for a travel company. She even leads some tours of Winnipeg. Her husband has kept a white man's name, Vernon and is a teacher in a Rez school."

"Near Little Bear?"

"The other side of town, to the west. She still has not forgiven Little Bear and hardly ever sees him, only on family gatherings. She loved Miriam, you know."

"I think everyone did. I'd like to talk with her. I've been to see Little Bear when I went to Amaranth after my visit to Bethany. Derry drove to see him on our last visit together to the Lake of the Woods.

"I think that talk helped stop him becoming suicidal. I had a good talk with him. He has turned his life round. He is unable to have children and is still single but he works to help young natives keep out of trouble. He goes to Court with them and instructs them."

"That's good. You must tell Silver Star but she will not want to come to Cairns; too many unhappy memories of how Little Bear behaved. She loved him a lot before that."

Alice understood that the hurting sister had not seen her handsome brother as a victim. She thought she might try to message her as it would be some time before she was likely to see her. Like Derry, she would make a plan.

Next morning, the woozy headed Mums had breakfast, fed their babies and helped with the buffet. Alice had made flans and pizzas for the freezer but needed to buy some salmon, salad and canapés.

"Do you want to shop with me? It will be a bit squashed with the buggies but we can manage."

"Why don't you go with Bethany and I'll stay here and take Claire for a walk."

"Take the buggy to the right, keep on the path and you will come to Palm Cove centre. We are going there for a meal together when Thomas arrives. I already have a baby sitter." Alice and Bethany went to the shopping centre just outside the town.

"There's the esplanade where we all went. We can take the babies there one day." Esther was asleep in the buggy as they packed the bags into the boot.

"Let's have a drink." suggested Alice. They sat outside in a smart, attractive cafe. "Bethany, I want to tell you something about our time in Uluru."

"It sounded great."

"It was. Bethany, darling, I had some time alone by a rock pool and I saw Miriam." She tried to explain that she was meditating and no one else was around. She described the wet hair and the white dress. Bethany did not know what to make of it.

"I have heard of such things." she said.

"It made me so peaceful and happy. I wondered why I had not seen Dad and Dawn Star. But it was so lovely to see her how she used to be."

"I'd like to tell Paul, Victor's Dad. He studies about spiritual things."

"Yes, do. It was so clear and real."

"Mum, I missed you at the birth of Esther. If I have another baby can you come and be with me"

"I hated not being there. Of course if I am still healthy I will come and be with you. Esther is so lovely."

Bright Star loved cooking and baked the side of salmon, cut it in pieces and arranged it on a bed of lettuce.

"I think you feed Joseph well."

"He's a good cook too." She smiled and put the big plate in the fridge.

Steve, Jeannie and Jonathan arrived with flowers and wine. Steve and Jeannie hugged Bethany and Bright Star.

"This is Jonathan, my brother. He is living with us while his house is being knocked into shape."

"Where's your house?" asked Bethany "Near your old one, opposite number 42."

"Really!"

He explained a little about his situation and how he had been left alone in the big family home in Townsville when his grown-up children had moved away with their partners. He had always loved Cairns so he decided to move nearer his sister.

"So you retired here like Mum and Dad?"

"Yes, but I' going to teach here when I am settled."

Alice overheard that phrase and introduced her daughter, her daughter-in-law and both babies who were on a cloth on the lawn.

"What are you going to teach?"

"Well, I was an English literature specialist so I taught seniors but I do voluntary work for both adults and adolescents who have missed out on the basics."

"I did EFL to Muslim ladies, I think you know. Do you know if there is anything similar in Cairns?"

"I can ask HQ in Townsville; they will have links with Cairns. I'm sure I can find you work if you want it."

"Thanks, when my family leaves I shall start looking."

"Where were the Muslims?"

"London, a ladies' group."

"There's a Mosque down the highway. Would you like me to take you there and have a look and see if there is a number or an email address?"

"That would be great." She picked up Esther and got him to interact with her. "Do you have grandchildren?"

"Not yet. Lisa wants a baby but she and Joseph are just setting up home and business. My son Anthony is with Liz but they haven't mentioned children yet."

"Our families are so scattered. I live in America with Victor, my husband, Joseph and Thomas, that's Hartleigh, both live in Oxford. Bright Star is Joseph's wife and Nathaniel is in Brisbane. Both brothers are coming to see me and meet their nieces."

"What a lovely family!" said Jonathan.

"Do you know about our sister who died?"

"No, but please don't tell me. It should be your mother who tells me. She must have suffered a lot."

"Very sensitive of you. She has. We all have and we only lost Dad three years ago."

"I lost my wife to cancer ten years ago so we are all bereaved and learning to get on with life."

"Can I ask a cheeky question? How are you and Jeannie so different in skin colour? Bright Star is native and Claire is quite dark skinned with black hair but blue eyes."

"Our mother was very dark, very pretty and totally Aborigine. My dad was blond and blue eyed. Look at Lisa and Anthony," he pulled out his phone, "They are both a pale coffee colour. I think I was born with more of my mother's genes. It caused me a lot of difficulties when I was growing up."

"In what way?"

He told Bethany that at school he had been treated differently as were the full Aborigines. "I once tried to scrub my skin with a scourer in the bath." My Dad yelled at me, "I chose your Mum. I loved her, never mind the skin colour."

"Are they still alive?"

"No, sadly they both passed away some years ago but they lived to see their grandchildren. They loved my wife, Helen and saw both babies."

Alice asked Jeannie to help her serve the food. Jonathan went to talk to Bright Star.

"I am pleased to meet you and to know you have joined this wonderful family. I am half white and half Aboriginal but I look totally Aboriginal."

“I am First Nation Canadian and so are both my parents and my brother and sister.”

“Tell me about them.”

“My father is Professor of Anthropology in Winnipeg University. He spent many years of working, researching and writing with Alice’s husband, Professor Derwent Barnes.”

“My son has heard of him and has followed his work a little.”

“My father is Koda Blackhill. My brother is in Social Work and works on a Rez with young boys heading for trouble. My older sister works for a Travel Company and is married to a native man. When you have a chance, look at the white bookshelf, there are books by them all.”

“Where’s the white bookshelf?”

She led him into the house and showed him the end of the lounge. There he saw the bookshelf in a long alcove. There are books by Derry, Alice’s husband and by her father, Professor Thomas Hartley and by all the people in the Cairns Anthropology Department, that includes Steve of course and by a Professor Beate from UK. Jonathan picked up Tribal Wisdom and saw their names and then other tomes by Derry and a Paul Rockingham.

“Bethany is a Rockingham. She is married to Paul’s son Victor.” Jonathan was rather overwhelmed.

“It sounds like a huge network across the world.”

“Derry called it Dreaming Tracks or Songlines.”

“I’ve heard of them. I need to find out more about them. My brain has been filled with literature and getting modern youth to sit and read and appreciate the treasures.”

Bright Star laughed, “All screens now. I must get Claire.”

Claire and Esther needed feeding while the adults ate the salmon and flans. For dessert, Alice had bought mangos and strawberries.

Alice found Jonathan talking with Steve and she heard him admiring both young Mums and both grandchildren.

“Alice, they are both remarkable young ladies.”

“Wait till you meet my sons. Nathaniel is coming from Art School in Brisbane and Thomas, actually he is Hartleigh, is coming from London but we are a stop-over for him as he is flying to New Zealand to research Māori culture. He is at the same college where my husband studied.”

Jeannie joined them.

"It's been great Alice. I am so pleased to see that Jonathan has mixed with you all. He can be a bit of a loner. The food was great. Thank you so much for inviting us."

Jonathan came up, "I shall have a party to celebrate moving in to my new house. Alice, you and whoever is with you must all come."

"A house warming. Great!"

"Warming! We shall need the air con by the time it is ready. I am waiting to paint and wall paper but I can't start until the windows are in properly. The garage is done, the shelves are up and the car goes in."

Alice smiled, "Are you a cook too? Shall I make some food?"

"Kind of you but I do cook and I cheat with ready-made."

All the adults kissed Alice and Bethany and Bright Star. Jonathan took Alice's shoulders and kissed her on both cheeks. She remembered kissing Derry like that the very first time and she found herself shaking a little. What a happy evening it had been. Claire and Esther went to bed and the three ladies sat with a glass of wine.

"Mum, he's really lovely!"

"I showed him your bookshelf and he saw all the books by Dad and granddad. He is curious about what Songlines are."

"He saw Miriam's picture and he told me not to tell him about her but to leave it until you were ready to talk."

"How thoughtful. Maybe one day."

Nathaniel flew in and went to the International airport to meet Thomas. So well arranged. He spotted Thomas and waved and yelled. They hugged for ages.

"Mum's coming to get us. She will meet us outside." Alice cried again when she saw her two sons together.

"Tap off, Mum. Let's see the girls and our nieces." Thomas hugged her and wiped her eyes. Brothers and sisters hugged and kissed.

"I am Hartleigh now. Where are my nieces?" Hartleigh and Nathaniel both bent down to the floor.

"Let's guess." He picked up Claire. "This is Claire, Joseph's daughter. Black hair, long legs, blue eyes."

"So you are Esther," said Nathaniel, "Look at those blue eyes." Both babies seemed happy to be played with, held and kissed by their uncles.

"Mum has a new friend. You have got to meet him." said Bethany. "Mum, can't you invite him?"

"I think we will all go to Steve and Jeannie's as he is still living with them."

"Good idea."

"We are going to eat in a restaurant in Palm Cove where we all used to go. Connie, who looked after you is going to look after the babies."

"But, I have never left her!" said Bright Star with anxiety.

Connie will come for the day and spend time with both babies to get to know them. We will slip out for a couple of hours."

Screens were used to contact the deserted husbands so Hartleigh and Nathaniel joined in. Alice arranged to call on Steve for a cuppa with her sons to introduce them to Jonathan.

Connie arrived after Hartleigh had recovered from jet lag. The bubbly, friendly Botanist was nearing retirement. She soon made friends with Claire and Esther. Hartleigh remembered her and Nathaniel thought she was familiar. Connie looked up at Miriam's photo and blew her a kiss.

Her blond hair was now grey but she was still as lively as ever.

"Glad to meet you, Connie. We've never left our babies before, so we are nervous."

"There has to be a first time. Just look at how content they are."

"You could give them lunch," suggested Bethany.

"Good idea and perhaps I could take them for a little walk one by one in their buggies. I'll play with them first."

Hartleigh and Nathaniel were re-bonding. They just wanted to talk to each other. They went swimming and strolled down the coast path. Nathaniel shared about his girlfriends. He had already had two different relationships but he felt they had not been serious. He liked the idea of having another artist for a girlfriend but he assured Hartleigh he was in no hurry. He wanted to establish his career first.

Hartleigh said he felt similarly. He would have to be abroad like his father and he did not want to leave a partner behind so frequently. He hoped he would meet another anthropologist. They also talked about meeting their mother's new friend, a widower. They had talked with Bethany and were very curious to meet him.

Connie's technique worked well. As the time to leave for the restaurant approached she said, "No big kisses and cuddles to say goodbye. Don't make a big thing of it. Wave perhaps and walk out. It nearly worked." Claire cried when

Bright Star left the room and did not return. She turned back and picked her up and handed her to Connie.

"Wave bye bye." She smiled and held her little arm as Claire waved and seemed to accept the she was now with Connie.

At the restaurant where she had eaten with her parents and Derry, she sat at the end of a table with her daughter, daughter-in-law and her two sons. There was a fair amount of banter between the siblings while Alice was remembering it was here that her father had first told them about the Canadian native Doctor of Anthropology.

A proud Alice sat listening to the chat.

"Who is the new friend that we are going to meet?" asked Hartleigh.

"His name is Jonathan and he is the younger brother of Jeannie. You'll meet him tomorrow at Steve's."

"He has two grown up children in Townsville and his wife died more than ten years ago." filled in Bethany. Alice felt that her children as well as her brother, were trying to match make.

"Have you met a partner yet, my darling?"

"Not a partner, a friend shares the flat but we are not an item. He is younger and just beginning the same course as me at Oxford."

"I am hoping for partners for you, Nathaniel and Little Bear."

"You saw him, didn't you?" Hartleigh's ears pricked up.

Alice outlined the talk she had had with him in Canada.

"He has changed. He is not behaving badly any more. He can't have kids but in his work he helps teenagers on the Rez." Bright Star was pleased to explain.

Hartleigh asked his Mum to give him all the details sometime before he flew off to New Zealand.

At the end of a very happy evening, Hartleigh spoke to Bethany.

"Don't push Mum over this guy. He could be the best guy on earth but I think Mum is saying she is not ready. She still misses Dad. What a wonderful Dad we had!"

"I will back off a bit, but she should marry again. She is so young and pretty, she should have 20 years of happiness and love."

"You romantic." They all took group photos before they went home where the young Mum's were relieved to find their little ones asleep.

"They were just fine. Not a single tear. They ate their tea, no problem."

Alice had baked a cake and then hired a taxi for the Mums, babies and buggies and drove her sons to Steve and Jeannie's house. Jeannie met the boys at the door and gave then a hug, "Jon can't wait to meet you."

She hugged Alice and then turned to the taxi to help unload.

They all walked through to the garden, admiring the big clock on the way. "Steve and Jon will be here soon. Steve is helping with the house."

They drank their cuppa and chatted in the garden but waited for the cakes until the others arrived.

"We are sorry we are late. The workmen messed up one window and we had to wait." Steve explained.

"Here are two of my sons, Hartleigh and Nathaniel." Alice took them over to Jonathan. They all shook hands and Hartleigh sat next to Jon getting ready to grill him.

"I am doing anthropology like my Dad. In fact I am at the same college and I'm off in a couple of days to research Maoris in New Zealand and the Pacific Islands. Have you travelled much?"

"Not as much as your family but we did go to New Zealand twice for holidays. It is beautiful. We went to several other parts of Australia. After my wife died we went to more local places. New Zealand, in fact it made my son interested in tribal culture for a while. We often came to Cairns to see Jeannie and I have always loved it."

"What was your job?"

"I taught English literature. My wife taught Maths in the same school at the beginning."

"I loved music and took English Literature to A level but in the end I chose anthropology. I sometimes read a novel but there is so much reading on my course."

"What are you researching in New Zealand?"

"Present day Māori culture. My Dad didn't really touch that much but his colleague Dr Beate did her PhD Thesis on it, but from a woman's point of view. Dad did much more in Australia, Canada and Peru."

"Interesting. I'm sure you will love it. I love their music, the Hukkah. They are very different from Australian Aborigines. There are more links with the Polynesians."

"Do you think Maoris will be your main focus?"

"Not sure. Mum wants me to go to Uluru and research the Anungu tribes. She really loved it."

"I'm ashamed to say I have never been."

"Where are your children?"

"Lisa is with Joseph near Townsville and Anthony is with Liz not far away. They are partners but have not married, yet."

"Where will you live?"

"Opposite number 42, your old house."

"Never."

"I love old Queenslanders but 63 was a bit of a wreck. I bought it cheap when I sold our family home so that I could give my children a sum to start them off."

"That's just what my Dad did! That's great Jonathan. Are you ever just Jon?"

"Of course. I love DIY but the house was beyond me. I had to call in help."

"My father named me Hartleigh Thomas after Alice's father but when he died he used my middle name. Now, I like Hartleigh! My grandfather was Professor Thomas Hartley." He spelled it out.

"It's a cooler name because I play in a music group and with my brother Joseph, a real musician, in Oxford."

"I feel I am getting to know your father through meeting his children."

"We were five and now we are four. We are in America, England and Australia but we have a close bond and keep in touch."

"Nathaniel went to Uluru with Mum and my uncles and he is an artist. He is bound to make some paintings and Uncle Daniel and his partner Charles are composing an Uluru melody."

"Where is your uncle?"

"London. He is in a Civil Partnership and they perform in England and Germany."

"There is no end to the talents and achievements of your family!"

"My Dad used to say, 'We are blessed'. He used that a lot, even when our sister died."

"I said to Bethany that I should leave that to your mother to tell me when she is ready. I know it is very sensitive."

"Well said. Like some cake?"

"Yes please." Hartleigh fetched some slices of Alice's cake and handed them round. He then went to find Bethany.

"See what you mean!" he whispered and then went to chat to Steve on the other side. "You are beginning to look like your Dad. Not so thin and longer hair but your face!"

"It's all the tribal people we look at!" he laughed. Nathaniel spent time with Esther and then went to speak with Jon.

"Are you working on Uluru?"

"In a way. I draw first. I have made sketches and taken photos. It is so magnificent I don't know where to start."

"What kind of art do you do? I am a bit ignorant. I like some well-known paintings and my favourites are the Australian Impressionists."

"I love them too. I like landscapes but I also like ethnic art and some of the abstract painting. I am not too keen on Picasso and company. Just don't get it but I like the Bauhaus."

"Bauhaus? German? Oh, dear I shall have to look them up."

"Yes, a whole movement about a hundred years ago. Klee, Kandinsky, Miro."

"I recognise the names, vaguely."

"Think triangles, circles, arrows, rectangles in bold colours and no connections spread across a huge coloured canvas. It was an interesting period philosophically and culturally. Women were just about included and that was new. I love doing my version of their work."

"Do you know how you will use your art studies?"

"I'd love to paint full time but I shall probably have to teach to earn my living."

"I used to teach, so did my wife. She did Maths. I don't understand them either."

"My Mum wants to teach EFL to foreigners."

"I'm working on it. I did some voluntary teaching in Townsville, so I have contacts. That reminds me," he leant over to Alice, "When do you want to go to the Mosque?"

Everyone looked surprised and they all laughed.

At home time Steve said he would take the boys in the van with the buggies and Alice could take Mums and babies in her car.

"I'll take them." Jon offered.

He helped pack the buggies and then the boys shook hands and Jon kissed the girls and Alice. She once again felt shaky, half in pleasure and half in fear.

They had agreed on a date to visit the Mosque after his house was finished in about a month.

The time of their departure came. "I must see them grow up. I'll come and see you all."

"You'll be a working woman!"

"I hope, but I need to see you and your babies."

"Early days yet, Mum." Nathaniel smiled.

Thomas was last to catch his plane. "Mum, you have a wonderful friend in Jon. I hope it works out well for you."

"Thanks, Hartleigh. He is a lovely man. He has brought up his children on his own from teenage years."

Alone in her own home, Alice wrote down her memories of her experiences at Uluru. She had not told her sons. She thought about Jon and agreed he was an unusual and lovely man. She even welcomed his touch on her arms when he greeted her but the other part of her emotions was fearful in a way she did not fully understand.

5 The Vicar's Proposal

Between the Uluru trip and her children's arrival Alice had a session of Spiritual Direction with Philip. As she arrived in the room she noticed he looked different. He was wearing a smart, beige jacket, pale trousers and a very white shirt. Then it struck her that he had had a different haircut. It was combed differently and his brown shoes were highly polished. She nearly commented but she stopped herself.

She sat down as he lit the candle.

"I am so glad you found the meditations helpful."

"Have you been there?"

"Many years ago with my wife and daughter."

"What did you think?"

"Rather a lot of tourists. So much heathen tourist tat and native paintings."

"And the Rock?"

"Ayers Rock, the Olgas, huge mysterious and stark."

"I have a huge Aboriginal canvas which my husband gave us over 30 years ago, I love it. I have not put it up yet as it was in our room which is now the guest room. I think I might put it in the lounge."

"You tolerate ancestor worship and spirit creatures?"

"Of course I do. Derry's studies taught us to respect native spirituality and even learn from it. Have you ever heard of dadirri?"

"No."

"It's the Aboriginal word for silent contemplation and meditation. Silence, stillness and listening to nature."

"I don't know about all that. It has not been in my tradition." He explained that he thought it was too dangerous to open our minds to spirits and heathen and pagan practice but that Christian Meditation should always be based on Scripture.

"Tell me what you felt at Uluru." She explained that as she read about God our Stronghold, she had felt His presence and His love for her. She felt she actually mattered to the Creator of the Rock, the earth and the universe. He was moved but she hesitated to share her experience of seeing Miriam.

"That's the most important thing, God made everything, not ancestral spirits and He loves you."

"But God is too great for us to understand, He made the world with Christ and the Holy Spirit. He used water and wind and all the spirits they acknowledge long before He made human beings."

"Very true."

"I never want to be narrow minded in my faith. I've seen some great sadness in people's lives because of well-meaning Christians who tried to change how they lived. I have seen break downs and family break up." He had nothing else to say but he repeated, "Keep hold of God as your stronghold."

"Something else happened" She was hesitant but his silence made her continue. "I saw my dead daughter, actually."

"I have heard of that. I had some people in my church who spoke of seeing their departed loved ones, and even hearing them in the house."

"She had wet hair and looked just like she did at 15. She loved swimming and often came home with wet hair. She was wearing her white party dress and dragged her hands over the grasses just like she did in the woods in England." Tears ran down her cheeks.

She was beautiful, a lovely girl and a loving girl. She was walking by a rock pool and she seemed to walk right into the rocks and disappear. Alice wiped her eyes. "It was lovely. I felt such peace about her."

"It was a love-gift from God to you."

"Why didn't I see Derry and the baby?"

"God knew you needed to see her."

"I do hold on to God as my stronghold and St Teresa's words. 'God alone suffices' and to the reality of mystery."

After the prayer, she packed her bag and stood up.

"Alice, we have a couple of scheduled sessions left. I do not think it would be inappropriate to invite you to my home to meet my daughter and her husband. Would you join us for afternoon tea one day?"

"How very kind. I'd love to. Thank you very much."

"I shall be free after all my children have returned. I am going to look for a voluntary teaching job teaching English to foreigners. I am waiting for a friend to give me a contact."

"How interesting. I will ring you with a date when Geraldine and Len are free. Their son has moved to Babinda and has a job there. He seems to like the town."

Alice left him grateful that he had handled her experience well and even thought it was valid. She took down the address and looked it up on the map to see it was near the Catholic Church where they were meeting. Philip gave a Saturday after the departure of all her children and grandchildren.

She found little housing estates like her own on the edges of the sugar cane fields. They lived in a very pleasant, comfortable house with a large garden. Alice parked and stood looking at the miles of sugar cane stretching behind the estate. Philip opened the door and ushered her in. The house was spotless and decorated like a Victorian house with wall-hanging with embroidered flowers, framed pictures of flowers and Bible texts. Family photos were on every table and shelf.

"Come in Alice, this is Geraldine, my daughter."

"Pleased to meet you, Geraldine. I am so grateful to have had Spiritual Direction with your father."

"He told us he had invited you but he isn't allowed to talk about the clients so we know nothing about you."

"I'm the widow of Sundale Court. I live alone now as my husband has died but I have four children and their husbands and wives and children, as well as friends do come to visit me. I decided not to downsize so that I would always have room for them."

"Four children! You don't look old enough."

"Do sit down, or would you prefer to go into the garden? It's rather hot but we do have shade."

"I'd love to." Alice left the chintz armchair and passed the chintz settee and stepped into a beautifully kept garden.

"You can see what my hobby is." said Philip.

"Isn't it great? Dad works wonders with it. We are both still working so we don't have time. Len's coming back soon, he had to go to the shops."

"I am amazed by the sugar cane. Are there any disadvantages to being so close at harvest time?"

"We are used to the smell when they burn off. It's like treacle in the air. We are also used to the noise of those gigantic machines but it only lasts a few days. The worst is when they kill the Cane Toads. Bodies all over the place."

“I heard about them when we first came to Cairns. We lived in the centre of town and were not so near.”

Suddenly Len appeared, “Glad to meet you, Alice.” Geraldine went to make the drinks as they sat under the awning.

“What’s your work?” she asked.

“Gerry does secretarial work in town near the Casino. She used to do hairdressing but this was better pay.”

“Can I come for a haircut?”

“She still does private clients. Of course you could. I work near the marina. I am a food order supervisor for a big company which supplies the hotels and the boats.”

“I remember when I first saw those gigantic, luxury boats. I could not believe it. Such wealth.”

“They are good customers.”

“And your son?”

“Terry has moved to Babinda and has a good job as a stockman for the railway and the coast. He’s not married yet but we are longing for grandchildren. He is our only son.”

“I have two, both girls. They were with me last week and they are both one year old.” She had to explain where they lived and shocked this very traditional family. Gerry explained that when Terry moved away they used the biggest room, did it up and made an en suite bathroom so Dad could come and live with them. He remained in the vicarage although he had retired. The new vicar was a lady who already had a family home. Being alone in the large vicarage did not suit him but it was Gerry who persuaded him to live with them as he was getting older.

“I still have good health but in a few years that might not be the case. It was kind of them to take me in.”

Alice noted that rooms seemed generally bigger in Australian houses and she could imagine that he would have a desk, a television, a bookshelf and a bed.

“I have my own television but I don’t watch much except sport. Len likes that too so we watch on the big screen in the lounge.”

“And I go into Dad’s room to see my dramas.” Gerry smiled. “Where is your youngest son studying?”

“Brisbane Art College. He is very talented but unless you become ‘flavour of the year’, it is hard to make a living, so he is training to teach.”

"There are a lot of Jewish names in your family," noted Gerry. "My mother was Jewish."

"That makes you Jewish, the lineage comes through the mother."

"She was rescued from the Nazis when she was five and was brought up by Christians. She went to a Messianic Jewish group in her last years.

"I did not realise you were Jewish but you do have the looks, the hair. Who was your father?" said Philip.

"Professor of Anthropology at Oxford. As English as they come. Do tell me about your wife. Is that her photo in the lounge?"

Philip answered, "We had our portraits taken when Gerry was twenty-one. Len is in the others. She died of cancer some years ago."

They chatted easily about Philip's wife and Derry. Gerry and Len were surprised that she was the daughter and the wife of a professor.

"And possibly the mother of another one. My eldest son is now in New Zealand studying Māori life today."

"What does that mean?" Alice realised that they were in danger of being overwhelmed by academic matters so she simplified her answers and asked them about their church.

"It's an Anglican church similar to the one I grew up in when Dad was Vicar for many years."

"Are you involved in many activities?"

"The fete, the jumble sales, the Harvest, Christmas. I used to take Sunday School when I was younger. Len is in the choir. He has a good voice."

"We mainly went to Christian meditation. We held a meeting each week in our home in Oxford and went to one in Cairns. Derry even took a Day of Reflection in the Catholic church where I meet your father.

"What does that involve?" Alice explained the John Main system of meditation but avoided using the word 'mantra' in case it caused offence. "I use a prayer word which I repeat until I can be totally still in God's presence."

"A prayer word?"

"John Main advises us to use the word' Maranatha' but I chose some German words from a hymn by Bonhoeffer and now I use the Spanish phrase from St Teresa of Avila.

"Solo Dios basta, God alone suffices." Philip was quite pleased with himself.
"Would you all like to have a meal with me in my house?" asked Alice.

"I'm sure we would.", "Yes please." Philip and Gerry responded. "I like cooking. Is there anything you don't eat?"

"No problems. I think we eat anything." Alice had her salmon dish in mind.

She left the house, thanking them and shaking hands. *How twee.* she thought, *like 1950s furniture in a modern home. Perhaps it came from the vicarage.* She was relieved to leave them. She felt somewhat stifled by their attitudes.

On Sundays she went to Mass at the Catholic Cathedral and enjoyed the warmth of her memories of first seeing the beautiful stained-glass windows of the creation. She felt rather sad as she thought of the little Anglican Church that was their spiritual home but had no knowledge of meditation and only negative views of indigenous spirituality.

She felt refreshed by going to her Meditation Group. There were a few new people who had joined recently.

Simon came to lunch and she told him about the retired vicar and his family. She invited him to lunch with them and he gladly accepted.

Simon brought some wooden gifts for them all and one for their son. Philip was surprised to see him in her home.

"This is my friend Simon from Meditation Group."

"Pleased to meet you." They all said together.

Philip sat next to Simon as they drank Prosecco. "Are you retired too?"

"Yes. I used to teach English language and literature and woodwork."

"Alice has so many professors in her family that I thought you might be another one."

"I did not go that far, but my partner did. He was a surgeon, a spine specialist in Cairns hospital and in a private clinic."

"Alice also has gay people in her family, a gay brother."

"And a gay son." she yelled from the garden. "He's the one doing anthropology."

"I'm amazed. I've heard of a recently deceased Professor Eugene something." Philip recalled.

"That's my beloved. We were together for over forty years. Has your son got a partner?"

"Not yet," Alice said. "He has friends but wants to concentrate on his studies."

"I don't think we know any gay people." said Gerry.

"My brother was 20 when he told us. He had had such a hard time. He went to the kind of charismatic church that believed you could change someone's sexual orientation by prayer and exorcism."

There was a silence. Simon came in to break the embarrassment.

"I never encountered that myself and I spent many years reading and studying about the issue. I did a lot of research on nature and nurture and genetics. I was so blessed to meet Eugene. We had a wonderful life together and I miss him so much."

They ate keeping the conversation away from the gay issue. Simon got his big bag from the car and distributed the gifts, birds, lizards and small koalas.

"We made these in our workshop and I would like to give them to you as gifts. I have made one for your son. Would he like a lizard on his wall?"

"He will. Absolutely. Thank-you."

"I wonder if their son is gay." whispered Simon to Alice in the kitchen.

"Something's wrong. You can pick up the vibes. It could just be that he is not as religious as them."

They sat indoors for a coffee as the heat outside was oppressive.

"Thank-you so much for coming. It is good to meet you and see how well my director is being looked after."

Philip was last to go through the door.

"We'll arrange the next session in three weeks." he said to her.

"Yes, Philip, I only have one commitment, the Mosque." She laughed, "A possible teaching opportunity."

Philip looked surprised. "You are looking for more Muslim ladies like the ones in London.?"

"Sort of. Just following a lead." Gerry took his arm to lead him to the car.

"Goodbye, God bless."

Alice was already working out a way to ask Philip about his grandson and wanted to find a way of wording it. She could not be too direct.

Simon kissed her goodbye and leant over to her ear. "You do realise that the elderly vicar is sweet on you?"

"Never!" she laughed. She then looked on line to see if there were any translation jobs around.

Philip had talks with his daughter in his room.

"Dad, she is so beautiful. She is surrounded by intelligent people and I think she is younger than me."

"I know all that. You did encourage me to try when I told you that I thought so highly of her that I'd like to ask her to marry me."

"I had not met her then. She's gorgeous and she was so kind to invite us. I am not so sure now. Do you think she has feelings for you?"

"She took my meditations to Uluru with her and she seemed so pleased that I had given them to her. I was so moved to see her weeping over her dead husband and her daughter who died in her teens. I felt I could comfort her. She is very caring and I think she would do her best to care for me. I do love her and I think we could have a love life together."

"You can but try but she has very liberal views on certain things."

"She would soon change them as she got involved with the church, and saw the love and good works there."

"I don't want you to get hurt. You have no home to offer her."

"I think she would have me in that big house of hers."

Philip rang to make a date for the next session.

"Alice, I would like to take you for a meal in the Botanical Gardens for our next session. Are you happy with that? A more informal session?"

"That's kind of you but you don't need to do that, Philip, we can meet in the church as usual." She was having a little panic inside, remembering Simon's words.

"I'd really like to. I shall drive you there. I have no car now, but Gerry will lend me hers."

"No need. I would pick you up but I really would much rather meet in our usual place."

"That's alright Alice, if that's what you prefer."

"Thanks, Philip. I was hoping to share something with you before I become a working girl."

Philip was happy to hear that and Alice was relieved and feared that Simon had been right. "Was he trying to make a date with her?"

She had hoped to share about her friendship with Jon and to pray about the pressure from her children and her own feelings that he was not necessarily interested in a romance but that he was just a good friend. She knew that she would not touch on that subject with him at all.

She went to the church with some trepidation. They started in the usual way and when he asked her what was on her minds, she spoke the words she had rehearsed in her head.

"Can you tell me about Terry, your grandson?"

"Does that impinge on your walk with God?"

"Yes, it does. I'll explain later but I would be glad if you could tell me about him and your relationship with him."

Philip hung his head and was quiet for too long. Alice sat and waited.

"He was given an ultimatum." He stopped. "His Dad found him outside the church. He had gone to one of the sheds in the grounds to get something and he saw Terry cuddling someone and then they were really kissing and doing other things. Len called out to him and saw he was kissing a boy from the choir."

Alice sat quietly. Simon had had some good, instinctive insights. "What was the ultimatum? Did his parents ask him to leave home?"

"They were very upset. Terry said that he loved the boy and that they were both 19 and so they planned to be together. Len and Gerry called me and we talked with them. Len and Gerry told them that what they were doing was wrong and that they should stop."

"My brother went through that. My son will not have to." She said clearly trying to make him understand that she disagreed with him entirely.

"Terry chose for himself. The boy had an uncle in Babinda so they both went there. Terry found a job and they rented a flat. The other lad also got a job but I don't even know his name."

"I'm so sorry to hear that. I hope you will accept Terry as he is and support him." There was another long silence.

"Is that what you wanted to talk about?"

"I just want to say thank-you for all your support over the past months. You have helped me through some very difficult times of grief. We can make this our last session but we will keep in touch."

"Alice, I have something to say." He drew a box from his pocket and held it in his hand. Her heart sank.

"Alice, I have grown very fond of you over the months. I think you are the most wonderful woman I have ever met. I'm older than you but age does not matter. I love you Alice and I think we will iron out our theological differences if we love each other and live together."

She could not speak as he opened the box and showed her an antique diamond ring. "Alice Barnes, please will you marry me?"

She lowered he head. How could she avoid hurting him?

"Philip I feel very honoured. Age does not matter if people are in love. Different belief systems can even be overcome with love, but Philip, I cannot accept your proposal. I do not love you in the way needed to marry you. Please accept my apologies if I have given you the wrong impression. I did not mean to." She stood up and stepped away and walked towards the door. She pulled the envelope with her final fees from her bag and put it on the table.

"I wanted to pray for Terry. I pray that you will all love and accept him. I am sorry Philip. God bless you and your family."

She didn't look up. She left quickly, walked to her car and drove to the university car park. She needed space, fresh air to cry and to walk in open fields. Above the university the hills of Cairns stood dark and green and high. She left her car and started for the foothills. In the trees she could cry. She felt so sorry for this man more than twenty years her senior, who had so humiliated himself. She stopped her weeping and tried to analyse her emotions. She decided to write them a letter to thank them and to plead with them on Terry's behalf.

How did Simon guess? She did not guess but she had been aware that there was a conflict of some sort. She recalled that there were not photos of Terry on the walls. She would have liked to talk to Abigail but she did not feel comfortable with a screen talk. She was short of 'girly talks. She walked across the foothills and looked at the sugar cane waving. She sat on a log, "I don't want to be a burden but I really need to talk to someone." She thought of Jeannie but she knew Jon would be there and she could not possibly share with him nearby.

She decided to ring Jeannie and ask her if she would come to her house for a talk. "Of course I'll come, Alice."

"In about half an hour? I'm at the university walking on the hills right now."

Jeannie drove over and they sat inside. "I'm sorry you are upset. Is one of the children sick?"

"No, a sick me. I am not ill but I had a horrible shock today."

Alice explained about the months of Spiritual Direction where she had walked through her grief with an elderly, retired Vicar. She mentioned his invitation to his home and her reciprocal invitation to him, his daughter and son-in-law.

"Then he offered me a diamond ring and asked me to marry him." Jeannie laughed aloud and strangely it helped Alice.

"How old is he?"

"Seventy-seven."

"Old enough to be your father. Alice you are a very beautiful woman. He might well fall in love with you, but to propose marriage, just not on unless you fell in love with him too."

"I don't love him, of course but I did not want him to feel I had been angling to attract him to me. I had to share painful stuff with him and he helped with praying through my loss, but I was never attracted to him." Jeannie thought it would help to have a glass of wine. Alice sipped as she told her about the traditional family and their traditional views.

"We had nothing in common, no real connection to lead to marriage." Jeannie hugged her and said that she and Steve had loved Derry and her too, and all their children and that she was welcome to have a chat about anything at all at any time. Alice was relieved that Jeannie agreed that a letter would be the right response.

As she stood in the garden after Jeannie left, she realised that Jon mattered to her. She felt some attraction to him and knew that they were at ease in each other's company, but the idea of any love or romance somehow frightened her.

6 The Mosque

Alice was exhausted by her emotional response to Philip's proposal. She was upset to upset him, a kind, elderly gentleman.
She left it a day or two and then she wrote to Geraldine and put in a little card for Philip. She thanked him once more, apologised once more and suggested he had a talk with his Supervisor in the Spiritual Direction circle. She then added that she hoped he would find some information about Christians who accepted gay people. She pointed out that we had all learned more about it in recent years and that many Christians saw that they had misinterpreted some Bible verses.

In her letter to Geraldine and Len, she mentioned her gay brother and what she had learned as she saw him wrestle with his sexuality and his Christian faith. She then informed them that there were some very helpful books to give them a different understanding of the Bible.

Thousands of churches now accepted gay relationships.

She ended, "It's not an abomination in the sight of God. There are many worse things in life, but that the Scriptures were about abuse and not orientation. Please love your son and let him know you have changed your mind and will accept him as he is."

She felt pleased when she put the letter in the post and went back to looking for translation firms. She tried the old ones but most had closed so she drafted a letter to send off to whatever companies were relevant in Cairns.

She contacted Abigail and had a screen chat about the vicar's proposal. It helped her to share with her oldest friend and confidante.

Abigail told her that she was expecting a third child. "I'm catching up with you." she laughed.

"Congratulations, dear Abigail! I do miss you. I'm going on a little trip tomorrow with another widower. He is not likely to propose but he is very good company. He is mixed race but he looks like a full Aborigine."

"It's another boy. We have chosen Marcus."

"How old fashioned of you."

"I know. We wanted Mar to go with Marlow and Marilla and we went through several possibilities but Marcus seemed the best."

Abigail said that Justin's work was still thriving, that he was doing one exhibition after another with smaller and smaller gaps between but most of all he was selling. Galleries were buying as well as the public.

"What's his name?"

"Who?"

"Your widower."

"Jonathan O'Neill. His mother was a very dark Aborigine and his father was a blond, blue-eyed Irishman. His children are both light as his wife was white and blond."

"All the best. I wish for you to find love again!"

"Thanks, Abigail. I feel very unsure about it."

"You would. That's you. Try for some happiness!"

"Bye, dear Abigail."

With these words ringing in her ears, she chose her clothes for the Mosque visit, long sleeves, covered legs and a scarf. She tried her blue silk Pakistani outfit but the trousers were no longer a good fit. She had kept it 27 years. She could wear the top and she chose white trousers. The scarf was still usable. Jon tooted and got out of his car and walked into the garden. The little boys next door were playing with a ball in the garden. They both stared at Jon. One called his Mum, Carol. She came out and said 'Hello'.

"Hi, I'm Jon." They had had no direct contact with an Aborigine except the mixed-race boys at school. A tall, dark stranger, and so dark, and so close, shocked them. Alice came out to greet Jon and spoke to her neighbour. Carol heard his voice and calmed herself. She called the boys to get ready for school.

Alice kissed his cheeks, "Sorry! They've surely seen you here before."

"Ready, Muslim lady? You have done well!"

"This was my going away outfit over 27 years ago. The trousers no longer fit." She locked up and got into his car.

"It's on the main highway south. We passed it on the way to Townsville." She tried to relax and looked out of the window.

"I only came this way once, when my mother was here. We went to a garden while Derry and Thomas were working together."

"Paranella Park?"

“That’s the one!” The new buildings, the vineyards, the big warehouses all flashed past and they were soon on more open road.

“Look, a Sikh Gurdwara.”

“They’re all arriving here now.”

Soon the familiar shape of the Mosque, the dome and minarets appeared before them. They parked and got out to read the notice board. A bearded man came out to meet them.

“Asalaam alekum.” said Alice.

“Valekum salaam.” he responded.

“Good morning,” said Jon, “we would like some information and we would like to visit your Mosque.”

“How can I help?” his English was very good.

“This is Mrs Barnes from Cairns. She would like to know if any Muslim ladies would like a tutor of English. She is a voluntary teacher, no money required.”

“What an offer!” he smiled at Alice. She put her scarf over her head.

“I used to run a class for Muslim ladies in London. I even learned some Urdu as they were from Pakistan.”

“Ap Urdu bolsakta hain?”

“Main chota Urdu bolsakta houn.” Jon looked on with surprise. “But I’d rather speak English. It was a long time ago.”

“Well, Madam, you are very welcome. Not many white people speak Urdu.”

“Where are you all from?”

“Mostly Pakistan but also Bangladesh and now we also have refugees from Sudan, after their war.”

“And you?”

“Pakistan, Karachi.”

“My class was mostly from Rawalpindi.”

“And they spoke Urdu?”

“Some did but they had their own dialect.”

“Where is the class?”

“It doesn’t exist yet. I am alone now my husband has died. Most of my children are abroad and I would like to do some work. If you have a group of ladies who would like to practice or learn English I could begin a class in a hall, somewhere near the Mosque. Would that be acceptable?”

"I'd have to ask the leadership team." Alice had anticipated and typed out her name, email address and phone number so he could let her know if there were some ladies available for lessons. She gave him a sheet.

"We need men too for the Sudanese. A woman would not be allowed."

"I might be able to help. I am a retired English teacher and I am happy to volunteer. I did some voluntary teaching in Townsville. No money needed. I have some books but I would possibly need more copies and the use of a photocopier if there are more students."

"I need to talk with my brothers. The Sudanese are free in the day. They have nothing to do in the camp. The women would also have class in the day. They never go out in the dark."

"When we leave you we will have a look round in the nearest village and see what halls are available. If we have to pay for a hall, would the Mosque cover the cost?"

"I think so. Give me time."

Jon took Alice's paper and wrote his details with his pen. "Do you have halls here?"

"We do. You could possibly use one. I am not sure about Madam. If she has ladies, it could be possible."

"Could we visit?"

"I will take you. Madam you have already covered your head, please just take off shoes."

"What's your name?"

"Mohammed Ali Sadik."

"Pleased to meet you Mr Sadik." Jon bowed his head a little.

They went inside the silent place, light, well decorated, clean and shiny. Alice was impressed. She stood alone gazing around the roof, admiring the designs and recalling her knowledge of Islamic art. She felt the calmness and the stillness, almost like the water hole at Uluru.

"I do not have books and papers but if there are some ladies, I will get some."

"They do not read and write. Just a few of them know a little."

"My London class was the same. I loved the ladies and we had parties together. We were in a church hall."

Sadik smiled, "You have been sent by Allah. We need your help."

"Could we propose one lesson a week?"

"You have come from Cairns, so about 40 minutes. It is a lot to ask of you."

"I could offer once a week to begin with." said Jon.

"So could I," Alice said, "if we do the same day we could travel together and save time and petrol."

"Sir, Madam you are so kind. Are you related?"

"Nearly. Mr O'Neill is the brother of a lady I have been close to for over 27 years." They said goodbye and she remembered not to shake his hand. He did shake hands with Jon.

"Sir, it is the will of Allah. I am so happy." On the way to the car Jon said, "That was very well put. If they thought we were having an illicit affair that would be that." He smiled and she smiled back. "It will be more complicated if we turn up together every week."

"Sudanese. I have never met any. We had a few Muslim boys in Townsville so I learned a little about their expectations and behaviour."

"Well, we are the will of Allah. I loved the Mosque."

"Village and halls?"

They drove back to a turning inland off the highway. There was a small row of shops, a church, a few other buildings that could contain halls and then open farm land.

"A drink first?" They found a pub like cafe and had some cold drinks. Jon chatted with the waiter and asked if there were halls to hire. Alice had forgotten to bring a lighter top and was feeling far too hot in her long sleeves. The waiter mentioned the church hall, the library with a hall and the Farmers' Union Hall.

"I wonder if any of them would allow Sudanese refugees from the camp to come inside?" They found the Farmers' hall and wrote down the number for hiring. It was all locked up. "It looks like one large hall. I bet it is used like a drinking club."

They went into the library and found the hall which was more a like a meeting room. It would hold about 6 people. The church was open but no one was around. They looked for a notice board but it was old and faded and scratched. They looked around the pews at the windows and then at the tomb stones outside. An elderly lady came up.

"Are you visitors?" Jon nearly said 'The will of Allah', but instead he said

"We are so pleased to see you. We want some information on your church hall. We might be interested in hiring it."

"I'm a church warden. Here is the number for the vicar and on the back is my number."

“Could you let us see it?” Alice asked. The lady pulled out a key.

“It’s at the back.” It was a modern, well-kept hall big enough to hold about 40 people or a class of about 10.

“Do you want it for a party?”

“No, we are teachers and we are possibly setting up some English lessons for the ladies at the Mosque and the men in the refugee camp.”

“Those refugees, they cause such trouble.”

“I understand that but they have suffered so much in their war, lost so much and they have nothing to do all day.”

“Why not teach them in the camp?”

“Why not indeed? Where is it? Thank-you so much for your help. We need two places for a couple of hours once a week. We started at the Mosque.” The lady seemed shocked. “You went to the Mosque?”

“It’s lovely. God is God whatever name.”

“Keep driving down this road and after the last farm buildings there is nothing else but the camp on your left.”

“Thank you very much. We did not think of the camp. Is there a shop with tee shirts?” Alice asked. They were directed back towards the Farmers’ Hall and a few doors down was a small haberdashery reminding Alice of the sewing shop near Amaranth. They sold a few items like nightdresses and tee-shirt.

“I know a place like this in a tiny town in the Prairies in Canada.” Alice laughed as she recalled her time there with Pearl. “I’ll pop in and see if I can get one.”

“I’ll get it for you.”

“I’ll have to change and take this off.”

“Didn’t think.” he laughed.

She looked through the clothes which were mainly for children. “I need a tee shirt for me. I am too hot.”

“Muslim top?”

“Yes.”

“We sell them sometimes now there’s a Mosque.” She went into the back. “I’ve only got this.” She held up a black sun top with thin straps.

“Can I put it on?” Here, behind the shelves. Alice changed and the top fitted and made her look like a bathing beauty. She paid and went to join Jon who had wandered down the street.

“What a difference. You look great!”

"Thank you, Sir." She smiled.

"Camp next? You had better have your scarf handy in case we are let in. This is a sad little village that has seen better days."

After the last farm buildings there were fields of cattle with those iconic water wheels and other fields of crops. Suddenly the wire fence of the camp appeared. They parked on the road opposite the gates and went up to the guard.

"Good morning. We'd like to speak to someone in authority in the camp or have an email or phone number to contact them?"

The guard made a phone call. "He's coming to you. You could not come in looking like that." He nodded to Alice.

"I changed too soon!" She wrapped the large scarf round her shoulders.

The guard was an Aboriginal soldier who smiled to meet Jon. He explained their mission. "English lessons, they certainly need them."

"We went to the Mosque as Mrs Barnes is interested in teaching some Muslim ladies and they told us about the Sudanese who attend from the camp."

"We could teach at the Mosque or the village hall. We are investigating where to take classes."

"Are you religious out to convert them?"

"Certainly not! I am a retired teacher and have just moved to Cairns. I took voluntary classes in Townsville. Mrs Barnes taught ladies in London. We are both offering to teach again as we just want to be of use."

"How much do you charge?"

"Nothing. We are volunteers. No charge for us but if we have to hire a hall, I hope the camp would cover the cost."

"You have made my day; two volunteers willing to teach refugees."

"Let me consult the team. What exactly do you have in mind?"

"To start with, two hours a week."

"OK, thanks. Got your details?" Alice got out another paper and handed it to Jon to write on his.

"Lunch?" he asked.

"Not round here. Too sad. Back to town or…"

"Paranella Park?" Alice was happy with that idea.

"It is a special place for me. I sat there with my mother and talked to her about my longing to have a baby. Shortly after that I was expecting Miriam."

They were relaxed and chatting about their calls that morning. Paranella was looking rather neglected as they walked through the areas of bamboo and through the stone arches.

"I'll get lunch. You are spending on petrol."

"No way, Madam. It will be my pleasure. Soon I can invite you all to open number 63."

"Well done!"

"I still have to get some furniture. I have the basics for me but I need chairs, table and settee."

They sat in the shade on the terrace overlooking the sea. They ate salads and Alice had a glass of cool white wine. He drank fruit juice.

Alice had no idea what the rest of the day would bring and that this day would change the rest of her life.

"Can we talk?" Jon asked. "About something serious?"

"There are two matters I would like to discuss with you. The first one might mean that we stop talking and do not go on to the second."

"I am intrigued. Do you want to deal with the first one and leave the second for another time?"

"Perhaps, but I am afraid you might not talk to me."

"You are worrying me."

"Sorry. I had lovely chats with your daughter Bethany and son Hartleigh and they both tried to tell me about Miriam. I stopped them and told them that I thought it should be you who tells me when you are ready."

"Dear Bethany and dear Hartleigh. They both suffered badly. Jon, I am a bit afraid of spoiling a lovely day. Jon, I love being with you but talking about Miriam will be hard and it will be even harder to listen and you would get upset too."

She felt him take her hands and hold them. She looked down and felt surprised to see his black hands holding her white hands. She realised that she had totally forgotten that he was black. She smiled and kept her hands in his.

"We'll find a time when it is right. She was a beautiful girl, just like her mother."

"Thank-you. Do you want to go on to item two?"

"Can I keep holding your hands?" She nodded and gave his hands a squeeze.

"Alice, I have real fears about a new relationship but I so appreciate meeting you and spending time with you. There's a possibility of us working together regularly after today and I want you to know that I admire you, respect you and I am beginning to fall in love with you. If you do not like that idea I hope it won't stop us being friends, companions."

Alice was not expecting anything like that. She took in a deep breath as Jon continued.

"My wife died just over ten years ago and since then I have not made love to any woman. I have been celibate for twelve years and my fear is that I am no longer capable, I might not be up to it any more. I'd like to get to know you more and spend more time with you but I don't want to hurt you and feel that I am fooling you or that I am pretending and offering something I cannot deliver. I am so attracted to you and feel I am falling in love with you so I want to be honest."

Alice pulled one hand away and touched his mouth and stroked his face.

"What a lovely thing to say. How honest of you. Jon I am attracted to you and I loved it when you held my shoulders to kiss me on the cheeks. I have the same problem. I have not made love for nearly five years and I have a similar problem, I am afraid. I love our friendship and companionship but like you I had a very happy marriage and I am not sure I could let anyone make love to me again."

Jon took her free hand back and smiled, "That's the worst bit over." He smiled. "My children are encouraging me to 'court' you."

"So are mine!"

"There's no rush. We meet regularly and perhaps we can experience loving touch again after our sufferings. We both know that it might not end in a love affair."

"That's so good to hear, Jon. You are an amazing man. I love how you handled today."

"And you are an amazing and very beautiful woman."

"Can I have a kiss before we go? No one around."

She remembered how she was with Derry after he had declared his love for her, an unusual boldness to encourage an unsure man.

He let go of her hands and she put her arms around his neck and she let him kiss her lips. He remained in that position and kissed her lips, her neck, her shoulders and then he put a hand behind her head and kissed her with an open mouth and she responded with some passion.

Slowly they pulled apart and both had tears running down their cheeks. "Alice, Alice, I love you." He wiped her tears.

"I love you Jonathan. I have fallen in love with you." She wiped his tears. "I am so happy. This is the answer to a friend's prayers for me."

"It is the will of Allah and of the ancestral spirits and of the Creator God. I wish we could make love right now. Good job we are in a park. Would it bother you to make love before a marriage?"

"No longer. I'd like to do that. Are you sleeping in number 63?"

"Yes, but it is not fit for visitors yet. It soon will be."

"Let's go to Sundale Court then." She shocked herself but she thought that this man was worth the risk. It could liberate him and possibly take away her fear. He drove with one hand on her knee most of the way. In the house, she took him to the guest room where the double bed was made up. They both had the same hesitancy and the same desire. Alice was concerned that after the four or five years she would not be able to give herself to another man. Jon had had 13-14 years of abstinence. In the newly designated guest room they discovered that their fears were groundless. Touch and caressing removed the hesitancy and they were able to make love. They were overwhelmed with emotion and joy. They had both wept together.

"I'd love you to stay but the neighbours will see your car and I could get a bad reputation as the widow of Sundale Court."

"Me too. I'd love to stay the night with you, but I'd better go to 63." They dressed, had a coffee and tried to calm down.

"I am so glad we made it. Please don't feel that I used you, Alice, I love you."

"Derry could not make love in the last two years so it was about five years of abstinence for me. I missed Derry and didn't want any other relationship. I was happy alone but meeting you changed all that."

"Who do we tell when? And what?" he asked.

"We can say we are dating. That's enough for now, I think, dearest Jon." Next morning, Steve rang, "How was the Mosque?"

7 Number 63

Sadik contacted them within days. The leaders had approved the lessons subject to the usual police checks. The ladies could use the hall in a little hut where the kitchen was. They cooked there for special communal meals. Jon would have the hall in the Mosque itself, to one side with other small rooms. He had phoned Jon, always men first and gave him a list of times and days to choose from. Jon asked for a list of names and then they would come to meet the students and make a timetable with them. Jon then went to Sundale Court for a planning session.

They chose two hours on a Thursday morning. "When can I see 63?"

"When we have finished our planning. You need some materials. I don't think you will find them in Cairns but I know a shop in Townsville. That is where my brother is and my children. We could spend a couple of days as it is a fair drive, or we could fly."

"I can't think."

"Are you OK? Am I going too fast?"

"I could cope without materials for a good month. I have a series of techniques without using aids."

"Would you like to start first and then get materials later when we know who we have and what their levels are."

"That sounds better. I don't feel ready yet to meet your family and make announcements."

"Are you having doubts?"

"There are things to share between us. Not doubts but if we share first we shall feel more comfortable together to make bigger decisions."

"You are so thoughtful and sensitive. Do you regret making love?"

She left her chair and went over to him and put her arms round him and they held each other. "No dear Jon, I don't regret making love with you, it was a wonderful experience. It is not my usual way of behaving and outside my comfort zone. I need time to get used to something so new." He stroked her hair and they kissed deeply.

"Alice, I do not want to lose you. I do not want to pressurise you. We'll take it slowly until we are both at ease, at peace."

"I love you Jon, I do not want to lose you. I want to be with you. I have four children, two partners and two grandchildren to consider."

"Let's go to 63, I have a meal ready for you. We can start sharing what is on our hearts." They decided on separate cars and she followed him to the road of old Queenslanders. She parked on the verge outside 63 and got out of the car and found herself opposite the garden of 42. She was overwhelmed by emotion and found herself sobbing. Jon left her alone for a while as he did not know what he was dealing with. Nor did Alice. Why ever was she weeping? She felt bad for Jon and thought she must be disturbing him.

"I'm sorry," she let him take her hand and lead her up the steps to the door.

"No arm chairs yet. Have a lie down on the bed." She cried into the pillow. He brought a glass of water and a box of tissues. He sat in the lounge and put on some classical music. He recalled Helen weeping like that when she learned that her cancer had returned.

Alice loved the Mozart and took a good half an hour to compose herself.

"I am so sorry dear Jonathan. I don't know what came over me. It was looking at 42, remembering Miriam going up the steps. We had such happy times there at the start of our marriage. I remember arriving there and then Derry had to go away and leave me for months. I saw little Thomas bounding around the rooms with toy cars. I had even put in a white bookcase and made a study for Derry. It was our first home together. I remembered how sad I was to leave it and return to Oxford. When we sold it I suffered from terrible insecurity. I remember Derry trying to comfort me."

Jon sat on the bed and cradled her in his arms. She asked if he knew Thala. He had never been there. She asked if he had ever had a massage.

"A physio massage for sport injury."

"We used healing massage with perfumed oils. One day I'll show you." Alice smiled, "Could I have a coffee?"

He showed her round the house, the spare rooms, his study, the bathroom and the kitchen end of the open plan lounge.

"Coffee out here?" He opened the balcony doors to the two little garden chairs. She sat looking over the Cairns hills and the cane fields stretching into the distance. As she sat sipping the delicious coffee she realised what she had experienced in the last few weeks. She explained to Jon as best she could that she had been emotionally stirred up to say goodbye to her beloved children and grandchildren.

Then there was the proposal of marriage from the elderly vicar who had been her spiritual director.

"He proposed to you? How old is he?"

"Seventy-seven. It shocked me that I had not realised that he had feelings for me. He had been kind and helpful but we were on very different wavelengths, even spiritually, or theologically. There was also the trip to Uluru. My brother and his partner and Hartleigh and Joseph are working on a musical composition. They loved it and I did too, even with something strange that happened to me." She hoped she would not be horrifying him by telling him about seeing Miriam.

"Did you ever see Helen?"

"Not see her. I felt her presence and I heard her walking down the stairs although for the last year she was bed ridden and did not come downstairs. She suffered terrible pain and was on morphine. She was like the living dead."

"How did you cope?"

"I prayed every prayer I knew, every prayer I'd ever been taught."

"I suppose I was praying when I saw Miriam."

"Can you tell me about her?"

Alice was calm and exhausted by her deep weeping. She spoke softly and slowly as she began to tell Jon the tragic story. When she reached her suicide and the murder of her child, he was weeping too, upset and shocked.

"How does anyone get through that? How did you all survive? No wonder you get overwhelmed by emotions but it is better to weep, to let it out or you would have a break down."

"It caused the strain on Derry's heart. He so loved her and the baby."

"Alice I cannot imagine how you got through such a terrible tragedy; only just 16, ignorant of the ways of boys and sex, guilty for her baby's blindness and no courage to cope with her life ahead. I am so sorry. No wonder you are feeling emotionally disturbed, delicate and overwhelmed. Alice continued to tell him of Little Bear's rehabilitation, how Derry had spoken with him and how she had also spoken with him a few months ago.

"No wonder you talk of our need of sharing. It would be terrible if you suffered all that and tried to relate to me without me knowing. I wish I knew what to do to help."

“There is something you can do. I’ll show you first.” Alice went to the bathroom and opened the cabinets. She found no oils but the nearest was a bottle of moisturising cream, thin and light with a little perfume. She found two big towels in the cupboard. She called Jon to come to the bedroom. “Can you put the Mozart back on?”

“I am going to give you a healing massage and then you can give me one.” She spread a towel on the bed and asked him to take his top off. He sat on the bed as she started to pour the cream on her hands. She gave him a fairly gentle massage back and front, got him to lie face down and then massaged his back more strongly. She asked him to turn over so she massaged his chest and could not stop herself leaning over to give him kisses. She said they should change roles and change towels. She gave him the cream and removed her own clothes.

“Tension is in my neck and shoulders. Do start there. Not too much cream, a little blob.” He turned out to be quite good. He was afraid of hurting her but she encouraged him to press harder on the muscles at the nape of her neck. They progressed to massaging each other everywhere and of course could not stop themselves making love.

“That’s so healing.” he whispered

“We had trained people giving spiritual massage at the Healing Centre, without the sex of course.”

“You must tell me about that one day.”

“There is nothing else so terrible to tell you about after Miriam. Be reassured, but we can share our past, our family life, our jobs and our spirituality, our views on things. I have oils from Thala at home for another occasion.”

“Would you like the lunch I prepared?”

“A little. Thanks. It will give me strength to drive home” She gathered up the cream covered towels.

“No worries, I have a machine.”

“How did you learn to love classical music?”

“My father. He loved it, I grew up with it. When the teachers at school realised I was intelligent and interested they put me with the white boys and pushed me on. I hated being black and I did all I could to be like a white boy. I copied the language and the accent and really worked on it. You and Derry knew much more than I did about Aboriginal culture and music. I copied my father. I was so badly treated at the junior school when they thought I was a full Aborigine, I decided to beat them at their own game and learn English literature and do better than the white boys. I succeeded! Marrying a beautiful, blond white girl was my crowning glory. Dealing with racist attitudes was very painful."

"You have overcome all that and I see no bitterness, resentment or anger in you."

"Not now. The church helped and Mum and Dad and the people there. They really encouraged me, even though the other members often commented on the darkness of my skin compared to my brother and sister."

"Jon, I love you so much and I am very sorry to have to leave you."

"Perhaps we could have a weekend away soon."

"I like that idea." She held on to him as they went to the door. "I am so aware that we have big decisions to make. We have a home each, what do we do about that? We have families to consider."

"We can't possibly decide any of that right now. We probably don't even know what we think."

"Where could we go?"

"Do you know Kuranda, Lake Placid on the Tablelands?"

"Yes, we did go. They are lovely places. The lake reminds me of Lake of the Woods in Canada."

"I'll give it some thought. Let's get the Mosque visit sorted first and then I must get this house fit for human habitation and a family party."

Alice had some days to herself before they went back to the Mosque. She recovered emotionally and felt stronger and did some freezer cooking to feel normal.

The post arrived just as she was leaving the house to meet Jon for the Mosque trip. She put two letters in her bag to read later. If she had known what they contained she would have torn them open immediately. In the end she was pleased that she had not done that because she could fully concentrate on meeting Sadik and the pupils.

Alice had 5 Muslim ladies, three from Pakistan and two from Bangladesh. Jon had 15 young men from Sudan. They chose those who already had permission to stay in Australia and were working through the processes, the paperwork involved. Jon offered to do two lessons a week eventually so he could get them to work in two groups or at different levels. Some could speak a little English.

Alice had worn a long-sleeved blouse and long trousers and had her scarf. They knew they had to wait a few weeks for the police check so they had time to make lesson plans and time to get materials.

"Mr O'Neill and Mrs Barnes, we are very grateful" Sadik shook Jon's hand. They drove back to Cairns to find a cafe for lunch. They chose a simple coffee bar in a shopping centre. At the table Jon stretched his hand out and she took it and held it until they ordered. Suddenly she remembered the letter.

"Sorry, can I read my letters?"

"Of course you can." She opened them while he ordered Panini and cappuccino.

She saw the first one was from Beate. Inside was a photocopy of a letter to Beate from Cairns University. She was called for an interview and was being offered a Professorship. Alice was so thrilled and exclaimed with great pleasure that her husband's colleague was coming to work at the University and was being offered a post as Professor.

"You recall seeing her thesis on our shelf? I can put her up until she gets settled and finds her own home."

"When?"

"Probably a few months' time. She is a very interesting, intelligent and forceful lady."

"I can't wait. Decisions to make before then!"

"Can we go back to 63 after lunch. I have some thoughts to share?"

"You don't mind the chaos? Go on, read your other letter."

She opened it to see that it was from Geraldine the daughter of the Rev Philip Browne. She expressed sorrow that her father had proposed to her, 'The foolish dream of a lonely old man'. She said she thought it was right to stop the sessions with him. He would make a recovery and then carry on serving the church. The second half of the letter amazed her. She was responding to the carefully worded plea from Alice that she reconcile with her son and accept him as a gay man. This had touched Gerry's heart and she had found some helpful books in a Christian bookshop in a church in Cairns. She said that she had always doubted that it was right for Christians to treat gay people in this way. She read the books and completely changed her mind.

She had shown it to Len, read bits out to him and persuaded him to go with her to Babinda and speak to Terry. They talked to Philip who was more understanding than they expected. Without conflict the parents drove to Babinda and spent time with their son and his partner. They hugged, said sorry and pleaded with him to forgive them and come back into their lives. The choirboy was called Phil!

Alice passed Jon the letter and she ate her Panini while he read. "That's remarkable, wonderful. Will you see him again?"

"I don't think so. I hope he does not write to me either, to save him embarrassment. Another Philip. Life is odd."

"Alice, you did very well with that letter. You handle everything so well, my darling." They walked out hand in hand and drove back to his home, number 63.

They parked and walked up the steps. He looked at her.

"No tears?" She smiled and took his hand as they walked into the unfurnished lounge. "Come on then. What do you want to say to me?"

"I think we both know that we have fallen in love and that we are compatible in many ways. I feel that so far, most of our relationship has been about me, my family, my emotions, my needs and I want it now to be more about you." He smiled and held her hand again and stroked her hair and face.

"What you need and want matter to me more than anything else."

"You have put in such effort to make this your home, this number 63. When we get to the stage that we want to live together, we should live here, make this our home together."

He was deeply moved by her respect and understanding. He would have no hesitation in living in Sundale Court but she had given him such honour.

"You have been thinking about our houses…"

"I was thinking that I could rent my house in a way that saves it for my children's visits. There must be a system of short term lets or half lets. The letter from Beate might be an answer initially. She knows all my children and she was very fond of Derry. She could have some rooms and share it when they come, until she is established"

"The will of Allah again."

"Where did you get married?"

"Helen was Catholic so we married in the Cathedral."

"I go there on Sundays. I love it, but I am not Catholic, I am an ecumenical Christian."

"I am not Catholic either but the children had to be brought up as Catholic. They are free spirits but they often go to Mass. I am interested in your Meditation

Group. I would like to understand more and come along sometime. Are you happy with that?"

"Delighted. I would never have survived without the Meditation Groups."

"So one day it could be the O'Neills of number 63?"

"I really hope so, Jonathan dear. I shall let my children know soon that we are an 'item' as Hartleigh Thomas says. I think I'd better go now, or I never will." They stood up and kissed passionately before he saw her to her car.

8 Preparing for a New Life

Nathaniel was the first to know. He told Alice he was coming for the weekend. She asked him to delay his visit for a week because she was now dating Jonathan and they were going away for a weekend.

"We are not rushing things but we are planning a future together."

"Well done, Mum! Can I bring a girlfriend with me?"

"Of course, dear. What's her name?"

"Magda. She's Polish." Alice thought that he would spread the news like wildfire so she spoke to all her children and to Abigail. There was not a single negative reaction until she spoke to Maddy. It was difficult to convince her that this black man was more English than the English in his voice, his education, his teaching. She did her best to explain that she had never intended to re-marry. This man had brought up a son and daughter after his wife had died ten years ago. Maddy just wished her well and hoped it worked out.

Jonathan was told by Jeannie that he looked very different and was clearly in love with Alice. Jonathan contacted his delighted children and promised to bring her to see them in the next two months.

The next Meditation Group was just before the weekend away. She did not know where Jon had booked. She told Fiona she was bringing a widower who she was dating, a mixed-race man, the brother of a good friend.

Jon was surprised at the large, luxurious home of the hosts and then was surprised again when two Aborigines walked in. They were a husband and wife, Elders from a local tribe on a Reservation. Alice was so pleased to see them, having met them before on one of their infrequent visits.

There was also a new couple who had recently moved to Cairns and attended the Cathedral. Richard explained the format of the evening for new people. They sat round a small table with a large candle. After the music and reading they meditated in silence for 30 minutes.

Jonathan listened intently and remained silent and still. He was moved and fascinated. At the end he had a conversation with the Aborigines and told them about his mother Ngala, a stolen child from the Townsville area.

"She married a rich white man who lost his inheritance due to the racism of his father and grandfather. Ngala had been a maid in his brother's house." He then spoke with the new Catholic couple.

"I live in a road near the Cathedral and Alice often goes to Mass there. I'd like to join her one Sunday."

"It's a great place to worship," said Colin, "Isn't it Patty?"

"Yes, we love it. Do come to lunch after the late morning Mass."

"Thank-you. We are actually away this weekend and on the following, Alice's son is coming with his girlfriend."

"Bring them, or come the following week."

"Are you a meditator?"

"No, but Alice is and so was her late husband. Where are you from?"

"Originally England, but we have been in Sydney many years and Colin has a contract to work in Cairns. I don't think we'll ever leave. It is paradise."

"Have you been in a cyclone yet? Alice was in one a few weeks after arriving here when her husband was away in the Bush?"

"A miner?"

"No, a Professor of Anthropology."

"What was his name?"

"Derwent Barnes. Her father was also a Professor, Thomas Hartley."

"What a small world. We lived near Oxford and a friend was at Marsden when Thomas Hartley was there. They talked of the professor who died and another one from a different college who was injured in some way in the rainforest. They ran some sort of charity." Jon called Alice over to tell them about her late husband and the charity.

"You are both invited to lunch in a couple of weeks and you can bring your son."

"How very kind. He is an artist studying in Brisbane."

Simon sat quietly during refreshments. Alice stood talking to Sandrine when Jon joined her and put his arm around her shoulders.

"I don't need to whisper to you that this one is sweet on you!" They both laughed. She had already told him of the Vicar's proposal and that she was dating another widower.

"Well, you are both radiant. All my very best wishes."

"Jon, Simon was also a teacher of English literature so you can swop notes." They did just that at great length.

Sandrine said to Alice, “He’s so easy to talk to. How did you meet him” Alice told her the story. Jon felt so at home and asked Richard if he had a book on Meditation that he could read. Richard was very pleased to give him one.

“Keep coming. You get more into it and get more from it by practising regularly.”

“I’m just fascinated. I can see how Alice has got through so much sorrow because of the practice of meditation.”

He drove her home before he returned to town. He told her he wanted to go to Mass with her. “Is that too soon? Is that OK? Do you want me to wait a bit?”

“Darling, Jon, so thoughtful. No it’s not too soon. It’s just right. My adopted Granny in Oxford became a Catholic in her last 20 years.”

“Adopted Granny?”

“Another time, dear, one of the many things to share with you.”

They kissed in the car for a long time. She reluctantly got out and waved him off. He would be back on Friday for their weekend away.

She rang to ask him what to pack; beach, rainforest, Tablelands walks? He said no beach, plenty of rainforest but a lake, so perhaps swim things. She packed walking shoes and swimsuit with sun clothes.

The car wound up and up the mountain passing the Barron River, so she guessed Kuranda. They drove through Kuranda and continued into the rainforest. They arrived at a resort near Lake Placid. There were little cabins, a restaurant and a pool.

“It’s lovely!” Their cabin had a view over the mountains. They unpacked and went for lunch and to explore the resort. It was not Thala but it was beautiful. The buildings were all in wood and the restaurant was open to the elements. They followed one of the forest tracks which was marked out. They saw lizards and unidentified scuttling creatures.

“We’ll go to the Lake Placid tomorrow.”

“I went once, years ago, on a boat ride. Can we swim there?”

“Not sure. We can bring our things in case.”

“Have you been before?”

“No. Steve told me about it. It is fairly new. He was in the forest with colleagues picking plants.”

“That’s him! Did you ever go to the township where he helped run a charity for buildings and education”

"No, but I think you did." She told him about the efforts of Kyle, Derry's nephew, the clinic and the new school. She described the deprivation, the poverty and the drugs. They saw streams and wild flowers as they walked.

Jon felt disturbed. He had tried so hard to live like a white man that he had paid scant attention to his cultural roots through his mother. He remembered that his father had taken his mother to find her tribe and that she had spent time with her parents and sometimes took him and Jeannie with her. He was small and could not remember much. She stopped the trips and he no longer knew which tribe it was, or where it was.

The walk led them out to a clearing on occasions and they were able to look out across the mountains. They took notice of the birds which were unfamiliar to them and stood listening to their song as they noted the roofs of cabins in the trees.

They had seen a poster in the restaurant advertising musical entertainment that evening.

"I wonder what type of music it is. By the way, that haunting music at Meditation. Do you know what it is?"

"Einaudi, or Hawes, or Whitacre. We'll ask next week. I have some at home as Derry often used it for our group."

"Tell me about your Oxford home and the Healing Centre."

Fortunately there were a few benches in the clearings, so they sat holding hands while Alice recounted the story of her childhood home, the Granny flat, the study with the white bookshelf, and then the development of the Hartley Barnes centre in the garden.

"Did you want to live with your parents?"

"Actually, no, but when my mother became ill this was my father's solution. They had their flat built and let Derry and I and the children live in the rest of the house. She explained about their unexpected deaths, Derry's new post at St Marcus, the Spiritual Direction Training and her client Louisa. He was fascinated by the strange turn of events in her life. She saved her mother's story for another occasion.

"Now what would you like to share from your life?"

He described his mother's visits to her tribe and how he and Jeannie often went with her. James had been but he was then in education so it was Jeannie and Jonathan who were sometimes left with other relatives while his mother spent time with her parents. He had hated the tribal way of life. He returned to his school experiences. With a rich, white Dad, he had enjoyed a better experience than other Aboriginal or mixed-race children, but he had been very hurt by their treatment in class. He observed the abuse rather than experienced it because the teachers knew who his father was. If a new white teacher came, he could still recall being humiliated and beaten and stood in a corner. Frederick had truly loved his wife and children and had done his best for them to give them a good education. He recalled that one day his mother decided she would no longer visit her tribe. She returned alone for her mother's funeral. Jon and Jeannie did not mind because they did not enjoy being with the tribal people. Jonathan told Alice that he felt uncomfortable about it all because he did not understand. She suggested that they talk with Jeannie to see if she could enlighten him more. Alice wondered if his father had maintained any contact with the four O'Neill children for whom Ngala had been a maid. He remembered that his father had been in contact with one of the children who never married and who had remained living in the house. She was Clementine, one of the two daughters who had always loved their uncle Frederick. She would be about 80 now.

On the last two occasions when Jon had made love to her, she had been aware of his hesitancy and even fear of impotence. He had been very relieved when he realised that he had not lost his capability. Now they were alone, uninterrupted and had no time limits, she realised that he had become demanding, even desperate. It worried her a little, although she could understand that he was undoing years of abstinence and grief. Nevertheless, she decided to talk to him.

"Jon, I love you. It has been less than a year since we first met and we have talked about taking things slowly. Here we are making love three times within a few hours. I am a little concerned."

Jon took the coffee cup and sipped before he put it down to speak to his beloved Alice. "I am sorry. Please forgive me" He described that over nearly 14 years he had done everything to prevent his desire. Hundreds of times he had woken up full of love and desire but Helen was dying of cancer. He loved her and stifled his desires over many years. He believed he would never make love again.

"When I met you, desires stirred but I feared being impotent. Now you have made me so happy, the floodgates have opened and I feel out of control."

"I do understand, my love. Let's see how we can handle this. You must not allow me to feel like an impersonal sex object."

"Would you like me to stop making love to you?"

"No, don't go back to killing your desire. We will get through this and you will be calmer and learn to control the excessive need to open the floodgates."

Alice described how she had lost her trust in men for many years and that Derry has waited 8 years before he declared his love for her. He had had such control that it restored her trust in him, in men. They had learned about spiritual healing massage and brought love and healing to each other.

"That's lovely," Jon said, "Can you help me too?"

"I think so. There are a couple of things to check. Jon, please do not feel ashamed. Of course you are aware of the floodgates after so long. You must not let them destroy you, dominate you."

He took her hands. "You are the most precious thing in my life. I do not want to lose you."

"I do not want to lose you. I love you so deeply. My desire for you is also very strong. I thought I would never make love again."

He asked her what she wanted to check and she told him about how Little Bear had ended up in sex addiction because of the suppressed anger over racism and appalling treatment by white people.

"You mentioned that marrying Helen, a blond, white woman was a 'crowning glory' and that you wanted to beat the white boys at their own game. This was a similar psychology to Little Bear who abused white girls to feel he was conquering racism."

Jon recalled her account of how he had turned his life around and had to learn how to love and respect women. He felt that Alice was speaking the truth to him.

"Dear Alice, I will find a counsellor to help me work through these issues."

"I think it would help you to experience being loved, receiving love instead of trying, pushing, demanding. After our trip today I will give you an oil massage and I will make love, express my love to you without you doing anything at all. You remain still and let love come to you."

The day at the lake went well and all they had spoken of took place. The boat ride gave them spectacular scenery, flocks of cormorants and pelicans.

After the massage Jon remained totally impassive and allowed her to express her love without him moving his arms.

"You are a healer, Alice. You have a gift."

The next day they went to Kuranda and wandered round the little town, listened to street music by some Aborigines. They ate in a modern restaurant with an open back overlooking flowering trees and colourful birds. Opposite one end was a mural of dancing Aboriginal figures on a plain wall. Alice took a photo for Nathaniel.

"I have brought something with me to give you. I don't know if this is the right time to give it to you." She sensed his hesitance and regret for how he had treated her. His grips had hurt her and had made her anxious.

"I note that we both still wear our wedding rings. Do you also have an engagement ring?"

"Yes, I preserve it perhaps for a son to give to a fiancée or for a grandchild."

"Lovely. I see no reason to change our wedding rings. They can represent our two marriages. I have bought you an engagement ring because although we might wait a bit, I would like to marry you, Alice, my love. Would you become engaged to me or do you want to wait until I have seen a counsellor?"

Alice was taken by surprise but was convinced that he would overcome his suppressed anger and 'floodgates' issues, and that they would make a good marriage and continue to do voluntary teaching and other activities which would be of help to others in need; this would be a way of celebrating their happiness.

"Dearest Jonathan, I will gladly accept your proposal." He opened the box to show a large ruby surrounded by little diamonds.

"What a fantastic choice! Could we announce our engagement at your party?" He slipped on the ring and discovered it needed to be made a little smaller. "We have time to get it done but I think we need to go furniture buying before the party."

"Thank-you, dear Alice for accepting me. Good idea about the furniture."

"You chose a most wonderful ring."

They left Kuranda and returned for their final night at the resort.

The next few weeks were very busy. They bought furniture after measuring up in every room. His single bed became a guest bed. They bought another one for the other spare room, a double bed for their room and for the lounge a double futon and two smaller, single futons, a big dining-table with 6 chairs. In the shop he took her over to the bookcases.

"Which one?" She laughed and looked at them all. "You mustn't live with me without a white bookshelf." She chose one with some small sections to break up the lines of books on two of the shelves.

9 Ngala

Nathaniel's weekend was very pleasant. Magda was charming and polite, friendly and helpful. They did not want to sleep in the same room. Magda helped with everything she could. She talked about her family in Poland and her art studies. Alice showed her the engagement ring and said the news was being announced at the party at number 63 next weekend.

"You can't stay, I suppose?"

"Stay, no, but I could come back. I am thinking of fares. I really want to return for the wedding."

"Good idea. It won't be for a few months. We are working now, only once a week. Beate is arriving soon and we have lots of things to sort out with Jon's children and mine." She explained that they would live at number 63 and that Beate would rent some of the rooms for a while until she was established in Cairns. She assured him that his room would always be his and that the house was available for his sister and brothers. Jon was having them to lunch to show them where Alice would be living. Alice had helped prepare the food.

The party day for 63 arrived. There were the members of the Meditation Group, Jon's son and daughter and partners as well as Steve and family. His brother James and family drove over as well. They were able to spill into the garden and sit on the steps.

"That's next, garden furniture!" Jon said before he called everyone to bring their drinks into the lounge.

"Thank-you for coming! Thank you for the gifts to welcome me to my new home. I wish to announce that I will not live here alone. This beautiful lady, my dearest love, Alice has agreed to marry me."

There was cheering, cat-calls, clapping and hugging.

"Well done, Dad!"

"Dad you crafty man!", "Congratulations!" filled the air.

In the conversation afterwards friends wanted to know what she would do with her house. She explained she was keeping it for her children and that soon, Dr Beate von Friedland would rent it while she settled in her new job.

"When's the wedding?" and "Where's the wedding?" Jon explained it was a work in progress.

After all the clearing up Alice made a time to talk to Jeannie. She hesitated to tell her all her thinking, but she asked about the O'Neills and their contacts with her father, Frederick and she asked her to tell her about the visits to the tribe.

Jeannie said that Ngala did not enjoy going and nor did the two children. Jeannie was about 8 at that time so she understood more. She spoke of the elders who were unpleasant to her mother because she had married a white man. Jeannie shouted to the elders that the white man was her wonderful Daddy and that he had brought his wife to find her family. She said he was not like the usual white men. They heeded the little girl and talked less against her mother and father. She said she was not sure where the tribe was but she thought that if she went back to Townsville she would remember some names and bus routes.

"Your mother was a maid to the O'Neill children. Did she keep in touch with them after she married?"

"Yes, with Clementine. She remained in the house as she did not marry. The others had married and moved away. Clemmy invited Mum and Dad to visit her after the father died.

"I'd like to find her. Jon wants to go to Townsville soon, would you like to come? I shall research Clemmy on line."

"Why are you doing this?" asked Jeannie.

"Something has been troubling Jon. He has some hurt feelings he needs to deal with, something about your mother."

"I'd be happy to come if Jon does not mind."

"Is there anything else you remember?"

She remembered how her father had taken them round the grounds of the house and met Clemmy outside while the old man was alive. She remembered Jon being born and everyone calling him 'your black brother' as they grew up.

Jon and Alice returned to the Mosque for their lessons. They met Mr Sadik and Jon told him that he wanted to explain that he and Mrs Barnes were going to get married in a few months. "Congratulations. A widow and a widower together now. That's very good." He blessed them in Urdu.

The first lesson for Jon was demanding as the young men were not very disciplined. They interrupted and asked questions, cutting across him. He put them in pairs and got them to find out the name, age and town of origin of their partner. They then had to introduce their partner. It worked a treat. Jon could listen to them and get an idea of their level.

Alice had an easier time with the ladies. They tried to say, ‘My name is. I’m from…’ and then learn the names of the objects she placed before them. There was a pen and pencil, kitchen items and a dozen household items including a doll and a baby shawl. They loved handling the familiar things and saying their names. Jon was convinced he would need a second lesson to work in two groups. He planned to go down on a second morning.

At home, Alice researched Clementine O’Neill on line. She found the O’Neill family, their large house and the companies they had run. The house had been sold and Clementine had moved into a Care Home. She looked up Care Home details and printed them off. She thought that Jon would be happy with her research and would agree to follow it up when they went to Townsville for materials. She chose an evening when they had a massage session in 63. She began the massage after they talked about a possible trip and sensed that he was tense.

They flew and hired a car. They would naturally visit Jon’s son and daughter and were delighted to get two supper invitations from them.

Finding Clemmy was not so hard. They rang down the list of homes, a few each and discovered the Home she was in. Clementine O’Neill was in her early 80s but was mentally alert. She could no longer walk unaided. They all went on the visit and saw Clemmy clap her hand over her mouth when she saw Jeannie and Jonathan.

“You were my little dears!” she exclaimed. She held out her hands and shed some tears. “You remember us!” said Jeannie.

“Ngala used to bring her babies to meet me secretly. Later I was able to invite you into the house. Ngala was very happy with Frederick and loved her babies.

“Do you know what happened to my mother?” asked Jeannie. “Frederick had found her tribe and reunited her with her parents.”

“We know that, Clemmy. Can we call you that?”

“Yes, I’m Clemmy the single one.”

“Do you remember the name of the tribe or where she went to visit them?”

“Oh dear. She took a bus and walked from a town when Frederick could not take her. The tribe…some strange sound…” Alice slowly read a list she had got from the internet, the Townsville area tribes. She stopped Alice when she reached Njuta. “Something like that.”

"Why did our mother stop going?"

"You don't know?"

"I was 8 and Jon was 5. We didn't like going so we were pleased when we stopped going there."

"She should have stopped long before." Clemmy gripped Jeannie's hand and looked at Jon. "Could I tell Jeannie without you here?"

"Of course, Alice and I will go to the sitting room."

Alice knew. She had guessed and was filled with dread. Jon noticed her anxiety.

"I think this is going to be very hard for you, Jon. I think I have understood, but I'll wait for Jeannie. Jon was silent and she wondered if he had understood too. It was more than half an hour before Jeannie came out. She was upset and had been crying. She asked them to go to Clemmy and explain that they had come from Cairns and would probably not be able to return very often to Townsville. Clemmy had been crying too and they took her hands and wished her well as they were leaving.

"God bless you all." she said. Jonathan had started to tremble.

They did not need to find the tribe now but they had enough details to go if they wished. They walked to a bench in the beautiful garden. Jeannie saw that Jon was uncomfortable and even trembling. She put her arms around him. Alice held his hands. She wanted to check that Jeannie was ready to explain. Alice was sure she knew what was coming.

"Our mother was badly treated by the tribal people who saw her as a traitor. Her brothers and sisters had been lost forever. Her father taunted her about her rich life-style and asked her to bring money. One relative, a cousin or a nephew started hitting her so she tried to run and find her children, James and Jeannie. He chased her and beat her and then he violated her. He raped her."

Jon broke down and sobbed. Jeannie continued, "She found her little ones and left as quickly as possible. She took her children to Clemmy and told her what had happened. She was able to be cleaned up and as all the bruises were hidden she told Clemmy never to tell Frederick. She returned to Clemmy when she discovered she was pregnant.

"Don't tell Frederick. The baby could be his."

"When you were born, Ngala knew that you were the son of an Aborigine but she laughed off the dark skin as a fluke of genetics, as did everyone else. Our father never knew. You were always his son and he loved you. And now you find out for the first time. It's heart-breaking, but Jon he was your father in every way."

They all sat crying and Alice felt bad that an action which was meant to help him, turned out to be so devastating.

"I want to go to the tribe." he said. They asked around and found the area. Jeannie remembered the village and the path to the tribal area. It was looking very different after nearly 60 years.

"They are all dead now, Jon."

"I need to see it." Jeannie and Alice comforted each other. Neither of them thought they should go at all but they wanted to help Jon get over the shock and they wanted to do anything that would bring healing.

They walked around the buildings where there were now modern shacks and smart houses and a shop. Jon asked to see an Elder. A wizened, grey haired, bearded little man came over to him.

"How old are you, please?" asked Jon. "Over 85. I am not sure."

"Do you remember Ngala who married a white man?" The old man trembled and wobbled. They fetched him a chair. He did not speak and he began to chant.

"I am her son." said Jon loudly. The elder bent and touched the earth and rubbed soil into his hands. He stood up and rubbed the soil on to Jon's hands and tried to reach his head. Jon bent down and the soil was rubbed across his forehead.

"Who was my father?"

"An evil, angry cousin of a cousin."

"What happened to him?"

"He died."

"He is dead now of course. When did he die?"

"Our tribe had their own punishment. Own court. We killed him. Court decided."

"But my mother came back here for 5 years and brought me and my sister here. Five years! Why?"

"Tribal tradition. She knew the laws from child time. She honoured her father and mother. They lost all other children. She knew evil man was dead so no danger, no fear."

Jon sobbed and sobbed and roared his pain while his sister and fiancée held him. "You are our tribe." said the Elder. Something strange happened. There was sudden silence. Jon walked to some trees and picked up two fallen branches.

“String?” he asked the elder who pointed to the shack. He came out with a cross in his hands. He had made a rudimentary cross with the string. He picked up a metal bar from the shack, probably a door lock and walked towards some trees.

“Please come.” Jon spoke to Jeannie and Alice. He stood by a tree which stood on its own and thudded the ground with the metal bar until there was a hole big enough for the branch cross. He put the bar aside and pressed the branch down into the hole and patted the earth so it stood upright. Then he knelt down and made the sign of the cross. Jeannie and Alice joined him as he recited the Lord’s Prayer, just about, with a quivering voice.

The Elder stood behind them.

“God have mercy on this tribe. No more curses. God bless my mother’s family and any descendants. God bless my relatives that I do not know. Thank you God for giving me a wonderful white father and a beautiful, faithful mother.” He stood up and helped Jeannie and Alice stand up. They stood in a hugging ring for several minutes then pulled out tissues to wipe their tear-stained faces. Jon did not wipe off the soil. The Elder was also weeping and stood leaning on a chair.

“Thank you for telling me the truth. God bless you too.” He held the gnarled and bony hands.

“He does. He does bless me and this is a great blessing.”

“We are due at Anthony’s in a few hours. Do you want me to phone and cancel?” Jeannie asked. Jon stood very straight and upright.

“No. He needs to know the truth; that matters. We’ll tell him the truth.” He held hands with Jeannie and Alice as they found their hire care where they had left it on a road in the village.

“Shall I drive?” Alice offered.

“Would you?” She spent a moment working out the controls and they drove back to the hotel. They were silent. Alice hunted for a music station on the radio and found one to accompany their drive.

They all showered and changed and had a siesta before they left for their supper with Anthony and Liz. They all did their best to hide the redness of their eyes.

Alice was very impressed by the way Jon had responded and recalled Derry’s prayers for the Barnes family and for each child.

They stood at the window, arms around each other.

"Jon, that was a holy moment, a holy prayer and a healing action. Don't be afraid to weep more, it is important to let it out."

He waited until after supper to tell Anthony where they had been that day. Alice noticed that he held back his tears and let Jeannie help explain. Anthony felt for his father who had discovered the truth at 62. He knew he would have some thinking to do as he processed the fact that his lovely, white grandfather was not his real grandfather. They were all subdued as they left. Liz had another look at the ruby ring and admired her Dad's choice.

The next day, Jeannie walked around the big stores while Jon and Alice chose teaching materials from the big bookshop. They drove to Lisa and Joseph and Jon was determined to face it all again. They ate another delicious meal and they sat to hear what he had to say.

Jeannie had to help out again.

"You mean my favourite granddad was not my real granddad? But he loved you, he loved all of us."

"We will always remember him. He was my father and your grandfather in the real sense. Your grandma was one very brave lady. She let him die never knowing about the rape and that I was not his biological son."

Their farewells were very tender.

Alice suggested to Jon in their hotel room that they had a meditation and a good night's sleep. She had a John Main booklet with her, chose a reading and they sat in silence for fifteen minutes. They kissed each other gently and slept.

At breakfast, he leaned over to Alice. "Can we go to Uluru for our honeymoon? I need to discover more about my roots and my mother's roots."

"We shall find a way of honouring her. Find some of your photos, dear Jon and we shall have a photo of your parents in a place of honour in our home. Uluru, wonderful idea."

10 Beate and Wedding Blessings

Jonathan was subdued for days. He was relieved to be home and to go to the English classes. Alice waited and gave him space and encouraged him to see his counsellor. They both enjoyed the teaching and using the new materials. They loved Meditation Group and Mass on Sundays. They delayed their visit to Clive and Patty. After the Thursday classes, they returned to Sundale Court and sat watching the lapping waves of Palm Cove.

"Alice, could we become Catholics?" She was so happy and told him she had been thinking of this for some time. They would make enquiries next Sunday. After coffee she asked him to come for a massage.

"Are you sure?" She saw he was trembling.

"My love, I am sure. I am a healer, remember." She smiled and hand in hand they walked in. She gave him as always a gentle, loving massage ending with love making. This was another step to healing.

They agreed that massages and love-making would only take place in 63 after Beate had arrived.

On Beate's first evening they had a 'girlie' evening over a bottle of wine in the garden, under the gazebo. Beate admired the ruby engagement ring. "Beautiful. Not my style." she smiled. "I would choose a silver, modern design, no stones!"

"Any lovers?"

"Two, not serious. Girls I mean. When do I meet Jonathan?"

"Tomorrow. I wanted time to catch up with you this evening. How's the jet lag?"

"I stopped over in Sydney for 3 nights in a hotel and slept. It was only 7 hours to Cairns so I am fine."

Beate told her that her mother had died a few months ago so now she felt free to change jobs and even countries. She talked with Koda, Paul, Jane and Steve. They greatly appreciated her work on tribal women with Paul and Jane and invited her to have her base in Cairns and become Professor of Anthropology. She could continue her work in Peru if she wished.

Alice shared about her teaching, her relationship with Steve's brother-in-law and their plans to join the Catholic Church. As Beate was such a direct and open person, Alice mentioned the plans for this big house.

"Would you like to rent part of it while you settle in? I am keeping it for my children and they are bound to use it for the wedding. Nathaniel lives here for college holidays. The double room is a guest room for couples but there is no reason why it cannot be your room when no one is around. Tonight you are in the big bedroom next to Nathaniel's."

"Alice, that is a great idea. We have time to look round and see how to use the rooms." Alice smiled. Beate would soon organise it all.

"Tomorrow Jonathan will come to meet you, Last week he had a terrible shock concerning his mother and father who died some years ago. He might not be his usual self. He is a big, strong black man, brought up very like a white man but he is very sensitive inside. Perhaps you could avoid asking him about his parents. He has grown up children. Do you know, his children and mine all pressurised us to get together!"

"That's good."

They drank away the next few hours and shared the other aspects of their lives, the Vicar's proposal to Alice, the funeral of Beate's mother, Alice's other children in America and Oxford.

Alice slept in the big bedroom. At breakfast time Joseph had a screen chat with his mother. He told her that Bright Star was pregnant but it was too early to know the gender. Baby Barnes was due in 6-7 months.

"Bright Star is missing the open spaces of Canada so we are looking for a new house in the countryside, not far from Oxford. I am looking south so we can more easily drive to London. We are still working on the Uluru Melody and we have nearly finished. Charles is trying to find us a venue for the premier in a London Church."

Alice was so proud of them all. Joseph wanted a date.

"Sorry, darling. We are speaking to the priest on Sunday and we may get one. We are going to Uluru for our honeymoon. Could you all think about performing your music at our wedding?"

Beate rose for breakfast and Jon drove up. He came in to meet her and held out his hand and said, "Glad to meet you, interesting and intelligent lady!"

"Is that what she said?" Beate hugged him and kissed him. "Congratulations on your engagement!"

"And on your professorship. Well done."

Beate asked him about his children and told him a little about her mother. "Von Friedland. Your mother is German?" asked Jon.

"It's quite a story. Perhaps over a wine after supper." she smiled. "I suppose you have heard about Alice's German mother."

Jon looked at Alice quizzically.

"We are gradually sharing parts of our lives with each other. She hasn't got to that bit yet." Alice took his hand.

"One day soon. It is a sad story with a happy ending."

After supper, under the gazebo Beate told Jon the story of her Nazi father and grandfather and what they had done. Then she told him how they had escaped the terrorism in the 1960s and 1970s.

"I think I will become a writer. There are so many extraordinary stories."

"I had a complete breakdown in England. The shock, the shame and the guilt were all terrible for me in my early school years. I hated anything German and refused to go to lessons if Germany was mentioned. I had some good counsellors and therapists so in senior school, after very wobbly days, I lost myself in my studies and was able to control my anger and pain."

Alice and Jon looked at each other, said nothing, but smiled.

"You can both come to my house tomorrow. Alice is moving in after the marriage. Beate, thank you so much for being so frank and open. It does me good. I am still working through a family trauma."

"And I am renting this, I think." She waved her arms around and smiled. "I am going to bed and letting you two lovebirds say goodnight.

"See you tomorrow."

"Beate, I am so pleased you are here. You always did us good in Oxford." They had a hug and Jon soon went on his way.

He cooked them all a meal with chicken and they chatted about what they could bring from Alice's house. Miriam's portrait and some artefacts were top of the list. The cutlery from Oxford and some crockery were next on her list.

On Sunday, Clive and Patty helped them find a priest to talk to.

The priest was very pleased that they wanted to become Catholic and said he would arrange an adult training course for them. They explained that they were getting married as a widow and widower and asked if they could marry in the Cathedral. Once again the priest could not hide his delight. They found a date in four months' time.

There were wedding invitations to order, a restaurant for the reception to book and accommodation and travel plans for her children and friends. Daniel said he had a venue in London for the Premier of Uluru Melody and Dawn Star Lament. They had all agreed to perform them for the wedding. They would come early to rehearse and get over Jet lag. It would mean Joseph leaving his pregnant wife and baby Claire. Bethany had screen time to asked her what she was going to wear.

"No idea yet. A plain re-wearable dress to match Jon's suit, probably. Jeannie and I will have a look round. We have time."

She was unsure about travel arrangements for getting to the wedding.

Then Hartleigh Thomas rang with a brilliant suggestion. "Could you and Jon factor in a visit to London and possibly Oxford before you go on honeymoon?"

This was discussed by the siblings and they thought it was the answer to several difficulties. In London Jon and Alice could stay in a hotel and hire a room for a celebration for all those who could not make it to Cairns; Maddy and Roy, Kyle and family if he could have a holiday from Romania, Abigail and Justin and family, probably with their new baby and friends from St Marcus Anthropology Department. Bethany would travel to London and fly to Cairns with her brothers on her own. Victor and Esther, Paul and Vivienne would travel to London and stay with her uncles and join them in the hotel celebration. Koda and the rest of the family had not yet made any arrangements.

"That was a brainwave! I've never been to England." Jon said.

They decided to fly from London to Sydney and then direct to Uluru instead of returning to Cairns.

In number 63 at the end of a tiring day of planning, Jon took Alice into his arms, "Alice, darling, can you tell me now about your parents?"

Alice realised that he was surprised that she had left it so long but she knew there were painful parts to tell and could not deal with them while she was setting up her class and handling Jon's own family issues which had shocked them both.

She leaned back on him on the futon as he held her. She thought that the Second World War, the Nazis, the holocaust and the Berlin Wall would not mean much to him.

"What do you understand about the holocaust and the War?" she asked.

"I read a lot of books about it, including Winston Churchill and several biographies. I learned about it at school and watched the television news when the Berlin Wall came down and the country was united."

Alice was impressed and pleasantly surprised.

"I am Jewish, Jon, because my mother was Jewish."

She slowly told him her mother's story and explained that she had always had a deep pain, right from childhood when she first learned about how her mother had come to England. She picked up the horror not spoken of and had a fear of finding out more about what her mother was feeling. She described the visit to Leipzig and that after that, Esther had identified with Jews by attending a group of Messianic Jews in Oxford. She showed him the doll and the photos which she had already brought from her house and put in a drawer.

"Seriously, Alice, we should write a book about your family and friends. Nothing is straightforward but it is wonderful."

"Well, Mr English teacher, a retirement job for you and you must include your family."

"We both had good and loving parents and a very good education."

"Thomas, my father worked in Nigeria and helped set up museums of the Benin brasses and bronzes. He wrote several books on them, still had African academics working with him to near the end of his life. He saw the poverty and set up a charity in the country. Another time I will tell you about the charity we have set up. Beate is a big part of it. I loved my father very much. Both of us could talk to him about anything at all. He always had words of wisdom." Alice explained about the last trip to Cairns and Nigeria and then how the house was altered just before they both died within a few weeks of each other.

Their quiet chat was interrupted by a call from Joseph. Baby Barnes was a boy and they had chosen the name Jacy, a Lakota Sioux name meaning 'Moon'.

"It goes with all the Stars in Koda's family and it will be cool in UK." Joseph announced.

Beate had her interview and was formally offered the post in Cairns. "How shall we celebrate? Can I take you for a meal?"

"We could always book a meal at Thala. Jon has not been there."

Jon and Beate both loved Thala. Over the meal he admitted to some misgivings about going to England, the colonial country, but they both tried to reassure him.

The next Sunday was the date with Clive and Patty. At last they had a free time to spend time with this new couple who had moved from Sydney. Clive advised Jon on what to see in Sydney, what not to miss. Patty was a born cook with a gift of hospitality. Jon relaxed and felt welcome, accepted, included. His inner healing was progressing.

Alice was able to explain to them a little of the work her father was involved with and the African charity. She mentioned the Hartley Barnes charity in Cairns and they said they would like to know more and take an interest in the work. Alice promised to get them some literature to read. It was still daylight when they left. Jon suggested that after the meal they should have a beach walk near the esplanade.

They walked dreamily along the beach, watching the boats, the windsurfers, the hills and the off shore islands.

They had a coffee on the esplanade and watched the little children on the swings. Jon seemed in a good frame of mind and asked her about the charity in Oxford and Cairns.

She told him that anthropology had led to charity because of the tender consciences of the people involved. Derry had a big heart because he had some family issues like Jon's. They sat with arms around shoulders as she mentioned Derry's pain and shame and what it had done to him.

"He had to learn that his grandfather had been a rapist and murderer and that knowing this had harmed his father and made his father intolerant and aggressive towards his son. There was a lot of healing to work through over the years."

"Two husbands with scandals in their families, Alice, what have you done to deserve that?"

"Let me tell you about the Hartley Barnes Foundation and the Spiritual Healing Centre in our garden. When we are in London we shall go to Oxford and show it to you." Alice mentioned Derry's team who set up the Foundation in the University. Part of it was the work done by Steve in Cairns and by Koda in Canada. She told him what a big part Beate had played, how she had taken the responsibility for the Queensland work and inspired all the teams to put training and education before new buildings.

"I am so impressed. What a family! What a lady!"

"She is a very special person. She loved Derry and was a great support to him. She is a feminist activist and gears her research to women. She was in a lesbian relationship when we met her but sadly it broke up. She needs another relationship now."

"Beate will be in the book!" he smiled and started talking about his childhood again. Alice understood more deeply about the natives who were badly treated by the Europeans and considered to be less than human, sub-humans, incompletely evolved. He talked a little about the tribe and that some were positively influenced by the Christian presence but that others had turned to bitterness and even hatred.

"After our wedding and trips, I'd like to visit Clemmy again in Townsville. She played a big part in my mother's life and helped her through. It's too far to go often but before she becomes too ill and is near death, I think she would be happy to see us."

Alice held his head in her hands and caressed his cheeks, his neck, his eyes. She kissed him lightly considering they were in a children's playground.

"Jonathan O'Neill, you are a wonderful man and I consider it a great blessing to be with you and to know that you love me. Thank you my darling." He embraced her too and they held each other for a while.

"Healing from deep injury leads to gratitude and care and compassion for others." She whispered in his ear. They walked back to his house and went in and made love after opening the futon and trying it out as a double bed.

"This is a holy time, Alice dear. Our love is so deep and full of understanding. My holy healer, my love."

She left him reluctantly again and drove home. She could hardly concentrate and felt she was in a dream. Beate was in the lounge watching television. Alice sat next to her and put her arms round her.

"He is such a wonderful man, Beate. I am so privileged to have him." Beate let her cry tears of joy and overwhelming emotion as they hugged. Alice wiped her eyes and needed to sleep.

"I'll pray you find a soul mate, Beate." She went to her room and slept deeply without even undressing.

Jon drove them down the highway to the next lesson and before it started Alice asked Mr Sadik if it would be possible to invite her class to the wedding. He promised to ask the leaders. If they agree I will bring the minibus and take them to the Cathedral.

"Thank-you so much." Jon was using some of his new materials in his lesson and played them some CDs with simple stories. They listened and then he replayed it bit by bit, getting them to repeat. They saw the pictures and followed the text. They had never done anything like that before so they tried hard and enjoyed the challenge. Alice had some similar CDs for the ladies but deemed it too soon to use them. She wanted to do more pair work and really needed another lady. She asked them to try and invite another lady to work with them.

In the car, Alice, sitting with a hand on Jon's shoulder as they drove, told him about the Cairns charity work and said that Beate had been the inspiration and that there just could be a role for them in the future.

Daniel rang to say that he had a commission in Cairns to perform the two pieces in a music venue. He had talked to Nathaniel who was only too pleased to have an exhibition of his Uluru paintings in the vestibule. It was to take place the day after the wedding.

There was a crowning glory for Jon and Alice when Koda rang and said that he and Paul were coming to Cairns with the whole family. Little Bear had decided to come too. His news was that in the court work he met a native lady with two children who needed to work for an income because her husband had been killed in a road accident. She had worked with Little Bear; heard his story and they fell in love and would soon get married. Alice was overjoyed. They were all going to stay in the holiday flats because they felt that being there would bring some closure to the painful incident which affected them all.

The Confirmation of Alice and Jon took place in the Cathedral with three other candidates. A golden sun shone through the stained glass.

The entire meditation group had come along and so had Beate, Steve and Jeannie. The golden light and the beauty of the liturgy and music made it a special, magic-like event, a spiritually healing event. Clive and Patty were in the congregation and had bought a bouquet of flowers to welcome them. Alice put it in Jon's house.

Some days later Jeannie and Alice went into the Cairns Central Shopping Centre to look for a dress. Jon had decided on a pale blue suit and white shirt so Alice was looking for a blue dress to match, a simple dress to be used for future occasions. Jeannie flicked through the rows of dresses. They pulled out a few to look at and then she found a powder blue dress, sleeveless, scoop necked and fairly tight fitting with no decorations, a plain design. Alice tried it on.

"Wow, Alice. You look wonderful!" She bought it.

Beate admired her dress when she reached home and then wanted to review the wedding plans.

"So, an Aboriginal man and a Jewish woman are getting married in an Australian Cathedral with relatives from Canada, America and England and friends from those same places?"

"That's about it!"

"Do wear some flowers in your hair. Justin and I will make you a tiara and send it." Abigail said.

The 5 Muslim ladies were allowed to come to their teacher's wedding. They would come in the Mosque minibus. Alice knew they would wear their colourful silk shalwa chemises.

A few days before the ceremony Alice and Jon tried to pack for England and for Uluru. Beate offered to co-ordinate all the wedding gifts and make sure they got to Sundale Court. What a treasure she was.

Alice had already introduced Beate to her next-door neighbours, told them she was getting married again and that she was moving to central Cairns while Beate would live in the house. She warned them that her family would stay there sometimes, especially the weekend of the wedding. They were pleasant and helpful. They even offered to put up a guest if they needed more beds that night and offered to let them leave their wedding gifts in their garage. How kind people could be!

Daniel, Charles, Hartleigh and Joseph arrived two days earlier to recover and to rehearse. They said the concert Premier had gone very well in London, with invitations for them to make a recording.

Magda had come with Nathaniel to help carry his paintings and to hear the rehearsal. They all squeezed into the big house but Magda took up the offer of the neighbours with the baby Perry. The lovely tiara of blue and white silk flowers arrived in good time, packed so thoughtfully.

No guest would ever forget a wedding like theirs. Golden light streamed in again as the liturgy began. At the part 'With this ring…' they had removed their wedding rings so Steve could pass them to be put back on. The beauty of the Catholic liturgy moved everyone. The music of Daniel, Charles and the two brothers moved just about everyone to tears. They played Dawn Star Lament first dedicated to Alice's deceased daughter and granddaughter and then followed the tribute to Uluru where the four musicians had captured the mysterious, magic and haunting atmosphere of the Rock. There were beautiful melodies on piano and on flute with a strumming guitar underneath the melody. Rightly or wrongly, they were applauded in spontaneous appreciation.

They little realised that the Press would spread the news about a musical piece depicting indigenous Australia, composed by four English men. As a result they were invited to perform in other Australian cities and in Germany and

London. The link with the university and the Hartley Barnes Foundation meant that journalists were sent so Alice and Jon had their pictures in several local papers.

Alice was just thinking that this meant that the Reverend Philip Browne and family would probably see it and she felt a little sorry for him. She then caught sight of a lady in a wheelchair. It was Clementine O'Neill.

Jon had asked Anthony to arrange to bring her to the wedding at his expense. They drove her and her chair to the airport and organised transport for the disabled and then drove her in a special taxi from Cairns airport. They had even booked her into a hotel with them. She was wearing a very beautiful silk dress in pale blue so she matched the bride and groom. Jon had left this to be a surprise for Alice. Clemmy was crying with joy to see the poor little boy she loved find such happiness after the loss of his parents and then his wife. She sat holding his hand.

"You look so handsome in that suit, Jonathan; your hair is not quite all grey. Together you both look wonderful."

Jeannie came to spend time with her and they both promised to come to Townsville to see her.

The Muslim ladies, resplendent as expected, were very excited and happy. Sadik was very helpful with their transport and he was invited to stay for the ceremony and the reception. It was held in a local restaurant. Speeches will be kept to a minimum, had been said, but both Koda and Steve had lovely comments to make and Bethany thanked her mother for her brilliant childhood and said that she was thrilled that she had found such a fantastic new husband. Hartleigh Thomas could not remain silent and added his thanks on behalf of his brothers.

"I had wonderful parents," he added and now Mum has a second chance at happiness after losing Dad. "Welcome to the family, Jonathan O'Neill."

Alice had a quiet moment as she looked round the room.

"Derry, you are here in everyone, Miriam you are with us today." She whispered, and then looked up to see Little Bear approaching.

She had a special hug for him and led him over to Jon. Beate in her long, green, hippy style dress sorted out the guests for Sundale and the guests for 63 and made sure that others could find their flats and hotels. Alice and Jon went back to Sundale to spend time with their sons and daughters. They had booked their flights to London for the next day so they would all have time together.

11 London and Oxford

Bethany flew to London with her mother and new husband to meet her own husband and daughter. Paul and the rest of the family flew back to America.

Koda and family came to London to see their daughter and granddaughter. Bright Star and her daughter were the only missing members. She was pregnant with Jacy and she decided the risk of long haul was too much, especially as Joseph had to go so early and return later due to his musical commitments. Joseph would pick her up in Oxford to bring her to the hotel.

From Heathrow they took a taxi to the hotel in Westminster. Multiple rooms had been booked for 4 days. The reception was to be held on the third day so those still in Australia could get there in good time. Jon had looked out at the familiar buildings of central London and was relieved to see how multicultural the streets were. He had feared standing out in the crowd.

The musicians arrived with tales of the great reception they had received at their concert in Cairns. The Press had been there too and featured the art work of Nathaniel. Magda had been at the concert with him and helped get the paintings back to Brisbane. He was sorry that she had not been able to come to London. He was beginning to feel that he loved her enough to want to spend his life with her.

How could they spend a day in Oxford? Alice spoke to her sons. Joseph had gone straight to Oxford to fetch his wife and little Claire but was happy to return after the reception to show Alice the house he was buying. Hartleigh Thomas said he would drive them to Oxford to visit the Spiritual Healing Centre and would take them to the station to go back to London for the last night in England. Alice contacted Peter to tell him she wanted to call in and show the centre to her new husband.

Alice was so happy to see her other granddaughter and Bright Star. She described the wedding, showed her photos and told her about her brother.

"Will your mother come for the birth of Jacy?"

"Yes, she is planning to. I am so pleased. I think you are coming to Oxford for a day. You will love our new house. We will not move in until after the birth."

For the reception, Alice wore her wedding dress and Jon wore his blue suit. Kyle and Adina arrived with Maddy. They greeted each other with smiles.

"Jon sounds so English!" Maddy noted. Kyle had had a long chat with him and introduced his Romanian wife. They had left their three children behind in Romania with grandparents.

"He's a lovely man. All good wishes to you both!" Kyle smiled to Alice. Maddy had to agree as she quickly saw the kindness and friendliness in Jon and found him easy to speak to.

Abigail and Justin brought the three little ones and had several photos taken with the bride and groom. Alice put on the tiara for these.

Jon tried to grasp the three names, Marlow, Marilla and Marcus as Alice held the baby and kissed him. He concluded that they represented nothing special except the eccentric character of the artist.

Justin wanted to tell her that both his parents were reconciled to him now they had children.

"The newspapers and television coverage helps!" he added. He has something to boast of to his work colleagues at the golf course.

Quietly, Abigail spoke to Alice about her mother who had also thawed somewhat and came to see her and the children in their flat.

"Father still refuses but she does not want to miss out on the grandchildren." Her mother had accepted Abigail's choice of husband and could appreciate that he didn't have to be a fundamentalist evangelical to be a loving and good man.

"Families. An odd phenomenon." Jon added.

"I am persuading him to write a memoir about our families." said Alice. They chatted happily together. Abigail went round to Jon's side and pulled him aside.

She handed him little Marcus. "Alice is my best friend. She is a wonderful woman and she has suffered a lot. I am so pleased she has married you and that you will love her and take care of her. God bless you both. I wish you a lovely, lovely life together." She held him and kissed his cheeks. Jon was very touched, kissed the baby and handed him back.

Separating was very hard. Alice knew that it would be a long time before they met again as they were leaving for different countries.

Victor came over with Esther and Bethany.

"I want to follow Joseph's example and have another baby." Victor put his arm around Bethany.

"I miss you so much, Mum. Please come to America when we have another baby. I'd like a son but I would be just as happy with a healthy girl. You look so happy."

"We are." Jon and Alice spoke together. "I shall always let your mother travel to see her children. Mine are only a couple of hour's flight away!"

Hartleigh Thomas had recovered in his uncle's house and drove to the hotel to pick Alice and Jon up for the journey to Oxford. He told them about his researches and said that he might have to come to Cairns sometimes although he thought his main topic would be Polynesia and the Maoris.

"Are you going to have a cry, my darling, when you see your house?" Jon asked Alice as they drove up the Woodstock Road.

"I hope not. I get taken by surprise; I am ready this time."

The car turned into the drive and the saw immediately that the new owners had made huge changes. There was a swimming pool instead of a tennis court. They passed the stony drive to the car park. Alice got out and turned back to see that the study had gone. The conservatory was the dining room now.

"That's where the bookshelf was. It was my special place and now it is in Sundale and another in 63." She smiled and held Jon's arm.

Peter was walking towards them with a beaming smile.

He hugged Alice and shook Jon's hand. Hartleigh Thomas was looking back at the house and then gave his attention to the Centre.

Jon saw over the entrance doors Hartley Barnes Spiritual Healing Centre. They sat inside for coffee and cake.

Peter passed the program to Jon who read down the lists; bereavement counselling, trauma counselling, spiritual massage, retreats, Days of Reflection, physiotherapy, Art therapy.

"I am so impressed. Can we do something like this in Cairns?"

"Why not? We undercut the private professionals because they are so expensive. We only take people who cannot afford to pay for the help."

"Sometimes we treat people who are rich and are willing to pay more because they like our work ethic and they love the atmosphere. They trust us because we are not out for profit." Peter explained and went on to say that they had recruited many new staff after the legacy from Louisa.

"We have two regular art therapists now. We have stuck with Christian meditation and not ventured into other kinds of therapy because we have a full timetable as it is."

Jon turned to Hartleigh, "How are you feeling? Is it hard for you to be here again?"

"Yes, it is. I have so many memories of Dad and Miriam. We had a privileged life before all the tragedies. It does not feel like home any more. I did not miss it when Mum and Dad went to Cairns. They bought me a flat in Oxford so I could be independent. I grieved for Miriam for a long time and I was so excited about my studies that I was pleased not to be in this house anymore." He let Jon hug him.

"Talk, Hartleigh, share. Don't hold it in or let it become so deep down you forget it is all there. It will surface if it is not dealt with."

"That makes sense. I did realise that and I found a listening partner at Oxford. They have moved with the times."

"I am pleased to hear that. Thank you so much for bringing us and thank you for your amazing music."

"Thanks, Jon, step-dad! We'll go to Joseph's now."

Joseph's flat was well organised and well decorated. He had many photos of Miriam on the wall, pictures with him going back years.

Bright Star was happy to welcome them and show them all the rooms. Claire had her own room and they had a double bedroom. The lounge was quite large but had Joseph's instruments in one corner with the electric keyboard that Daniel had given.

Bright Star had prepared them a meal so they squashed around the small dining table at one end of the lounge.

"Trout, but I didn't fish for it like I did in Canada."

"I am sorry I won't see Jacy, our Moon. I am sure we will make another trip to England and of course there is always a home for you in Cairns." Bright Star and Alice talked about Little Bear and his native widow.

"He has waited so long. He wanted a native wife and she already has two children. I do hope they accept him and get on well with him." Bright Star held Claire who was walking well and speaking well.

"It is never easy but he has changed his life so much that I am sure he will make a big effort to be a father to them."

After the meal Joseph drove Alice and Jon to the new house, planning to go straight to a station from there. Alice hugged and kissed Claire and Bright Star. The new house stood detached in its own grounds. It was a chalet bungalow, surrounded by garden and a low wooden fence. All around was farmland; fields with cows and others with crops sloping into the distance.

"Bright Star can breathe here and I can easily travel to music venues. I am actually doing an education course so I can teach piano and flute." The owners were at home and they could see packing cases inside and outside the house.

"There are four rooms upstairs so one can be a music room. Claire has a room and Jacy will also have one. I think we agree to just have two children. There is a big lounge with a screen that can make it into two rooms." Alice told him that he had done well to choose this house and looked forward to staying there one day. Joseph took them back to the flat and Thomas drove them to the station as he was spending a few days with his brother.

In the train, Jon asked about the birthmarks on Joseph's head and wanted to know if he had had difficulties at school. Alice told him about Derry's prayer and how they had always made light of the 'maps' he had. She laughed as she remembered Bright Star drawing the shape and finding his matching island in the Lake of the Woods.

"He managed very well. He made light of any comments and after a while no one noticed them. Bethany has some on her arms and legs but Nathaniel had nothing. Isn't it strange?

"Claire is dark skinned with dark hair but has blue eyes."

"You are the United Nations!"

12 Honeymoon in Uluru

Alice and Jon had a long wait at the airport for the plane to Sydney. Neither of them knew the city. They slept in the hotel to overcome the tiredness and visited the Harbour Bridge and the Opera House. They both loved the magnificent harbour and went to see the Rock art which was on boulders by the water side.

"I expect Derry understood this art."

"Yes, he did. You can read his book and one day you must meet Mary Ruth, the Aboriginal teacher and artist who is in the Northern Territory. She often gives talks at institutions in Darwin and she knows Beate."

"My life is being so enriched."

Jon had chosen a retreat after the traumatic emotional upheaval he had been through, knowing that it would not be luxurious. He had added three days of luxury at the end to celebrate their marriage. Alice was quite content with that. They had a little cabin and a bus to take them to the Rock each day. It was clean and comfortable, sparsely furnished. Meals were taken in a communal hut. There were about 12 people in their group. The emphasis was on silence so they did not speak over meals. They would have to make an effort to engage in conversation, but like most of the others, they did not want to. They wanted to concentrate on meditation and prayer. They could choose to see the Rock at night, taking a picnic. After the silent supper they were given cards to prepare them for the next day, the early rise at 5.30 and the names of the stopping places at the base of the Rock.

That night Jon made love to Alice in the little cabin and they relaxed into a deep sleep.

Apart from experiencing a lot of silence, the retreat was challenging. On the first day they were asked to sit apart and contemplate something nearby in nature; they could choose a leaf, a stone, a flower, a blade of grass. The leader had tried to get them to understand how to look, how to observe. Each day there was a music retreat using both Aboriginal and European music, a poem or meditative paragraph to read and consider at length and on the fourth day there was a feedback session for any who wanted to attend.

Some people expressed that they felt very uncomfortable with silence, others, more experienced could share a little of their thinking when they observed, when they felt challenged and their experience of deep inner peace and awareness of a spiritual power.

The leader gave them advice on breathing techniques and introduced them to the word 'dadirri' and then gave a session of sitting apart and listening to nature, not just birds, insects and running water, but leaves, grasses, soil, rocks. There were movements everywhere.

On the 5th day there were tougher challenges; they should spread far apart and consider their inner pain, sufferings caused by others, guilt, regret and disappointment. They walked to some higher ground where they could look down without walking up the Rock itself. The music was below them and then came a silence of over an hour. As they were far apart and silence filled the air, weeping, sniffing and stifled sobs could be heard.

Alice was concerned about how Jon was managing but she put this aside and concentrated on her own pain. Her guilt came to the surface; she had been absent when her mother died, she had not realised that her daughter was sexually active at 15 and she had not prevented her daughter's suicide. Her guilt was overwhelming. Miriam's baby had lost her life, murdered by her mother when she had jumped from a height. Why had Alice not stopped her going out? Why had she not realised?

She moved on to more recent events. She had initiated the family searches that had led to Jon discovering dark truths about his family. This had caused him deep pain. Would it have been better not to know? She wept bitterly. Then she turned to find gratitude for all the people who had come into her life and helped her though the dark times. Finally she spoke her gratitude for Jon, her new love and a wonderful man.

Far from her, too far to hear her weeping, he was weeping too. He was facing the recent revelation that the man he had believed to be his father all his life was not. This great father had never known that Jon was not his son. Instead he had discovered that his biological father had been from his mother's tribe. This bitter cousin had beaten and raped his mother and was then executed under tribal law. When his mother became pregnant she hoped it was her white husband's son but although she saw the black skin and black eyes, and knew that it was the Aborigine's son, she told no one, except Clemmy O'Neill and spoke of genetics, as did everyone else and Jon was accepted by all the family as Frederick's son.

Jon wept for his mother and for himself and was glad that his father never knew. His brother and sister had never known either, nor his children until he told them a few weeks ago. He felt guilty that he had let out some of his anger in a way that hurt his new wife. He felt guilty that he had spent his life trying to be a white man and had ignored the state of his mother's people, ignored the culture and the religion, the loss of land, the history of bad treatment.

He turned to consider his counsellor and the love of his wife who had helped him through and prevented his anger coming out in worse ways in later years. He felt her love and healing power flowing through him. He was so grateful for his sister's love and his children, all supporting him through the shock.

The music below started up again, gentle and vague, deep and with a tuneless rhythm. He decided he needed more time alone in a wilderness. At the end of the day he and Alice held each other without speaking for hours.

For the last two days they had some choices, more silence alone, more music or more directed prayer and worship. Jon chose silence for both days and Alice chose music and worship. They both rejected the feedback session. They had enough voices in their heads already. They loved staring at the Rock and the surrounding strange landscape during those last days. Jon tried to understand why climbing was no longer allowed and could not grasp the concept of sacred ground and ancestral spirits. He decided he must read Derry's book. There were adverts for other retreat venues, Tasmania, the coast, the rainforest given out at the end of the retreat. They took them and thanked the leader. A bus then took them to their hotel further away from the Rock. From the window, they could just make out the shape of the Rock in the distance.

It really was luxury, a huge bed all decked in soft white sheets, a gold decorated shower, a fridge with drinks, a menu of wonderful choices.

The brochure offered massages, swimming in the pool, manicure and hair dressing. They had a swim and went for supper. Classical music was playing live in one corner of the splendid room with large windows shaded but open to the wilderness.

"I'm sorry we cannot climb the Rock. I shall read Derry's book to understand about ancestral spirits and sacred ground."

"Shall we try a massage here?"

"I like yours."

"I'll book one and report back."

"I want to walk and think."

The first walk was to the pool where Alice had seen the vision of Miriam. She stood staring for a long time. Two Aborigines stood and played music and then told stories and myths as they waited by the still water. Alice whispered to Jon, "This is where I saw Miriam."

He knelt down and bowed his head and made the sign of the cross. She joined him but did not want to intrude on his holy moment.

They had another swim and went for supper. There was a string quartet playing this time. They held hands and just stared into each other's eyes for a very long time.

Alice appreciated the deep tissue massage of her neck, shoulders and back. She was told she needed this treatment regularly as she had a lot of tension in the nape of her neck and shoulders. She recommended it to Jon who had a similar experience and was told more of less the same.

"We must build in more silence and more meditation for ourselves." Jon said on the last day. "It was good to swim and have a massage but there is a missing element for me."

"Worship, prayer?"

"I think that's it, a missing Presence."

Night fell with a deep darkness. They were lying on the very soft, wide bed, naked, still, not speaking.

"Alice I love you, your love making, your healing, your teaching, everything about you, I love."

"Jonathan O'Neill, you were made especially for me. I love you deeply and it hurts my head and nearly makes me faint. There is nothing about you that I don't love."

It took a long time for their hearts to stop racing and they fell into sleep.

Reality, the everyday, work, house cleaning, cooking and eating, speaking to others; it took a while. Steve collected them at the airport and took them to 63. Beate had brought round the wedding gifts and had needed Steve's help with the van to bring the garden furniture and gazebo.

"Just what we needed!" Jon said.

"Professor von Friedland has made you a supper in Sundale Court. Then you get your first night in your Queenslander as a married couple." They thanked Steve, hugged him.

"When do we go for supper?"

"Sevenish."

The gazebo was put up with the garden table and chairs. They sat on the swinging chair under the gazebo and counted their blessings.

Their love for each other was strong and stable, the more so because they had faced their inner pains, their pasts, their losses and overcome them. Uppermost in their minds as they began married life was their desire to give, to help, to encourage and to bring healing to others.

13 The Reunion

Everyone looks askance at the phrase 'Happy ever after'. The O'Neills had had experiences which had made them much more realistic and yet there is not another phrase to describe the next 25 years of their time together.

Jon read Derry's book on Aboriginal culture and spirituality. They both joined AIATSIS (Australian Institute of Aboriginal and Torres Strait Islanders Studies). They visited the HQ in Canberra and attended conferences. They took the materials to the Hartley Barnes Foundation at the University.

They both continued with the teaching at the Mosque for several years. They both helped at the charity at the township where Jon took some English teaching and literacy in the school. Jon started a branch on women's issues with Beate and they called it the Ngala O'Neill Centre.

Professor Beate formed a close friendship with Connie in spite of the age difference and they shared a house together. They recalled sharing the Granny flat in Oxford some years earlier. Lisa, Jon's daughter, presented her father with little Jack, his first grandchild.

Alice made trips to England and America on alternate years as her family grew. Bethany had two more children, both boys, Jeremy and Vince, so Alice made the trips to be with her for the births. Victor was delighted with his three children and Esther ruled the roost with her younger brothers. (Just like Miriam.) The twin, Nicholas also married and had a family in USA. Cristina married a Spanish man and lived in Spain for long periods.

Paul and Vivienne carried on meeting up with Koda and family. One year, they had a holiday at Lake of the Woods and invited Alice and Jon to join them. That was a precious time together.

Little Bear married his widow and settled to be a good, loving and trustworthy step-father. Hartleigh continued as expected to a PhD and worked mainly in New Zealand and Polynesia but made frequent trips to Cairns. He had a haircut, no more man-bun and in his late thirties he met a partner, Henry, who worked with him in Polynesia and New Zealand.

When he was in Oxford he made music with Joseph and spent time with Daniel and Charles who had decided to retire. They left their London flat and moved to a house not far from Joseph and Bright Star in Oxfordshire. They played occasional concerts, but had left the fast-paced rat race. They both enjoyed good health for some years so they made regular trips to Cairns to see Alice and Jon.

Joseph and Bright Star kept to their intention of having just two children. He did some teaching and formed a new music group which performed in London and Oxford and sometimes in other towns.

Shining Star and Koda stayed with them for Jacy's birth. The lovely dancer and singer went back to dance classes and music when her children were old enough. Daniel and Charles were good baby sitters.

Nathaniel married Magda and remained in Australia. Their first home was in Brisbane as most of his opportunities of work were in that city.

"The reunion was definitely Daniel's idea!" said Hartleigh. "He has done so much to keep us all in touch."

"We are never out of touch but we are never all together." said Joseph. "I think we should do it, make it happen while Mum and Jon are still able to travel. Who knows? Both Daniel and Jon are approaching seventy."

Hartleigh counted up how many of them were in England. He and Henry shared a flat in Oxford, Bright Star and Joseph and Daniel and Charles had country houses outside the city. Bethany was in America and Nathaniel was in Brisbane. The Barnes siblings all respected their uncle's suggestion of a reunion.

Alice had five grandchildren and would no doubt have more when Nathaniel and Magda started a family.

Daniel had a sense that a reunion for the family would be important while they were still young enough to enjoy such an occasion. They planned for next summer when Miriam would have been 32 and her daughter would have been in her teens.

Alice enjoyed visiting them all and Jon gave her the freedom to go without him on some of the trips. She was thrilled at the idea of getting all her children together.

After retiring and moving to Oxfordshire, Daniel and Charles spread their musical wings somewhat. They had 'jamming' sessions with Hartleigh and Joseph. After their successful collaboration in composing Uluru Melody and Dawn Star Lament they worked together to compose music to go with the art exhibitions at de Boyadere gallery. Justin mounted an exhibition called Angst and Agony, depicting the work of the Art Therapy Group. He chose the works of the most capable and dynamic of the clients. Some of the works had the power of Picasso's Guernica so music to accompany the disturbing images was composed.

When Justin's father started to visit the gallery, he called his show 'World of Values'. The sculptures and paintings depicted the values he was rejecting, materialism and commercialism, greed and the destruction of natural beauty. He made architectural models with blood dripping down the walls and canvases of beautiful landscapes being dug up and exploded. Some of the Press found it too disturbing, especially with the discordant music in the background.

His own children inspired 'By and About Kidz' exhibition. He asked for portraits of parents, families and pets among other subjects and was overwhelmed by entries.

"The Royal Academy televises their team making choices for the Summer Show!" commented Daniel looking through the piles of papers.

Daniel and Charles had come to Cairns to see Alice and Nathaniel and to enjoy a stay in Thala. This was his next idea for musical collaboration, a tribute to Thala. Beate was still renting Sundale Court when a letter for Alice arrived. She went round to have a coffee with Beate and collect the letter. She did not recognise the handwriting and opened it without realising she was in for a shock. She had been married to Jonathan for over two years when she received the letter from her old Spiritual Director, Philip Browne.

Alice, you have sunk to the lowest level of degradation. You, one of God's chosen people, a Jew, have linked yourself with a dark, black pagan, a heathen, a tribal savage. This is an offence to God. It is condemned by the Word of God. A red ring is what he bought you. The colour of blood, the colour of death and murder. They kill with spears. You would have been safe with my antique diamond. At least you cannot bear children. Your line is at an end. Your promiscuous daughter linked herself with a savage. God was not pleased. Savages and heathens are evil. I cannot love a woman who loves a heathen. You have condemned yourself to live with evil. You are in bed with evil. You allow evil to come into your body. God have mercy on you and save you from dark, dark evil. Philip.

Beate came in with the coffee and found her white and trembling.

"Alice, destroy this letter. Do not let Jon or any of your children see this. He is mad and demented." Beate hugged her weeping friend. He must have seen the beautiful portrait of the bride and groom in the local paper. Perhaps his daughter had kept it from him, or in his dementia he had suddenly decided to write after two years.

"I will share it with Daniel. We are close and share everything."

"I will ring him and tell him to come here. No way must Jon know. It will only cause harm."

Daniel was able to drive over from Thala and comfort his sister. Beate brought in a lighted candle and a metal oven dish. Alice held the letter in the flames and saw it turn to ash.

"There is the dark evil!" Daniel smiled, "It's gone!"

Alice remembered how Jon's mother had kept her terrible secret all her life and decided she would do the same.

When she was next in England with Joseph and Bright Star, Daniel checked up on how she was and on how she had managed to get over the shock without telling Jon.

"I said nothing but I think he picked up on my emotions as he asked me if I would like a healing massage in our charity healing centre in Cairns. I said I would prefer one from him but I was afraid that I would weep. I did not! He was so gentle that I felt the pain leave me."

"I am so pleased. Now we really must plan a reunion. Hartleigh and Joseph want to go to Dorset where you had such happy holidays when they were small."

"We had a dog with us. I have been thinking of getting a dog." Joseph heard the last part of the conversation.

It was not long before Joseph took his family to a kennel and chose a Springer Spaniel. Jacy and Claire were thrilled with him. Bright Star suggested they called him Hunter, Hunter 2.

It took longer than they had imagined but the reunion eventually happened. They chose 6 lodges near Lulworth, high on the cliffs overlooking the sea. They hired two People Carriers. Daniel and Charles drove one with Alice and Jon, Nathaniel and Magda collected from Heathrow. The other was driven by Henry with Hartleigh who collected the Americans and Bethany. Joseph and Bright Star drove themselves down to Dorset from Oxfordshire.

They chose four small lodges for the couples and two large lodges for the families.

The modern facilities were much more advanced than when they had stayed there as children. For 12 days they spent time together in the local beauty spots, Jurassic Coast, Corfe Castle, Monkey World and the Tank Museum.

The English summer weather was as good as it could be as they swam in the sea, walked on the cliffs and explored the beautiful countryside. Buddleia was in bloom everywhere, the mauve flowers contrasting with the white of the large banks of daisies by the road side.

Daniel took several portraits of the siblings together and with Alice. They chatted together about their childhood, their times with their father and the way he always made time for them as individuals, especially after he returned from a jungle or rainforest.

Daniel promised to make a photo book for them all.

He had come to Swanage earlier to find a hotel where they could stay for the last night after booking a large room for a celebratory meal. He found the ideal hotel on the top of the last cliff out of town with views over the bay. He booked 6 rooms and the conservatory dining room for the party. In the lounge was a grand piano so Daniel and Charles gave a recital before the meal. The meal was a buffet organised by the hotel catering team and reminded them of the Thala buffet.

Alice wondered how Jon was feeling. He did not look as if he felt like an outsider as the Barnes family reminisced and honoured their father. He chatted freely with all of the children at different times. He made sure he thanked Daniel for the idea and the organisation.

"I have become aware how Alice has adjusted over the years to living in a way she did not always choose. Her father's plan for the house, meant she had little choice about living in her childhood home when she was longing to have her own home. Her husband's job meant she could not stay in Cairns when she was longing to do that. Her children married close friends of his colleagues and ended up in America and England and fortunately for me, in Australia. She just accepted it all and coped!"

"That's my sister!" Daniel clapped his shoulder. "And she now has you and she loves you so much!"

There were speeches after the meal. Jonathan gave a moving and amazing speech about his own losses and family traumas and the treasure he now had in marrying Alice and joining the Barnes family. In Daniel's speech, he agreed that it was too expensive to have many such reunions but that they should do at least one more on a special birthday, a 70th for Alice, or Daniel or Jon. Hartleigh ended the formal speeches by honouring Jonathan.

"You must consider yourself head of the Barnes clan Mr O'Neill!"

The party finished when Hartleigh brought in his guitar and Joseph brought out some percussion instruments and invited all the children to dance. Hunter then got his run on the beach and his food. They had to decide who would stay with him in a vehicle overnight. Joseph thought he would be more at home and more settled if he slept in their own vehicle. There was clapping, hugging, kissing and weeping as the three vehicles left in the morning. Alice and Jonathan spent a few more days with both of her sons while all the others left from Heathrow. Their last two days were with Daniel and Charles who had begun working on music for a tribute to Thala. That was not the final reunion. Hartleigh took over the task when Daniel became too old. Over the next ten years they had a reunion in Lake of the Woods in Canada, in Cairns and their beloved Dorset.

Jonathan pointed out to Alice an announcement in the local paper when they reached number 63. She was relieved to read of the death of the much-loved Reverend Philip Browne who was suffering from dementia and had a stroke. With peace of mind and joy in her heart she was able to take up her weekly teaching and charity work with her husband.

Number 63 was the home of Jon and Alice until their old age when they needed a house without steps.

They swopped over and let out 63 and lived in Sundale Court once more. Their children used both houses on their visits and there was usually a student from the university, happy to rent a room in the Queenslander.

Jon did find time to write a memoir. He began with the O'Neill's, getting more information from Clemmy during his visits every two months until she passed away. He covered the Hartleys next and ended with a eulogy for Daniel Robert Hartley the well-known musician. He described the link with the Barnes; Alice Leah Hartley had married Derwent Barnes and he began by recounting the Hartley's visit to Leipzig when the Berlin Wall had opened. He told of the huge impact on their lives made by this trip where they learned of the sad deaths of Mrs Esther Hartley's parents, a Jewish family, killed by the Nazis.

Towards the end of his account of the life and work of Professor Barnes and his retirement in Australia he wrote of the symbolic significance of the white bookshelf in the life of Alice, his wife. Many houses of academics had a similar bookshelf in a study. To Alice, the corner of the white bookshelf with a leather chair to the side had been a place of comfort, security, familiarity and also adventure and privilege. She had loved her father's books and all the weird and wonderful artefacts which spoke of faraway places. Many a student had sat there over the years and benefitted from Professor Thomas' patience, knowledge and helpfulness. All through her life, Alice had made sure she had a white bookshelf. The second was in 42, her first marital home in Cairns and after leaving Oxford, she had two others in 63 and Sundale Court.

They were tokens and she had grown out of the need for that kind of security. She had found it once more in her marriage to Jon and her ongoing work for the Hartley Barnes Foundation and the Ngala O'Neill Centre.

In the final weeks of her life, Alice and Jon sat in their garden watching the waves. Alice thought back over her first honeymoon in Thala and her second in Uluru.

"Our marriage has been longer than my first one to Derry. I have been blessed with two wonderful husbands! I was the widow of Sundale Court and you will be the widower of Sundale Court."

"I have loved every part of our life together. We leave two growing families and two growing charities."

They heard their names, "Jonathan, Alice!" Their carer had arrived.

"Can you see the waves? Another cyclone on the way! Let's get you ready for bed and shut down all the windows and doors."

She remembered lying on the bed with Connie during her first cyclone as a young bride after her first few weeks in Cairns while Derry was in the outback. She cuddled Jon as they listened to the thrashing waves.

THE END